TO SO FEW

Richard Powell

ALSO BY RICHARD POWELL

THE JERGEN COUNTY SERIES:

Murder Club

The Gingerbread man

The Jergen County War

Deadly Discovery

An Eye For An Eye

THE BRIDGE CLUB SERIES

Old Age and Treachery

Harvesting the Angels

Little Lucifer

Truths, Lies & Trolls

PIRATES OF BARATARIA

A Rescue In Time

TIGERS ON THE ROAD

A Journey To Destiny

THE DEVIL'S PLAYGROUND

Pact With The Devil

This is a work of historical fiction. What does that mean? I weave real people into the plot. Claire Chennault, Harvey Greenlaw, Paul Frillman, Dick Rossi, Greg Boyington, and Erik Schilling lived the real stuff. Olga Greenlaw chronicled the units War Diary and Rose Mok, as Olga claimed, had to make a living. Also, many events in the story came from these people's own accounts gleaned from histories produced by themselves or others. While the events are based on true events in history, I have also taken liberty with time frames to fit the story. Other characters are figments of my imagination. Any resemblance to actual people you meet or in my life is purely coincidental.

I don't claim to be an expert on this band of men and women who risked so much when others cared so little about the plight of the Chinese. For factual material, I would encourage you to seek out the works of Daniel Ford, Terry Anderson, or Jack Samson.

I also hope the reader can forgive what many might consider insensitive language in the dialog. But people back then talked that way. We know better now. Right?

After Rangoon's fall, Winston Churchill compared the Flying Tigers to the brave airmen who flew in the Battle of Britain. Of those brave souls he said, "Never in the field of human conflict have so many owed so much, **to so few**."

DEDICATION

This book is dedicated to all the brave men and women who failed to come home after serving their country. They gave so much and never had the chance to enjoy what they defended. You are in our hearts forever.

CHAPTER ONE

KUNMING, CHINA DECEMBER 1941

The P-40's tracers ripped into the Japanese bomber, setting it ablaze. As his plane dove beneath the burning bomber, Joe glanced up. Completely engulfed in flames, hanging out of the shattered turret above him, the gunner grinned. Beckoned Joe to join him in his flaming coffin. Instead of passing beneath, Joe's plane paused under the flaming wreck, floating underneath, as if trapped in some force field from a *Buck Rogers* serial. The burning gunner dropped onto Joe's cowling, crawled toward him, the man's eyes vacant sockets. The wind from Joe's propeller fanned the flames surrounding the gunner as his mouth opened in a scream drowned out by Joe's engine's roar. Bathed in sweat, but shivering, Joe bolted up in the bed.

As he shivered, Ann's hand caressed his shoulder. "Joe, what's wrong?"

Even though he couldn't see her face, he imagined it etched in the concern echoed in her voice.

He glanced around the darkened room. Instead of being strapped into his fighter, he lay beside Ann in a hotel bed. Reassured, he leaned back. As his head rested once more on the pillow, she moved against him, her warm flesh easing his chill. As he closed his eyes, the horrible image reappeared. He sat up again and scanned the room. "A dream. That's all it was. It all seemed so real."

Ann rubbed his back. "Tell me about it. It might help."

"I was up there. In the attack. Saw one guy I killed. But it was different."

"Different?"

"The guy acted like I should join him. In the burning plane. When I didn't, he came for me."

She gasped. Still shaking, he slipped from the bed, found his flight jacket on the floor where he'd tossed it as they ripped off their clothes before falling into bed together. Found the flask in the pocket. His hands trembled as he removed the cap and brought it to his lips. The whiskey warmed his throat, but still, he shivered.

"Come back to bed. Let me hold you."

He ran his fingers through his black hair as his teeth chattered. "I'm sweatin' like mad, but I'm freezin'."

The bedclothes rustled in the dark room. Her hands found him in the dark and drew him close. The lilac smell in her hair, her smooth, warm skin pressed against him radiated, quelling the chills as she rocked him gently in her arms.

"In my nurse's training, they talked about the problems a lot of soldiers had when they came back from the Great war. They said the terrible things they saw and did, haunted them."

"Did they get over it?"

"Most did, but some... Come on back to bed."

As they snuggled, Joe ran his hand down her back. "I'm sorry. This should be special tonight. And here I am doin' this crazy crap."

Ann kissed his cheek. "It was special. It still is."

"Despite my craziness?"

"Besides being kinda cute, I find your wackiness appealing."

"At the rate I'm goin', I'll rival Clark Gable."

She poked him. "Stop that. Now you sound like a crybaby, instead of the manly cur, I let steal my virtue."

He drew her close. "When we got to bouncin' here earlier, I thought I heard some high notes you sang during services on the boat coming here. Probably *Rock of Ages*."

Her hand drifted down his chest, and she chuckled. "More like *Amazing Grace*." Her hand found his manhood, "Oh my, there might be hope yet, though." She chuckled. "Ooh, yes. Mr. Joe Stuart, I feel a hint of the man I fell for."

****

"Colonel the folks back home are eager to hear more about your boys here."

Claire Chennault's eyes narrowed as he pondered the reporter's question. "I'm not sure what I can tell ya. Our presence here was supposed to be a secret. But after the attack on Pearl Harbor it appears things have changed" Chennault held up the letter the man gave him earlier.. "I can keep this so anything I tell ya doesn't come back to bite me?"

The reporter nodded as he scribbled notes on his pad. "With all the success the Japs are having, the folks in Washington are desperate for anything that doesn't look like Western democracy is goin' down the toilet."

"To save us time tell me what Currie told you."

"Your boys were recruited from the military. Army and Navy reserved officers and enlisted."

Chennault, his ever-present cigarette trapped between two extended fingers shook them in the air towards the reporter as if pounding home his point. "We have Marines as well. All resigned before joining. They accepted employment as independent contractors with Central Aircraft Manufacturing Company."

"CAMCO?"

Chennault nodded. "Officially we're the American Volunteer Group or AVG."

"So, none of your guys are actual American Military."

"That's right. They have contracts for one year. At the end of that time, they're free to go where they want."

6

"Huh, for a buncha civilians they've made quite an impact."

Chennault shrugged. "One contact with the Japanese can hardly be described as that. We'll see. We just sent a squadron to Rangoon to help the British down there at the other end of the Road. Gotta have both ends working in order to keep the Chinese in the fight. We'll have to see how that goes before we can brag."

The reporter cocked his head. "That's it?"

Chennault's eyes narrowed. "Enough for now. Like I said, if we can help hold Rangoon come on back for the party."

As both men rose, the reporter slipped his pen and pad inside his suitcoat jacket. "I and my readers back home will be followin' the news from Rangoon. Thanks, Colonel for your time."

Outside Chennault's door, Harvey Greenlaw, Chennault's adjutant, trailed the exiting reporter with his eyes as the man strode away.

"You got something for me, Harvey?"

Greenlaw held up the dispatch. "Just came in."

A frown crept across Chennault's leather pace as Greenlaw handed the sheet to him. "Good news?"

Greenlaw shrugged as he seated himself across from Chennault. "How'd it go?"

"He wanted me to brag, but I gave it to him straight. Hope it helps."

"Even about the spotter network?"

"Hell no. Took me five years to get that set up. That's our one ace in the hole here. The Japanese find out about that, we're screwed."

"True, thanks to them we know there comin' as soon as they take off. They ever catch on hard tellin' what they might do."

Chennault scowled. "Probably wipe out every village between here and Hanoi. Japanese claim they want Asia for Asians and they're just liberators. I guess they don't consider the Chinese, Asians."

Seated Harvey removed his pipe. "Whattya think they'll pull next?"

"The Chinese seem to be holdin' their land forces off for once. Till they figure out what we're up to, their air force'll probably leave us alone here for a while. Want the guys alert, though."

Greenlaw puffed on his pipe and nodded. "The spotter network gives us plenty of warning. Reporters came through last week, said the Japs are making a push in Burma."

Chennault stubbed out the cigarette in the ashtray, scowled. "If they take Rangoon that cuts off the other end of the Burma Road. Only way to supply the Chinese since the Japs hold all the other harbors in the area."

"So, our guys in Rangoon are in for it."

"Let's hope they can get along now with the Brits. They haven't helped our guys much before."

Harvey nodded. "But now we're all on the same side."

Chennault passed the sheet back to Greenlaw. "Did you read this?"

Greenlaw shrugged. "It was for you. I figured if I needed to know you'd tell me."

"Pfft. Japs know more about what goes on here than I do. This came in this morning from our spotter in Hanoi."

Greenlaw's eyebrow arched as he studied the sheet. "Only one bomber returned from the raid here?"

Chennault nodded. "Our boys shot down six near here but said they damaged some. So, it looks like they might have damaged three more so bad they never made it back."

"And we lost one ship."

"Guy bellied into a rice paddy. Lamison checked it out. Props bent pretty bad, but he figures him and that Chinese crew they call the cannibals can fix it."

Greenlaw nodded. "Not bad for our first action. Hope it continues."

The desk phone rang. As Chennault listened to the caller, he turned to the window. Outside, two P-40s taxied from their dispersal areas towards the runway. A frown crept over his face as he listened. Even though things here in Kunming seemed orderly, they could not say the same for his unit in Burma.

Chennault slammed the phone down. Spun his chair around to face his adjutant studying the spotter's report. "Son of a bitch, Harvey. What am I runnin' here a fighting unit or a goddamn orphanage?"

Greenlaw's head snapped up. "So, it's true."

"Sounds like it."

"If this Ed Burton clown's working the black market, discharge him. Turn it over to the Brits. Let it be their problem."

Chennault leaned back in his chair, ran his fingers over his tan, leathery face, scowled. "Shit, we brought him over here, sent him out on a training mission that got fucked up. He was doin' his duty. We put the kid in harm's way. It's our responsibility."

"We never told him to turn into some Rangoon gangster. That seems to be his choice."

"While serving in this unit, he got forced down and kidnapped by bandits. According to Olsen, his squadron leader, the only thing that saves him is cooperating with the assholes that nabbed him."

"Burton's squadron's in Rangoon now. If he's in Rangoon, why doesn't he merely walk onto the base, turn himself over to Olsen, and be done with it?"

Chennault drummed his fingers on the desk. "Olsen claims it's complicated. He only heard it secondhand from Jenson."

"Jenson?"

"Burton cornered him at that bar they all like down in Rangoon."

"The Silver Grill?"

"Yeah that one. Apparently, he told Jenson the story, and he passed it on to Olsen."

Greenlaw leaned back. "Want someone to go straighten it out?"

"Who?"

Greenlaw shrugged. "Me or the padre."

"Nah, it's in Olsen's hands. He's down there. Hell, I don't even remember the kid. He was only here for a couple of weeks before he disappeared. We still got more pilots than planes, and you two will have your hands full once the Japs make a move."

"Olga could call down there. She's always houndin' me about the guys. His disappearance shook her up."

"Your wife is supposed to be keepin' the war diary, not playin' the goddamn housemother." Chennault chewed his lip while he pondered Greenlaw's suggestion. "Yeah, have her call down there. Talk to Olsen, and I guess Jenson too. He's the one Burton talked to. Shit, I always thought R.H.I.P. meant rank has its privileges. It seems like it should be R.H.I.P.A."

A puzzled frown creeped over Greenlaw's face. "What?"

"Rank has its pains in the ass."

"That should have another 'I' in it."

Chennault shrugged turned back to the window to survey his domain once again. "Crossin' the 'T' s is your job. You can add 'I's as well. Comes with your lofty position."

****

After dropping Ann off at the hospital, the next morning, the car took Joe to the base. Her passion the night before surprised him. Not what he expected from a Boston missionary. She had not mentioned his proposal but seemed content to be with him. For now, that would be enough.

On the flight line, Russ Lamison stood on the X-plane's wing, talking with the pilot in the cockpit. In the daylight, Russ's face, framed by his uneven hair looking as if it had been trimmed by a drunken barber, halted Joe in his tracks. Gaunt and pale, Russ looked worse than when he saw him a few days earlier before the Japanese attacked. Determined to check on his friend, Joe trailed Russ as he strode to the hangar.

Joe caught up with him at a workbench inside covered with airplane parts. Russ glanced up as Joe approached and nodded.

"Hey, Russ. What you got there?"

"Supercharger. Schilling thinks we can get more boost with some minor changes here and there," Russ replied, pointing at the parts arranged on the bench. "He's right, it'll up the horsepower, but it will increase wear. Might even blow the engine."

Russ turned to Ang Su, standing beside him. As he talked to his Chinese assistant who co-led the group the men called Lamison's Cannibals, Russ pointed at the same parts he showed Joe. Ang Su studied the scattered pieces, then shrugged.

Finished, Russ turned back to Joe. "The bearings we made are stronger than the originals, but even Ang Su is not sure they would handle that added power. Usually, we test one small part at a time, so the chances of total engine failure would be minimal. If this is wrong, the whole engine goes. We don't have enough spares to risk blowing one up. If it passed the initial trial and failed in the air, we might lose both the plane and the pilot."

"So, what're you going to do?"

"I guess explain it to Schilling like that. Wouldn't wanna piss him off. The guy helps us a lot, and he's a helluva pilot."

Joe nodded. "I know what ya mean. Most pilots are a bunch of know it all prima-donnas, but of the bunch, he'd be the most likely to understand. Listen, I got the duty today, but I'm off tomorrow. How about goin' into town?"

"I'm off today myself, but on tomorrow, thanks anyway. I'd like to get away tonight though. Got a standing invitation for dinner in town, but no way to get there."

Joe grinned. "Bet I could get wheels for ya. Invitation in town, huh?"

"Yeah, folks I met after the decoy attack. Did some work for 'em and they invited me as payback. Didn't have to, but they were so great I hate to leave 'em hangin'."

"Well, count on goin'. I'm sure I can spring you some wheels."

Joe rushed back to search for Paul Frillman, the Chaplain. Between himself and the chaplain, they could come through for Russ. After finding Frillman's office empty, he hurried down the hall hoping to find the Chaplain in Olga Greenlaw's office. Inside the office, she sat alone, writing in a giant ledger.

At Joe's arrival, she looked up and smiled. Sloe-eyed, with dark hair, the woman's exotic beauty entranced the unit's males. In spite of her marriage to Chennault's adjutant, most gravitated to her office, like bees to a nectar filled blossom. She smiled. "You shot down a Jap the other day? Here to check on your bonus?"

Her statement made him pause. Had not considered the promised bonus of five hundred dollars for each plane shot down. The offer sounded great when they recruited him, but the reality of killing for money now hit an uncomfortable chord. "Uh, no, ma'am. I guess it slipped my mind."

She leaned forward giving him a glimpse down her blouse, gazed into his eyes. "Then what can I do for you?"

Joe cleared his throat, shuffled his feet. "I'm looking for the Reverend. Do you know where he is?"

Amused at Joe's discomfort she leaned back, gave him an appraising glance. "Paul and Harvey went into town. They should be back later tonight."

Joe's shoulders slumped, and a frown crept over his face.

Olga cocked her head, her brow furrowed. "Can I help you?"

"I'm not sure. I'm worried about Russ."

"Russ Lamison?" She beckoned him to the vacant chair before her desk. "That's right. You were there when Paul and I told him about his wife's death. God, that was awful. I feel guilty. With the move and all, I haven't checked up on him since we got here. You're worried about him?"

After dropping into the vacant chair, he shared his concerns about his friend. When he finished Olga made a wry face. "And he's made friends in town, and the only reason he hasn't been able to visit them is he doesn't have a car?"

"That's about it. Yes."

She stood, and as she passed Joe, she squeezed his shoulder. "Let me go talk to the boss."

Shit! Joe thought to himself, what kind of mess have I stirred up now?

Olga returned, smiling. "We have the staff car assigned to Harvey and me. Like I said he and Paul wouldn't be back until late tonight, so he can use that today if he likes. Tell him to get the keys from me when he's ready. Okay?"

"The Colonel is all right with that? I know he wouldn't let the guys do this in Toungoo."

"Let's say this case deserved special consideration."

Joe rose, and as he moved to the door, he paused. "Thank you, ma'am. I'll let Russ know right away!"

"I wish you guys would quit calling me ma'am. Makes me feel like an old woman. Mrs. Greenlaw makes me feel like your mother. Call me Olga. Please."

"Yes, Ma'am. Er, I mean Olga. Sure! And thanks again."

When Russ arrived at Olga's office later that day, she beckoned him in. "Ed Burton was a friend of yours, right?"

"They found him? He's okay?"

Olga shrugged. "Sort of. He's in Rangoon. He's become a black-market tycoon."

"What? How?"

"It's a long story, but essentially his kidnappers got nabbed by a bandit chief. Apparently, he agreed to work for this bandit to save the original group."

"He did what?"

She nodded. "Agreed to work for the bandit, so this cutthroat wouldn't harm Ed's original kidnappers."

"Why would Ed do that?"

Olga smiled. "I don't have all the details, but I understand it involves a woman."

"Is he comin' back to the unit?"

"Let's hope." She gave him an appraising glance. "You like your heading out for a date, Mister Lamison."

"Oh, no, ma'am. I mean, Mrs. Greenlaw. I'm having dinner with the folks who run the mission hospital. Dr. Ross and his daughter, Ann. Thought I should be at my best. Right?"

"Well, I'm impressed. If I weren't a married woman, I'd go out with you." She chuckled as he blushed and fidgeted. "Here are the keys. Also, when you need to go to town, let me know, and I can make sure you get there, okay?"

Russ nodded as he took the keys from her hand. As she led him to the door, she gave him a peck on the cheek. "Russ, anything else you need come and see me. I said we'd be your family now, and I meant it. But be home at a decent hour or your coach will turn into a pumpkin. Even you won't be able to fix that."

He smiled and waved as he walked down the hall. She returned his wave with a smile, then walked to Chennault's office.

"Thanks for taking care of that, Mother Greenlaw." Chennault's gruff tone not matching his smile as she walked into the office. "He's a good man. We need him at his best.

He's gotta be hurting from his wife's death. A break from here might be what he needs."

As she leaned in Chennault's doorway, she glanced down the hall after Russ's departing figure. "Also, I heard the man who runs that hospital has a gorgeous daughter Russ's age."

Chennault shook his head. "It might be too early for him to look around. Frillman claims the guy was a newlywed and still very much in the honeymoon period."

Olga scoffed. "Well, I overheard my Dad tell my older brother that women were like streetcars. If you miss one another will be along shortly. When I reached the dating age, he told me the same about men."

****

Several days later Russ hummed a Christmas tune as he strode to Olga's station wagon. This would be his second trip to visit Ann and her father, Dr. Ross. He admired her father for the work he did and when around Ann, his wife's ghost stayed in the recesses of his mind. As Russ made his way to the car, Joe jogged to his side. "So, ya got wheels."

Russ nodded. "Mrs. Greenlaw lets me use her car as long as I bring it back early. No duty tonight?"

"Nah. And am I ready to cut loose. Since you're goin' to town can I hitch a ride?"

Russ nodded. "But like I said, I need to get back early. That a problem?"

"Nah. Drop me at the hotel."

As Russ started the vehicle, he turned to Joe. "You hangin' with the guys there?"

"I hope not. I met someone who works here, and with any luck, I can coax her out for a night on the town."

"If you know where she's at, I can drop you there."

"That wouldn't work. I plan on spendin' a little time with her and her family. Then take her out on the town. They don't have a car, so I need a set of wheels. The lady that runs the hotel is more than happy to help me out with that."

As they pulled up outside the hotel, Joe reached for the door handle. "Thanks for the lift."

"I'm not gonna head back before midnight. I could pick you up here if you need a ride back?"

Joe grinned and arched his eyebrows. "Nah. Actually, I'm hopin' to coax her back to the hotel. With any luck, I won't be headin' back before tomorrow." He gave Russ a wink. "You know what I mean?"

Inside the hotel, Rose Mok sat in the bar. Alone in the corner, this petite and pretty Chinese lady kept a watchful eye on her customers and staff. Besides this hotel, Rose owned a trucking company engaged in transporting supplies up the Burma Road. Ann also claimed the woman had designs on her father. After ordering at the bar, he strode to her table. "I need a ride out to the hospital. Can it be arranged?"

Rose smiled. "I was going out there myself to bring Dr. Ross his scotch." Rose gave him a sly wink. "Maybe we both get lucky tonight, and you can have car."

CHAPTER TWO

The sound of a car pulling up outside drew Ann to the window. Her father, Dr. Ross, glanced up from the child he tended. "Is that Rose? She mentioned she'd be by later with my scotch."

"No, it's Russ. Did you call him?"

Dr. Ross arched an eyebrow as he studied his daughter still at the window. "Nothing's broke. Must be a social call. Think your young man might have a rival?"

She rolled her eyes. "Dad, don't start. He's lonesome is all. I'm sure it's hit all those guys at the airfield. Especially this time of year."

"In that case, you better run out there and make sure he knows he's welcome, while I finish off here."

As Russ strode to the cottage, Ann stepped out of the hospital next door. "Russ, Merry Christmas!"

Her call prompted him to turn and smile. After trotting down the hospital steps she joined him near the car and gave him a peck on the cheek. "We're finishing up, so if you want to go on in the house we'll be there in a minute."

"I'll come along. Can't hurt to check on that generator."

"I was checking on the children. With no more attacks, we're emptying the place."

"Does that mean they might move you?"

Ann cocked her head and frowned. "Gee, I never thought about that."

"Word at the base is that the Japs are gettin' ready to move into Burma. That might slow 'em down here in China. If they close that end on the Burma road, they wouldn't need to bomb here anymore."

Inside the ward, only children remained. None appeared badly injured. Some sat on beds, alone or with others talking or playing cards. Others scampered around the room. One sat alone in the corner. Her broken-hearted cry unheeded by the others.

"Where're their folks?" Russ asked looking at the gathered little ones all staring at him in wonder.

"These are the ones who don't have parents. As soon as they're well, they go to an orphanage the mission runs on the other side of town."

Russ slipped up to the crying child, scooped her up and whispered to her in Chinese. She nodded, wiped her eyes and smiled.

"Who wants to hear the story of baby Jesus," Russ called out to the children in Chinese.

A few trickled to Russ's side then others rushed close as he described the story, he would tell them. With the little girl clutched in his arms, Russ sat down on the bed. As the rest gathered round, he told the story of the first Christmas.

****

Perched on a cushion, Rose's head barely cleared the steering wheel. In the passenger seat Joe, gazed out over the darkened country side. Since lurking Japanese planes might be drawn to them in the dark, they followed blackout restrictions. Without headlights, they relied on the moonlight to guide them down the dark road. Outside the hospital, the AVG station wagon sat.

Rose frowned. "Ah, It looks like Olga is here already. She mentioned she was coming out to see the children, but I thought that would be tomorrow."

"No, I think it's the guy that gave me a lift into town."

Rose gave Joe a puzzled glance. "Let's go find out what is going on, okay? Might be a big party."

As they climbed the cottage's stairs, Rose carried two liquor bottles while Joe lugged a heavy wicker basket packed with foodstuffs from the hotel. When no one answered their knock, Rose opened the door. "Put the basket on the table."

After Joe placed it there, she set a few items next to it, then lit the oven. "While I warm these up, you go find the Doctor and your girlfriend."

After giving her a mock salute, he trotted to the larger building both eager to see Ann and curious about Russ's presence. Inside the ward, Ann sat on a bed near the entrance. She greeted him with a smile, put a finger to her lips, and pointed across the room.

Seated on a bed with a little girl staring up at him, Russ spoke to the children gathered around him. Quietly Joe moved next to Ann and joined her on the bed.

She leaned close to Joe "He is telling them about Jesus' birth. They love it."

Two children exchanged smiles, then looked back to the storyteller. When Russ mooed then brayed, giggles erupted among his audience while a few shared grins. As he continued, two of the youngest put their thumbs in their mouths. Their eyelids drooped as they struggled to stay awake.

Two nurses drifted into the room and stood at the door watching as Russ spun his tale. Finally, he paused, the little girl on his lap gave him a hug. Two of the older ones clapped while several others groaned and chattered.

"They're begging for another story," Ann whispered as Russ glanced in their direction, his jaw dropped.

"It's time for a bedtime snack," Ann called out to the children in Chinese, "Thank Mr. Lamison for his story and invite him back again for another."

As they rose to follow the nurses from the room, several waved or called out to him. Russ followed carrying the little girl who now rested her head on his shoulder sound asleep.

15

Ann leaned close to Joe. As she ran her fingers through his hair. "Oh, I so hoped you would make it tonight." She kissed his cheek and nodded towards the door where the children had exited. "You must know Russ from the base."

"Yeah, as a matter of fact, he gave me a lift into town, so I could get here. I didn't know he was coming here. He said he was visiting friends in town."

Ann ran her fingers through her hair. "They brought him in unconscious after an attack. He must have been close to a bomb blast because it singed his hair. He had a concussion and had trouble hearing for a few days, but while he was here, he fixed our generator."

"He and his cannibals are great fixin' stuff."

"Cannibal's?"

Joe shook his head. "His Chinese crew. They fix a lot a planes by taking parts from wrecks and stuff. Cause of that a lotta guys call 'em Lamison's Cannibals."

Ann chuckled. "So, they don't eat people."

"Nah, it's slang. In truth it's probably more like *Frankenstein*. Buildin' a new one from other parts."

She chuckled. "Gee Mr. Stuart, a literary side as well. What else don't I know about you?"

"A lot madam. You should be aware that I'm more than a handsome, dashing aviator. Russ fixed your generator?"

"If he hadn't, I don't know what might have happened. We needed it for a lot of the equipment. Probably saved a few lives. Dad gave him an open invitation for dinner, as a reward. He is such a nice man, is he married?"

"He was." Russ appeared at the door looking sheepish as he approached, "It's a long story. I'll tell you later."

As both rose to greet him, Ann took Russ's hand. "That was beautiful. We need to make you our master of stories in addition to our master of repair."

After giving Joe a sideways glance, Russ turned to Ann. "My mom told me that every year at Christmas. I hope they understood my Chinese."

She took Joe's arm. "From where I sat it sounded beautiful. I take it you also are responsible for bringing this heathen."

"Well, I gave him a lift to town. Didn't know where he headed," as Russ now glanced at Joe, Joe recalled his conversation about his plans for the night and worried what Russ might now say.

"We should probably find your Dad," Joe interjected to deflect the conversation. "Rose is inside fixing a Christmas feast. Knowin' her she probably is in no mood to wait."

"I'll go round him up." As she left the room, she called over her shoulder. Why don't you two boys head on up to the house and keep Rose company till I can drag him away?"

****

An uneasy silence hung over them as they strolled to the house.

Halfway to the house Joe took Russ's arm. "Look Russ, I'm glad you've met Ann and her Dad."

Russ glanced up, sighed. "When I'm here the pain goes away."

"That's a good thing. Ann says she enjoys your comin' out here too. You should keep it up."

"You don't think I'm hornin' in on your girl?"

"She is gorgeous. A lot of guys on the trip here put the moves on her, but for some reason she picked me, I've never met anyone like her and I've asked her to marry me."

"So, you're engaged?"

"I asked. She hasn't said no. I guess that means a kind of yes."

Russ gazed off as he spoke. "Don't tell anyone, especially her, it's kind of embarrassing. See, when I first came to, after the attack, I opened my eyes and there she was above me. Honest to God, I thought I died and she was an angel. First thing I did was ask her where my wife was."

"Shit, Russ! Honest?

Russ shrugged.

"I won't tell a soul."

"Thanks, she probably thinks I'm a little bit off." Russ failed to mention how disappointed he had been to discover he had not died. "Listen, I know you got plans for later. How about I shove off? Don't wanna mess up your night."

"No, I'm glad you're here, man. You need something besides work and your crew. You've been dealt a shitty deal. Bein' here around these people is right for you. But, if you put the moves on my girl, I will kick the shit out of you."

Russ scoffed. "Now you're sounding like that asshole, Boyington. If you ask me, you hang around with him way too much."

Joe put his arm around Russ's shoulder and together they walked the rest of the way back to the house.

****

Later at the hotel after their lovemaking, Ann rested her head on Joe's shoulder. She stroked the hair on his chest as he ran his fingers along the smooth skin on her back.

As his hand traced her bottom's curve, he whispered, "Nicest Christmas present I've had in a long time,"

She tugged his chest hair, and he winced. "When's the last time you had anything as nice? And who gave it to you?"

"My big brother when I was ten."

Wide-eyed she raised up. "Your brother?"

"Gave me his electric train. Course it only went round and round." He chuckled then squeezed her bottom. "This moves in a lot of nice directions."

"I am not sure what I see in you, Joe Stuart!"

"You missin' Johnathan?"

Her grin vanished. "Sometimes, I feel guilty about that."

"Why?"

She hung head. "Remember, his mother only allowed me to come on the voyage here with the understanding he and I would marry."

"Since that didn't happen and you're here, there's no problem."

"I'm not sure. She runs the Society that sponsors the hospital. Hard telling what she might do if she doesn't get her way. Remember Java?"

Joe recalled Mrs. Morgan's stranding Ann and her near marooning on the island during the voyage over. All because Mrs. Morgan heard a rumor of Ann's involvement with Joe.

"But she's nowhere around. Still no problem, right?"

Ann nodded. "Not yet. She and Johnathan haven't come this way for inspections because of the bombings. If the Japanese don't return, they might show up."

"I'll tell the boss. Have the spotters put the Morgans on their threat list."

"Then what? You guys scramble and shoot her down?"

"After the way her and Johnathan treated the guys on the ship, they'd probably even forgo the bonus for 'em."

She settled her head again on his chest before kissing him lightly on the cheek. "Tell me about Russ."

"God, now you wanna talk about some other guy? Sorry I brought up the subject."

She poked him in the side. "Jealous?"

"What? Here I am, begging for your hand in marriage. The man who would leap through flames to be at your side? And you ask me about some other guy?"

"Joe, you know how I feel about you. Besides, you promised."

"What do you want to know?"

"I'm merely curious about him. He seems nice, and he's not bad looking. Why doesn't he have someone? Is he a hidden monster?"

Joe shrugged. "Nah. He's a swell guy. Loves machines. And is handy as hell with 'em."

She raised her head, placed her chin on his chest. "At times, I think he is dead inside. With no feelings at all, but then you saw him with those children tonight."

"Russ recently lost his wife."

"That explains a lot. How did it happen?"

Joe put his hand behind his head. "She taught school in the country. Got caught in a blizzard while drivin' home. Car went into a ditch and stranded her. Guess she either froze to death or suffocated from carbon monoxide."

A tear glistened in her eye. "Oh, God, that's awful."

"What's worse, she was pregnant."

Joe then told her what he knew about Lamison's history, including his growing up as an orphan. As he finished, Ann sighed. "That makes sense now. After the attack, those Chinese brought him in unconscious. He came to as I was cleaning him up, and he asked if he could see his wife."

"So, you know?"

"Know what?"

"He told me some other stuff that I promised not to tell."

"I guess he thought he died and went to heaven. That happens a lot with people coming out of something like that. They often think they are dead and ask questions about heaven."

Breaking his promise to Russ, he told Ann what Russ told him earlier about seeing her as an angel. When he finished, she gently rested her head on Joe's shoulders. As her tears flowed onto his chest, he ran his fingers through her hair. "Sometimes, I wonder if there is a God. And if he is so powerful, how can he let all this wickedness happen."

****

OULOON, CHINA

"We sent you here to save souls, not start a harem." Gwen Morgan scowled down her nose at the man standing before her table, doing her best to channel the rage passed down from her Puritan ancestors.

The man's blond hair, and freckles incongruent with his black Chinese peasant garb and sandals. He squared his shoulders, his blue eyes meeting her gaze. At his side, a petite Chinese girl with downcast eyes cradled an infant.

Defiant, the man thrust out his chin. "Mei is my wife."

Mrs. Morgan gasped. "Your wife? How? There is no ordained clergy within miles of this place."

"The village priest officiated."

"Him? He's not Christian. That's outrageous."

"While not recognizing our deities, his beliefs are consistent with our own."

Mrs. Morgan turned to the bald man seated next to her. "Mr. Gant, have all of your people gone native?"

Gant's eyelids fluttered behind his wire-rimmed spectacles. He tugged at his collar and cleared his throat. "But I agreed to officiate when I arrived for this inspection. Give their union a true Christian blessing."

"You knew of this abomination?"

19

Gant pursed his lips. "Mr. Turner's wife passed away three years ago. I believed his forbearance from carnal pleasures all this time had been admirable. His new bride is, after all, a convert. I can attest to that myself."

"So, just like that, you intended to come here and consecrate this union. Did you also plan on baptizing this... this..." Her face flushed as she gestured to the infant. She tossed up her hands, shoved away from the table and stomped out.

Gant her exit with his eyes, then turned back to the couple before the table. "Doesn't sound too positive."

The man before him shook his head.

Gant sighed. "Don't worry, Mr. Turner. After she leaves, we will proceed as discussed."

The young woman at Turner's side looked up, a worried frown on her face. "Will she make trouble for us, Mr. Gant?"

"Most likely. She heads the society that sponsors all these missions. Because of that, she has a lot of power."

"Isn't my visa dependent on being with the mission?" Turner asked

Gant nodded. "But the government has other priorities. Deporting one missionary is probably not high on their list right now."

"Chiang Kai-shek approved my visa. The Kuomintang abandoned the village yesterday. Mao's Communists will be arriving soon to take control."

Gant's eyebrows rose with Turner's statement. "I will share that information with Mrs. Morgan. That might blunt her fury a bit." He rose to his feet. "You folks run along. I'll keep you informed."

As Gant followed Mrs. Morgan's exit, Turner put his arm around his wife's shoulders and left by an outside door.

In the adjacent room, Mrs. Morgan paced. She fanned herself while mumbling. Aware of Gant's entrance, she turned. "I'm going at once to the province offices. I should have no trouble having this man's visa revoked. I'm also putting you on notice. Any more of this gross misconduct, and I'll send you packing as well."

Gant went to the sideboard containing several crystal liquor decanters. "You look as if you could use a brandy."

Her head snapped around. "Do all men believe they can solve a problem with a quick drink?" She scowled as she brushed her gray curls from her face.

He shook his head as he filled a brandy snifter. "Solves nothing, but can calm the emotions. Prevent a person from making irrational decisions in the moment's heat."

She placed her hands on her hips. "You're saying I'm irrational?"

Before taking a sip, Gant shook his head. "No, but you should consider some things before you rush over to government house."

"What's that?"

"Our visas were all sanctioned by Chiang's Kuomintang."

"Yes. Is that important?"

"The province here is now under the control of Mao's Communists. While they have yet to arrive here in the town, they need not be reminded that there is a nest of missionaries in their midst. Last bunch they discovered are sitting in camps."

Mrs. Morgan rolled her eyes. "And you planned on telling me this when?"

Gant took a long drink from his snifter. Cocked his head. "If you recall when you announced your intention to inspect here, I mentioned that the timing might not be the best." He shrugged as he poured another drink. "But you insisted on coming, anyway."

The entrance by a young, man with slicked back dark hair in a white linen suit trailed by a casually attired Chinese youth. interrupted their conversation. Seeing the two already there, the dark-haired man paused. "Chen and I were out looking over the town. Did you know that the Communists have arrived, mother?"

Mrs. Morgan glared in Gant's direction. "So, I have been informed. Did you have problems, Johnathan?"

The two young men shared smiles. Johnathan turned to his mother. "No, Chen spotted them right off. That's why we didn't stay out long."

Mrs. Morgan turned to Chen. "Don't bother unpacking the car. We'll be leaving soon."

Chen nodded as Johnathan poured them both drinks from a decanter. As he passed the glass to Chen, Johnathan turned to his mother. "Where we headed next?"

Gant raised his glass. "I would suggest you go to Chintzu next. You could reach there before nightfall."

Chen nodded. "Even with the Red Brigades running things here, bandits still work the roads at night."

Mrs. Morgan sighed. "I do wish the bombing at Kunming would abate." She went to the sideboard herself and poured a brandy. "I'm sure you are anxious to check on your fiance'."

"Ann?"

Mrs. Morgan placed her hand on her chest. "Such a brave girl. The news I heard recently claimed she and her father moved the hospital twice since she arrived."

Gant nodded. "Yes, the bombing there has been relentless. I admire Dr. Ross for his courage. Remaining there with those constant attacks. But I understood that a new group of pilots might come there to protect the city."

Mrs. Morgan rolled her eyes. "I hope they aren't the same ones we met on the boat." She fanned herself, wrinkled her nose. "Disgusting degenerates."

CHAPTER THREE

RANGOON, BURMA

"I still find your claims a little hard to believe."

As Glenn Miller's *In The Mood* played softly on the radio, Ed Burton folded his arms, leaned back in his chair as he waited for Thiri's reply.

Seated at the adjacent desk in their warehouse office, Thiri looked up from her ledger. "You merely want me to feed your male ego. Make yourself believe you are more than adequate."

"Adequate? What about what you said last night?"

She flipped her black hair over her shoulder, gave him a wicked grin. "Amid passion, one says many things. True, you get better, but..." She winked. "You could do with more practice."

"As I said, I still find your little scheme hard to believe."

"That I arranged your kidnapping?"

Ed nodded. "Sounds so..."

"Machiavellian?"

"Where do you come up with these words?"

"I graduated from University, remember? And why not? I studied you closely after you landed in our village. Strong, almost good looking."

"Almost?"

She nodded. "Not like Burmese men." She shrugged. "But not bad in your way. I thought you might be a good lover."

"And arranging my kidnapping was the only way for you to have your way with me?"

"I wanted you to appreciate what I offered."

Ed rolled his eyes.

Thiri continued, her face serious, but stole a glance in his direction, judging his reaction. "Zeya was the revolutionary bent on running the British from Burma. Then he convinced the others to wander around in the forest, pretending to be great fighters. It suited my plans to convince him to grab you when he had the chance. I told him it might help him and his little band to get noticed. That was easy."

"And you figured he and the others would eventually give up trying to get the insurgency leader's attention. Then you'd step in and rescue me."

Thiri batted her eyes. "Why not? You are a man and easily manipulated."

Her lip quivered, her cheery disposition vanished beneath a wave of sadness. Silent she gazed off. A tear ran down her cheek. "I didn't mean for it to go so wrong."

Ed rolled his chair to her side. Wrapped her in his arms. "It wasn't your fault the plan fell apart. None of you knew the truth about Zeya."

She buried her head against his shoulder. Her shoulders quaked as she sobbed.

He ran his fingers through her hair, then drew back. "I'm sorry. Damn."

"No, it is all right. You may touch my head. No one is around, and Buddha may not be right about that. It comforts me."

"Look, we've made the best of the whole thing. You and the others are safe from Thiha for now. Hopefully, we'll be able to escape soon and get on with our lives."

She raised her eyes to him, stroked his cheek. "I still cannot accept that about Zeya."

"That he's a British spy?"

"My father, if nothing else, taught us to cherish our heritage. To work for the day when our country could be free of these British and their lackeys. I cannot accept that my brother has become one."

Ed shrugged. "People change. We've not talked with him since Thiha captured us."

"True. And we only have Thiha's word that Zeya is a spy."

"Thiha's a bandit and a killer. Lying wouldn't be a far stretch for him."

"True. If Zeya and I talked, I might understand."

She raised her lips to him, and they kissed. As their lips parted, Ed smiled. "Remember, I've told you I want you in my life for as long as you want."

A twinkle reappeared in her eyes. She grinned. "Are you sure I will not tire of you and cast you aside?"

"Rest assured. I will work hard at bein' all the love slave you need."

As she drew away, he passed her his handkerchief. After drying her eyes, she glanced at the clock. "You need to hurry, or you will miss your appointment at the airbase. If we don't keep moving these goods out, Thiha might close our shop."

As Ed rose, the music on the radio ended, he rolled his eyes. "If Radio Tokyo didn't have the best music, I'd never had it on, but the announcers..." A woman's voice on the radio interrupted him:

"People of Rangoon, we are coming to liberate you from your British masters. To free your country, though, you must make sacrifices. To spare yourselves, loyal Burmese should leave the city for your safety. The Imperial forces will first drop poison gas as we did in Manchuria. When this clears, our paratroopers will rain down from the skies. They will deal harshly with all who resist. After your liberation, you may safely return and join us in celebrating your new liberty!"

As the Banzai chant began, Ed switched off the radio.

****

At the police station soldiers scurried past the commander's office door preparing for the operation. With his hat in hand, Zeya stood just inside awaiting his orders.

"Constable, as you brought evidence on this Thiha and his associates, I want you to lead the raid on his warehouse." As he said this the uniformed officer closed his office door to reduce the noise from the crowded police station waiting room.

Zeya acknowledged the British officer's command with a nod.

In his khaki uniform and cavalry boots, the blond Englishman stroked his mustache as he paced. He tapped a quirt against his boots as he talked as if the rhythm might make his points. He turned to the Gurkha at attention next to Zeya with Sergeant Stripes on his sleeve. "Your squad will provide backup on the operation."

Zeya thrust back his shoulders. "What about the American's warehouse?"

The officer's head cocked back, his eyes narrowed. "Ah yes. Can't have that one slipping away either. Take his after you finish with this Thiha chap. I want him first. After all, he's the one running the show. Been a pain in our arses for years. The Yank's just a thief. That Thiha bloke's a murderer as well."

As Zeya headed out the door, the officer called out. "Remember, I want them brought in alive. Put `em in the docket, make an example of `em, then we can hang `em, eh?"

Zeya nodded as he put on his straw fedora and exited the office. Outside at the base of the station house stairs a truck with Gurkha seated in back idled at the curb. After the Sergeant leaped in to join his comrades in the rear, Zeya climbed into the passenger's seat and the truck roared off down the street.

As they turned down the street leading to Thiha's warehouse, an aircraft passed low overhead dropping leaflets. Once their truck screeched to a halt outside the warehouse, Zeya, along with the Gurkha leaped out. One Gurkha retrieved a sheet blowing along the pavement and passed it to Zeya. As Zeya read it the Sergeant peered over his shoulder.

"Do you think they mean it, Sah?" The Sergeant asked.

Zeya sneered as he wadded the sheet. "It doesn't matter. For now, we have work to do."

While people gathered up the sheets on the street, the Sergeant kicked open the Judas gate in one large door, allowing the others to stream in behind, their rifles poised for action. As the Gurkha rounded up the warehouse workers, Zeya, gun drawn, with the Sergeant trailing, charged up the stairs to the warehouse office. Inside, a young Burmese male leaped to his feet. "Zeya! You've come to free us?"

"Place your hands on your head," The Sergeant barked.

The young man gave Zeya a puzzled frown as he followed the Sergeant's order.

Zeya approached the young man as the Sergeant cuffed his hands behind his back. "Where's Thiha?"

"He left early this morning for Mandalay. Zeya, what's going on?"

Zeya ignored the question, turned to the Sergeant. "Pay no mind to what he said. Check the rest of the building. Thiha might be hiding."

Once the Sergeant left, Zeya turned to the young man. "Where are the others?"

"Jun and Shung are downstairs. The rest are with the American and Thiri at the other warehouse. Have you come to free us at last?"

Zeya nodded. "But, I need to deal with the man who defiled my sister."

"But Thiha escaped."

"Thiha is not the one who must pay."

As Zeya led the young man in handcuffs down the stairs, a crowd gathered outside. The Sergeant joined him. "We've rounded up everyone here. The others confirmed that Thiha is not here." He nodded to the people clustered in the street. "If we leave now there will be looting."

"Our orders were to catch the crooks. What happens now is not our concern."

****

The British Major frowned as he studied Ed's price list. "How you seem to have what we need at the best price amazes me."

What could Ed say? Thiha stole it from the British, whatever they got for it would be profit. They kept the prices low but not low enough to draw suspicion. The sound of an airplane passing low overhead prompted both men to glance up as if they might see through the ceiling. As the air-raid siren sounded, all activity in the office ceased as everyone ducked beneath their desks. Once the all-clear sounded, one clerk rose and glanced out the window. "The bastard dumped paper."

As Ed and the Major rose from beneath the table where they had taken cover, an enlisted man hurried in, clutching a handful of leaflets. After laying one on the desk, he scurried out. Ed stepped behind the Major and read over the officer's shoulder.

The Major bared his teeth. "Can't read this other gibberish. Probably says the same thing in all these Wog lingoes."

"They said the same thing earlier on the radio about poison gas and paratroopers."

"Probably want to make sure that everybody hears about it. Not just the folks who own a wireless." The Major tossed the sheet in the trash. "Surprised, they mentioned the butchery in Nanking. Bloody cheek!"

With his meeting concluded at the airbase, Ed descended the stairs to his waiting car. The leaflets triggered immediate panic. Now thousands took to the streets. Some carried suitcases and bags while others wandered surveying the skies. Once they left the airfield, he and Thant, Ed's Burmese driver, and bodyguard, headed towards the warehouse through the throng.

Thant leaned on the horn as if the noise might clear a path through the crowd flowing around them. Blocked by the foot traffic, the car stopped creeping forward. After two hours, the usual thirty-minute trip left them a mile from their destination.

Frustrated and fearing for Thiri's safety, Ed leaped from the back seat and called over his shoulder. "Stay with the car. I'll walk the rest of the way. Join me when you can."

As he pushed through the crowd, he glanced down the side street towards Thiha's storehouse. Flames roared from his partner's structure, while a smoke column soared into the sky above. Sirens blared behind him. The crowd's movement halted in a confused crush as frantic people made way for the fire trucks, fled the fire, or continued their panicked travels through the street.

At one point, the crowd swept Ed along like a cork floating on a confused sea. One second forward, then back, or breaking against a wall. At one point, he braced his back against a wall then pushed the nearest person with both feet to keep from being smothered. The air filled with screams and wails, punctuated by angry outbursts.

Gradually the press of bodies subsided. Able to move, Joe shoved through the crowd, now, as if a swimmer, struggling upstream or gliding downstream, but headed to his destination.

At his warehouse, he stepped through one large door's Judas gate. The faint glow coming from the office windows upstairs illuminated the piled crates awaiting delivery. Deserted and quiet, he wondered where his crew had gone.

His footsteps rang out on the iron stairway, as he trotted up. Out of breath at the top, he listened — silence, not even the usual music from Thiri's desk radio. His panting the only sounds reaching his ears.

As he approached the office door, his footsteps clanging on the iron catwalk echoed. When he swung the door open, he spied black hair just above the back of his desk chair, facing away from the door. His relief changed to shock as the chair turned, and he found himself face to face with Zeya holding a huge pistol.

"I thought you might have slipped away like, Thiha," Zeya hissed as he held the gun aimed at Ed, "I am glad you didn't. At least I can deal with you. There is joy in that."

Ed glanced around the vacant office. "Where is Thiri?"

"The Gurkha came and took them all away. They are safe from you and Thiha. I stayed here, hoping you might return."

"Zeya, what's goin' on?"

"What is going on? You do not know? Did you think you could go on thieving with Thiha forever? Or are you going to pretend that you did not know he was a thief and a murderer?" Zeya cocked the pistol. "He paid you money and gave you a fine place to live because he was a generous man?"

"Zeya, you know damn well how I got in this situation. I'm sure Thiri explained what we had to do."

"That is a lie. You made this arrangement with Thiha to make yourself rich. Plus, you persuaded him to give you my sister as a concubine to sweeten the deal."

"Thiri said this?"

"No, your abuse has unbalanced her mind. Made wild claims you did this to protect her and the others. Became aggressive. She even attacked me! Her brother." The pistol shook in Zeya's hands as his finger tightened on the trigger." The Gurkhas sedated her before they took her away."

"But what she said is true. I love Thiri, and she loves me. We performed this charade to protect her and the others from Thiha after you fucked everything up."

As soon as he spoke, Ed realized he said the wrong thing. Zeya's face flushed. The gun trembled in his hands. Ed stepped sideways out the doorway as Zeya's weapon roared. The bullet passed through the now empty space pinging as it ricocheted off the steel catwalk handrail.

"On top of everything else, you defiled my sister!" Zeya screamed as he fired again. Ed dropped to the catwalk's floor as the office window shattered above him. Zeya fired again. This time the bullet shattered the wood in the wall just inches from Ed's head, splattering wood chips in his eyes.

"The others are safe, but because of you, she is insane. Even if she recovers, no decent Burmese man will want her because of you and Thiha's treachery."

The sound of Zeya's footsteps approached the door. Unable to cross the doorway to escape down the stairs, he crawled towards the catwalk's dead end. A one-story drop to the floor below would be less dangerous than trying to dodge bullets from Zeya's gun on the narrow catwalk.

Below, a stack of boxes came to within six feet of the catwalk's floor. Zeya stepped out and peered into the darkness.

"You look like a real gangster in that white suit. It shows up well in this darkness," Zeya snarled as he cocked the pistol, "It's a shame it has gotten so dirty today."

At that moment, one large warehouse door swung open, bathing the building in light. Distracted, Zeya looked away. Seizing the opportunity, Ed plunged over the catwalk's edge, dropping to the boxes stacked below. Desperate, he rolled off the stack's edge. Ed clutched the top to break his fall, allowing him to land on his feet on the side opposite Zeya. As he reached out to maintain his balance, hands pinned his arms.

"Stand down, Constable!" a voice called up to Zeya from behind him.

CHAPTER FOUR

As Ed leaned against the cell wall, he recalled yesterday's events. After disarming Zeya, the British officer had posted guards at the warehouse. The officer then escorted Ed to the police car while Zeya followed them to the station in a truck.

As they traveled through the crowded streets, Ed described his kidnapping and the arrangement he made with Thiha for his and the group's safety. But the officer ignored him as he studied Ed's papers identifying him as Travers.

At the police station, two Gurkha jerked him from the car. With shoves and clubs, they herded him down the jailhouse hallway. Outside the cell, they removed his shoes and his belt before shoving him inside and locking the door.

Throughout the night, screams and ranting came from nearby cells. The noise, coupled with his worries about himself and Thiri, prevented sleep on the wooden planks that served as a bunk. Just before dawn, he dozed. Jerked awake by the sound of boots marching down the hall, he bolted upright on his bed.

"His circumstances are suspicious," The voice of the British officer from yesterday trailed up the hallway as the footsteps grew louder. "He claims to be one of your pilots, but he carries papers identifying him as a Swiss by the name of Travers. Appropriate, given it originally meant someone who collected tolls at bridges. Probably a common one for a black marketer, but hardly a Swiss surname."

Olsen, his squadron leader, accompanied by the British officer, and a short, stout, bald man in a rumpled gray suit appeared outside his cell.

After peering into the cell, Olsen shook his head. "That's our guy. He might look like a bum, but bandits kidnapped him several weeks ago. I'm surprised you found him alive."

The bald man at Olsen's side wiped his brow and scowled at the British officer. "I will interview him right away, Captain, and if I discover that your people have brutalized him, my government will protest. These accommodations are frightful. I demand you release him at once."

The British officer shrugged, then beckoned a Gurkha holding keys to approach the cell. As the guard opened the door, his glance gave Ed shivers.

While clutching his pants to keep them up, Ed shuffled to the door. "I need my shoes and my belt."

The guard removed a bag from a hook on the wall. After tossing it to Ed, he stomped off.

While Ed replaced his belt and tied his shoes, the British officer turned to Olsen and the other man. "I am releasing him to your custody while we investigate further. You will make him available should we need to speak to him later?"

The short bald man scowled. "He is an American citizen. I find your attitude in the matter atrocious."

The British officer pulled himself to attention and scowled. "I don't care what your government might say or do at this point. I am releasing him because we have more serious concerns than dealing with the small-time crooks you brought here."

Finished, the officer followed the guard down the hallway without a backward glance.

Olsen shook his head. "Jesus, Burton, I can hardly wait for your story." He gestured to the man at his side. "This is Carl Edelston from the US embassy." Olsen turned to Edelston. "Can you do your interview while we drive? With the traffic mess, you should have ample time. That way, we can both hear what he has to say."

The man nodded as he stepped aside to allow Ed out of the cell. Ed and Olsen walked side by side as they left with the man from the Consulate scurrying behind.

Before he climbed into the car's backseat, Ed turned to Olsen. "Can we stop at the apartment I was using on the way? I need to grab some clothes."

Olsen nodded as he climbed into the front passenger seat while Edelston took the wheel.

Ed stepped from the car as it stopped in front of his apartment building. "I'll only be a second," he called over his shoulder as he trotted up the stairs. In his apartment, he shook his head as he surveyed the chaos wrought by the police.

He grabbed a pillowcase and gathered clothing items. After removing his torn and stained suit, he redressed in the flying gear he wore when kidnapped. He wondered if they would let him fly again as he pulled on his flight boots.

Finished dressing, he went to the door. Once the bolted the door, he moved to the to the now empty closet. On his hands and knees, he pried a board from the closet floor and set it aside. From the hole, he pulled out wads of currency Thiri stashed there.

Satisfied he had it all, he then pulled another board loose. From this spot, he pulled out four small gold bars also hidden by her. After dropping the cash and the gold into a pillowcase, he pushed the boards back in place. He now filled the pillowcase with his remaining clothes.

He paused at the door before leaving. A lump formed in his throat as he surveyed the room. Thiri's clothes scattered everywhere. Her perfume bottle shattered against the wall filling the air with the aroma of her presence. On the dresser set her copy of the *Kama Sutra*. Filled with exotic sexual positions that she loved to study, then try with him in their evenings together.

"One gains much by studying different belief systems. This Hindu holy book is one that could inspire one throughout the lifetime." She'd say, looking up from the book. Then she'd laugh and drag him to the bed for what she described as the evening's lesson.

As he slipped it inside the pillowcase, he vowed to find her no matter where she might be in this chaotic city.

****

The sound of a passing car jarred Thant awake. He rubbed his eyes as he sat up on the car seat. As the sky lightened with the dawn, the passing vehicle stopped a half-block away in front of Ed and Thiri's apartment building. After sleeping in the car, Thant's body ached. His rumpled suit smelled foul. As his stomach growled, reminding him he had not eaten since Ed's arrest, Ed emerged from the car and jogged inside the building.

Prepared to rescue Ed, he started the car. If Ed stayed, Thant would go to him for instructions. If his boss left, he would trail behind, hoping to help him escape.

Yesterday, Thant arrived at the warehouse as the police took Ed away. He crouched behind the dash as the police car passed, but as he looked up to track its passage, a large truck stopped beside his vehicle. As Zeya leaped from the vehicle's back and charged his auto, Thant trembled. Enraged, Zeya threw open the door, yanked him out by his lapels, and slammed him against the car. Zeya pressed his face against his. "Where have you been, you disgusting little worm?"

"The traffic. You have seen the streets. The boss walked, and I caught up with him only now. What is happening?"

Zeya's face a scornful mask. "I've arrested your boss. His little scheme with Thiha is at an end. He will rot in jail, or maybe I will arrange for him to have an accident. It is not your concern."

"Why is the boss being arrested? He only agreed to work with Thiha to save us from being sold in Bangkok. I told you that. I'm sure Thiri said the same thing."

Zeya slapped him. "That is even worse. The American's abuse has left her unbalanced. She is out of her mind."

"That's not true. Why are you doing this?"

He shoved Thant to the pavement. "Now go. Meet the others at the train station."

Thant brought his hands together like a supplicant at the altar. "You are making this all up. Why? I have been with them. They are in love. She gives herself freely."

Zeya sneered. "Love? What does a disgusting little sodomite like you know of such things? I want no more arguments. Go, or I will turn you over to the men in the truck. They know how to deal with your kind."

Thant shook his head and shrugged. Helpless, he returned to the car and called over his shoulder. "I will go to the station. Drive the others home. The trains are full."

At the station, the others from their group stood outside on the crowded sidewalk. As he stepped from the vehicle, they gathered around.

One girl clutched his hand. "It was horrible. Zeya arrived with the police. As they arrested us the crowd broke in and started looting."

A boy at her side nodded. "Zeya gave me and the others' money and told us to come here and catch a train back home. The Japanese would come, and we needed to be out of the city."

Thant frowned. "What about the other warehouse?"

The boy at his side nudged the one beside him, he stepped forward. "I was there, Zeya came with the Ghurka. Thiri attacked him, and they subdued her. She told them she and the boss had been doing all this to keep us safe before we escaped, but Zeya called her a liar. Told the Gurkha that the boss and Thiha's abuse had unbalanced her mind. "

A second girl stepped forward. "Yes, he said she was crazy, and they would find her a place to straighten out her thinking. The Gurkha held her arms and put her in a jacket that fastened in the back, and the sleeves trapped her arms."

The boy nodded. "She kicked and screamed. Called Zeya a traitor, and he slapped her before they took her away."

"Where did they take her?"

The others all exchanged glances then one boy stepped forward. "I believe they took her to the asylum."

These words sent a shiver down Thant's spine. His stomach churned as he recalled once passing by this isolated prison. The frightening sounds drifting out from the eerie structure set his teeth on edge. Remembered stories from others who shared his passions about their own experiences while undergoing their so-called rehabilitation in that hellish dungeon.

The train sitting at the platform's whistle sounded prompting the others to turn. A girl clutched Thant's hand. "We must hurry. The train is about to leave."

The boy at her side nodded. "Yes. Leave the car here. We have tickets, but they are letting anyone on that can squeeze in. We must catch this one before they bomb the station."

Thant pulled away from the girl. "No, I must stay. You all go on ahead. When I find Thiri, I will drive her and the boss to the village. Tell her father, please."

And so began his lonely vigil the evening before. Posted here on the street, sleeping fitfully, as he worried about Ed and Thiri and what he may have to do to lead them to safety.

Now instead of driving away, the car that brought Ed remained at the curb. Finally, Ed emerged dressed in the clothes he wore when captured, lugging two packed pillowcases.

Thant drew the pistol from his shoulder holster, prepared to cover the boss if he bolted from his captors. As he clutched the gun in his sweaty hands, he placed his other on the car's horn ring. A quick toot of the horn might alert the boss to his presence, he told himself. Prompt Ed to dash in his direction. He would use the gun to cover the boss' retreat. Possibly disable the other vehicle, allowing them to escape.

He had never fired the weapon before and wondered if now he would be up to the task before him. He set his jaw. It didn't matter; he told himself. He could not abandon this man who sacrificed so much to save him and the others from Thiha. If required, he would lay down his life for this man.

As his hand moved to the horn ring, Ed glanced in his direction. Without showing a sign of recognition, Ed ducked inside the other car's back seat.

Thant groaned as he set the gun on the seat beside him, put the car in gear, and trailed Ed's captors through the streets to the airfield gates. As the vehicle carrying his boss passed through the gates, Thant stopped down the road.

His mind raced. Without money to bribe the guards, he could not get in without the boss. Also, since they arrested the boss and brought him here, would they detain him as an accomplice as well? Convinced he could do nothing here, he drove off determined to find Thiri. Perhaps together they could save the boss.

****

The next morning, as Thant studied the streets below the apartment dawn broke outside. He sighed while the man behind him continued his questioning as he massaged Thant's neck. "What will you do? If your policeman friend discovers you failed to leave with the others, he might guess you came here. If so, he would arrest us both."

Thant turned and nodded. Drew the man close, ran his fingers through the man's salt and pepper hair. "I'm sorry Cho. Taking me in has put you in great danger."

"Despite everything, you know how I feel. I did not betray you to that policeman. He remembered our relationship from university."

Thant stepped back. With his hand beneath Cho's chin, Thant gently tipped his lover's head back to gaze into his eyes. "I know. He threatened me as well. A lifetime in prison merely because you love someone? It is evil."

Cho drew away, fumbled with his robe's sash, with one hand as he poured tea from a ceramic pot with the other. "Do you think the Comrades will treat us better? Allow us to openly declare our love?" He passed the filled cup to Thant.

As Thant raised the steaming cup to his lips he frowned. "They promised. In the meantime, I need information about Thiri."

"Thiri? Zeya's sister?"

"The Gurkha took her away. The others claim she is in the asylum, but I need to know for sure."

"Why?"

He told Cho of his plan to rescue Ed and Thiri.

"But why? Stay here until the Japanese come. I am still free to come and go. You will want for nothing. Then we can be safe."

Thant shook his head. "The boss treated me with respect and honor. He and Thiri are in love. I feel obligated."

Cho dropped into a chair at the kitchen table. "With all the chaos in the city who would know?"

"The police."

Cho's head snapped around, his jaw dropped. "You cannot go there. What if you are seen? If not by Zeya, the Gurkha."

"I hate to ask this of you, but would you go there in my stead?"

Cho rose, took Thant in his arms. "If you are set on this course. But it seems madness and for what?"

"To me it seems the right thing to do. How often do we get those chances?"

****

Alone in her cell, Thiri huddled against the wall. All around noises pierced the darkness. Both screams and laughter sent chills down her spine. Some babbled. Their droning conversations, illogical or rambling. Others revealed a dark and frightening personal reality. Either railing against this world or describing other universes populated by outrageous and skillful clowns or filled with evil demons. The odor of urine, feces, and stale vomit filled the air.

Last night the lights remained on all night. She guessed this allowed the attendants to observe the inmates. The evening before, two women fought in the common area for almost an hour before four burly men arrived. They placed both in jackets, like the one they put on her when they took her away. These heavy canvas jackets pinned their arms inside, strapped behind. When the two continued kicking and screaming, the attendants dragged them out. Because the fight lasted so long before they intervened, Thiri guessed the attendants did not watch constantly but checked at intervals. If she had problems with another inmate, help might not come in time.

Also, the attendants provided no comfort. Merely brought the three meal buckets or hosed down the walls and floors daily. During this ritual, they sometimes sprayed inmates and laughed as the hapless soul captured in the water blast crashed into the wall.

All but one attendant appeared aloof to the surrounding misery as if they viewed the people here as no different from livestock. Instead, when he entered the ward, he studied her like a wolf watching a small animal. Later he returned and stood outside her cell, leering and rubbing his crotch. After that, he grabbed another young female inmate wandering by. He led her away while staring back at Thiri as if taking a photograph in his mind. Later, he shoved the young woman back into the common area, then turned and winked at Thiri. The memory made her shiver.

Tonight, the lights went out at dusk right after they emptied the food bucket and left the cell doors unlocked. No trace of light penetrated the surrounding darkness. A shuffling nearby made her draw even closer to herself. Her bunk creaked. She sensed movement nearby as if someone perched at the plank bed's other end. Once again, the bed creaked along with the sound of someone sliding across the board. Still unable to make out any forms in the darkness, a body brushed against hers. A hand touched her knee then stroked her thigh. She shuddered as an arm embraced her shoulder, a rough tongue thrust into her ear.

A woman's voice whispered in the dark. "Ah, granddaughter, you are so fine. I would be your friend, make you safe, make you happy."

The woman cackled in the dark as Thiri squirmed trapped by her unseen suitor against the wall. The woman pressed her hard against the wall pinning her immobile.

"I thought you would struggle. That is good. If you make it too hard for me, I will cut your throat. It would be messy, but I still would enjoy you. They might lock me up for a week or so, but I don't mind the privacy. It would give me time to recall our little time together."

A flashlight's beam cut the darkness. The light, revealed the woman's face. The big woman, who prowled the ward or stayed by herself against the wall while studying the others. A straight razor gleamed in her attacker's hand.

Thiri never saw it but heard the thud of the truncheon strike the back of the woman's head. As she toppled against Thiri, she tasted the woman's foul breath. The woman's eyes now sightless as she crumbled to the floor. The light in Thiri's eyes blinded her.

"Well, it looks like I got here in time," a man's voice came from the darkness. "It appears someone else thought they might enjoy the first serving."

CHAPTER FIVE

As the flashlight tumbled to the floor, her attacker pressed Thiri's shoulders back on the plank. Despite the beam's focus on the wall, the reflected light revealed her attacker as the same man who leered at her earlier while escorting the girl out. His teeth bared in a wicked grin. His eyes riveted on hers as he pressed her back on the bunk. "Hold still bitch, or I'll hurt you."

He released one shoulder as he pressed her down with his weight to tug at the hem of her dress.

His hand slipped up her thigh while she strained to keep her knees together as she beat on his chest. "No. Stop."

Tears streamed down her cheeks while his hand slipped higher. As he wedged her knees apart with his, she kneed his groin.

"Bitch." He lunged back, backhanded her across the face. "Lie still. Who knows? You might enjoy it."

She clawed at his face. "Never."

He pinned her arms once more. His weight on her chest suffocating. "The others don't complain. I should choke the shit outta you and do it while you're still warm, but I like a little fight. Adds to the fun."

With her arms pinned by his forearm, he again grasped the hem of her dress. Her dress now at her waist, he again pinned her arms to the plank. Slipped one hand to where he gripped a finger and bent it back.

As she howled with pain, he leered into her eyes. "I'm gonna let go of the other hand. If you fight me, I'll twist this finger off."

"No. Please."

Pinned on the bed, unable to hit or claw. His teeth flashed as her attacker smiled in the dim light. "You might find you like it."

"Never." she hissed.

He jammed a finger inside her. "Damn, girl, you're wet already. Must like it rough. That, right?" He slapped her again before resuming his probing.

Unable to look in her assailant's face, Thiri turned her head. A shadow appeared at the cell doorway. The silhouette bent over as if picking something up, before slipping behind the man looming over her.

Still grasping her finger, the man undid his trousers. As he raised up to pull them down, a hand slipped under his chin, jerking his head back. The razor flashed in the dim light as the shadow drew it across his throat. Blood fountained from his neck, air rushed from his lungs as his eyes rolled back in his head.

The shadow shoved her attacker aside while his blood flowed across the floor, pooling around his inert form.

As the shadow retreated into the darkness, Thiri sat up and pulled her blood-soaked dress down. "Who are you? What do you want?"

A voice replied from the darkness. "I want nothing. You are safe now."

Thiri snatched up the flashlight and aimed it in the voice's direction. Outside her cell stood the girl her attacker raped earlier that day. Covered in blood, the old woman's razor clutched in her hand, she pointed to the older woman's body crumpled on the floor next to the man. "These two have been our nightmare."

Other figures emerged from the shadows. Gathered around the young girl holding the razor. Her long black hair shimmered as she turned her head to them. "We must block the door. If they discover what we've done, they will punish us."

One turned to Thiri, her face illuminated by the flashlight. Her short black hair sticking out like a lion's mane she pointed in Thiri's direction. "But you merely protected this one. We will tell them." Several nodded in agreement.

Still clutching the razor, the killer shook her head. "They won't listen. We are crazy."

****

When Cho, Thant's lover, returned last evening, he claimed the Gurkhas took Thiri to the asylum outside town. Thant needed to confirm it and learn more. Stopped a few yards down the road the following morning, Thant studied the asylum. Surrounded by a ten-foot stone wall, only the upper stories of the institution's building appeared above it. Once again, he recalled the stories others who shared his passion told about their experiences here. The humiliating manipulations used by the staff to enhance their desires for the opposite sex. Their horrific treatments to discourage their attraction to their own gender. His stomach churned as he imagined what treatment lay in store for Thiri, or what he risked freeing her. But she and Ed had stood by him. Trusted him to protect them. He must not back away. With his jaw clenched he put the car in gear and drove to the gate.

The man inside the gatehouse stepped up to his car. "I am here to visit."

The guard scowled. "I must see a pass."

Thant retrieved a handful of shillings from his jacket pocket and held them out. "Please."

The guard glanced around before taking the coins. With a nod, he opened the gate and waved Thant's car through.

Parked in the semicircular drive before the main building, Thant rushed up the stairs. Once inside, Thant slipped from doorway to doorway, taking cover when footsteps approached. At the end of a long hallway, a woman typed at a desk before a door marked "Director."

Hidden in the shadow, Thant waited until the woman left the area. Seizing his opportunity, he barged through the door.

Inside, the man behind the desk lunged back in his chair. His jaw dropped as he gazed at Thant through the pince-nez perched on his nose. "What's the meaning of this?"

Thant planted his feet. He removed his fedora and fidgeted with the brim. "Please, sir, I seek my fiance'. I fear she may be here."

"Fear? Young man, we provide nothing but the finest care here for our charges." He glanced past Thant then turned his gaze back to him. "How did you get in here?"

"Please, sir. I only want to make sure she is all right."

"Unless you are family, I can tell you nothing. I can neither confirm nor deny the person you are seeking is here, so if you have no other business, I must ask you to leave."

The Director's eyes narrowed as he straightened his vest and pressed the button on the intercom. "Officer, to my office at once." He scowled as he studied Thant standing at attention before him, his hat in hand. "I am not sure how you got in here or who told you that this young woman might be here. If she is here, you will need to talk to her family. If they agree, they can add you to the permissible visitor's list. But, as I said, I cannot tell you if she is here or not."

Thant opened his wallet, removed a ten-pound note, his last week's pay, which he laid on the man's desk.

"Her name is Thiri. Please, sir, my fiancé's family does not approve of me because I am a Christian. We fled here to hide in the city while we received instruction from the priest, so the Church would accept our marriage. Her brother pursued us and used his connections with the police to have her arrested and brought here. I only want to make sure she is all right."

The man peered at the bill lying on his desk, but his hands made no move toward the currency. Instead, he glanced up at Thant. "I realize the ethnic animosity that exists here. Buddhist against Hindu. Hindu against Sikh. Sikh against Muslim and everyone against the Christian. I am truly sorry for your position, but again I cannot tell you if she is here or not, but she is all right. Please take your money."

A hulking man entered the office and loomed over Thant.

"Officer, this man was about to leave. Could you make sure he gets safely to the gate?"

As Thant exited, the phone rang. After putting the phone to his ear, he frowned as he listened. "No, don't break down the door. I'll call the police and be right down."

As he replaced the phone, a tall, dark-haired woman entered. "Herbert, remember we have the governor's banquet this evening."

He held up his hand as he spoke again into the phone. "Yes, give me the police station. This is Director Ralston at the Asylum. It's urgent."

"What's wrong, Herbert?"

He covered the mouthpiece. "Please, Sylvia, I need to take care of this." He uncovered the mouthpiece. "This is Director Ralston at the Asylum. I need to speak with whoever is in charge. We have an emergency."

Sylvia placed a hand to her chest, her eyes opened wide. "Are we in danger?"

"Leftenant Murphy? Yes, we have a rather serious situation here."

Ralston listened. "A riot in the women's ward. The attendant on duty is missing. The patients barricaded the door and are refusing entrance."

"Yes, other orderlies deserted with the panic and all, so possibly he deserted. I only have two security guards and may need your people to back us up if we have to go in."

He listened. "How many patients? I believe there is around seventy-five on the roster, but that changes from day to day with illness and death."

He nodded now as he listened. "Yes, this ward contains several considered violent to others."

Ralston rolled his eyes. "A guard will meet you at the gate. They will direct you to the proper building. In the meantime, I'm going down there to assess the situation."

He turned to Sylvia, his wife, who stood now silent, her eyes opened wide. "Go back to the house. Lock the doors and keep the children inside. You know where the revolver is. If they break out, you may have to use it."

As Sylvia scurried away, Ralston retrieved a cattle prod from a desk drawer. He peered at the metal tube's prongs. As he pressed a button on the handle, a spark snapped between prongs. Satisfied with its performance, he strode out.

****

With a quick glance over his shoulder, checking for surveillance, Zeya ducked into the tea shop. Wide-eyed, the man behind the counter beckoned Zeya to follow him. Before escorting Zeya to the back, he turned to his only customers, a couple seated at a table near the door. "Excuse me, I shall return shortly. If I may, I recommend the raisin tea cakes. My daughter baked them, but an hour ago."

He took Zeya by the arm, leading him towards the shop's back area. "Comrade, where have you been?"

Zeya removed his straw fedora, ran his fingers through his hair. "Things have gotten out of control."

The man frowned as he unlocked the back door. "I will call the others. Have a cup of tea while you wait, or if you want something stronger, there is whiskey in the cupboard. Wait here while I finish upfront."

Once the door closed behind him, Zeya set his hat on the table and dropped onto a chair. Had he ever had anything under control, he asked himself. First, kidnapping the American, then Thiha nabbing them all. And now his sister in the asylum... He drummed his fingers on the table as he scanned the room. He leaped to his feet and went to the cupboard. After taking down the bottle, he uncorked it and filled a glass.

He tossed the contents down in one gulp. Coughed and thumped his chest. While puffing his cheeks from the burn, he poured another. His hand trembled as he raised the drink to his lips. Now sipping, he paced, mumbled, and massaged his forehead.

How could this have happened? Instead of driving the British from his country, he tossed his sister into debauchery, driving her insane.

The officer who stopped him from killing the American had kept him for hours, questioning him about the fire at Thiha's warehouse. Berated him for not remaining there to prevent the looting and vandalism. Allowing the warehouse's contents to be destroyed. Instead, he had rushed off to the other warehouse, leaving Thiha's unguarded. When the reprimand session ended, he worked through the night with other policemen quelling disturbances that broke out throughout the city overnight.

As the door opened behind him, he turned. The shopkeeper trailed by another Burmese man in a three-piece suit entered the room. The second man's face broke into a smile. "Comrade Zeya, I and the others worried about you."

"Me?"

The man placed his hand on Zeya's shoulder, stared into his eyes as the shopkeeper brewed tea. "Yes, word came to us that the Gurkha had arrested you at the American's warehouse. We feared they compromised you."

"No, I caught that American gangster there." Zeya sipped his drink and shrugged. "The Officer in charge allowed the criminal to ride in his car, leaving me to ride with the Gurkha." He shrugged. "You know how they are."

The man nodded. "But it all goes well, does it not? This disruption in British supplies caused by Thiha and the American. The others admire that coup you so skillfully arranged."

Zeya swallowed the urge to scream. Instead, these words roared in his head. *No, I kidnapped the American to lure Thiha into a police trap. Instead, he escaped, captured my band, and become even more successful in his thievery.* But the party had spun this tale as Zeya's great coup so many times the man would think him unbalanced for mentioning it. Remind them that this had all been, as the American, Ed Burton, claimed, his fuck up.

As the shopkeeper poured tea, the man beckoned Zeya to a chair as he talked. "And now the chaos created by the leaflets. You'll see, soon we will drive the British out. As our Japanese friends have promised, Asia for Asians."

A rumbling like thunder came from above. The building shook rattling plates in the cupboard.

****

As Ed entered the alert shack, most of the pilot's inside greeted him with wide-eyed stares as if they saw a ghost. Jenson, wearing his trademark cowboy hat, boots, and shorts, shoved his way through the crowd gathered around Ed.

As Jensen pumped Ed's hand, a broad grin spread on his face. "Shit Burton! Haven't seen you since that night at the Silver Grill. Rejoined the flock?"

"It's good to be back, but it's a real mess."

Jensen nodded, still grinning. "I'll say. The CO was pissed when he got the message to bail you out."

"Well, I didn't think it pleased the Old Man I turned up either." Finished shaking hands, Ed dropped into a vacant chair. "After they told Chennault what happened, Greenlaw notified Olson that I should consider myself under arrest while the matter is under investigation. Said something about a court-martial."

As he set a steaming coffee mug in front of Ed, one pilot shook his head. "Under arrest? What the hell does that mean?"

A pilot leaning against the wall with his arms folded across his chest scowled. "Oh, hell. That's just Greenlaw's usual shtick. He's threatened me with that twice already."

Jenson tipped his hat back on his head and laughed. "Yeah! Remember, he had a shit-fit when Boyington wrestled the water buffalo. It took four of us to keep Boyington from doing to Greenlaw what he did to the buffalo. Scared Greenlaw so bad he hid in his office for a week."

Ed frowned. "Who's Boyington?"

Jenson nodded. "A Marine. Arrived after you disappeared. Big mean bastard, but he's old. Twenty-six."

Ed rose and strolled to the window. As he studied the airfield outside, Jenson joined him. The aircraft parked outside appeared evenly divided between the two runways. His squadrons P-40s on one and the British Brewster Buffaloes on the other. Ed nodded towards the runways. "So, how does it work around here?"

"Our runway crosses the British runway with half the planes at either end."

"How in the hell do you keep from ramming each other at the intersection during a scramble?"

"Everybody stays to the right. Brits roll through the intersection, and we fly over. Hairy, but we had one false alarm, and it worked okay. Just keep an eye out for the Brits. Sometimes one of them gets up early before the crossing, cause of the atmospherics, I guess."

The phone's peal silenced the room. All turned towards it, as Jenson picked up the receiver. Silent, he listened, then set the phone back in its cradle. "We got bombers coming in from the East and Southeast. All planes up."

The shack emptied as pilots rushed out the door. Half the men scurried to the P-40s parked near the building while the other half leaped into a car that raced to the planes parked at the far end. Since they got the signal first and with ground crewman to start the aircraft, the British Buffaloes engines roared, and two rolled down the runway. Soon the air filled with the whine of engine starters, the stuttering coughs of others as they caught or the roar of those that started.

Soon planes buzzed past each other on the runway. No collisions, but one Buffalo nearly flipped end over end as the pilot slammed on the brakes when one P-40 failed to flyover the intersection. His quick stop allowed him to cross behind the speeding P-40 before the Buffalo's tail slammed down. Once the pilot released the brake, he rolled forward. With the shortened takeoff run it overran the runway before rising in the air, skimming trees surrounding the field. Once the fighters disappeared in the sky, a deathly silence fell over the base.

As Ed emerged from the shack, two men raced up on bicycles. After dumping the bikes, they sprinted to two P-40s still parked on the flight line. Ed trotted over to them.

"Burton! Jesus, where did you come from?" one asked as he pulled a parachute from the plane and strapped it on.

"It's complicated. We'll talk later. Japs are comin'."

The other pilot donned his helmet as he climbed on the wing. Once he plugged his radio into the plane's dash, he listened over his headset. As he strapped on his parachute, he turned to Ed and the other pilot. "We're supposed to join up with 'em over the oil refinery." He pointed to the blocks of wood wedged against the plane's tires. "Can you pull the wheel chocks for us, fellah?"

Ed scurried around the plane's wing while yanking the blocks away from the wheel on one, then the other.

"Good huntin' guys!" he shouted as the two engine starters brought the warbirds to life.

As the two taxied to the runway, the air-raid siren sounded. The sound of planes overhead prompted him to glance upwards. A mass of dots approached from the East. After dropping the wheel chocks, Ed sprinted to a pile of sandbags nearby and leaped into the slit trench on the other side of the bags. As the bombs whistled down from above, he crouched and covered his head.

CHAPTER SIX

As light streamed through the barred windows, Thiri's head sunk to her chest, and her eyelids drooped. Laughter and shouting at the ward door made her head pop up, and she glanced around. The attendant's nearly decapitated body remained on the floor by her bunk, while they dragged her first attacker's body to a nearby wall. The dead woman's sightless eyes stared at Thiri as if she could rise any movement and resume her attack. As Thiri rose from the bunk, she clutched the flashlight in her hand while stepping over the attendant's body.

The young woman, who killed the attendant, now stood with two others near the door. They turned in unison as Thiri emerged from her cell. The remaining inmates either sat along the wall or wandered around the floor.

The attendant's killer slipped the razor into her pocket. She tossed the black hair that hung down to her waist, over her shoulder as she approached. Instead of making eye contact with Thiri, the killer's eyes appeared glued to the ceiling while her lips moved as she mumbled to herself.

As Thiri stepped back inside her cell, she slipped on the wet blood pooled on the floor and gasped. The young woman ceased mumbling and rushed to her side to break Thiri's fall. "Don't worry. The bad ones can't bother you anymore."

Another at the door nodded. "That's right, and we won't let the devils outside, in either."

The guard's killer pointed to herself. "I'm Sanda."

Thiri tried a weak smile. "I'm Thiri. What's going on?"

Sanda glanced back to the door. "They tried to bring in the food bucket, but we won't let them. It's filthy anyway. Not fit for pigs."

"What will they do?"

"Who knows? That bitch that watches us during the day said she would call the director. What's he going to do? Put us in here?"

Sanda's eyes rolled up, and she frowned. "She won't hurt us. She is one of us. No! I can't. I believe she is a friend." Sanda now looked into Thiri's eyes and smiled. "I was telling Carl that you're not like the others."

Thiri's hand went to her mouth. "Carl?"

Sanda smiled. "He looks out for me." Sanda nodded to the attendant's body. "Carl warned me all the time about Johan, but he couldn't do anything to protect me until last night. When Johan hit her and made her drop the razor, Carl saw his chance and took care of Johan."

"And Carl is warning you about me?"

Sanda made a wry face. "He can be a little oversensitive, but I have watched you, and I believe we can trust you."

"Tell Carl, thank you for saving me."

Sanda grinned. "I don't have to. He can hear and see you, but he only talks to me."

Outside, came a distant thunder-like rumbling. Sanda grinned as her eyes again rolled up. "Carl says God is angry. He will also protect us."

****

With the guard at his side, Thant strode to his car parked on the circular drive. Had the man slipped up? Telling him Thiri was safe? Relieved that he now knew where they held Thiri, he started the car to drive back into town. As he drove through the gate in the surrounding wall, a multitude of specks appeared in the sky heading towards the city.

From out of a cloud, smaller fast-moving specks approached the giant flock. One in the flock's midst erupted in an orange flash trailing smoke as it fell. His hands trembled as he watched the aerial combat. What is going on? He accelerated towards the city.

On the outskirts of town, he crested a hill overlooking both the city and the harbor. Traffic halted as people filled the road, dancing, and cheering. Children in the crowd giggled as they pointed to the sky.

Unable to drive through the celebrating throng, Thant stepped out and scanned the sky, searching for the cause of this jubilation. As the crowd cheered and waved, someone cried out, "The Liberators are coming."

As he shielded his eyes with his hand, Thant turned to the sound of approaching airplanes. Except for the metallic glint reflecting off some, they looked like a flock of birds. As they approached, the large red balls on the twin engine planes wings became visible.

"It's our brothers, the Japanese, " a voice called from the crowd.

"Oh, look here comes the enemy," someone shouted as smaller planes darted among the twin-engine craft. Balls of fire shot from the little planes towards the twin-engine planes. The larger airplanes, in turn, squirted fireballs back. One Japanese bomber smoked while it lagged behind the others. The smaller planes swarmed around it like angry bees, and soon this plane burned.

As it tumbled to the ground, the crowd groaned. Then cheers rang out as two smaller planes burst into flame, and a third exploded. A parachute now floated down. When puffs of smoke appeared around the bigger aircraft, the small ones dove away. Soon booms echoed in the sky like the report from an aerial fireworks display, while small objects rained down from the twin-engine planes. As they settled on the city ahead, puffs of smoke marched across the landscape.

The sky soon rumbled as if an enormous thunderstorm approached.

Several in the crowd screamed. Many ran. Some towards the columns of smoke, others away, jostling Thant as they passed. To his right, another group of twin-engine planes headed toward the city. As this group dropped their bombs, Thant leaped back into the car.

With planes roaring overhead, Thant raced towards the city. At the city's edge, smoke obscured the road, forcing him to slow. He wove the car around rubble heaps from destroyed and burning buildings. At times, he drove on the sidewalk to avoid obstructions. One road, choked with flaming vehicles and rubble, forced him to reverse direction and seek a detour.

People lay everywhere. Some still in death while others wailed in agony or crawled desperately out of the street. The rotten egg smell from natural gas filled the air along with the cries and wails of the injured and dying.

Near Cho's apartment, a man, severed in half, laid with the body's top half thrown against a wall as if sitting beside it. His lower half set on the road's opposite side. His entrails smeared across the street as if connecting the two halves together. Next to the man's upper body, a baby, blackened, and missing an arm, screamed. A teenager lay as if sleeping peacefully on the sidewalk. She looked uninjured, except for not breathing.

After parking the car, he rushed to the screaming infant. As he kneeled, the baby's cries ceased. He clutched the limp body to his chest as airplane engines again roared overhead.

****

With the prod resting on his shoulder, Ralston, the director, marched to the building housing the women's ward like a soldier on parade. The sound of aircraft passing over, prompted him to glance up. As he shielded his eyes from the sun, the twin-engine planes with the Red Ball markings on the wings banked over the facility. Tiny specks spewing fireballs swarmed around the bombers, and fireballs, in turn, spit back from the bombers. One bomber trailing smoke lagged behind the rest, and the tiny specks circled like sharks moving in for the kill. One passed through the bomber formation. Its path continued until it swooped not more than a hundred feet above his head.

Different from the British planes he'd seen before, this craft had a gaping mouth with fang-like teeth. The odd-shaped star on the wings, coupled with the reclining damsel with horns painted on the side, puzzled him. Its engine roared as it passed over him before it soared nearly straight up to rejoin the battle. As two more dove through the twin-engine formation overhead, fountains of dust kicked up nearby, prompting him to race for shelter in the building ahead. As he passed inside, the engines roared overhead. He glanced outside in time to see these two, painted the same as the first, also soar upward.

"Are they attacking us?" A woman's voice behind him asked.

Ralston turned to an obese woman in a white smock. Her black hair tied back in a bun she gazed skyward.

"I'm not sure. I've not seen those planes with the teeth before. They are not ours, but they also do not have the same markings as the bombers. If I had to guess, they might be that bunch I heard came from China to help."

"But they shot at you."

"Probably stray bullets from the battle up there. If they miss their target, the bullet has to go somewhere." He nodded to the ward door. "So, what's going on here, Eka?"

The woman threw her hands up. "I am not sure. I arrived this morning for my shift, and Johan was not at the desk. I thought he might be on the ward, checking the patients."

She pointed to two large pails filled with steaming gruel by the door. "But he failed to come out even when the food buckets arrived. I tried to open the door, but it was jammed, and one inmate told me to go away."

"What else did they say?"

The woman's eyes moved from side to side as if she looked to see who else might overhear her conversation. "The woman said they had taken care of Johan and would do the same to anyone who enters."

"Taken care?"

Eka nodded.

"Does that mean he's in there with them?"

Eka shrugged. "I believe so."

Herbert held out his hand. "Give me the keys." As he clutched the door key in his hand, he strode to the wooden door and inserted it in the lock. He rapped on the door with the butt of the prod. "This is Director Ralston. I'm coming in."

He turned the key, held the prod up like a fighter at a shield wall preparing for a killing thrust, and shoved on the door. It didn't budge. He rapped on the door again, only this time louder and shouted. "See here. If you don't stop this nonsense right now, I will have no choice but to have the police break down the door. If it comes to that, there will be severe consequences."

"Like what?" A voice on the other side howled back. "I would rather be dead than be in this shit hole."

"Yeah. They gonna put us in jail?" Another shouted through the door. "That would be like a vacation compared with what we put up with in here."

Ralston squared his shoulders and drew himself up to his entire five-foot height. "Your food is out here. You must be hungry."

"Keep it. Of course, it might even be fit to eat this morning seein' how Johan didn't piss in it like usual."

Ralston scowled and turned to Eka. She shrugged. "Johan jokes with them about it, but I have never seen him do it."

He turned back to the door. "Eka said that Johan never does it, he merely jokes about it."

"Well, he will not joke about anything anymore."

"What? What do you mean?"

"Sanda."

A second woman responded behind the door. Her voice soft. "Yes?"

"Did Johan rape you yesterday, or was that a joke too?"

"You know it was not a joke, and he won't be doing that anymore either."

Several cackled behind the door.

Ralston turned to Eka. "Do you know anything about this?"

Eka hung her head. "He claimed he needed to discipline her. He took her there to the isolation room. I assumed he merely spanked her or something. I didn't know."

"That's right, Mr. Director." A gravelly woman's voice came through the door. "He never used the rubber hose. Just that little weenie that dangled between his legs. But it ain't danglin' there anymore."

Again the cackles came through the door.

Ralston's brow furrowed. He turned to the door. "Is he in there now?"

"Sorta." The voice on the other side spit back. "He came in here last night and tried it on with one of us. Kinda lost his head."

CHAPTER SEVEN

Despite covering his ears, Ed's ears ached and rang from the explosions. The surrounding ground trembled, worse than the earthquake he experienced when stationed in San Francisco. Clods from nearby blasts rained into the trench while loose dirt cascaded down the trench's sides. Afraid these small landslides heralded a complete cave-in, he inched away from them. Between the explosions, machine guns chattered, adding a staccato to the bombs booming bass line.

He had taken part in ground attack exercises. Seen the devastation caused by bombing and strafing from the air, but had never experienced them on the ground in the target area. Helpless as death rained down, fear's bitter bile taste rose in his mouth.

Unwilling to stay in this ready-made grave, he poised to bolt and run from the shelter, but the roar diminished. Like an evil giant marching away, the explosions faded. The machine gun chatter tapered off, replaced by the roar of planes swooping across the field. Flames crackled in the stillness. Above, smoke trailed across the blue sky overhead.

Slowly, he peered over the trench's edge. Two fuel trucks burned on the deserted field. One hangar had collapsed. Gradually, heads appeared from behind sandbags. Over the faint ringing in his ears, screams and shouts came from somewhere nearby.

Inside one sandbag enclosure, a large gun barrel bent like a giant bow leaned against the bags. Men leaped from trenches, racing to the spot to check for damage and wounded. Bomb craters marred one runway while the other appeared pristine. A Jeep's approach prompted him to turn as he climbed over the singed bags. Olsen, his squadron leader, seated behind the wheel, peered at him, "You okay, Burton?" Olsen's voice sounded far away.

"Yeah, I think so." Ed brushed dirt out of his hair. "Sure as hell don't wanna be on the ground if they come again, though."

"As soon as we have a plane ready, I want you to take it out. Get the feel back. I'm sure you're rusty with the lay-off."

"Sure, skipper. Any word from the guys?"

"The Brits radioed back, claimed two of our guys got shot down. Don't know if they got out or not. With these crappy radios, we won't know a thing until they come back."

A plane sputtered overhead, trailing smoke interrupted their conversation. As it banked to approach, the engine died as it passed through the smoke from the blazing building to land. Still rolling out, its tail wheel not yet settled on the runway, it lurched forward as the wheels fell into a bomb crater. The nose dropped, bending the propeller as the landing gear collapsed. It screeched down the runway on its belly, trailing sparks.

Before the slide ended, Ed and Olson ran to the Jeep. As they raced to the downed plane, the pilot scrambled from the cockpit before trotting away from the smoking plane. A fire truck, its bell clanging, skidded to a stop beside the aircraft.

"You okay?" Olson shouted to the pilot as he pulled off his helmet while glancing back, disgusted with the wreck. After tossing his parachute into the Jeep's rear seat, he climbed in. "Yeah, Shit! You can't see those craters through the smoke. What a fucking mess."

Two P-40s appeared overhead. The first banked to line up with the damaged runway, but before touching down, the pilot gunned the engine and soared up. The other raised his landing gear and orbited the field.

"That's Mack! Hopefully, he radios the others about the field," Olson said as they watched the other plane set down on the undamaged runway. "Let's head over to the dispersal area to get the news from the rest."

The remaining planes arrived, either in pairs or alone. As soon as the aircraft parked, the ground crew swarmed them, snaking machine gun belts into the wings and nose mounts, or patching gunshot holes. While fuel trucks refilled the planes' tanks, the pilots gathered, discussing the day's action.

"Seemed like Martin got nailed by every bomber in their formation. He dove away like we're supposed to, but his plane caught fire and went down," one pilot said, shuffling the ground with his foot. As he stared off, he swallowed as if choking something back. "I didn't see a chute."

"What about Green and Gilbert," Olson asked, looking to the faces of the men gathered around.

"They were both late gettin' into the air," one flight leader reported. "Never saw either one after we attacked either."

"So, we have one down and two missing," Olson announced as he made notes on his clipboard, "Okay, how did we do."

Olson's questions energized the sullen gathering as the men described the day's action. As he listened to the accounts, Ed wondered if he would share the same enthusiasm as the rest. Could he close for the kill? Before his kidnapping, he had been eager to be at the Japanese. Had never considered killing or dying. One thing for sure, he would never again ride out another attack on the ground.

****

Director Ralston scowled as he held the phone to his ear. "I appreciate the situation in the city, but we have a serious situation here, and I haven't the resources or staff to contain it."

As he listened, his wife, Sylvia, sat across from him, clutching a revolver while two little girls played at her feet.

"I see no humor in this." He slammed the phone down.

"What did the governor say?"

"With the bombings and all the looting in town, they can't send either the police or the army to quell a riot here. They have other priorities besides dealing with a bunch of lunatics."

"Did he offer any suggestions?"

"He said to turn on the lights after dark and evacuate all the staff. Might attract the Japs to the building, and they could solve the problem."

"What a dreadful thing to say."

Ralston shrugged.

"What shall we do?"

Ralston massaged his brow as if fighting off a headache. One little girl stood, brushed back her cap of golden-brown curls from her forehead while holding up a sheet of paper. "See? That's the pony I want."

"That's lovely, darling. Can you draw a house for him too? That way, he won't get caught in the monsoons."

With grin the child resumed her drawing. Sylvia turned back to her husband. "Well?"

"I haven't a clue. The night attendant was not at his post this morning. They've blocked the entrance and only talked to me through the door."

"What did they say?"

Ralston glanced down at the children at his wife's feet. He leaned close, whispered "What they told me makes me believe they might have killed the attendant."

Sylvia's hand rose to her chest. "Would they break out? Attack us as well?"

"The windows are all barred, and I had them place a barricade on the door."

"What then? You can't keep them penned up in there forever. What will they eat?"

"There is no water on the ward either. They damaged all the sinks, and we had to remove them. They urinate and defecate on the floors, and the staff hose the place down several times a day. But if we cannot get in, that will not be possible."

"Perhaps you should reason with them."

"Reason? Sylvia, they are insane."

"Herbert, there must be some there that you can talk to."

Ralston sighed and rose from his chair. "I suppose you're right. Bolt the door behind me and don't open it to anyone but me."

The sun set as he strode across the grounds to the women's ward. Smoke rose from the city. The governor's words echoed in his head. Would the Japanese bomb the asylum? He asked himself. Newsreels had been full of their atrocities elsewhere. The leaflets dropped a few days ago promised that anyone remaining in the city when they arrived would meet the same fate as Nanking's people. There, the Japanese murdered over two hundred thousand. He shuddered as he recalled the reports of rape. Women and female children in the thousands. Here he sat. A civil servant with a wife and two daughters.

He attempted to rouse his courage as he walked. Now the Japanese faced a real army. Soldiers of the mightiest empire on the planet. British troops, not some Chinese peasant army. Nothing to worry about. He told himself.

****

"Bogies at three o'clock low!" The voice on Ed's headset called out. As he glanced to his right, he dipped the wing. On a course that would intersect theirs, he spotted the Japanese bombers as they dropped their bombs. Black smudges appeared around the formation as anti-aircraft guns fired at the fleeing unescorted attackers.

After the attack two days ago, Ed had taken a plane up twice. First, he familiarized himself with the area, following a British flight over the town to avoid setting off the now trigger-happy anti-aircraft gunners below. Then he and Olson did a mock dogfight in the afternoon, to make sure he worked off the rust from his absence. Confidant, he still had the skills, he headed into his first action today.

"Stay in formation and prepare to attack," The section leader ordered over the radio as he led them around to the right side of the formation below. With the sun at their backs, they dove as a group.

Ed eased the stick, leveling his swooping craft about five hundred yards from the bombers. Through his gunsight, he aimed at the large red ball on the attacker ahead. When he pressed the trigger on the control stick, his plane shuddered as the fifty calibers in the nose spit out their deadly projectiles. A slight movement of the rudder pedal swung the tracer's fireballs, spitting from his guns to rake the plane ahead from nose to tail. As he swooped below the bomber, his head swiveled as he searched both for targets and threats.

Tracers streaked across his front from the left. He dove below their path as a shadow passed overhead. He turned towards the shadow's path and found himself behind, but slightly below another bomber. After squeezing the trigger again, his tracers slammed into its fuselage, at the wing root, then straight into the rear of his target as he aligned his plane dead astern.

As the bomber's wing separated from the fuselage, the damaged plane spun into his path, forcing him to bank away to avoid colliding with the wreckage.

"Burton, break left!" Jenson shouted over his headphones as bullets slammed into the armor shield at his hack. Tracers now streaked by from behind as he banked to the left while descending to build speed.

As he glanced over his shoulder, Jensen's plane fired into a fixed-gear open cockpit fighter that had been on Ed's tail. The Japanese disappeared in a fireball.

Two similar fighters descended on Jensen's plane, their guns blazing. Smoke trailed from Jensen's plane as he swerved to avoid the trap.

As Ed completed his turn, he now faced the two Japanese fighters heading at him on a near-collision course. Ed fired, hoping his guns range outmatched the smaller weapons these fighters carried. Both swerved away without shooting.

He banked while searching for signs of Jensen's plane, but only saw a smoke trail descending towards the earth below. As he continued his descent, a parachute floated near the smoke trail. As he spiraled down, he circled the chute where Jensen grasped the lines attached to the umbrella. Several panels appeared missing in the wispy, white canopy, and Jensen stared up at the damage. He grinned and waved as Ed passed, even though Ed's slipstream whipped the dangling airman from side to side.

With sufficient fuel, he would remain to guard Jenson until he reached the ground. As he ascended, a Japanese fighter dove toward the parachute, its guns blazing.

As Ed turned to head off the attacking Japanese, Jensen tugged on the parachute's cords, collapsing the canopy. After dropping below the stream of tracer bullets seeking to find him, Jensen released the shrouds. As the chute re-opened, the enemy fighter turned to make another pass at the helpless, dangling American.

Without aiming, Ed fired, hoping to distract Jensen's attacker. Aware of Ed's presence, the attacker climbed away, but a second Japanese dropped out of the sky, firing. Again, Jensen collapsed the canopy, his fall avoiding the tracer stream. This time the Japanese fighter dove at the fall, firing as if leading a clay pigeon. Again, the canopy opened, slowing Jensen's descent, but now Jensen no longer grasped the shrouds. Instead, his arms hung at his sides. His head slumped forward. His legs swayed in the breeze.

Screaming into his oxygen mask, Ed pivoted towards the Japanese fighter as it prepared to attack the dangling figure below the parachute again. Once more, Ed fired without aiming, hoping to distract Jensen's attacker. His guns coughed a few times, then went silent. Either they jammed, or he had used up his ammunition.

Aware of Ed's presence, the Japanese pilot turned to meet Ed. As the bullets whizzed by Ed's windscreen, the Japanese fighter exploded as an RAF Buffalo's machine guns raked it.

Jensen's parachute collapsed as he hit the ground. As Ed passed over the still figure lying on the ground, his fuel light came on. He turned away to head back to the base, a sick feeling in the pit of his stomach.

CHAPTER EIGHT

KUNMING, CHINA

"Close it up, Junior," Greg Boyington's voice crackled over Joe's headphones. He nudged the rudder, sliding the plane right, putting him just off the other plane's wing-tip. His head swiveled right, left, up and down, searching for threats. Ahead, Kunming airfield appeared through a break in the clouds. Their dawn patrol almost finished, his stomach growled. Late returning to the base this morning, Joe had merely grabbed a donut, which he washed down with coffee from a cardboard cup while trotting to the flight line. Once they landed, he'd head straight to the mess. With luck, the cooks would still have food waiting.

As Boyington's plane peeled off to land, Joe maintained his vigil above. When his replacement joined up on him, he waggled his wings, gave the other pilot a wave, then turned towards the field for his own landing.

After parking next to Boyington's plane, he spied the big man talking to his crew chief. Joe wondered if Boyington's surliness today stemmed from his background as a Marine aviator. Gung-ho jarheads, the other services referred to them. Or did it come from his need to supplement his pay with the promised bonuses for kills? As Joe approached, Boyington turned. With his high cheek bones and prominent nose Boyington's expression conjured up images of an Apache warrior ready to claim a scalp. "You day dreamin' about your girl?"

Joe shook his head. "Hard to keep track of everything at once. Doin' the swivel neck watchin' for Japs, flying the plane, and keepin' formation is somethin' I need to get used to."

"Shit, Japs ain't nowhere around. If they were, the old man's spotters would give us an hour's notice."

"Don't matter. Gotta keep the habits. I'm headin' to the mess hall."

"Give me a minute, I'll join ya." Boyington turned back to the crew chief. "Check the charger. Manifold pressure kept droppin'."

The man nodded and strode off.

Boyington took off his flying helmet, beckoned Joe to follow. "Those of us maintaining celibacy had time for a hearty repast with our comrades at the appointed hour. But I'll join ya for a cup of joe while you feed your face. Hate to see ya lonesome."

"You're all heart. Why you so grumpy, old man?"

"Cause I chewed your ass on the radio?"

Joe nodded.

"These damn patrols."

"It's flyin' otherwise we'd be sittin' around on our asses doin' nothin'."

"Shit, Japs ain't comin' back here since we kicked their asses. We oughta be in Rangoon." He nudged Joe in the side, winked. "Can't let the Hell's Angels have all the fun."

"Sounds like they're catchin' hell down there."

"Yeah, Brits got caught on the ground during the raid yesterday, only got two planes left. Lost a couple of our guys, too. But they're kickin' ass."

Inside the mess hall, the aroma of fresh baking, coffee brewing, and bacon filled the air. While Joe went through the line, Boyington filled a mug from the coffee urn. As they scanned the room, Russ, seated alone, beckoned them over. As Boyington settled into his chair, he returned Russ's smile with a scowl. "Whatta you so chipper about? Get a new wrench?"

"Nah, got news from a buddy a mine. Ed Burton."

Boyington cocked his head. "Who?"

"He was before your time. Was in the third squadron. Got forced down and kidnapped."

Joe nodded. "I heard about that. You heard from him?"

"Yeah, he called in the combat report yesterday. He's back and flyin' with the squadron down in Rangoon."

Boyington slammed down his cup. "Shit. Is that what it takes to get into the action?"

Russ gave Joe a puzzled frown.

Joe shrugged. "Don't mind him. He's eager to see a little action." Joe nudged Boyington in the ribs. "Don't worry old fellah, you'll get your chance."

"Shit, by the time my hair turns gray." Boyington rose, leaving his mug on the table, he strode off.

Russ shook his head. "I'd be happy to never see a Jap plane again in my life. He don't know what he's in for."

"I've seen what damage planes do in a ground attack, and I'd never wanna be in one either, but it's different up there."

Russ frowned. "Different?"

"Yeah, you can shoot back, and if it gets too hairy, you can vamoose. Beats the shit outta coverin' your head in some shitty slit trench."

"Who's Mrs. Morgan?"

Joe set his fork down and frowned. "What brings that up?"

"I was out at the hospital yesterday. Ann mentioned the woman might be comin' on an inspection."

"Shit."

"You know her?"

Joe nodded as he jabbed at a piece of fried egg on his plate. "She stranded Ann in Java."

"She what?"

"Stranded her." Joe then described how Mrs. Morgan arranged for the ship to leave Ann behind in Surabaya.

"But she got back to the boat, right?"

"Yeah. Thanks to this brothel owner."

Russ's eyebrows rose. "A brothel owner?"

Joe chuckled. "Ann claims the guy offered her a job. Even gave her a standing offer. Said if she changed her mind, he'd pay her way back to Java."

"This Morgan woman some crazy psycho?"

"Nah, a concerned mother."

"What the heck does that mean?"

Joe wondered how much to tell Russ. After all the woman couldn't be all bad. But then again?...."She didn't like the fact that Ann and I spent time together. Guess she has plans for Ann and her son."

"Plans?"

"Ann claims the only reason this Morgan dame allowed her to come to China was she figured Ann and her son would get hitched."

Russ shook his head. "Guy can't find a wife on his own? What's the matter with him?"

"Kind of a snooty rich asshole, but other than that, I don't know..."

"But he's back there, and you're here."

Joe shook his head. "See that's the thing, this Morgan dame brought him along. Figured the voyage would light the romantic fires, but Johnathan never stepped up to the plate."

"And instead, you and she hit it off."

"That's about the size of it."

"But now Ann's here. Nothin' this woman can do now, right?"

Joe shrugged. "Don't matter. This Morgan broad runs all the missions. Guess she can jerk the funds from the hospital if she doesn't like what she finds there."

****

That evening after arriving in town for the Christmas celebration at Rose's hotel, Joe and Russ entered the crowded hotel dining room. As they passed through bustling waiters lugging trays packed with bottles or food, Joe scanned the boisterous crowd. Fueled with holiday spirit and relief from the respite from the relentless Japanese attacks, laughter and joyous chatter filled the air. With no new casualties flooding the hospital, Rose had coaxed Ann and her father into town for the holiday festivities, and Ann invited them to this party.

Through the room's smoky haze, Joe glimpsed Ann at a large table near the back. Seated along with her father and Rose, Ann leaned close to Greg Boyington's hulking figure seated at her side. When she leaned back to laugh, she glanced in his direction. A welcoming smile captured her face as her father beckoned them over.

"I was telling the princess here that if you didn't show up shortly, she would have to settle on me for the first dance." Boyington rose, gave Russ a nod.

"Are you sure your sect allows such heathen displays, Reverend?" Ann replied, a mischievous grin on her face, "I would hate to think I might contribute to your moral downfall."

Boyington shook his head and sighed. "The Lord might forget and forgive my transgressions before you do. Or is it because you're a woman you think you can get away with bustin' my chops?"

She patted his arm. "Oh! I am just concerned with your spiritual well-being."

"Well, I'm gonna run along now and commune with the spirits l worship the most." Boyington raised his glass in emphasis as he strolled away. "I also intend to find a lass with a less sharp tongue to help me stay in the holiday mood."

The big man waved over his shoulder as he moved away from the table. Joe bent down and kissed Ann as he reached her side. She stood and gave Russ a hug, and he blushed. Still holding his hand, she gazed into his eyes. "I am so glad Joe talked you into coming."

Russ turned to Joe. "What was that all about?"

"What?"

Russ nodded towards Ann. "Callin' Boyington, Reverend."

Joe and Ann exchanged smiles before Joe turned back to Russ. "On the trip here, they had us pose as different professions. We could pick anything we wanted as long as it wasn't pilots. Figured it would keep us all hush-hush."

Russ nodded. "We came in with a bunch of troops, so they didn't have us do anything."

"Well, we came on this civilian liner. Had an assortment of civilians as passengers."

"Assortment?" Ann poked him. "I was part of an assortment?"

Joe shook his head. "Most were missionaries." He nodded towards Ann. "Like her."

Ann squeezed Joe's hand. "This guy pretended to be a tractor salesman. And his rowdy friend tried to pass himself off as a missionary."

Russ's jaw dropped, glanced in Boyington's direction as the big man waved to the bartender for a refill. "Boyington? A missionary?"

Ann grinned. "He is quite an actor. Did such a good job, one of our group's leaders insisted he lead a Sunday service."

"And he did it?"

Ann continued her story with a sad frown. "He made a lot of excuses to delay the experience. I'm afraid after only a few days, everyone, not with your group, figured out the truth. Greg finally made it to a service, and unfortunately, the man conducting the service treated him with contempt. I was ashamed."

Joe shook his head. "Greg used the experience as another reason to get drunk. Don't think it fazed him much at the time, and he seems to enjoy your teasing him about it. But speaking of your little Christian band, have you heard anything from Johnathan or his mother?"

"Father got a telegram yesterday. They're doing inspections in the Northern provinces."

"Far away from the fighting and the bombing."

"Oh, Joe, they are civilians. Not warriors like yourselves. They're here to save souls."

Joe shrugged. "Mrs. Morgan and her son both gave me the creeps."

Joe waived down a passing waiter. "I'd like a bourbon on ice." He turned to Russ. "How about you?"

"A Coke, if you got it, please."

The waiter nodded before turning away.

Dr. Ross raised his champagne glass and nodded. "Everything as quiet at the base, as they have been out at the hospital?"

"Well, no Japs have been headin' our way. The guys are chompin' at the bit, but the Japs are avoiding us like the plague up here," Joe replied.

Rose cocked her head, and her brow creased. "I understand they attacked Rangoon."

As Joe described what he had heard in dispatches and gossip back at the base, Ann studied Russ. Most evenings, he had returned to the hospital. Particularly popular on the children's ward, he spent his time telling them stories or making little toys. A favorite was a flat wooden square made of what looked like plywood. He drilled two holes side by side near the square's center. He then had the children paint designs on the wooden plaques, then after the paint dried, they tied a looping string through the wood. While holding a side of the loop in each hand, he showed them how to twirl the wood in the middle until the cord had several twists. As they pulled their hands outward, the wood spun. When they brought their hands back together, the string rewound, so the twirling continued as they pulled it outward again.

As if playing accordions, the little ones would spin their small blocks for hours watching the designs they made change shape with the spinning. Or having contests to see who could keep theirs moving the longest.

"The children loved the puppet show," she said to Russ, "A little violent, but the kids loved the characters' antics."

"Actually, the puppets belong to one of the Chinese workers," Russ replied, "He does it as a hobby at festivals. It would have been better if he had done it, but he was away visiting family. So, Ang Su borrowed the stuff."

"Well, tell Ang Su. He provided a superb performance."

"Thanks, I will. Ang Su made me practice with him all afternoon. I didn't think I would ever remember the script."

"Here's the puppet master!" A woman's voice exclaimed close by.

Russ and Ann turned as Olga joined them. "I hope the kids enjoyed the show as much as I did." She patted Russ on the shoulder. "Russ and Ang Su made me watch three times before they were sure they had it right."

"Lamison, I need a word," her husband added as he joined Olga standing near the table. Russ stood, and the two moved away to talk.

"The play was just a scream. Paul had me and a few others who understand Chinese sit in on their rehearsals. Even after the third time through, I was laughing so hard my side hurt," Olga continued talking to Ann.

"What's that?" Joe said, turning to the two women.

Ann and Olga told Joe about Russ's visits to the hospital and the puppet show they had done that afternoon. As he listened, he watched Russ and Greenlaw in the corner. Greenlaw talked while Russ nodded his head, saying nothing.

Finally, Russ returned. Olga bid them goodbye and joined her husband, searching for their own table in the crowded room.

"What's going on?" Joe asked as Russ sat down.

"I guess it's no big secret. The docks are a mess in Rangoon, and we're hurtin' for supplies. The boss wants me and Frillman to take my crew down there and bring back all we can."

"When?"

"Sometime this week. He'll let me know."

"Tell the kids I won't be back for a while," he continued turning now to Ann. "But make sure they know I'll be back as soon as I can. Okay?"

"Be careful." She squeezed his hand. "I'll make sure they know."

****

BWOLIN, CHINA

"Now where has that boy gone off to?" Mrs. Morgan scowled as she turned away from the unanswered hotel room door. With her back turned to him, Chen stepped out of the next room. Wide-eyed, he stuck his head back into the room and whispered to someone inside, before turning back to Mrs. Morgan. "You are looking for your son?"

She gave a slight start, then turned to him. "Yes, I can't imagine where he's gone off to so early."

"He mentioned he might go to the shops. Something about a present."

Mrs. Morgan placed her hand to her ample bosom, gave Chen a slight smile, and her eyelashes fluttered. "Probably a trinket for his betrothed. We should arrive in Kunming in a few days."

Chen's eyebrows arched. "The nurse there, whose father has the mission hospital?"

"A delightful girl. Johnathan wanted to wed her before, even considered a shipboard wedding, but she desired to have her father's blessing before she would agree. Have you met Dr. Ross?"

"No, ma'am. Heard of him, though."

"You'll like him. Skilled physician. If it hadn't been for some unpleasantness in Boston, we might never have gotten his services."

Chen cocked his head. "Unpleasantness?"

"Nothing related to his clinical skills. Merely an under-appreciation of local customs."

"Her father has not met your son?"

She gave a dismissive wave. "Oh, years ago, before he came out here. Johnathan would have been a young boy. I'm sure he wouldn't recall him."

Chen nodded. "Nor would he realize yet what a fine young man he's become."

Mrs. Morgan patted his arm, grinned. "How kind of you to say so. I'm going down to breakfast. I packed my bags. Please, put them in the car."

As she strode away, Chen trailed her with his eyes. When she passed out of sight, he again opened his door. Johnathan peeked out, and he scanned the hallway. Satisfied his mother had left, he turned to Chen. "What will we do now?"

"After you dress, you must go down the back stairs and come in the front door. I told your mother you went shopping. She believes you seek something for the nurse in Kunming."

Johnathan frowned. "Shopping? I didn't buy anything."

"No matter. Tell her you found nothing suitable."

Johnathan gave Chen a peck on the cheek. "You're a sly fox. I should be wary of you."

After loading the luggage, Chen leaned against the car's fender parked outside the hotel. Soon Mrs. Morgan emerged, trailed by Johnathan. As they climbed into the vehicle, Johnathan turned to his mother. "Where are we visiting today?"

She turned to Chen. "What's the nearest mission from here?"

"Sinkang, we could reach there well before dusk."

She pulled a sheet from her purse, raised her reading glasses attached to a tether around her neck, and peered at the document. "Yes, Lottie Johnson's there. Fine Christian woman. I'm certain she'll be pleased to see us."

"Should we wire ahead?"

She patted Johnathan's thigh in response to his question. "No, like the others, I want to arrive unannounced. See how they normally operate instead of witnessing some dog and pony show they put on to impress."

****

RANGOON, BURMA

"So, they agreed to accept food and water." Sylvia Ralston frowned as she gazed out the window.

Ralston poured a drink from a crystal decanter. "Yes, and I allowed them the use of the hose and cleaning supplies to clean the ward."

"And what about the attendant? That Johan fellow?"

"They killed him." Ralston sipped his drink, grimaced. "Gruesome. They claimed he killed an older inmate. Hazel, I believe, was her name."

"So, they might have been merely defending themselves."

"Hard to say, Sylvia. They are all considered insane."

Sylvia's hand flew to her mouth. "And the two dead, their bodies are on the ward?"

"No, they hauled them out sometime during the night. Put them in the foyer."

"I thought you had them locked in?"

"They managed somehow. Might have had help from the staff."

"What are you going to do?"

Ralston took another sip. His lip curled in a wry expression. "For now, give them what they want. Keep them barricaded inside and hope for the best."

She touched his shoulder. "For how long?"

His brow furrowed. "Not sure. Once things settle in the city, perhaps the police can come in and help me restore order. We don't have enough staff now to take care of them all. More dessert every day."

"That's outrageous. Who will take care of them?"

Ralston's face flushed. He tossed his hands in the air. "The government is falling apart around our ears, Sylvia. The Indians who work in the civil service are fleeing. They pile the docks with food that goes nowhere. Left to rot. Ships are leaving port because they can't be unloaded. The police and firemen remaining on their posts are occupied with protecting the city. We are simply on our own."

For the next six days, Ralston posted himself at the ward door at mealtimes. While those who came out to retrieve the food refused to talk, once the door closed, some conversed with him from behind the locked door. On the seventh day, the inmates agreed to send out a delegation to meet with the stipulation that if he harmed either, the rest would break out of the ward and attack. The two young girls they selected as delegates surprised him. One, an inmate that had resided there since childhood, named Sanda. The other a new admission named Thiri. He had not yet interviewed the new arrival but recalled her name from her fiancé's earlier visit.

Once they emerged from the ward, the two young women followed him across the grounds to his office. After serving them tea, his wife left them alone.

Director Ralston steepled his fingers as he studied the two young women seated on the opposite side of his desk. Dressed in the brown, almost canvas-like gown uniform, the inmates wore, Thiri's shoulder-length black hair, while uncombed, shined as if it had been well cared for recently. Her brown eyes twinkled with an intelligence not seen in his other patients. Silent, she merely studied his face as if peering into his soul.

Sanda's long, tangled black hair fell down her back nearly to her waist. She scratched at a spot above her forehead. She picked at the area, then gazed at her pinched finger and scowled. Turning to Thiri, Sanda held her hand out for Thiri's inspection. After peering at the girl's fingers, Thiri covered her mouth. Sanda then held her hand out so Ralston could view it. "See? Lice."

Ralston jerked back in his chair. "Impossible, we have everyone inspected for that daily and treated when identified."

Sanda tossed her head back. "Ha. That's not true. All of us have them. I have not had a bath in over a month unless you count the times the staff spray us with the hose."

"But that has been my orders." He opened a notebook and passed it across to her. "Sanda, right?"

The girl nodded.

He pointed to the page. "See, it's in the operating order right here."

Sanda frowned and nodded to Thiri, who pulled the book before her and studied the page.

She nodded. "That is what it says. But I had been here several days before the disturbance. In that time, no one checked me, and I saw no one else inspected. The ones working our ward are not following this directive."

Sanda frowned. "But as the Director says, that is their order?"

Thiri nodded and glanced at Ralston.

Ralston removed his pince-nez and scowled. "You've not had a bath in over a month?"

Sanda thrust her shoulders back. "That is correct."

"But your treatment plan requires hydrotherapy at least once a week. Possibly that's why?"

Sanda cocked her head. "Hydrotherapy? What's that?"

Ralston tossed his hands in the air. "That's when you sit in the bathtubs in the therapy area. They cover the tub, so only your head sticks out. Then they regulate the temperature according to the plan. It facilitates the humors' flow through your body, strengthening your psyche."

Sanda shook her head. "I have never had this done with me. Neither have any of my fellow inmates."

"Inmates? You ladies are not inmates. You are patients in my care. Where do you come up with this language?"

Sanda and Thiri exchanged glances before Sanda turned back to Ralston. "That is what we call ourselves."

"That's terrible. I strictly instructed the staff to refer to you all as patients. Inmates. That makes this sound like it's a jail, and you're all criminals. Did the staff call you that?"

Sanda shook her head. "No, they call us loonies, crazies, and bitches. We call each other inmates out of respect.

Ralston buried his face in his hands.

****

With the Japanese attacking daily, Ed had no time to search for Thiri. Even though they had no formal arrangement. Not talked about marriage. He wanted her back in his life now and forever. Also, the British failed to recover Jensen's body. Thiri's and Jensen's disappearance weighed heavily as he strode down the barracks' hallway carrying his parachute.

Ahead in the hallway, four pilots gathered outside an open door. Someone inside passed a bottle out to one. The recipient wiped the top with his sleeve, then hoisted the bottle as if offering a toast. After taking a large swig, the man passed it to the man next to him. As Ed approached, the hum of conversation punctuated by laughter came from the room.

"Damn! Should we check 'em all? I'm not sure I can repack it."

"One guy in our crew is a helluva rigger. If he doesn't have time to do it himself, I'll bet he would talk you through it." Came the reply as Ed arrived at the doorway.

Inside, Jensen sat on his bed, his Stetson pulled down low over his eyes. He held an open bottle on his knee, a large bandage on his thigh. As Ed arrived in the doorway, Jensen raised the bottle in greeting and waved Ed in, while those clustered in the hallway stood aside.

"I think I'm gonna dump mine out and replace it with one of them soft Limey pillows," Jenson said while pointing to the British parachute Ed carried. "It looks like Saville Row outfitted our Prodigal. Did they require you to join his Majesty's finest to score that fine parachute?"

"Oley got the Brits to loan me the gear I needed, but I'm still on our side of the pond,"

"If it's a British chute, I'll bet it's the finest Umbrella Insurance a man can acquire," one pilot quipped from the hall referring to the Chinese label on the unit's parachutes.

Another shook his head. "Nah. I heard those Chinese letters are instruction for returning the chute if it fails to open. Money-back guarantee."

A pilot beside Jenson clapped him on the shoulder. "Here that Jenson? You might be entitled to a partial refund at least."

"Well, I shouldn't, bitch. If mine had been right, I'd be dead." As Jensen took another swig, his Stetson fell off, exposing the gauze wrapped around his head.

"You just wander in, or did the Gurkha have to drag you back?" Ed quipped relieved that the cowboy, while slightly banged up, appeared to have little damage. "We all gave you up for dead last week."

Jensen grinned as he leaned back against the wall. "Been on R and R. Came down hard. No thanks to that sorry ass parachute. Plus, having to dump air to keep out of those Jap's sights."

"Yeah, your chute looked all fucked up. When I made that last pass at you, I thought you had had it."

Jensen waved his hand dismissively. "Hey, thanks for scarin' that one bastard off. I was playin' possum in case anymore made a pass while I was still hangin' there, but still, I hit the ground so hard knocked me out. Brit that found me thought I was dead at first. Then when I came to, he stuck this gun in my face."

"Must have spotted that Blood Chit on your jacket," one man commented, "Probably figured it was Japanese writing and you were a mercenary flyin' for the Japs."

"Maybe they should put English on it. Convert the reward to tea and crumpets for the Raj," another grumbled.

"When I explained who I was, he got all smarmy. Apologized for his poor manners and such. For a moment, I worried he might kiss me. Turned out to be a good Joe. Took me to his place, brought over a Doctor that lived next door to check me out, and patch me up. Made me stay with him till I quit havin' headaches."

"But you've been gone a whole week!"

Jensen grinned. "The guy was gettin' ready to leave town and needed to empty his wine cellar. Said he'd be damn if he'd let the Japs have it. He and I and the Doc tried to get it done, but there was just too much. So, they loaded it all on a truck and delivered the wine and me here before they scrammed."

Olsen pushed through the crowd at the door, shook his head as he glanced around the room.

"Just notified Kunming about your return. Second Pursuit will be here either tomorrow or the day after to relieve us. The old man wants two of you guys to hang back for a while to get the new guys squared away."

Jensen gestured to Ed with the bottle in his hand. "Did Greenlaw say I should consider myself under arrest like Burton for bein' AWOL or somethin'? Oh, and there's a case of this stuff over there by the wall. Help yourself, skipper. A gift from His Majesty's grateful subjects."

Olson moved to the case and peered inside. "I'm having the ground crew concentrate on getting the planes in good enough shape to fly them to Kunming." He pulled out a bottle and studied the label. "I guess we should stand down for now. Let the Brits cover the city for the next two days."

After selecting a bottle, Olsen exited the room with Ed following close behind. Ed caught him in the hallway. "Sir, I'd like to volunteer to stick around and help the new guys get settled in."

"Fine, see who else might stay. Actually, ask your buddy, Jensen. He looks well-rested."

CHAPTER NINE

Tears rolled down her cheeks as the tiny Burmese woman clutched the infant to her breast. With one leg a bloody stump, the baby made no sound. All around in the crowded hospital hallway, moans and weeping filled the air, along with the coppery odor of blood, feces, and charred flesh.

"Please, someone, help my baby." The woman wailed.

Thant and a European woman wearing a nurse's cap rushed to the woman. The nurse nodded to Thant. "Let the Doctor take him."

The mother clutched the child to her breast. "You must save him, please."

The nurse gave Thant a pleading look as she reached for the infant, turned to the mother. "We will do our best. The treatment rooms are crowded. Trust us. While he examines him, why don't you go have a cup of tea."

After releasing the limp infant to the nurse, tears ran down her face as she turned away to the table where a young woman poured tea.

After giving the nurse a puzzled frown, Thant scurried away with the child to one of the curtained areas. As he laid the dead baby on the examining table, the nurse joined him. "I am not a doctor."

The nurse brushed back a loose strand of hair from her forehead. "It doesn't matter. At least that woman can have a moment's peace before we break her heart."

"But why did you tell her I am a doctor?"

"You were in medical school, right?"

Thant nodded. "But I never finished."

"It doesn't matter, Professor Williams claimed you were one of his brightest students."

"But I only volunteered to help on the ambulance."

"Dr. Mortinson is the only physician left. You know more than any of the aides. With all these traumatic amputations, all we're doing is cleaning up afterward, anyway. The work you did yesterday, I am certain, saved at least five patients. Plus, you're Burmese, the people trust you. That goes a long way in helping them."

Thant looked down at the tiny body on the examination table. His lip quivered. "All this makes no sense, Stella."

Stella, the nurse, placed her hand on his. "War seldom does."

"But the Japanese promised to help the people of Burma. Run the British out. Give us our country back. They promised Asia for Asians."

Stella shook her head. "Bombs don't discriminate. When they go off, they destroy everything around them."

"But they shoot at crowds of people fleeing the city."

She placed her hand on his. "I know. I've heard all the locals talk about the Japanese as if they are coming to save them. Perhaps they will, but in the meantime, they are driving we Gweilos out."

Thant shook his head. "I never thought of you as a Gweilo. The foreign devils were the soldiers and the police."

"In the time I've been here, I've seen things my countrymen have done to your people that shamed me. So, I understand."

"But yet you stay. Have not run away, like others. Maybe you have become Burmese."

"I remember back when we worked together at the hospital. Most of the nurses found you quite attractive. Don't tell her I told you, but Wren is the one who kept putting the panties in your mailbox."

Thant's jaw dropped. "What? That was her?"

"Broke her heart when you disappeared. Where did you go?"

Thant hung his head. "I had a change in priorities."

"Someone claimed you ran off to join the insurgency."

Her statement sent a chill down Thant's spine. For all, he knew there remained a price on his head, along with the others for their alleged attack on the supply depot. Along with his work with Thiha, he had become a criminal. After witnessing Ed's arrest, he wanted to keep his involvement quiet. Still hoped to help them. "What? Can you imagine me as some fearsome freedom fighter?"

"Why not? I heard how you evacuated that ambulance yesterday. The people inside would have died if you hadn't kept carrying them out. Planes swooping down, their machine guns blazing, while you carried the people inside to safety."

Thant shrugged. "That made no sense either. The red crosses all over the ambulance should have been visible even from the air, but those Japanese planes swarmed it like it was a target."

Stella nodded. "That's why we repainted the remaining two and are only using plain trucks now. But as I said, you're very brave. So, yes, I could imagine you as a fierce warrior."

He volunteered for this work, hoping as an ambulance driver, he could gain access to the airfield. Contact his boss, then together they could free Thiri from her imprisonment. Perhaps the people at the asylum would respond to a request from an American more readily. Only last week, he made two runs to the airfield to pick up wounded from the air strikes. While helping clear injured from a bombed-out trench, he glimpsed his old boss walking with other pilots to the planes. It seemed bloodthirsty to hope for a calamity at the airbase to allow him access to Ed. But at the moment, he saw no alternative.

"I merely considered it my duty." Thant glanced down at the tiny body before him. With a sigh, he placed a sheet over the dead infant. "Shall I tell the mother, or will you?"

"Let me go get another. In the meantime, tell the mother we're doing all we can. Give her a little more time to gather her strength."

****

The Sergeant nudged Zeya seated beside him at the reception desk as he set down the phone. "Can you imagine? The Director out at the looney bin is wantin' a detachment sent out, chop-chop. Claims the inmates are rebellin'. Like we got nothin' else on our plates, right, laddie?"

"He said what?"

A uniformed officer standing nearby turned to them. "He calls almost daily with the same request. I gave him instructions on dealing with it. Apparently, he didn't follow-up.

The Sergeant scoffed. "Except for all the criminals we got here, everyone else seems crazy. Oughta just let 'em go. Nobody'd notice."

The officer turned to Zeya. "Have you finished that homicide report?"

The Sergeants brow furrowed. "Homicide? How would a feller know a murder with all the killin' the Jappos are doin'?."

Zeya glanced up from his report. "I witnessed the man shooting the store clerk. The clerk tried to stop him from leaving without purchasing an item."

"And the thief shot him?"

Zeya nodded.

"And you arrested him?"

"No, before I could catch him, a strafing plane killed him."

The Sergeant turned to the officer. "And he's sittin' here on his arse fillin' out a report?"

"While the rest of the world is in chaos, I will maintain order within this unit." The officer turned to Zeya. "Carry on, constable."

Zeya glanced at the Sergeant, who rolled his eyes.

Once the officer left, Zeya set aside his pen. "There are problems at the asylum?"

"Aye, lad. Like everywhere else, things are goin' to hell no matter what the Leftenant says."

Zeya scratched his signature on the form before him, tossed it in a basket on the Sergeant's desk. After rising to his feet, he put on his straw fedora. The Sergeant glanced over at the form, arched an eyebrow. "Headin' out again to maintain the order?"

"Yes, I will need my sidearm."

The Sergeant shrugged. "Ain't got it. The officer still has it while he considers the shootin' you did the other day at the warehouse. You're gonna have to settle for quellin' the disturbances with the force of your badge and personality till he gives it back."

Once outside the police station, Zeya hurried along the busy street. The crowds on the sidewalk, thinned by the flight of the city's inhabitants, failed to impede his progress. Overhead, smoke drifted across the sky. Sirens from emergency vehicles wailed, but there had not been an alert since the two days of bombing around Christmas.

With the force busy discouraging looting, directing traffic, and the other chaos from the attacks, he had no fear of surveillance. Without the usual tactics he used to avoid followers, he made it to the tea shop in less than a quarter-hour.

With no customers to serve, the owner hammered boards outside over the windows. As Zeya approached, he set his tools aside and entered the shop. Inside, the man stepped behind the counter, pulled a bottle from beneath the bar, along with two glasses. After filling both tumblers, he pushed one across to Zeya. "I believe this might be more fitting than tea."

With a nod, Zeya tossed back the drink and set the glass back on the counter. When the man began to refill Zeya's glass, Zeya covered it with his hand. "Thank you, but one is enough. Can I get a pistol?"

The man cocked his head. "With all that's going on, I thought they armed all the police."

"They removed mine after the shooting at the warehouse, and it has yet to be returned."

"Even now? With all that is going on?"

Zeya sighed, shoved his hat back on his head. "I believe some British would stand in a sinking boat at teatime and not set aside the cup even with the water near their ears."

The shop owner nodded. "That will end soon. You watch. Which reminds me. I received a message from the Comrades. Aung San is forming a force in Bangkok to assist in the liberation. He wants all who can, to join him there."

"Bangkok? It may as well be on the moon. Besides, there is still much to be done here."

The shop owner shrugged as he poured another drink. "With all the dockworkers leaving, nothing is being unloaded. Ships come into the harbor and leave because no one is available to take the cargo."

"But the British remain."

"The Japanese will invade soon. I and others are leaving in three days to join Aung San along with the rest in Bangkok." He placed his hand on Zeya's. "Join us. Become a soldier. We will march alongside our Japanese brothers."

Zeya stared off, lost in thought. The moment he had waited for. He and the others originally kidnapped the American, hoping to attract Aung San or one of his follower's attention. That bore no fruit. Led to his current problems. Now the chance to fight alongside his idol. The man who promised to lead Burma out of its oppression. It seemed too good to be true.

But then what about Thiri? Her words came back to haunt him. In love with that foreigner? With her mind unbalanced by the American, she seemed a stranger to him now. Eventually, their father would find her. If he left soon to join Aung San, she would poison the old man's mind against him. Fill their father's account with the lies the American coerced her into believing. He couldn't allow that. He turned to the shopkeeper. "I agree. It is time we join up with others in the movement. You are leaving in three days?"

"At midnight, we will meet here at the shop. To make sure no one stops us, we will walk or ride bicycles to the edge of town. There a truck will meet us."

"Before I go, I need to take care of a few things. For that, I will need a pistol."

The shopkeeper unlocked a cabinet. On tip-toe, he removed a cloth bag from the top shelf. Once he loosened the bag's drawstring, he removed a large pistol. "I purchased this many years ago when I first joined the movement. My work has not required its use, but I am certain it still functions."

Zeya took the revolver, expertly exposed the cartridge cylinder. Dumped the bullets into his hand before dry firing it several times. As he replaced the cartridges, he smiled. "This should do nicely."

He slipped the gun into his empty shoulder holster. "Once I finish my errands, I will return."

CHAPTER TEN

After putting the children down for their nap, Sylvia entered Ralston's office. "So, what are they like?"

Seated at his desk, Ralston set aside the notes he studied. Ralston's wife's question triggered a torrent of images. All turned his belief in the asylum's mission upside down. "The two they sent to negotiate seemed almost lucid."

"But you spent almost two hours with them. Surely you formed some impressions other than that."

"Sanda, the one that did most of the talking has a long, disturbing history."

"In what way?"

"We admitted her when she was a mere teenager. Couldn't have been over twelve or thirteen. Her mother's employer abused her."

"He beat her?"

Ralston cleared his throat. "No, he had sexual relations with her. Started when she must have been only five or six."

Sylvia's face blanched, placed a hand on her chest. "Oh, dear. That would unbalance anyone. But is she violent?"

"It's not really clear. Apparently, someone emasculated her abuser. He bled to death." Ralston, shook his head. "She accused the butler of doing it."

Wide-eyed, Sylvia gasped. "The butler?"

Ralston scoffed. "Like a dime novel. But it seemed consistent with the facts at the time. Chap named Carl. She claims she still talks to him. Other than that, she seems all right."

"Has she been violent since she came here?"

"Not to my knowledge."

"What about the other one?"

"She's one I'm uncertain about. The Gurkha brought her in after a disturbance before the bombings." He then shared Thiri's story Thant told him earlier.

"That's awful? All because she wanted to marry this nice young man and convert?"

"That's about the size of it. The story is consistent with her commitment papers. Signed by her brother. Apparently, he's a police constable."

"And what are you supposed to do? Persuade her to not convert?" Sylvia scoffed. "I'll admit she would do better with Church of England, but last I heard Catholics were considered Christian as well."

"Her commitment is legal. There are protocols, dear, that must be followed."

"So, she remains here on the ward until what?"

Ralston rubbed his forehead as if fending off a headache. "She attacked a policeman. Made herself a danger to others, it was all in the affidavit that accompanied her commitment order."

"You say her brother is a policeman?"

"Yes."

"Was he the one she attacked?"

"It doesn't say." Ralston sighed. "What would you have me do?"

Sylvia turned, strolled to the window, drew back the curtain, and gazed out across the asylum campus. "I often fought with my brother, but he never had me committed. When do you meet with them again?"

"In the morning. Why?"

"May I sit in with you?"

He turned to her and frowned. "What have you in mind?"

"They are women."

"Yes."

"And according to what you've shared with me, the staff have abused them terribly."

Ralston nodded. "A travesty. If Johan lived, I would have had him brought up on charges."

"My presence might help calm them. Plus, I might discern more about their character, being a woman myself."

The next morning, as he waited for his wife and daughters to finish breakfast, Ralston stood at his office window. Outside stood the buildings holding the nearly six hundred souls in his charge. Not a micro-manager during the five years he ran this hospital, he relied on writing clear directives to staff he had trained. As a former medical school instructor, he prided himself on his teaching abilities. Had laid out clear, humane care plans for the persons in his care and expected his staff to follow through.

The governor and others in the colonial offices kept him busy night and day with meetings and hearings over a myriad of issues. Called him frequently for his learned counsel over many matters besides the wellbeing of his charges. With trust in his staff, he rarely visited the wards. Not witnessed his directive's implementation. What he learned from the women shattered his world. Had his trust in his subordinates been naïve? Even negligent? With the women's ward, it appeared to be so. But what about the others?

Sylvia's entrance interrupted his thoughts, but not before he vowed to check the remaining units. Make sure the problems in the women's ward did not occur elsewhere.

"The children are with their tutor. Are you ready to go?"

He turned from his ruminations and nodded.

Outside the women's ward, a burly dark-haired man sat at a table outside the door surrounded by a pool of water. He glanced up at their entrance and scowled. "I've been here all night. The daytime woman didn't show."

Sylvia paused outside the pool and studied it as Ralston approached the seated man.

"I apologize, Ben. I'll make sure you have someone relieve you as soon as possible."

Ben nodded to Sylvia. "Beggin' the Missus pardon, but these bitches have been raisin' cane all night. Must be a full moon."

Herbert's face flushed. "We refer to women and men in our care as patients. I remind you it is our responsibility to care for them with dignity and respect."

Ben nodded towards a pile of bloody rags in the corner. "A few of your refined ladies in an ungenteel moment tossed their monthly visitor rags at me when I brought 'em breakfast. Had to use the fire hose to get 'em back inside."

"You are aware of the problems we've had in the last few days?"

Ben nodded. "Johan was well-liked by his mates."

Eka's arrival interrupted the conversation. She frowned as she scanned the bloody cloths and the pooled water. "Oh, what happened here?" Then she stepped back, and her eyes opened wide as she discovered Ralston and Sylvia. "I apologize for my tardiness. But I had to walk. There were no buses or taxis."

Ralston nodded. "At least you came."

Eka turned to Ben. "Has it started again?"

Ben shrugged. "I believe the ladies missed your presence. Now, if you all will excuse me. I'm headin' off." Before he exited, he gave Sylvia a half bow.

After Ben exited, Sylvia turned to her husband. "What do we do now?"

He turned to Eka. "It seems the ladies were disturbed last night."

"I'm not surprised. Ben and Johan were quite close. I suspect they might have done some things with the women together."

Ralston knocked on the ward door. "Hello? It's Dr. Ralston."

When no answer came from within, he knocked again. "Are you all right?"

"If that monster's still out there, we ain't openin' the door."

"Only Eka, my wife, Sylvia, and myself are here now."

"Your wife? Did ya hear that girl's? The governor's wife herself's here."

"S'pose she's here to invite us to tea?" A second voice replied from behind the door.

Sylvia stepped forward. "Please, I'm here with my husband to help."

"You're a little late. Dorie's dead, and Sanda's hurt real bad. That asshole knocked 'em down hard with the firehose."

Ralston's brow furrowed. "Please. I am a physician. Let me in. Possibly I can help."

"Let them in. Sanda needs help. Otherwise, she may lose her leg."

Ralston turned to Sylvia. "I recognize that voice. That's the one I told you about. Thiri."

With a creak, the door opened a crack. A young woman with short black hair, spiked out in all directions, peered out. Studied the entryway before opening the door.

With Ralston leading the way, Sylvia and Eka followed. Inside, water puddled over the entire floor as if a rainstorm had passed through. Several women ran mops over the floor, directing the water to floor drains, while the others lined the wall, or paced barefoot on the damp concrete floor. The women's clothing and hair appeared soaked. A body lay in the corner, her head bent at an awkward angle, and her eyes stared sightlessly. Thiri and two other women stood over Sanda lying on a bed. Her face etched in pain, Sanda peered upward, mumbling.

As they reached Sanda's bedside, Thiri turned. "I believe her leg might be broken. Can you help her?"

Ralston shook his head. "I can do little for her here. Can you help move her to the examination room down the hall?"

Sanda gasped. "No! I'll be good. Don't take me away."

Ralston peered down. "I'm not going to hurt you. I only want to make you better."

She frowned. "You can fix me?"

"I'll do my best."

Thiri and the other two patients exchanged glances. Sanda grasped Thiri's hand. "Carl wants you to come with me."

Thiri stroked Sanda's brow. "Don't worry, I'll be by your side."

After Ralston showed the women how to lift Sanda while supporting the injured leg, they moved her into the foyer. Once on the examination table, one woman turned to Thiri. "When you're ready to return, knock."

"That place is revolting." Sylvia paced as Ralston bent over Sanda lying on the examination table. Sanda mumbled and winced as Ralston ran his hand over her leg. Thiri, standing beside him, held Sanda's hand, and ran her fingers through the injured girl's hair. "He's not going to hurt me, Carl. He promised to make my leg better."

Sylvia rushed to the table, peered down. "That's right, darling. My husband's a great doctor. He'll have your leg right in no time."

Sanda's eyes shifted to Sylvia. "But he couldn't fix Dorie."

A tear formed in Sylvia's eye. "No, that's right. She broke her neck. No way to fix something like that."

"Dorie was nice. Even Carl liked her right off."

Ralston shook his head, stepped back. "She needs to go to hospital."

Sanda's head snapped around to him. The movement made her wince. "Hospital? What is that?"

"That is a place with skilled doctors and nurses. They can set this properly."

Ralston picked up the phone, arched his eyebrow. "At least this bloody one still works."

Sylvia frowned. "What are you doing?"

"Calling for an ambulance. Only way I can see to make sure she's cared for properly."

****

KUNMING, CHINA

While moving down the hotel hallway, Joe smiled as he recalled his evening with Ann. The desk bell pealed like a fire alarm as someone downstairs repeatedly rapped on it. "Hello. Is anyone here?"

Joe frowned, trying to place the familiar voice, but failed. Whoever it might be sounded annoyed. He paused as he rounded the landing, coming face to face with Mrs. Morgan at the stairway's base. Her jaw dropped as she stepped back, treating Joe to a scowl. Her son, Johnathan standing at the reception desk, with his back to Joe once more struck the bell as if dribbling a basketball across the counter. As Rose emerged from the dining room and stepped behind the desk, Johnathan tipped back his fedora. "Is all the service here as lackadaisical as registration?"

With her best inscrutable expression, Rose looked him in the eye. "You are wanting a room?"

Mrs. Morgan clutched her son's sleeve. Nodded toward the stairway. "Is the hotel filled with those awful men?"

After Rose glanced up, to see Joe on the landing, she gave Mrs. Morgan a puzzled frown. At the same moment, Joe did an about-face and raced back up the stairs, not waiting to hear Rose's answer. He needed to head Ann off from the confrontation waiting below. Ann emerged as Joe reached the door. He took her arm and escorted her back inside.

She grinned. "Joe, haven't you had enough? I've showered and dressed. Besides, I want breakfast before I head off to work."

"Mrs. Morgan is in the lobby."

Wide-eyed Ann's hand went to her mouth. "She's here?"

Joe nodded. "And Johnathan's with her."

"I heard they were out doing inspections, but they didn't say when they might show up here."

"Probably the idea. Listen, you wait here while I scout around downstairs. Find out what they're up to."

"But Joe, I need to get to the hospital. If I'm not there, they'll have questions."

He shoved his hat back on his head. "Don't worry. We'll come up with something. Just wait here. Lock the door behind me, and I'll be right back."

Outside the room, he passed Chen, who nodded and grinned while lugging two suitcases down the hall. Johnathan and his mother still stood before the reception desk.

At his approach, Rose gave him a mischievous grin. "Did you and your young lady have a pleasant evening?"

Mrs. Morgan rolled her eyes while Johnathan leered.

"Yes. As a matter of fact, we might need the room for a few more hours, if that's okay."

Rose winked. "No problem."

Mrs. Morgan tossed her head back, glared down her nose at Joe. "I believe I'll wait in the car while you settle here." And stomped out.

Joe leaned against the counter. "What brings you to Kunming?"

"Mother and I are inspecting all the missions sponsored by the society. While we want the missions providing services to the locals run well, we must ensure our staff present themselves as good role models. In the Christian sense, that is."

"You are traveling to the hospital?"

Rose's question prompted both to turn.

Johnathan nodded. "Yes, the one operated by the Ross's. Do you know them?"

Rose's grin vanished as she stole a glance at Joe before replying. "Yes, Dr. Ross is a very fine gentleman. Respected in the community."

"And his daughter? You familiar with her as well?"

"Of course. She has been a great asset to the hospital. The staff all speak highly of her."

Johnathan rubbed his chin as if pondering a great question. "Has she mentioned me? I'm her fiance. Johnathan."

Rose's eyes opened wide. "Uh, uh...."

"Remember the other day she mentioned her fiance," Joe interjected.

Rose nodded. "Ah, yes. And you are he?"

Johnathan stood straighter, his face took on a smug expression. "None other."

"So, this visit is to achieve an affair of the heart?"

Johnathan cleared his throat. "Mother believes the time might be right to press the issue while we're here."

Once again, Rose stole a glance in Joe's direction. "You have been here before?"

Johnathan shook his head. "First time."

"Then you might lose your way. I can lend you my driver. He is quite skillful. Plus, he is familiar with the safest route through town."

Johnathan frowned. "There are dangers here?"

Rose nodded. "Many of the bombs the Japanese dropped failed to explode. It would be unfortunate if you and the others came upon some of these as they are not clearly marked."

Johnathan's eyebrows rose. "Excuse me, I'll share your concerns with mother. It's up to her."

As Johnathan exited, Rose clutched Joe's sleeve. "You knew of this?"

"It's complicated. Ann might explain it better than me, but they're goin' to the hospital. How we gonna get her outta here and to the hospital without them seeing her."

Rose's brow furrowed. "That is what I am working on already."

"You mean?"

"That's right. I listened to what he said. Knew I must do something. What you think. As your friend Boyington say, you think I born yesterday?"

Johnathan's return interrupted their conversation. "Mother says that the car is crowded enough, and Chen, our driver, is quite capable."

Rose cocked her head. "Then perhaps I can draw you a map, showing the best route. Would that be satisfactory?"

As Chen came down the stairs, Johnathan turned to him. "This lady." He turned to her.

Rose smiled. "Rose. Rose Mok."

Chen smiled and gave her a half bow. "Pleased."

"Anyway, she says there are many unexploded bombs about. Wants to draw us a map of the safest way to the hospital."

Chen nodded to Rose. "Thank you. That would be most helpful."

The three men bent over the counter, watching Rose draw in the route on a sheet of paper. Joe backed up and shook his head as the two men peered at the drawing. Once she finished, Chen snatched it from her hand, gave her a half bow before the two strolled out the door.

Rose rushed out from behind the counter. "Now, you must hurry. Even with the path, I sent them on; you will need much joss to beat them to hospital."

****

"Where ya been? We got patrol in an hour." Boyington scowled as he watched the fifteen planes warming up on the field. The cute Panda bear painted on each plane's side incongruent with the wicked teeth on the craft's cowling. After waving off Rose's driver, Joe joined Boyington in his vigil next to the airstrip. "I thought they slated us for the Rangoon relief."

"Colonel changed his mind, plus he's sendin' 'em early. Guess they're gettin' a respite down there. Figured it might be timely to swap out with the Third."

"Ran into your old buddy."

Boyington arched an eyebrow. "Who?"

"Johnathan Morgan."

"That twerp? What the fuck is he doin' here?"

"He and his mother are on a morals inspection. Come to check out the mission. Make sure they are presenting themselves as good Christians."

"How long they here?"

Joe shook his head. "Not sure."

"Shit, you might as well head off with the Panda Bears. You're not gonna see any action in the romance department as long as they're around. Where were they?"

"Checkin' into the hotel right as Ann and I were gettin' ready to leave this mornin'."

"You got busted?"

Joe shook his head. "Rose sent 'em on a wild goose chase through town, while she and I high-tailed it back to the hospital. They got to the hospital just as our car left. Damn, I had to duck down in the seat as the car pulled out to keep 'em from spottin' me."

"You say Rose set this all up?"

Joe nodded.

"I've heard it's bad luck here to have somebody here save your bacon. Puts ya in debt to 'em for life. They claim folks commit suicide tryin' to get outta that obligation."

"Nah, Rose has her own reasons for keepin' the good Doctor Ross happy."

CHAPTER ELEVEN

RANGOON, BURMA

"We've had no raids for a few days perhaps this run will be uneventful." The orderly setting in the ambulance's passenger seat next to Thant scanned the sky.

Thant nodded. "Did they say what might have happened?"

The man shook his head. "Only that a patient met with an accident."

With ambulance's bell pealing, they raced out of town. The few people on the road moved aside to clear a path.

"Do they have a lot of calls from here?"

Thant's colleague shook his head. "Never been here before. Not sure why. Place is full of loonies. You would think they would hurt themselves more often."

The asylum loomed on the horizon. Thant slowed as they neared the gate. Stopped at the barrier, both scanned their surroundings. "No one is stationed at the gate. See if you can open it."

Once through the gate, Thant rolled down his window. "After you close the gate, we will cruise around the grounds. Hopefully, we will find who called."

After his passenger rejoined him, they scanned the surroundings. "Did they say which building?"

Thant's passenger shook his head. "Just that the injured person was a woman."

With the bell echoing off the surrounding buildings, Thant and his companion scanned the area, while the vehicle crept through the complex. Once they passed the main building, Thant cruised along the lane in front of the back buildings. As they neared the women's ward, Ralston emerged and waved them down.

As Thant stepped from the cab, Ralston's eyes opened wide. "You work at the hospital?"

"I volunteer."

"This is a very strange coincidence."

Thant cocked his head. "I'm sorry?"

"Follow me."

After retrieving the stretcher from the ambulance's back, both rushed after Ralston. Inside the foyer, strange cries and laughter came from behind a massive wooden door. Ralston beckoned them down a hallway on the right. As they followed him, Sylvia stepped out from a side room. She turned back to the doorway. "The ambulance is here, girls."

Following Ralston through the doorway, Thant froze in his tracks. Thiri's jaw dropped and her eyes opened wide. Ralston nodded to Thant. "I assume you know this young gentleman?"

Thant dropped the stretcher and rushed to embrace her. He put his lips to her ear. "He believes we are engaged. I will explain later."

He drew back, smiled into her eyes. "I have tried so hard to see you." He turned to Ralston. "Tell her, please."

"Yes, he came right after your admission. But we have rules about patient privacy. Without permission from your family I could not allow him to visit."

Thant nodded, turned to Ralston. "But I could tell you sympathized. I'm not sure you meant to, but I felt reassured that my beloved was safe and well cared for. So, who had the accident?"

Thiri stepped aside and gestured to Sanda, propped up on the table.

Ralston stepped forward. "She has a broken leg. I splinted it for support, but she will need it set. After that I'm not sure."

As Thant approached, he spoke softly in Burmese. Sanda smiled, laid back. Her eyes rolled up in her head. "He will not hurt me, Carl. He promised to make my leg better." She turned back to Thant. "Could you fix Dorie too?"

Thant gave Ralston a puzzled glance, Thiri took her hand. "Dorie was hurt too bad. She can't be fixed."

A tear ran down Sanda's cheek. "Dorie was nice. Everybody liked her, even Carl."

Thiri stroked her forehead. "I know. But they can fix you."

Sanda clutched Thiri's hand. "Will you come with me?"

Thiri turned to Ralston, he nodded.

"Yes."

****

Finished with the cable, Jenson set it on the table. "This says the transport should show up anytime."

Ed stared out the window at the airfield. "Did the message say who might be comin'?"

"I guess Frillman and Lamison along with his cannibals."

"Cannibals?"

"That Chinese crew of Lamison's. Guys got to callin' 'em the cannibals cause they repaired busted up planes with parts from wrecked birds."

"Be good to see Russ again. Even won't mind bein' around the padre. As long as he don't insist we do jumpin' jacks or some other weird shit designed to build strong bodies to house our clean Christian souls."

"Guess they're comin' to scrounge the docks for spares. Since CAMCO closed down, we got nothin'. Russ's bunch performs miracles, but there's limits."

"Sure as hell quiet with the rest of the guys gone."

"Pandas oughta be here around sundown. That'll liven things up."

Ed turned from the window. "I remember when we first got here, how eager everybody was to mix it up with the Japs. The guys that left this morning all sounded like they had their bellies full of fighting for a while."

Jenson itched beneath his head bandage as he nodded. "The reality of it's a helluva lot different than I figured."

"When I was a kid, I saw this movie. I think it was called Hell's Angels. Made air combat seem romantic. Knights of the air and all."

Jenson nodded. "Yeah, I read stories about `em. Made it all sound so glamorous."

"Wonder if that was all bullshit. Suppose it's because we're fightin' Japs instead of Germans?"

"Nah. Talked to some a the Brits who were in the Battle of Britain. Said the fightin' in Europe ain't much different, except the Jerries use parachutes just like us. Any luck findin' your girl?"

"Checked our apartment and the warehouse yesterday and saw nobody. Guy runs the hotel hadn't seen her either. Not sure what happened to the kids in that group that snatched me."

"Maybe they all got outta town like everybody else."

Ed closed his eyes, tried to bring up her face in his mind. Wished in their time together they had at least found time for a photo. If she left town, where would she have gone? Back to her village? If so, would he ever be able to find it or her again? He'd been lost when he landed there. Knew only that it had been within flying distance from Toungoo.

The engine's roar from a plane passing overhead interrupted their conversation. "Shit, that's twin engines. Are the Japs back?"

Both rushed to the window. Jenson shrugged. "It's CNAC must be the plane from Kunming."

As they emerged from the alert shack, the twin engine transport set down on the runway. While it taxied towards them, dust trailed in its wake. Near the shack, the airliner turned broadside. As the engines wound down, the side door opened. Someone inside dropped a ladder, and men scrambled down.

The first man on the ground, a tall Chinese, paused to stare at the big bird he had ridden in. A broad grin on his face. Next came Paul Frillman. He brushed back his wavy brown hair and marched towards them. After several more Chinese men emerged from the craft, Russ scrambled down the ladder. With the Chinese in tow, he trailed Frillman to the alert shack.

Frillman smiled and shook hands with Jenson, while studying Ed's face.

Finally, he turned to Ed. "We almost gave up on you."

"It's been quite a journey."

"I'm eager to hear about it."

As Russ greeted Jenson with a handshake. "Where do I put up the crew here?"

Jenson nodded to a set of tents near the barracks. "British put those fine abodes up in your honor."

"Are the rest of the ground crew there too?"

"Nah. RAF has 'em in their barracks, but you guys wouldn't wanna hang with them. Just a buncha snooty bastards, anyway."

Russ turned to the gathered Chinese. As he talked to them in their language, he pointed to the tents. Finished, he turned back to Jenson. "If there's an attack, what then?"

"Shelters are all over by those sand bags. Use any one you can get to. Brits aren't real fussy when the shit's flyin' around."

The tall Chinese at Russ's side chuckled at Jenson's comment.

As the Chinese headed towards the tents, Russ turned to Ed. "You look in pretty good shape."

Ed didn't know how to answer. Russ looked gaunt, and his face seemed to have aged. Ed wondered what kind of stress his friend might have faced since he last saw him. Couldn't say, yeah, and you seem like you've been through the wringer. So, he picked a subject Russ enjoyed discussing. "How's your wife?"

Russ hung his head. "Excuse me, I need to help the guys get settled."

As Russ strode away, Frillman shook his head. "I guess you hadn't heard."

Ed frowned. "What?"

"His wife died."

"Shit." Thiri's loss devastated him, but at least he held hope they would be together again. Russ didn't have that. "I wondered what might be wrong. He doesn't look good."

"He's carryin' a lot inside. Won't talk about it with me. You two were close before you went missing. Check in with him later. He might open up with ya."

Ed nodded. "Least I can do." He turned to Jenson. "I'm gonna run into town. I haven't checked in with the cops about Thiri. They might have answers or could help."

As Ed strode away. Frillman turned to Jenson. "Who's this Thiri he mentioned."

"Girl he was involved with when they kidnapped him. He's kinda obsessed with findin' her."

Frillman shoved his cap back on his head. "A woman? Instead of a combat unit, this whole bunch seems like a *Sob Sisters* episode."

****

Zeya crouched down in the car as Ed's vehicle passed. He had not seen the American since his arrest. Had posted himself outside the airbase waiting during his off-duty hours, but the man failed to emerge from this sanctuary until today. As he started his car to trail Ed, he grumbled to himself.

This man, he trailed, stole from the British. Gotten rich on his work with Thiha, now instead of prison, he roamed the streets freely. On top of his thievery, the man drove his sister to insanity with his depravity. For that he would pay. Thiha slipped his grasp for now. After the liberation, he would hunt him down. The Japanese would not tolerate his banditry either.

Zeya slowed as Ed parked outside the police station. What could the man be doing? Did the British not care about his crimes either? That made no sense.

Once past Ed's car, he parked ahead, still pointing in the same direction. If the American came out, he would continue his trail. Surely, he would eventually move to a spot where Zeya could safely take his revenge. But still, the problem presented by Thiri's insanity rose in his mind.

While at the University, he attended classes in psychology. Knew little about the field, except the instructor seemed adamant. Once a person went into the asylum, they rarely emerged healthy. The institution's purpose to provide a place where they would no longer pose a threat to themselves or others. But his father would find her. Listen to her lies. The old man always favored her over him. She would make him an outcast. He must prevent that. But how?

****

The British officer who had arrested him at the warehouse peered down his nose at Ed standing before his desk. The man sneered, as if Ed might be something foul he might step in. "I've more important things to do than keep track of every little piece of fluff that one of you might fancy."

"I was told the Gurkha took her away right before my arrest."

The officer turned to the desk Sergeant, who shrugged. "Saw nothin' in the report about it. Who told you?"

Ed squared his shoulders. "Your constable, Zeya. Girl's his sister."

The officer cocked an eyebrow. "No wonder he appeared in such a state when I showed up. Been my sister you were having your way with I would have wanted to shoot you myself. Should have let him finish the job." The officer turned to the desk Sergeant. "Inform Constable Zeya when he returns, he may have his pistol back. I consider the shooting justified." He turned back to Ed. "Now if there's nothing else, I would suggest you leave before the Constable returns."

"What? Listen, Mack..." His face flushed, Ed seized the officer's lapels. A Gurkha standing near stepped forward and whacked the back of Ed's knee with a club. As Ed's leg buckled, the Gurkha motioned two of his comrades to the spot. Together they hoisted Ed to his feet. The one who struck him shoved his face into Ed's. "You heard the officer." He nodded to the two holding Ed's arms. "Take him out."

As the Gurkha escorted the limping Ed out the door, the officer called after him. "And tell that little jerk at the consulate to not bother complaining. I should just toss you back in the cells where you belong."

****

Zeya reached inside his jacket as Ed limped down the station house steps. As his hand closed on the pistol's handle, two Gurkha emerged behind Ed. They gathered around as Ed opened his car door. Zeya crouched down in the seat. With his field of fire blocked, he waited for the Gurkha to move on.

Ed turned to face the Nepalese soldiers surrounding him. One shoved Ed inside the car, leaned close and spoke. When the man straightened up, Ed slumped in his seat. Zeya could not see Ed's face, but his shoulders shook. Could the man be crying? What had they told him inside?

After Ed started his car, the Gurkha remained in the street, trailing him with their eyes as he drove off. Blocked from pursuing by the men in the street, Zeya slipped the gun under the car seat, opened the door, and joined the Gurkha. "What did that scum want?"

One turned to him. "He came in making inquiries about that woman we took to the asylum. She is your sister?"

Zeya nodded.

"The Leftenant sent him away. Told him nothing, but I suggested you sent her away with the others. He will no longer trouble you. Also, the Leftenant believes discharging your weapon at the warehouse was justified, the desk Sergeant is to return your revolver."

CHAPTER TWELVE

KUNMING, CHINA

"The woman running the hotel speaks highly of you."

Dr. Ross nodded at Mrs. Morgan's comment as they marched to the hospital. "That's encouraging. We've tried our best."

Johnathan and Chen, trailing them, scanned the area. The surrounding trees towered above the buildings, making them nearly invisible from above. "I must say this location is picturesque. What do you think, mother?"

She paused, glanced around. "At least you've been spared the bombing."

"This location has. But our others were not as fortunate."

Her eyebrows arched. "They bombed the hospital?"

She turned to the hospital building and scowled. "We mark the others. Large red crosses on the roof as recommended in the Geneva Convention. Perhaps if you employed the same practice, they might spare you."

"We marked our first location like that. The Japanese made a point of attacking it. They want to make sure they destroy all the supports the Chinese have. Hospitals included."

"What? Savages." She turned to Johnathan. "Make a note. We need to register a complaint about that with our ambassador. He'll put a stop to that."

Dr. Ross turned away and rolled his eyes. "I wish you luck with that. But since we stopped marking the hospital, the only time they hit us is from stray droppings. Probably a new or incompetent bombardier." He shrugged. "But since those Americans chased them off, they haven't returned."

She snorted. "At least they have been good for something. Heathens, the lot of them."

Dr. Ross frowned. "You've had contact with them?"

Mrs. Morgan scoffed. "There was a bunch on our ship coming over. All they did was drink and chase every skirt they saw. Fortunately, Johnathan made sure Ann had no truck with those scoundrels."

Dr. Ross cleared his throat, nodded to Johnathan. "I'm pleased someone looked out for her."

"Let's move along. I need to see this place at work. I want to get back to the hotel before dark. Chen had enough trouble finding our way here in broad daylight. I can't imagine making the same trip in the dark."

Dr. Ross cocked his head. "You had a hard time finding us?"

"Yes, but that hotel owner." She turned to Johnathan. "What was her name again?"

Johnathan turned from Chen. "Rose, mother. Rose Mok."

"Yes, her. Drew us a map so we could avoid the unexploded bombs."

Dr. Ross bit his lip to suppress a smile and nodded. "Yes, those things pose a problem. Let's get you started then." He turned back to Johnathan and Chen. "You know that you shouldn't use the headlights either. Might attract the Japanese."

"Heavens, they attack at night as well?"

"We've been fortunate so far, but I'm sure our following the blackout procedures contribute to that. You must be careful to not show lights while traveling." Dr. Ross nodded toward the heavens "Never know who might lurk up there."

"You boys hear that?" She took Dr. Ross's arm. "We'd best get a move on then."

Inside, nurses gathered up food trays or changed bed linen.

As she scanned the room, Mrs. Morgan smiled. "It's all so clean. I'm pleased. Did they just finish breakfast?"

"Yes, and now they're doing the early morning treatments?"

Her smile vanished as a tiny girl missing a leg and arm huddled wide-eyed on a bed. The nurse, at her bedside, pulled on the girl's arm. Her chatter to the child sounded angry.

Mrs. Morgan rushed to the spot, barked out commands in Chinese, halting the nurse's struggle with the child. The girl glanced up, wide-eyed at Mrs. Morgan while the nurse stepped back. Mrs. Morgan eased down on the bed beside the child, wrapped her arms around the little one's shoulders, leaned close while murmuring to the tiny girl. A smile appeared on the tot's face as she snuggled against Mrs. Morgan, who beckoned the nurse forward. With the girl cradled in her arms, she ran her fingers through the tot's hair while the nurse did her treatment. Once finished, Mrs. Morgan hugged the girl, tucked her back onto her bed, and rose.

Once she rejoined the others, she turned to Dr. Ross. "Why are there so many children? Most don't appear to need medical treatment."

"They are all orphans. The orphanage is full, so they stay with us for now."

She turned to Johnathan. "Include the orphanage on our tour. We must see what we can do. A hospital is no place for them. They need to play, go to school."

Johnathan nodded, pointed to swinging doors in the back where nurses now carried trays. "Is that the kitchen?"

Dr. Ross nodded. "In the evening, it also serves as a laundry."

"Is Ann on duty?"

"I'm afraid she had the late shift last evening. I woke her when you arrived. She'll be down shortly."

Finished with their inspection, the group now approached the house. As they climbed the porch stairs, Ann appeared at the door. "I hope the hospital met with your approval."

She stepped aside and beckoned to the table. "I made coffee, and there's some coffee cake Rose sent from the hotel yesterday. Their cook is an excellent baker."

Mrs. Morgan's eyelashes fluttered. "That sounds wonderful." As she removed her gloves, she scanned the kitchen. "Quaint, but functional." She nodded to a flower-filled vase on the table. "I'm sure you're grateful for the woman's touch." She turned to Ann. "I ran into one of those disgusting men from the ship at the hotel. They aren't still bothering you, are they?"

Ann and her father exchanged glances before she replied. "No, I haven't had problems with them."

"Good. That's one of my greatest concerns with our people. Make sure they tend to their duties in a Christian manner. Along with our good works, we're obligated to provide a good moral example."

****

RANGOON, BURMA

"That Yank won't be botherin' your sister again. Officer set him straight on that." The desk Sergeant winked as he opened the desk drawer. Removed Zeya's pistol from a sack inside.

"What did he tell him?"

"Told him he shoulda let you shoot him."

The Gurkha standing by the desk nodded. "After what I told him he won't know where she is."

The Sergeant grinned as he held out the pistol, butt-first, to Zeya. "Leftenant also believes your shootin' other day justified. So, here's your piece."

After accepting the gun, Zeya broke it down to inspect the cartridge cylinder.

"It's not loaded. You gotta see the armorer for ammunition."

Zeya nodded as he slipped the weapon into his holster. After obtaining ammunition, Zeya rushed out to his car. Ed may not be available for his vengeance, but he must do something about Thiri. Perhaps persuade her to accompany him to Thailand. Once out of her father's reach until after the liberation, Zeya might have a chance. Redeem himself in his father's eyes before unveiling the ruin his foolishness had brought on her and the family.

Yes, that would be the answer, he told himself as he traveled through town. He had no idea how she might respond to him. Her attack during the raid surprised him. Instead of the relief, she should have expressed at his rescue, she insisted on waiting for the American. Spun the tale, the man forced into her mind with his debauchery.

Claimed they worked for that thief until they could escape. Said she loved the American. What craziness.

Perhaps while he strove to free their country, he could find a place where her mind might heal. One thing for sure, she had always been strong-willed. Perhaps given proper care, she might recover her senses. See that her brother and family loved her no matter what Ed had done to her.

Confidant, he ignored the ambulance as it roared past in the other direction. Yes, he told himself as the asylum loomed ahead, she might even welcome him with open arms. Grateful for his rescue.

He leaned on the horn at the entrance gate, but no one appeared to open the barrier. He stepped from the vehicle. Peered around the facility's grounds. Not a person anywhere. He shoved the gate upwards out of the way. Without closing the barrier, he followed the signs to the main building.

After parking in the circular drive before what appeared to be the main entrance, he leaped up the stairs, two at a time. Inside, he passed several vacant offices until he came to one with the Director's sign on the door. Since the assistant's desk outside the door set empty, he passed inside without knocking. Again found no one inside.

As he turned to leave, Ralston entered. The little man stepped back, and his jaw dropped. "May I help you?"

"Yes, I am here to take my sister out of here."

Ralston frowned. "Your sister?"

"Her name is Thiri. The Gurkha brought her here last week."

"And you want her discharged into your care?" Ralston removed his pince-nez. "You have some identification?"

Zeya nodded. As he reached inside his jacket, Ralston's eyebrows rose as he spied the pistol in the shoulder holster. After passing his warrant card to Ralston, Zeya removed his hat and ran his hand over his head as Ralston studied his credentials.

"Thiri, you say?"

"Yes."

Ralston passed the warrant card back, strolled behind his desk, beckoned Zeya to the empty chair before it. "Name's not familiar to me. I must check the ward rosters. Won't take a moment."

After Zeya seated himself, Ralston removed a leather-bound ledger from his desk drawer. After replacing his pince-nez, Ralston ran his finger down the page. "Ah, here it is. Yes, she is no longer with us, I'm afraid."

Zeya leaped to his feet. "That's impossible." He jabbed his finger at the ledger. "I demand to see your record."

Ralston drew the register back towards himself. "I'm sorry. That's not allowed. Patient privacy. Laws on that. I'm sure as a policeman, you understand."

Zeya drew his pistol from beneath his jacket. "No. You need to understand. I am serious. Now show me that record."

Ralston's eyebrows rose. "Our rules are to protect the people in our care from unwarranted intrusion into their lives. Now before you do something you regret, why don't you put away that gun. Let's discuss this like adults."

Sylvia appeared behind Zeya. Her eyes opened wide, and her hand went to her mouth. Without saying a word, she backed from the room unnoticed by Zeya.

The gun shook in Zeya's hand, his face flushed.

"Please constable. I'm certain you are concerned for your sister's wellbeing, but if you persist down this path..."

"I will see that record now." Zeya cocked the pistol.

"Constable. Consider what you're doing. Having you behind bars will only contribute to her stress. Might even trigger a relapse."

Tears streamed down Zeya's cheeks as he lowered the gun.

As he settled into the chair across from Ralston, he released the gun's hammer, before setting the pistol in his lap.

Ralston leaned back and sighed as Zeya hung his head.

Zeya's head snapped up. "Where is she?"

Ralston tugged at his collar. "I'm not sure."

"But they admitted her last week. She was violent. Attacked me."

Ralston nodded. "It was in the commitment order."

"Then why is she not here?"

"She seemed stable. Appeared before the magistrate, and he discharged her."

"Discharged her?"

"Yes."

Zeya ran his fingers through his hair. His stomach churned, *Could she already be back in their village poisoning their father' mind against him?* "Where did she go?"

"As an adult, she would be free to go anywhere she liked." Ralston rose. "You look pale, young man." He strolled to a table containing a crystal container. Filled a tumbler from it and passed it to Zeya. "It's brandy. Might settle your nerves a bit."

Zeya tossed it down. Ran his hand over his face, sighed, and slowly rose to his feet. Ralston moved to his side, patted him on the shoulder. "I'm certain your sister is all right. If there are further problems, though, bring her back. That's our job."

After Zeya left, Sylvia entered from a side door carrying a revolver. She passed it to Ralston, and he placed it in a desk drawer. "Thank you, dear. I didn't think I could have pulled that off without knowing you had that just outside the door."

As he poured them both measures from the bottle, Sylvia fanned herself. "But it's been so many years since I've handled one of those things."

"True, it's been a while since you dispatched that burglar, but I had faith."

"Now what?"

Ralston gave her a puzzled glance. "What do you mean?"

"With Thiri? Will you tell her about her brother?"

"No, she's better off re-united with her young man. Between her and her brother, she appears to be the most stable."

She sipped her brandy. "What was all that about the magistrate discharging her?"

Ralston swished his brandy in the glass, sniffed its bouquet, and smiled. "Did you forget? The governor appointed me six months ago. More convenient than running them into town for a hearing before some layman. Just never got around to using the authority before today."

****

As Ed strode down the hall to his room, voices trailed down the hallway. "How in the hell would anybody do that?"

A second chuckled. "Definitely need a good back for it. That's for sure."

Inside, a tall, blond-haired man stood holding Thiri's copy of the *Kama Sutra*. The second, a tall, lanky brown-haired man peered over his shoulder. Both looked up from the book as Ed entered.

The blond man's handsome face broke out in a grin as he held the book out to Ed, his words marked by a Texas drawl. "Seen some exotic stuff since I got here, but this takes the cake."

Ed's face flushed as he reached for the book. The Texan extended his hand. "Sorry about pokin' around in it, but found it layin' here on the bunk they assigned me. I'm David Hill, but most folks call me Tex." He nodded to his companion. "This here scoundrel's Jim Howard."

"I'm Ed. Ed Burton."

Ed slipped Thiri's copy of the *Kama Sutra* under his arm as he shook Tex's hand before doing the same with Howard.

Howard nodded. "Just plain Jim here. If you don't mind my askin', what is that thing?"

Ed's flush deepened. What could he say? Thiri treasured that book, filled with drawings depicting different sexual positions. Studied it every night before bed, memorizing the position she insisted they attempt each evening. A lump formed in his throat as he recalled their laughter as they struggled with the novel position. Usually breaking down in the throes of passion, tossing the book aside, and energetically romping in the moment's heat. "It-it's the *Kama Sutra*. Hindu holy book."

Howard tapped Tex's chest. "See? Told you it wasn't just some blue book. Drawin's seemed artful like."

Tex smirked. "Hindu, ya say? Sure as hell got it all over bein' a Baptist."

Jim nodded, turned to Ed. "Probably don't frown on dancin' either, right?"

"Don't really know. I, uh..." Ed slipped the book inside his dresser, turned back to the boisterous pair. "You guys with the Second Pursuit?"

Howard nodded. "Panda Bears. And proud of it."

Tex turned to Ed. "You're the guy got kidnapped, right?"

He nodded.

"This place got anything resemblin' an officers' club. Awful dry from suckin' on that oxygen all the way here."

"Sure. Out behind the barracks."

Tex tossed his flight jacket on a bunk, clapped Ed on the back. "Musta been a helluva an adventure. How bout you enlighten us over a few beers?"

After leaving the barracks, they made their way to the shack that served as the officer's club. As they approached in the gathering, dusk, talk, and laughter drifted out from inside.

Tex turned to Ed. "Sounds like the rest of the guys got in."

"How many of you guys come down?"

Tex shrugged. "Whole damn squadron. Seen a lotta action?"

"Had a couple attacks after I got back to the unit. But it's been quiet for the last few days."

Inside, several men still wearing flight gear stood at the bar, their parachute packs stacked in the corner. In his boots and cowboy hat, Jenson stood among the others leaning against the bar. As they entered, Jenson turned, and a grin spread on his face. "Hey, Burton, where d'you dig up that cowpoke?"

Tex pulled himself up to his full height and nudged Ed. "For the record that bum is all hat and no cattle."

Jenson shoved his Stetson back, placed his hands on his hips. "Ah, you're full of it. Down South, all ya got is them mangy longhorns. You want real beef, ya gotta come up to the Northern Panhandle."

Jim Howard shook his head and turned to Ed. "With these two, it's the first liar loses."

"How can you tell when a Texan is lyin'?" One airman shouted from the group at the bar.

"His lips are movin." This reply from another, spurred a chorus of hoots and laughs from the gathered men.

Tex's eyes turned up to the ceiling, and he frowned at the hole. "What the hell?"

Jenson grinned. "Jap bomb. Lucky it was a dud." His sweeping gesture encompassed the entire building. "Otherwise, it would have destroyed this fine British establishment."

At the bar, Howard ran his hand over the splintered countertop, then stuck a finger through several holes.

Jenson pointed to the ceiling. "Can't see the holes up there in the dark, but they're there. Jap strafed the place. Took out a whole week's grog ration."

Howard frowned. "Heathens."

As the bartender passed a beer bottle to Ed, Jenson turned to him and tipped back his Stetson. "Find anything out about your girl?"

"Cops claim they don't know. One of the Gurkha told me that her brother shipped them outta a town after the raid. He figured she might have gone with 'em."

"If that's the case, she's safe. Once things settle, you can hunt her up."

CHAPTER THIRTEEN

Thant bent over the table where Sanda lay Thiri at his side.

"You're my fiance'?"

Thant shrugged in response to Thiri's question. As he examined Sanda's leg, he told Thiri about his initial meeting with Ralston. "I volunteered for the ambulance because I hoped to free the boss from his confinement."

Thiri frowned. "He's in jail?"

"I guess it's like that. Some men came and took him away from the jail and took him to the airfield. I had to go there several times to pick up injured after the raids. Once I saw him walking with a group of men wearing leather helmets and these big pads down by their butts."

Thiri grinned. "Those pads are parachutes. They wear them in case the plane is damaged, and they have to jump out."

"How would they be certain they could land on their bottoms?"

"No, silly. They pull a string that unfolds this big umbrella that is packed inside those packs you saw. It allows them to float down safely."

Thant frowned. "That makes sense. The pads didn't look thick enough to provide much protection in a long fall."

"You're serious. You didn't know?"

He chuckled. "Of course not. I studied medicine. Had little time for frivolous things."

Thiri rolled her eyes.

Sanda mumbled and winced as Thant ran his hand over her leg. Beside him, Thiri stroked Sanda's head while holding her hand.

Sanda's eyes rolled back. "He will not hurt me, Carl. He promised to make my leg better."

Thiri peered down. "That's right. He'll have your leg right in no time."

From a cupboard, Thant retrieved a cone-shaped mask and a bottle. He bent over his patient. "I want to give you something to help you sleep. While you're out, I can fix your leg, and you won't feel a thing."

"Sleep?"

Thant nodded, held up the cone and the bottle. "I will place this over your nose and mouth. After that, I pour some of this liquid on the cone. You breathe it, and then you will go to sleep. When you wake up, I will have put your leg in a cast."

"A cast?"

"A hard plaster shell. It will hold the bones in place while they heal. Then in a few weeks, we crack off the plaster, and your leg will be good as new."

"Carl wants you to promise it will be better."

Thant and Thiri shared a glance before he looked back down at her. "Tell Carl, I promise."

Sanda squeezed Thiri's hand. "Okay."

Once sedated, Thant worked rapidly to set the leg and put on the cast. "I hate using ether. Her personal reality seems frightening enough without the hallucinations this sometimes causes, but I was afraid she wouldn't cooperate while conscious."

"What will happen to her?"

"I suppose she must return to the asylum."

"Can't she stay here?"

"For a broken leg? What beds we have are filled with people that need them. They are discharging people now that probably should remain."

Thiri looked down at the unconscious girl.

"Now that you're out of that awful place. Stay here with me. Together we'll rescue Ed and return to our village."

Thiri shook her head. "Sanda saved me. I promised to be with her."

****

Thiri, along with Thant and the orderly, stood to the side as Ralston and Sylvia stood over Sanda's unconscious form on the stretcher in the ward's foyer.

"She can't go to that awful ward. Not like this." Her hand to her chest, Sylvia turned wide-eyed to her husband.

"Are you suggesting something, Sylvia?"

"There is a spare room. Perhaps she could stay there while she recuperates."

"But dear, she requires care and supervision."

Sylvia placed her hands on her hips. "Isn't that what this place provides?"

"I barely have enough staff to cover the wards. Let alone provide her with a staff person."

"I'm sure we can manage."

"What about the children?"

Sylvia turned to Thiri. "Would you be willing to come along? Help her out? We could move a cot in the room for you."

Ralston grimaced. "Your young man here told me about the problems you had with your family about converting to Christianity. Was worried about you after your brother had you put in here."

As Ralston spoke, Thiri gave Thant a sideways glance. He bit his lip to suppress a smile. Ralston continued. "I don't hold with such things myself. Other families have tried the same thing. What I'm trying to say is, you seem stable, and what my wife proposes seems to be the only solution. Would you be willing to stay with us in the main house and nurse your friend here back to health?"

92

Thiri turned to Thant. He hung his head. "I promised her to stay by her side. I must keep my word."

Ralston turned to Thant. "Don't worry. We'll look after your intended. Plus, you can visit. How's that?"

Thant shrugged. Ralston leaned close. "I'm sure you had other things in mind, young man. But there will be plenty of time for that after the nuptials."

Thant blushed.

Sylvia huffed placed her hands on her hips. "What did you say to him, Herbert?"

"Just assured him that things would work out." He gave Thant a backhanded tap to his chest. "Right sport? In her case, Sylvia and I may have a sort of en loco parentis responsibility for her. So, we will allow you to take her to town for the instruction you both need for the conversion. Of course, one of us would chaperon, make sure everything remains on the up and up."

****

KUNMING, CHINA

"I just passed the mountains when I spotted twenty Jap fighters on my ten o'clock. They mighta been headin' here." Olson, the Hell's Angel squadron leader, shook his head, then sipped his beer.

Boyington scowled. "Get any?"

"Nah, ducked into a cloud till they passed, but radioed the sighting. Guess they headed somewhere else."

"You didn't even make a pass at 'em?" Boyington rolled his eyes. "One good burst mighta netted ya five hundred smackers."

Olson wiped the foam from his upper lip. "In this case, I heeded Madame Chiang's own words."

Boyington slammed his drink on the bar. "Madame Chiang? What the hell she got to do with it?"

Olson tipped back his cap. "Maybe you hadn't seen it. It was in all the papers down in Rangoon after you guys kicked their asses."

"What?"

"She said any one of her American flyers could take out ten Japanese."

"What's that got to do with it?"

Olson shrugged. "Didn't want to make Madame Chiang look bad. If there had been nine or ten of 'em, I would have engaged. But there was more than that. Plus, you know how the Japs exaggerate shit."

Boyington muttered under his breath while shaking his head.

Olson nudged Joe. "What's his problem?"

"He's dyin' for a chance to get at 'em."

"Might not get to either. Japs might be given up." Boyington growled.

Joe set down his drink, turned to Boyington. "What are you talkin' about?"

"Was over in the offices checkin' out Olga's legs and a cable come through. They ain't had a sniff from the Japs since the Panda's arrived. Been two weeks since they showed up here."

"They'll be back soon enough."

Olson clapped Boyington on the back. "Well, the old man got on the horn with some Limey officer down there. The guy wants our boys to do a run into Thailand. Jump one a their airfields."

Joe shook his head. "Sounds like fun."

Boyington rubbed his chin. "Wonder if that bonus applies to planes you shoot up on the ground."

Olson set down his drink. "I wouldn't ask the boss. I saw him this morning, and he seemed ready to chew somebody's tail."

Boyington nodded. "Yeah, the CAMCO guys are fallin' down on the job. Closed down the factory by Rangoon and hightailed it outta town. That's why he sent the Padre and Lamison to Rangoon."

"You could always ask Greenlaw about the bonus." Olson said

Boyington scoffed. "I doubt he'd give me the time of day. Got all huffy when he found me talkin' to his wife."

Joe groaned. "God, my hearts breakin' for ya."

"Easy for you to say. Got that honey of yours nearby. Oh, whoops, I'm sorry." Boyington chuckled nudge, Joe. "Forgot. Heard how that asshole Johnathan's comin' with his courtin'?"

****

In the cottage's kitchen, Dr. Ross and Johnathan sat at the table. "Your mother's a fine woman. Well respected in Boston."

"But you refuse to give your blessing to our marriage?" Johnathan sighed, ran his fingers through his hair. The movement hardly budged his slicked-back style. "Can I ask why?"

Dr. Ross set his pipe aside, leaned back. "I'm not refusing. I've not seen or talked to you in years. I know nothing about you, really."

"Hasn't Ann talked about me and how she feels?"

"Until recently, we've had little time to discuss anything besides patient care. Granted, in the last few days, there has been less stress there, but then with you and your mother showing up two days ago, there has been little private time either."

"But surely..."

Dr. Ross interrupted by holding up his hand. "After you and I have a chance to spend time together, I'm sure I'll have a better idea as to your character. Ann has spent more time with you, and I trust her judgment, but to ask me to support this union currently?" He shook his head. "I need more time."

Ann's entrance trailed by Mrs. Morgan interrupted their discussion. After removing her nurse's cap, Ann gave her father a peck on the cheek. Johnathan took her hand and drew her to his side. "What have you and mother been up to?"

"She wanted to review the patient records." She glanced at Mrs. Morgan. "She had several suggestions for tracking supplies that might improve our projections."

Mrs. Morgan nodded as she joined her son and Dr. Ross at the table. "Looking at your past usage of essential medicines should guarantee you don't run out of essential anesthetics and antibiotics. That would be catastrophic."

Dr. Ross shook his head. "Basically, we've merely requested all we could get and hoped that would be sufficient."

Mrs. Morgan tossed her head back, huffed. "If everyone did that, there would not be enough to go around. You must consider those things. The society has many hospitals to serve."

Ann placed her hands on her hips. Her face flushed. Angered at Mrs. Morgan's dismissal of her father's statement. "Besides Chunking, any of the others getting bombed almost daily?"

Mrs. Morgan frowned. "Well, no, but you might be beyond that here as well." She turned to her son. "Have you had a fruitful morning as well?"

Ann rolled her eyes before moving to fill a teakettle at the sink, Johnathan trailed her with his eyes. He turned back to his mother. "I think Dr. Ross and I have reached an understanding."

"Wonderful." She turned to Dr. Ross. "So, we have a wedding to plan?"

"As I told your young man, there is really no hurry."

Mrs. Morgan drew herself up in her chair. "What? Don't you think it's unseemly for a lovely young woman such as your daughter to remain unattached?"

"Unseemly?"

"The only available male companionship locally are those savages at the airfield."

Dr. Ross shrugged. "You see them as a threat to her virtue?"

Mrs. Morgan stole a glance toward the counter where Ann set out a teapot. She leaned close to Dr. Ross as if she might be about to reveal a secret. "She appeared tempted during the voyage over."

"And you're afraid that so much temptation nearby might be too great to resist?"

Mrs. Morgan drew back, gave a determined nod. "Exactly. Once married, those pressures might be avoided. A wedding band is a powerful reminder of one's moral responsibility."

Dr. Ross leaned back in his chair. Shot a glance at Johnathan. "After the wedding, your son would remain here? In Kunming?"

"Of course not. I can't travel around this countryside unescorted. It's just not done. He would come with me as I do my inspections."

"I suppose then Ann would go with you two?"

Mrs. Morgan turned to her son. He looked away. Avoided her gaze. "I'd not considered those things."

Dr. Ross nodded. "I recruited and trained nurses from the local population. I'm afraid to provide care and train at the same time... Well, let's say it produced less than ideal results. That all changed with her arrival.

Along with the welcome company she provided me, her ability to continue the staff's training has been a Godsend. We could go back to the way it was, I suppose, but." Dr. Ross shrugged.

"Johnathan, would you mind putting things off for now? Maybe wait until I've finished and ready to return to Boston?"

Dr. Ross smiled. "Perfect solution." He clapped Johnathan on the back. "Then, you could remain here with us after your mother leaves." He turned to Ann. Her head snapped around. "What do you think, dear? Would that prove satisfactory?"

The color drained from Johnathan's face.

****

Rose moved through the lobby into the Hotel's bar. "I understand the one's fighting in Rangoon returned yesterday. Make sure the bar is well stocked."

The barman nodded, and Rose left the lounge. Inside her hotel's dining room, she filled a mug with coffee from the urn. As Rose sipped, she inspected the dining room's condition. Stopped at tables to hold up a spoon or a fork to determine its cleanliness, while she strolled to the area where they cleaned the hotel's dishes and laundry. Inside, one woman scrubbed pots and pans at the sink, while a man used a washboard on bedsheets. As they worked, they chatted and laughed.

"It brings me joy to see my people happy in their work."

Both stopped laughing, like naughty school children, when the principal walks in. Rose frowned. "Do not stop on my account."

While a smile still played at the man's lips, he nodded his head to Rose as if saluting her. "I apologize. It is probably not a laughing matter. The Gweilo are peculiar. To laugh at our guest's habits might be unseemly."

"Their habits?"

"Yes."

"You mean the pilots?"

The man's eyebrows rose, "Oh, no. They seem like the rest of us. The new ones."

"New ones?"

The man nodded. "The old woman and her son."

Rose rolled her eyes. "The old woman is a Lǎobǎn. All the missionaries kowtow to her. We need to stay on her good side, or she might shut down the hospital and the orphanage."

The man pursed his lips, and shot a glance in the woman's direction.

"Is something wrong?"

"Her son. Is he powerful as well?"

"Do you mean, should we fear him?"

The man nodded.

"Only if what he does embarrasses his mother. Why?"

The man shrugged, shot a glance at the woman at the sink. "The son is different."

Rose scowled. "In what way?"

"I washed the sheets from their driver's bed. They bear the stains from lovemaking."

Rose scowled. "He is young, handsome. While I have not seen him with any maidens here, I am certain he has needs. Perhaps he pleasures himself."

The man and the women exchanged glances. A grin spread on the man's face. While the woman covered her mouth to suppress giggles.

Rose frowned. "What? I say something amusing."

"The sheets also were stained heavily with oil that smells like the kind the son wears."

CHAPTER FOURTEEN

RANGOON, BURMA

Thiri stood at the bedroom window staring out at the asylum's grounds. Sanda rising on the bed behind her prompted her to turn.

"What did they do to me?" A tear ran down Sanda's cheek as she stared wide-eyed at the cast.

Thiri moved to her side. "Remember, Thant, the young man who took you to the hospital and put you to sleep?

Sanda nodded.

"He said he would put a cast on your leg to make it better."

"Is that what it is?"

Thiri nodded.

Sanda ran her hand over the smooth white plaster. "It is hard." She rapped it with her knuckle, then grinned. "I felt nothing. It might be good to have this all over one's body. Then no one could hurt you."

"Is that what you want? To feel nothing?"

"No, I would like to be happy, but I meant no one could touch me. That would be a good thing."

"A good thing?"

Sanda nodded. "Whenever anyone touches you, they hurt you."

"Not everyone who touches you will hurt you."

"Ha! What about Johan and Hazel. They touched you. Wanted to hurt you."

Thiri frowned. "But I have had others touch me, and I liked it. Wonderful, in fact."

"Really?"

"Haven't you?"

Sanda shook her head. "Not that I remember."

"What about your mother or your father?"

"My father died before I was born. I don't remember my mother too well."

"What about Thant?"

"He hurt me when he checked my leg. And then he put me to sleep. Remember? So, he could work on it."

"How about tickling?" Thiri nudged Sanda's side.

Sanda lunged back as if struck, then winced when her leg moved. "No! Carl. She didn't mean it. She didn't know."

Thiri drew back. "I'm sorry. My father used to grab me there, and it made me giggle."

"Please, Carl. Let me explain it to her." Sanda blinked several times, her eyes cast upward as if staring at the ceiling. She turned to Thiri. "That is what the bad man did before he hurt me. Said, let's play. Then he grabbed me. His hands. Bad hands."

"I'm sorry. I didn't know. I won't hurt you. You must realize that. After all, you saved me from Hazel and Johan."

Sanda grinned. "That's right. You like me?"

Thiri nodded. "If I say or do something that scares you or hurts, tell me and I won't."

The door opening behind them prompted both to turn. A little girl wide-eyed peeked around the door. A grin spread on her face. "Hello. I'm Julie. Momma asked me to see if you needed anything."

Thiri nodded to the child. "I'm Thiri. This is Sanda." She turned to Sanda. "Are you hungry? Thirsty? You missed lunch."

Sanda nodded. "I would like something to drink, but my stomach seems funny. I'm not sure I should eat."

The girl approached, stared at Sanda's cast. "What happened to you?"

Sanda glanced at Thiri, then back at the child. "I fell and broke my leg."

"Does it hurt?"

"A little."

Sylvia entered the room, carrying a tray with a second girl trailing her. The first girl, Julie, turned. "Momma, Sanda said her leg hurts."

"Go tell your father." As Julie scampered off, Sylvia set the tray with a china teapot, cups, and a plate of cookies on the bedside. "I see you've already met Julie." She nodded to the second girl who peeked out, wide-eyed from behind her mother. "This is Victoria. She doesn't say much, too busy learning. Soaking everything in. I brought tea. It will please Herbert you are awake." Her brow furrowed. "You're in pain?"

"A little. Not like before."

"I hope the gown fits you all right. It's one of mine."

Sanda nodded. "It's lovely."

Sylvia turned to Thiri. "We must see about getting you something to wear as well. I'm sure you're used to better."

Julie appeared again, leading Ralston by the hand. "You're all right? Julie said you might be in pain."

Sanda nodded. "A little." She pointed to a spot on the cast. "It aches there."

"That's where it broke. Some aspirin will probably take care of that. Are you hungry? Thirsty?"

"My stomach seems dizzy. But I would like something to drink."

"The queasiness in your stomach is from the anesthetic they used to put you to sleep. That should ease in a few hours, probably before bedtime. If you think you can, I would like you to at least eat a couple of these biscuits before I give you the aspirin."

Sylvia poured a cup of tea. "Do you use cream or sugar?"

Sanda frowned. "I never tried either."

"Well, let's give you a little of both. The extra nutrition should do you well." Finished with her ministrations, she passed the cup on a saucer to Sanda. As she peered inside it, Sanda arched her eyebrows. "Thank you." She sipped and smiled. "This is wonderful."

Ralston pursed his lips as he turned. He called over his shoulder. "Have a biscuit, and I shall return shortly with the aspirin."

Sylvia held out her hand to Julie. "Come on, girls. Let these two enjoy their tea." As she exited, she glanced over her shoulder. "You both should take a little rest. I'll be up at suppertime."

Sylvia caught up with her husband in the hall. "Did you see that? She's like a feral child."

"Remember? She came here quite young."

"She seems almost like a child. How old is she now?"

"Twenty-five, I believe. Have to check the record to be certain."

Sylvia shook her head. "So innocent."

As Ralston turned to get Sanda's aspirin, he said nothing about the blood-stained razor he discovered in the pocket of Sanda's dress. But he would lock the bedroom door tonight.

****

As their flight soared over the Burma back country, Ed recalled this morning's briefing.

"Let's take it to 'em." Newkirk, the Panda Bears squadron leader, said as he finished. So, that's what they planned to do.

They had left Mingaladon before sunrise. Headed for the Japanese airfield at Tak in Thailand, they crossed the Dawna mountain range that marked the border as the sun's disk appeared ahead on the horizon. Since the Japanese stopped attacking, the British command insisted they take the offensive. Intelligence claimed this Japanese airfield had become active, so it became the first target in what the British called the "Lean Forward" initiative.

Ed focused on the plane off his right wing to avoid looking straight into the rising sun. As smoke trailed from this craft's engine, the pilot's voice came over his headset. "Engine's actin' up. Headin' back."

Newkirk replied. "Roger, Burton, close up on me."

100

Off to their left, smoke rose. "Looks like Moulmein airfield already got visited. Keep your eyes peeled, more might hang around."

Close to the border and vulnerable to strikes with little warning, Moulmein had been manned sparsely. Ed overheard two British say the Indians had stationed some biplanes there two days ago. Had they merely provided the same function as a canary in a coal mine? A sacrifice for the greater good?

The attack on this outpost might have signaled a major strike in their direction, so Ed's head now swiveled as he searched for threats. While Tak sat a mere fifty miles from the border, the P-40s took a circuitous path to round the Japanese airbase. Once they could put the sun at their backs, they would swing around to attack.

As the formation turned to attack, Ed armed the guns. Once sure of his position within the flight, he scanned the sky, searching for threats.

"Airfield at eleven o'clock."

One by one, the planes peeled off for their strafing run, leaving about two miles between each aircraft. "Holy shit looks like they're gettin' ready to take off." A voice he didn't recognize called out over his headset.

Tex Hill's drawl now broke through. "We got company."

"I got your back," Newkirk replied.

A metallic glint left and below prompted Ed to glance in that direction. A closer look revealed a speck zipping just above the trees. Within seconds the speck grew into a fixed gear fighter, banking on one P-40's tail as it lined up on its strafing run. Ed swerved behind the attacker and squeezed off a short burst. Aware now of Ed's presence, the Japanese flipped around to face him so fast Ed's jaw dropped. Head on with his opponent, Ed hit his trigger as tracers reached out from the opposing fighter. The Japanese pilot's shells passed above him, while his intersected the enemy's flight path. He broke right as the Japanese plane sprouted flames and spun into the ground below.

Before he could re-align with the airfield, it passed on his right. Three planes burned beside the runway as people below scattered.

Ahead, a P-40 banked to make another pass at the airfield, Ed duplicated the maneuver in the opposite direction. The plane ahead blocked his field of fire, so he moved his hand away from the trigger. The lead P-40 walked a long burst through the parked aircraft below. With their propellers spinning, one after another exploded or toppled. At the end of its strafing run, the P-40 ahead's propeller stopped spinning. For a moment, it soared between two Japanese fighters as if in formation. Without power, the P-40 fell behind the two Japanese, who swooped away at treetop level. Now, as the P-40 banked to pass over the airfield, a puff of smoke shot from its exhaust, and the propeller spun.

When Ed drew alongside the leading plane, the pilot glanced over and waved. As Ed returned the salute, Newkirk's voice came over his headphones. "Fun's over."

To avoid ground fire, they altered their course on the return flight. Instead of a staggered formation, they flew in a nearly straight line with Ed in trail.

"Hey, it's like old home week." Tex's drawl came through his headset."

"Whattya talkin' about cowboy?"

"Three o'clock."

Ed turned to the right. Below sat Toungoo. The airfield they had used for training before moving to China. He had flown from there when forced down and captured by Zeya. The sight sparked a plan in Ed's mind. While maintaining his position in the flight, he pulled out his area map. Now he studied the landmarks below, determined to memorize the route from here to Rangoon. Thiri might not be beyond his reach.

****

While having tea, Ralston and Sylvia discussed conditions on the women's ward. "Oh Ralston, can things be that bad in the other wards?" A tear formed in Sylvia's eye as she sat across from his desk.

"I'm not sure. I depended on the staff to follow through on my directives once I trained them. With everything else, I hope I have not misplaced my trust."

"Have there been other incidents?"

"None. But once again, with all the demands from government house, I failed to follow up. Possibly what we saw in the women's ward is not widespread, or perhaps it might have been brought about by our current staffing problems. Either way, I need to go out at once. See what's happening with my own eyes."

As he rose from his chair, she glanced up. "Be careful, darling." He squeezed her shoulder as he strode out, determined to discover the truth about the condition of his charges.

In the women's ward, Eka remained at her post. The hum of conversation mixed with the occasional laughter came from behind the door. "Has no one else come to help?"

She shook her head. "I've not had anyone with me since the disturbance. Ben relieved me last night, but he arrived late."

"Have you heard anything from the other wards?"

"No, but we seldom do."

"I'm going around to the other buildings. If you need help, call the other wards."

As he marched to the building housing the most dangerous males, he hoped what he found, put his fears aside. Inside the foyer, he discovered no one on duty. He peered through the observation grate in the door. Men wandered or sat against walls. The odor that drifted through the mesh made his stomach churn. Some wore the shabby canvas gowns similar to the females, but many wore nothing.

He stepped back from the door with a frown. "Hello. Anyone here?"

When no one responded, he opened a side door. As he rushed down the hallway, he hoped to find the attendants in the therapy area. Even if they had been shorthanded, he disliked the fact that no one observed the ward. Images of what might happen without supervision made him shudder. But at least his people must be trying their best.

At the end of the hallway, he entered the hydro-therapy room. The ten bathtubs along each wall stood empty. A glance inside one suggested they had not used it for a considerable time. One had at least an inch of dust in its bottom. What had Sanda said? She had no idea what hydro-therapy might be? Yet she had been here during his entire five-year tenure.

He retraced his steps to another room along the hall. They had recently delivered exercise equipment. He'd read in a journal about the effects of regular workouts on blood chemistry. With all the recent turmoil, he had not taken the time to follow-up on the effectiveness until now. Perhaps they might be here in the gym.

Instead, the room sat empty, except for one bed with stains that looked suspiciously like blood. Not a trace of the equipment Ralston signed for only three months ago. His heart raced as he scanned the empty room. Had they delivered it?

Back at the foyer, he moved to the desk and flipped open the logbook. No signatures in the last two days.

At a half trot, he moved to the next building. In the foyer, a Burmese man sat at the desk reading a book. At Ralston's entrance, he put the book aside. "Excuse me, this building is off-limits to everyone but staff."

Ralston stepped back, scowled. "I'm the director. And you?"

The man's eyes opened wide. His jaw dropped. "Van Twong."

"I don't recall you from training or your name from any staff rosters."

"Training?"

"Yes, the classes everyone takes when hired here."

"I know nothing about that."

"Who hired you?"

"A Scotsman named Ben."

Ralston scowled. "He hired you?"

Twong nodded. "He is married to my cousin. He also hired my brother for the night shift."

"How long have you worked here?"

"A year, next month."

Ralston massaged his forehead. "Who pays you?"

"Ben. Two rupees a week. Cash."

Ralston's mental calculations revealed this to be one-tenth of Ben's salary. "Does he pay your brother as well?"

"Yes, he is most generous. I have one other brother working here and several friends. The pay is much better than we get working for the Indians."

Ralston pulled out a book from a drawer in the desk. After opening it, he set it before Twong. "And this? The therapy directives?"

Twong peered down at the page and shrugged. "I'm sorry. I can't read."

"Do your shift mates do the therapy then?"

"I always work alone."

****

Later in his office, Ralston stared out at the grounds. He released the curtain. As it settled back in place, he turned. "I am afraid the care in the women's ward may have been the best we provided."

Sylvia gasped her eyes trailed Ralston as he paced. "What? You don't mean."

Paused at the sideboard, he filled a tall glass from a crystal decanter. He took a long drink, nodded. "Along with abuse and neglect, I uncovered fraud and embezzlement on a massive scale."

"Surely, it can't be that horrible."

"The most violent men's ward has not been staffed for two days."

"Since the attacks and the unrest, the staffing has been unreliable. I know the office staff has not been here for several days. That's not your fault."

"Equipment I ordered and paid for with hospital funds are gone. I'm not even certain it arrived."

He tossed back the rest of his drink, poured another.

"Oh, dear."

"I can't see that they implemented any of my treatment directives for months anywhere. And the staff working has been somehow subcontracted in by the ones on the payroll. In fact, all I am certain of is that Johan, the women murdered, and his friend Ben collected the rest of the staff's wages. They then hired these untrained, uneducated people off the streets."

"All of them?"

"Except for Eka on the women's ward, yes."

"How could that happen?"

"I trusted the people I hired. Thought they were people of good character. Instead, I harbored crooks, psychopaths, and rapists."

Sylvia rose, went to the sideboard herself, and poured a drink. "What shall we do?"

"I'm not sure. I suppose I should go to government house in the morning. Apprise them of the situation."

She set down her drink, took his, and drew him close. "Darling, don't worry, things will work out. You'll find the right thing to do."

Julie rushed in, leading her sister. Both children grinned. "The lady with the broken leg is funny."

Ralston frowned. "What do you mean, dear?"

"She's arguing with someone we can't see."
"Dear, that's part of her illness. Don't worry."
"Well, I worried. She seems nice."

CHAPTER FIFTEEN

Bone tired from the mission, Ed joined the crowd at the bar.

"I never aimed, just steered to follow the tracers like you do with a firehose. Flamed him, and he spun in." Tex shot a glance at Ed. He nodded, confirming to the others gathered at the bar Tex's victory claim.

Jim Howard clapped Ed on the shoulder. "Thanks for scarin' off those Japs."

Tex frowned. "Scared off Japs?"

"Yeah, I was on my second strafin' run. Musta caught some ground fire, and the engine quit. I pull up, dead stick, and I'm glidin' along between two Japs."

Tex tipped his cap back on his head. "This gonna be one a them stories that ends up with you bein' killed?"

Howard gave Ed a gentle backhand to his chest. "He's sore about a joke I told him the other day."

"He stole it from the Jack Benny show. Ya oughta have him do a Rochester imitation some time. You'll split a gut." Tex nudged Howard. "Go on, tell us about the Japs you was flyin' with. I can see they didn't kill ya."

"They was so busy checkin' out all the damage we did. They didn't notice me at first. One finally turns in my direction. Fucker goes round-eye on me, and his jaw dropped. Thought, oh shit, my number's up. But then he spots Burton here, and they hightailed it outta there."

Tex frowned. "But you said your engine died."

Howard nodded. "It did. Too low to bail out, so I figured I'd put down at the Jap airfield. Throw myself on their tender mercies."

One pilot grinned. "Yeah, just like in a movie I saw once, about the big one. This German's forced down on a British airfield. While they wait for the cops or whoever, to take the guy prisoner, they all sat and got drunk together."

Another shook his head. "You'd a had a better chance jumpin' out."

Tex shook his head. "Is this where you die?"

"Nah, for some reason, the engine kicked back in. Best sound I ever heard."

Ed frowned. "You tell the crew chief about it?"

Howard nodded. "They'll take a look at it, but..." He shrugged.

Ed cocked his head. "If you want, I'll talk to Lamison about it."

Howard's eyebrows rose. "He here?"

"Yep, him and his whole crew."

"Havin' him and his bunch check it out, would go a long way to settlin' my mind."

Outside the bar, Ed marched to the tents where Ed and his Chinese crew billeted. He'd not talked to Russ since the man arrived. Since he put his foot in his mouth that first day, he had avoided Russ. Unsure how to approach him. Talking about the plane's needed inspection would give him the excuse. Make amends, might even find words to comfort his old buddy.

But he had a selfish reason for talking to Russ. Chennault had sent Russ to retrieve Ed and his plane after his forced landing near Thiri's village. That meant Russ knew the location. If he could put it on the map, he made on the way back from the mission today, he could find it again from the air. He landed there once before. Why not again?

****

As the sun set, Zeya scanned the street behind him for watchers before slipping inside the tea shop.

Despite his cautious door opening, the bell tinkled, prompting the owner to turn from his station behind the counter. "Did you finish your errands?"

Zeya shook his head. What could he say? The American had not left the airbase in the last two days, and his search for Thiri fruitless in the chaotic city. "I am afraid I will have to leave some things undone and hope they settle themselves with the invasion."

"You will not need the gun. If the police stop us, it will arouse suspicion. Once we reach Bangkok, they will supply all the weapons we need."

Zeya set the pistol on the counter. "Where are the others?"

"They started out for the rendezvous already. We decided moving singly or in pairs would draw less attention than a dozen men marching together."

Zeya glanced around the shop. "You have someone looking after the shop?"

He nodded. "My wife and daughter." After picking up the pistol, the shopkeeper retrieved its bag from beneath the counter. Once he placed the weapon inside the bag, he locked it in an overhead cabinet near the back.

As if saying goodbye to the store, the man scanned the room before turning out the lights. Outside, while his companion locked the door behind him, Zeya scanned the street. "With the curfew, we will be obvious."

"Since many left there is little looting. The police seldom patrol here now." The shopkeeper placed the key on the sill above the door. "Shan't need this where we're going, eh comrade?"

Together they strode through the deserted street, careful to stay in the shadows. The smell of rotting garbage piled in alleyways and along the curbs filled the air. The only signs of life, rats squealing and dogs growled as they scrounged either for the rotting food or the rodents.

In an alcove they passed, a cat arched its back and hissed. A truck roared past without lights, forcing both men to duck into a shadow until it disappeared. Once it passed, Zeya glanced around, checking for a pursuer, finding none he once again strode with his companion.

Across the lane, a curtain moved, sending a flash of light into the street, lighting their faces for an instant. His companion gasped, quickened his pace.

Zeya caught the man's sleeve. "It might have only been a cat or a child brushing the curtain. Walk normally, rushing will draw attention."

"Sorry. I am but a shopkeeper. I'm certain a man with your experience as a policeman might think me foolishly timid."

Slow and deliberate, they moved through the night until they neared the city's edge. At an intersection, the shopkeeper extended his arm, blocking Zeya's advance. "The patrols are heavier here near the city limits."

Zeya nodded. "They are more interested in stopping infiltrators than people leaving. But those who flee are leaving from the other side of town."

The shopkeeper peered around the corner. "I see no one. Perhaps we can cross."

As they stepped into the street, a light pierced the darkness, illuminating them while casting their giant shadows down the pavement behind.

"Halt!" a voice boomed from behind the glaring light.

Both froze, holding up his hand to shield his eyes, Zeya turned toward the light. A Gurkha stepped from the shadows. His eyes narrowed while studying the shop keeper.

"It is that Constable, Zeya." A voice said from out of the shadows.

As the light extinguished, footsteps approached in the darkness. The Gurkha Sergeant from his station emerged from the shadows. A puzzled look on the man's face. "Inspecting the posts?"

Zeya shook his head. Gestured to his companion. "This merchant closed late. Asked me to escort him home."

After giving the shopkeeper an appraising glance, the Sergeant turned to Zeya. "Good idea. We nabbed several men a few minutes ago, sneaking through here. Don't know what they might have been about, but we are taking them to the station. Let the officer sort it out." He turned back to the shopkeeper, who stared back wide-eyed through his wire-rimmed spectacles. "You are fortunate to have him with you. Even with honest intentions, we keep curfew violators overnight."

The Sergeant nodded to Zeya. "Good evening to you, sah."

****

After lighting the pipe and passing it to Ed, Ang Su seated himself next to Russ. "Your Lǎobǎn will be pleased. We filled two trucks with spare parts from the dock."

Russ nodded as he inhaled the opium and passed the pipe to Ang Su.

"We should talk to your friend, Ed Burton. He might know where we might get more trucks."

Russ exhaled; a vague smile spread on his face. "True. He was on a mission today, probably at the officer's club getting drunk with the rest. I'll ask in the morning."

After toking from the pipe, Ang Su set it aside. "I wondered about you."

"Me?"

"Yes. Since you started going out to that Mission hospital, you stopped using the pipe."

Russ hung his head. "Had things to do."

"Got things to do now. Plenty, and here we are back using the pipe."

Russ removed his cap, brushed his hair back before replacing it. "It brings me peace."

"I thought perhaps that lady there might draw you back to the living."

"She is a wonderful woman."

"I see how you look at her. She like you too."

Russ leaned back against the hangar they sat beside. Stared off. "She's in love with a pilot."

Ang Su shrugged. "That can change."

"As well as a pilot he's handsome. Had some college."

"He is a warrior. Useful now, but maybe not forever. You are a man who fixes things. That is always needed."

An image of his dead wife floated up into his mind. He wondered what the baby, had it lived, would have been like. A girl like Marie? Blond hair, blue eyes, smart as a whip. Or a boy who loved tinkering with things. Have to lock up his tools to make sure the kid didn't take everything apart.

But that didn't happen. He wiped a tear from his eye with his sleeve. As Ang Su said, around Ann, he felt alive again. She liked him, he knew, but not in the way she cared for Joe. But since he spent time with her, he had not needed the pipe for a while. But here it seemed, the only way he could keep himself from drifting back into dark hole in his heart left by his wife's death.

Ang Su rose to his feet. He held out his hand to Russ. "Come. Time to head back to the tent."

After pulling Russ to his feet, he clapped him on the back. "Tomorrow, we get more trucks. When we got one for each man in the crew, we can head up the road to Kunming. Get you back to your angel at the mission."

****

With his hands on his hips, exasperated, Ed shoved his cap back on his head.

Without taking his eyes off the game arrayed on the crate before him, the Chinese man repeated his statement. "Lǎobǎn and Ang Su at hangar."

Inside the Chinese's tent, Ed loomed over two Chinese seated at a Mahjong board. He frowned and shook his head. "You don't understand. I'm lookin' for Russ."

The two Chinese seated on their cots in the tent exchanged grins. The one who had spoken turned back to Ed. "Russ is Lăobăn."

"Lăobăn?"

The man nodded, pointed to a building across the field. "Chief. Russ is Lăobăn."

"Where did you say he was?"

The men again exchanged glances. The one who had yet to speak shrugged, rolled his eyes. The first turned back to Ed. "He at hangar. You find him there."

After giving them a half bow, Ed exited the tent while the men returned to their game chattering and laughing. As he strode to the hangar, Russ, along with the tall Chinese man he often saw hanging around Russ, rounded the building he headed towards.

Russ appeared unsteady on his feet, while the Chinaman at his side steadied him. A grin spread on Russ's face as Ed neared. "Hey Burton, glad you made it back today." He clapped the Chinese man on the back. "This is my number one, best man, Ang Su." Russ turned to Ang Su and spoke to him in Chinese. Ang Su nodded. "Lăobăn says you might find us some trucks."

Ed's brow furrowed, puzzled not only by the two's slightly intoxicated appearance but also by the statement. "What?"

Russ nodded. "Yeah, folks said you had yourself a shipping' company."

"Brits confiscated 'em."

Russ frowned. "Can't ya get 'em back?"

Ed shook his head. "I don't have much pull with 'em. I think they'd lock me up if I went back to talk about 'em."

Russ made a wry face. "Where'd they stash 'em?"

"Not sure, but there's a bunch parked near the docks. Got all kinds of vehicles there. Must have unloaded 'em before all the crap started."

Russ grinned. "How 'bout you show us around tomorrow. We could use the orientation."

Ed nodded. "Long as I don't have flight duty. Listen, Howard's engine quit on him over the Jap airfield. Started back up, and he flew it home. Could you check it?"

"Sure. In the meantime, have 'em ground it. Listen, come around about sunrise tomorrow. We can head into town then."

As the sun rose next morning, Ed strode to the tent, billeting the Chinese. Finding the shelter empty, he moved on to the flight line. Here Russ and Ang Su stood on ladders beside Howard's plane. With the cowling removed, Russ turned a wrench, while Ang Su illuminated the work with a flashlight.

As he arrived, Russ glanced up. "Be done here in a second."

"Find somethin'?"

"Best guess is the engine overheated and seized. After it cooled down a bit, the wind spun the prop and started it again. Gonna have to tear it down. He's damn lucky. But they shouldn't fly it again till the overhaul's done." Russ spoke to Ang Su in Chinese. The Chinese man nodded, climbed down the ladder, and marched off.

"He'll get the crew started on the rebuild while we head into town."

"You got wheels?"

"Found one those snazzy little Jeeps down on the docks day before yesterday. One a the Brits showed us."

Ed nodded. "Trucks aren't too far away from there."

After climbing into the Jeep, Russ retrieved a Tommy gun from beneath the seat and passed it to Ed. "Ever use one a these before?"

Ed shook his head as he studied the gun.

"Somebody said you'd filled your time here as a gangster."

"Shady businessman is more like it. Just a minor thief."

As they drove to the dock, Ed described his adventures with Thiha and the black market, including his involvement with Thiri.

At the docks, Russ turned to Ed. "Sounds like somethin' right outta *Terry and the Pirates*. You oughta write a book. So, what about the girl?"

Ed shrugged. "I wanna find her."

"In the middle of all this? Got any idea where she might be?"

"A Gurkha at the police station claimed her brother sent her back to their village."

"Where you got forced down?"

Ed nodded. "Do you remember where it was?"

"I could find it on a map. Why?"

"I want to check on her."

Russ's brow furrowed. "How?"

"Fly in. Like I did before."

Russ shook his head. "Olson said you were damn lucky to set down on that road. Trees on both sides didn't leave much clearance."

"But I did it. And Olson flew it out, right?"

"Yeah. So how you gonna accomplish this? Go to Newkirk, say hey pop since it's Saturday night can I borrow a plane to go look up my girl?"

"I dunno. I'll think a somethin'."

Russ stared out over the wharf. Sighed. "I'll draw ya a map when we get back. But you gotta promise me if this goes all to hell you eat it, burn it, whatever it takes to keep me outta it. She must be one helluva girl. Now let's go find those trucks."

CHAPTER SIXTEEN

KUNMING, CHINA

Waiters rushed by carrying trays loaded with food or beverages, as Mrs. Morgan studied a menu and Johnathan sipped a cocktail. "But mother, remain here in Kunming?" Johnathan slumped forward in his chair. With his elbow resting on the table, he massaged his forehead.

Not wishing to cause a scene here in the hotel dining room, she moved close to her son. "How would it appear? Abandoning a new wife in this place. It's not done."

"Look around you. Everywhere you go. Stink, filth, beggars constantly. It's not Boston. God, It's not even New Jersey."

She placed her hand on his shoulder. "I could appoint you as an on-site director. A married man needs a career."

He pulled away. "A career? Here? You want me living in this squalid backwater."

"Well, at least until you and she have a child on the way. Couldn't have grandchildren growing up here amongst these... these..."

He leaned forward. "Heathens, mother? Is that the word you were searching for?"

"Well, the children would need to be back with their own kind. Civilized. Besides, as a newlywed, you probably won't even notice the surroundings. And there are other missions close by for social events and such.

He leaned back and sighed. "Actually, I don't believe Ann and her father are too keen on our marriage."

Mrs. Morgan gasped. A couple at a nearby table turned at his outburst. She gave them a scowl and turned back to her son. "Nonsense. Dr. Ross is merely concerned with his daughter's welfare and his patient's care."

Johnathan picked up his cocktail glass, drained it in one, held it up for a refill. "Oh yeah? You weren't there when I spoke to him. Refused to bless our engagement. Said he and Ann had not discussed it. Knew little about me. One excuse after another to put the whole thing off."

Mrs. Morgan fanned herself with her menu. Scanned the room, searching for eavesdroppers. "I really think you've had enough. We've not eaten yet. This much on an empty stomach..."

"Mother, I'm a grown man, well aware of his limits. Now, where is that waiter?" He scanned the room, still holding his glass high. A waiter scurried over, gave a half bow. "You want fresh one?"

"Yes. And tell the bartender to hold the water. I want a double straight up. Chop-chop."

****

Chennault's fingers drummed on his desk as he studied the radiogram from the Whitehouse. Across from him, Olga's fingers toyed with her blouse's top button. "So, your message to Roosevelt worked."

He tossed the sheet on the desk. "I guess. But it comes with a price. Not sure it'll sit well with the guys."

After picking up the sheet herself, she glanced at it, then frowned. "Six thousand pounds of supplies in Calcutta, five hundred pounds in Karachi. Plus, fifty new P-40s. Not the obsolete Tomahawks like we got, but the new Kittyhawks?"

Chennault nodded. "Faster, more maneuverable and armed with six fifty calibers in the wings. After the Army puts `em together in Africa, they'll deliver `em."

"It also says that fifteen of the ferry pilots will stay and join us here. What's the problem?"

"It means they'll induct us into the Army."

Olga's brow furrowed. "What's the problem with that?"

"The guys' contracts were for one year. That's it. They have no obligation to stay after that. Most signed on here to get out of the military. Others want to return to their old services. But the bottom line is when their contract expires, they're done."

"I still don't understand."

Chennault picked up the radiogram. Waved it like a baton to emphasize his points. "This would draft them into the Army. All of them."

"And that's a problem?"

"It won't thrill the Navy and Marine guys one bit. They might all quit. And the rest?" He shrugged.

She leaned back, chewed her lip. "They might surprise you. The guys all respect you."

"Just the same, keep this to yourself. Not a word to anyone, including your husband."

After she left, Chennault leaned back in his chair. He also hadn't mentioned the radiogram forwarded to him earlier by Madame Chiang, written by the general Washington assigned to study the situation in China. The man agreed that they should incorporate the AVG into the Army with Chennault as the commander. But he demanded a total overhaul of the command structure. The man wanted Greenlaw and the rest of the command staff replaced with regular staff officers. Plus, they would remove all the current squadron commanders. The officer stated that this would be the only way to move this rag-tag bunch seamlessly into a regular unit and shed its maverick atmosphere. Yes, if this leaked out, Chennault feared the men might not only quit but mutiny.

****

Dr. Ross set aside his journal to watch Ann change a child's bandage. As she worked, Ann talked to the child in Chinese. The little girl's eyes twinkled, and she grinned as the child listened to his daughter. He wondered what Ann might be telling the child.

He marveled at how much Ann resembled her mother. His late wife also had the looks that turned men's heads. He often wondered what about him attracted her? Certainly, not his looks. Tall and gangly, he began losing his hair in his early twenty's when they met.

The adage that opposites attract must have been right in their case. His wife, outgoing and charming. He, shy and socially awkward. His wife adored being around people while he preferred the company of his books. Then came religion. The big divide. While not an atheist, he rejected the formal beliefs. Found their doctrines of superiority repugnant.

Ann's mother, on the other hand, a staunch Catholic. While she maintained her religious practices, her family ostracized her for marrying outside the faith.

While he and his wife seemed comfortable together despite the contrasts, the scandal at his free clinic tore their marriage apart. The abortions cost him his medical license. Had she been a Protestant, she might have divorced him. Instead, their marriage became a hollow shell, with Ann at its center. To avoid criminal charges, he fled to the missionary service, where his lack of credentials mattered little.

Finished with her patient, Ann set the child back in her bed. She turned to him and gave him that look she often gave to trauma patients when they first arrived. She moved to his side. "What's wrong?"

"Wrong?"

She frowned. That same look, Ann's mother gave him when he avoided her questions about the clinic. "You looked troubled."

"I was remembering your mother."

She placed her hand on his. "Despite what happened, she never stopped loving you."

"But nothing stayed the same. You realize I had no choice but to come here."

She squeezed his hand. "It hurt. I missed you so much. At first, I thought I would die."

He hung his head. "You were always like my shadow. Even towards the end, watching the women's children at the clinic, while I saw them."

"I loved Mom dearly, but..."

He gave her a weak smile. "I always considered you Daddy's girl."

"After Mom died, and I went to stay with Aunt Jane, she had all these family albums. I would sit for hours going through them. She would tell me stories about you making me feel like you were always there."

"And that didn't set you against me?"

"When I was younger, I never understood what happened with the clinic and all. But now, I see you were only trying to help those women. And here you do wonders. On top of loving you with all my heart, I am proud to be your daughter."

He squeezed her hand. "Well, you're here now. I'm so pleased with the woman you've become."

She gave him a peck on the cheek. "Even though I might be a little wild and worldly?"

"You're different, but then again, your generation is so much different from mine. But so much is changing in this world, who am I to judge right or wrong. But I worry."

"Worry?"

He nodded. "You obviously care a great deal for this young flier. He cares deeply about you. In fact, Rose told me he asked you to marry him."

Ann sat up straight, frowned. "She said that?"

"Since she runs that hotel, there's little that goes on in this town that she doesn't find out."

"He's asked. I didn't say no. But..."

"But then there is Johnathan. His mother expects you and him to marry."

"Yes, and if I disappoint her, she may retaliate." Images of her marooning in Java flashed through her mind, but she didn't share that with her father.

"You're walking a tightrope."

"And now that I'm here, she might not only take out her wrath on me but also on you."

Dr. Ross massaged his forehead. He leaned back. "I'm an old man. Have made many choices in my life. Good or bad as others might claim, I have taken the consequences and survived."

"I only wanted to be here with you. The thing with Joe happened. Neither of us planned it."

"That's how life is. While we are busy making plans and dreams, life happens."

She hung her head. "Have I really made a mess of things?"

"You've done your best no matter how it turns out. If you continue doing the best you can, no matter how things turn out, you can take pride in that. Just remember, no matter what, I love you and would do whatever it takes to help you succeed."

"Again, I'm sorry for the mess I've caused."

Dr. Ross shrugged. "Nothing bad has happened yet. Thanks to Rose's quick thinking, you avoided a scandal. Plus, for now, Mrs. Morgan seems satisfied with us and the current situation. But a day of reckoning might come, and for that, we must prepare."

****

After shoving the sheet aside, Chen bolted upright on the bed. "You would really leave and return to Boston?"

Johnathan smoothed his hair back over his head, lit a cigarette, and nodded. "Come on back to bed. Let's not quarrel."

Seated with his back to Johnathan at the edge of the bed, Chen shook his head. "But I thought..."

"I would settle down here in China? Thought I would abandon my life in the States? Settle for this?"

"This means nothing to you? I give myself to you, and now I feel I am just some whore."

Johnathan reached out, ran his hands over Chen's skin. So exotic. He had experienced nothing like it. "Come back with me."

Chen turned frowned. "Leave my home? My family?"

"But we could still be together."

"Ha, your mother wants you married. If not to that... that... woman at the hospital, some other woman."

Johnathan smirked. "That's how it's done. You must know that by now."

"So, what would I be? Your driver? Maybe a butler? Or how about a gardener? I have an uncle who does that for rich people in Los Angeles."

"It beats the shit outta what's around here. God, Chen. The entire country is one gigantic shit hole."

"And then what? You sneak around on your wife. Come and see me for pleasure? All so I could live in America?"

"It's a marvelous place. There, a man can be whatever he wants to be?"

"In this marvelous place, can one be a homosexual openly?"

Johnathan scoffed. "Of course not. That's true anywhere. But at least there's stability, safety. There's no government here except for whatever warlord lives nearby. Why the Japanese want it is beyond me."

Chen thrust his shoulders back, sat up straight. "Here I am going to University. When I finish, an engineer. Then I can build things. Improve my country, make life easier for my people."

"And that's all funded by the mission, right?"

Chen nodded.

"You want to continue?"

"Of course."

"My mother runs the mission. What she says goes. Thanks to her good graces, you might continue your studies. Achieve those things you mentioned."

"What are you saying?"

"Nothing pleases her more than to see her boy happy. So, let's forget about this little argument for now." He patted the bed next to him. "Now, come on back to bed and make Mama's boy happy."

CHAPTER SEVENTEEN

RANGOON, BURMA

"I don't have an answer for you. I'm sorry." The governor shook his head. His wavy black hair, not a strand out of place. He removed his wire-rimmed glasses as if that might make Ralston disappear along with his demands. Surrounded by shelves lined with leather-bound books except in bare areas filled with photos of the governor with dignitaries, even Churchill himself, like a potentate ensconced in his throne room, the man folded his arms across his chest

Ralston, seated across the desk from the man, hung his head. "These people are in our care."

The red-haired officer with the Colonel's insignia on his epaulets standing at the governor's side pointed out the window overlooking the harbor. "All of Burma is our responsibility. People all over this city are going without food, medicine. And you want us also to care for your colony of lunatics?"

The governor nodded. "Certainly, you can see our point. Have you gone to the aid agencies?"

"Not yet. I hoped things would stabilize, and our own government could step up."

"If not for the current chaos from the attacks, it might have been possible. But now?" The governor sighed. "Now, have you considered yourself and your family?"

Ralston glanced up. "I'm sorry. What?"

"No matter what, the bloody Japs will start up their bombing again. They've already landed troops almost on our doorstep. They're moving against Singapore, we'll be next. Can't have your family in the middle of that, right?"

Ralston ran his hands over his head. "I really hadn't considered that."

"It's time. The government is ordering all civilians out. I'm expecting passenger liners soon. They are tasked with evacuating dependents. I suggest you go home and prepare to depart."

"But... But what about my patients?"

The man at the governor's side thrust his shoulders back, drew himself up to his full height. "If you leave them penned up, they'll die from thirst or starvation. Plus, everywhere they've been, the Japs have not been the kindest folks in dealing with people they feel are inferior."

Ralston frowned. "You mean?"

The Colonel continued. "Open the doors. Let 'em out. Put it in God's hands, as if he weren't busy enough."

The governor nodded. "No matter what, come to the house this evening. Along with planning the evacuation, you might plead your case with the aid people there."

As Ralston made his way down the stairs at government house, airplane engines droned overhead. The planes he saw the day before with the ferocious shark's teeth on the front, and the cute Panda bear on the side swooped up. Above them came a swarm of specks coming from the direction of Thailand. The bombing lull must be over, he told himself as he started his car and headed back to the asylum.

As the attack centered on the harbor area, the path back seemed clear. The problem of his patients nagged at him as he drove. He smiled as he considered Thiri and Sanda. Both a pleasant spark to their home. His children adored them both. Thiri, with her stories and Sanda like a big sister with a few strange habits. Her settlement in with the family also seemed to reduce her conversations with that Carl. Perhaps that might be the key to treating others. Get them in a safe place around ordinary people, instead of herding them all together, to infect each other with bizarre delusions. He might explore that later. That is if anyone left him in a position of authority after this debacle.

Once home, he found Sanda and his two daughters sitting at Thiri's feet as she read them a story.

He paused at the doorway to listen.

"And the giant roared, 'Fee, fi, fo, fum, I smell the blood of an Englishman,'" Thiri growled, using her best deep voice.

The three girls howled with laughter as she continued.

"And Jack hid behind the door and quaked with fear."

The little girls' eyes grew wide, and they held hands.

"Be he live or be he dead. I'll grind his bones to make my bread."

Sanda chuckled, and her eyes rolled up. "It's just a story, Carl." Then she patted Julie's hand. "Don't worry."

Thiri glanced up from the book. Aware of Ralston's presence, her eyebrows rose. She held the book up. "Is this all right?"

Ralston nodded. "You are a talented storyteller. If I had the time, I'd stay and listen." He nodded to the listeners. "Splendid story. You need to pay attention. Can never tell when you might need to deal with a giant."

As he left the room, Thiri continued the story. Now what to do about the rest of those in his care?

****

As the formation soared over the Burmese countryside, Ed eased his throttle.

"Close it up, Burton." Ed's flight leader barked over his headset.

"Engines runnin' rough. Like it won't hold power." Ed reached down and enriched the mixture. Flame and smoke poured from the exhaust.

"He's smokin'," Tex's drawl came over the air.

Ed leaned the mixture, and the flame and smoke subsided. "I may have to head back."

"Roger. Hill, form up on me." The flight leader replied.

Ed descended from the formation. Once clear of the rest, he banked towards Toungoo.

With his heading set, he unfolded the map Russ helped draw. His plane running well and nearly a full tank of gas, he should have no problem finding Thiri's village.

A thousand questions and doubts swirled through his mind. What would he do when he got there? Would Wunna, her father, approve of their relationship?"

Obsessed with George Washington and the American Revolution, Wunna had talked with Ed for hours. The old man shared with him the problems with British Colonial rule after Ed's forced landing. Seemed eager to discover ways to drive the British out as Ed's forefathers had. Ed felt the man considered him a friend. Would he also accept Ed as a son-in-law?"

And if he found her? Would she still feel the same? In her teasing, she always informed him he had been her choice. Would she even choose him after being back with her own people? Again, with her father?

Emotions he had not experienced since he met his first girlfriend's family in high school. That had been a disaster. He'd been a kid then. Now older, he might not appear as foolish. Foolish? Pfft. But what about this? Stealing a plane. Is that what this was?

Beyond that, what about the unit? Would they consider this desertion?

Foolish did not begin to describe his actions right now. But he must go through with this or regret it for the rest of his life.

He glanced over the side. Did anything below look familiar? Another look at the map. Yes, he seemed on course. He couldn't get lost now. Not with all the chances he had taken.

The engine stuttered. Oh, shit. Could he really have engine trouble? If he did, no one would find him. Then he remembered the blood chit sewn on his jacket. The Chinese writing offering a reward for his return.

But Burma lay below. Thanks to Thiri, he now had some proficiency in Burmese. Enough, possibly to find help on his own. But then what about the bandits that roamed the countryside? Especially in the areas close to the Thai border. After all, he'd been through with Zeya's band and Thiha, would this toss him into the same mess as before? Plus, they claimed the insurgents here sympathized with the Japanese, now thoroughly entrenched in neighboring Thailand.

His eyes scanned the gauges. All appeared normal. The engine smooth. The stutter might have merely been bad gas.

Toungoo's appearance, off to his left, energized him. Drove the thoughts and doubts from his head. Navigation from here to Thiri's village now a piece of cake, he told himself.

After checking his map, he adjusted his course, eagerly scanning the terrain below for landmarks. An ocean of green filled with trees below. No sign of the road. He lost altitude, removed the oxygen mask, no longer needed at this level. Leaned to the side, where it should appear. Frustrated, his breath fogged the canopy. He swore as he swiped away the frost with his gloves, smearing the Plexiglas without clearing his vision.

Desperate, he pulled down his goggles, pushed back the canopy. After dipping the left wing, he leaned out to glance ahead. A break in the forest appeared. With the wind whipping into the cockpit, he pinned the fluttering map on his leg, chancing a quick glance.

That had to be it. He nudged the stick to line up with the road, while he scanned ahead for the village.

Ahead, one appeared. He squinted. Could that be it, or might it be the one he and Wunna walked to? The one with the phone.

He dropped lower. Studied the structures below while he circled. Telephone lines ran from the village, but the structures looked unfamiliar.

He banked to circle one more time and spotted the sharp bend in the road. Neither village had been near such a turn. Also, the phone lines continued out the village's other side. He soared away, still following the road. The phone lines edging the road gave him hope. He had the right lane. He merely needed to press on.

Over a rise, a second village appeared. As he neared it, a grin spread on his face. The telephone lines ended here. This must be the village he phoned from. Thiri's must only be a short distance away.

The journey to this village took nearly six hours on foot. How fast did he and the old man walk? One or two miles an hour? Calculated in his head, he figured that amounted to roughly ten miles. His airspeed now at two hundred, meant he would be less than five minutes away from his destination. He craned his neck, desperate to spot her village.

To aid his navigation, he checked his watch. As he glanced up again, a village appeared ahead. The absence of phone lines made him smile. This must be it.

He dropped low, almost at tree-top level, announcing his presence to the villagers. After passing over the collection of huts, he circled as people poured from the buildings below. Yes, this had to be it. The hut where he and Wunna had passed the evenings set near the center, but no one below looked familiar.

Confident he had the right village, he bore off down the road looking for his previous landing site. As before, the road remained straight, and the trees bordering the road, far enough back, his wings would clear. As long as he stayed in the road's center.

After gaining altitude, he turned back for his landing. As he dropped his wheels and cut the power, the plane settled into a smooth glide. With a slight correction to stay centered, he set the wheels on the road's surface. Before the tail wheel touched down, blocking his forward vision, a crowd marched down the road from the village's direction, but too far away for him to spot anyone familiar.

After cutting the engine, Ed stepped onto the wing. Closer now, he saw no familiar faces in the approaching crowd. Still, at least this time, they appeared more curious than unfriendly.

An older man, not Wunna, paused the crowd with a hand gesture, then approached Ed alone. Ed removed his helmet, and the man frowned, peered closely, and then inquired in Burmese. "You were here before?"

Ed nodded and replied. "Yes, I flew in and talked with Wunna. In case you do not remember, my name is Ed. I came back to visit again with him and his family."

As Ed spoke, several in the crowd smiled. Some muttered to their neighbors. Apparently, several recalled his previous visit.

The man gave a half bow. "I am Hue. Wunna is unwell. But if you like, I will take you to him."

As they marched back to the village, children joined the crowd. The throng chattered excitedly amongst themselves, and they took on a festive mood. Like last time, he once again imagined himself leading a parade.

"Wunna is ill?"

Grave, the man, called Hue, nodded. "Sick at heart."

When the crowd paused outside Wunna's hut, Hue turned. "He is inside. Perhaps your coming might bring him joy."

After removing his flying boots, Ed followed Hue inside. The hut's interior had changed little since his last visit. Near the wall, facing the door, stood an altar depicting the Buddha in meditation. On the right stood another statue featuring a rather fat and cheerful standing Buddha that made Ed smile. On his left, an enormous portrait of George Washington hung on the wall. It, too, looked like an altar. The print, the Athenaeum, always made Ed think of Washington in the clouds. Wunna reclined on a mat at the standing Buddha's base. As he sat up, his lusterless eyes lit up, and a weak smile spread on his face. "Ed. My friend, you have returned?"

Wunna tossed back his coverlet, motioned Hue to his side. As the other helped Wunna to his feet, Wunna brushed his shoulder-length gray hair over his shoulder. Once upright, he hobbled to Ed and embraced him. "You must forgive me I have not been in the best spirits lately."

"What's wrong?"

"I have lost much of life's spark."

Ed nodded to Hue. "He told me you were sick at heart."

Wunna ran his fingers down the wispy gray beard dangling from his chin. Cast a sideways glance at the other man.

Hue cocked his head. "Forgive me if I shared too much."

Wunna patted him on the shoulder. "You are an excellent friend. You and your family take good care of me. If you said anything here to my friend, I am certain it comes from your concern."

With a puzzled frown, Wunna turned to Ed. "You have learned Burmese?"

"Didn't Thiri tell you?"

Wunna's smile faded, the sparkle left his eyes. He shook his head. "I have not spoken to her in a long time. She disappeared not long after you. I thought you might bring me news of her."

"But the Gurkha said Zeya returned her with the others."

"Others?"

"Yes, the ones in Zeya's band of insurgents. After they arrested me, the Gurkha said Zeya sent them all back here. That's why I came. To make sure she was all right."

"The Gurkha misled you."

"She's not here?"

Wunna shook his head. "So much sorrow." He staggered to a bench set before Washington's portrait and slumped down. "I fear I ignited a destructive spark in my son. I merely wanted my children to respect our heritage. Instead, I unleashed a terrible force." He glanced at the Buddha. "Karma."

Ed moved to Wunna's side, placed his hand on his shoulder. "Then you know about Thiri and me?"

He nodded. "The others said, despite Zeya's treachery, you two fell in love. That you took a great risk to save her and them from that evil man."

"Did the others say where she might be?"

"They claimed my son locked her away in the lunatic asylum."

"Asylum?"

"Yes, in Rangoon."

"She's not here?"

Wunna shook his head. "Besides losing Zeya to this craziness, I fear I have lost her to that awful place." A tear formed in his eye. "Thiri." He turned to Ed. "You know that means Splendor." He shook his head. "What I would give to have her here again." Wunna nodded. "Just knowing she was alive and well would bring the joy back to my heart."

****

RANGOON, BURMA

With her hand to her chest, Sylvia dropped into the chair across from Ralston. "Are things in town really that bad?"

Grim, he nodded. "The governor suggested that we prepare ourselves for evacuation. A passenger liner will arrive within the week to take senior administration staff and dependents on to India."

"India?"

"I imagine that's the closest British safe-haven for now."

Sylvia gasped. "Safe? Darling, we've been there. Beggars in the streets. Those filthy cows everywhere, disease. Compared to that, Rangoon is paradise."

"Anyway, there is a meeting at the governor's mansion this evening. He suggested that we both attend. Get the information firsthand."

"What about the children?"

"Doreen can mind them. We won't be gone over two hours."

Sylvia's hand went to her mouth. "Doreen hasn't been here for two days. I believe she's left."

Ralston scowled, drummed his fingers on the desk. "What about Thiri?"

"Leave our children in the care of a patient?"

"Dear, she's as sane as you and I."

Sylvia arched her eyebrows. "I know. The children adore her and Sanda."

He placed her hand on hers. "They will be fine, I'm sure. Also, the people from the relief agencies might be there. Perhaps they might have answers for our patients."

CHAPTER EIGHTEEN

After Ed parked his plane at Mingaladon, Russ climbed up and leaned over the cockpit. "Did you find her?"

Ed leaned back in the pilot's seat. Shook his head in response to Russ's question. "Her Dad said she's here in Rangoon."

"Here?"

"The lunatic asylum."

"Jesus, Ed, Newkirk's shittin' bricks." Russ shook his head as he reached in to help Ed unstrap his parachute harness. "The rest of the flight got back three hours ago. They already put you down as missing."

"Probably shoulda ditched and called in, but I wanted back in a hurry."

"Not sure what you can tell 'em. If you'd been in the air, you woulda been outta gas by the time the others got back. So, they ain't gonna buy that you got lost."

Ed shrugged as he stood up in the cockpit, joined Russ on the wing. "Might as well tell the truth. What they gonna do?"

As they stepped off the plane's wing, a Jeep driven by Jenson pulled up next to the aircraft. After donning his Stetson, he joined them near the plane. "You been glidin'?"

Ed told him what he'd done.

Jenson gave Ed's shoulder a playful tap. "What's a few hours? I was gone for a week helping those Brits evacuate their wine cellar. At least you didn't lose the plane like I did."

"Yeah, but I ducked out on a mission. That's different."

"You're gonna get an ass chewin'. If Newkirk reports it to Kunming..."

Ed scoffed. "Greenlaw already told me to consider myself under arrest pending a full inquiry."

Jenson shrugged. "This ain't the military. Greenlaw's just full of himself."

Russ jumped down from the wing. "I'll go along with ya. I can tell the boss the plane's fine that might lighten the blow."

"We can stop off at the barracks, I still got a few bottles of that wine left. Help set the mood."

Ed smiled. "With all this support, they might even let me have a blindfold before they shoot me."

As they drove, Ed recalled his last talk with Wunna. How the man's eyes lit up and energized as Ed swore to find Thiri. Rescue her from whatever hell Zeya condemned her to. But first, he had to face the consequences here.

After retrieving the wine from Jenson's room, the three drove to the alert shed. Parked at the shed, the three piled out of the jeep and marched inside.

Newkirk, pacing inside, halted, spun around. His eyes narrowed, his pencil-thin mustache curled up as he bared his teeth. "Where the fuck you been?"

Jenson stepped between Ed and Newkirk. Held up a wine bottle. "Remember Burton, here's a special case."

Newkirk's eyes turned to Jenson, then the wine bottle. "Special case?"

Jenson held out the bottle. "Let's uncork this bottle. Discuss it like gentlemen. Give the man a fair hearin' and all. You're not an asshole like Greenlaw."

Russ stepped forward. "That's right, Burton's had a rough go of it since he arrived here. Bein' kidnapped and all. We gotta give him a little slack."

Newkirk scowled. "Slack? He turns back from a mission with engine trouble. Shows up here two hours after he shoulda been outta gas." Newkirk planted his hands on his hips. "I already turned him in as missing."

Jenson nodded. "And here he is. Safe and sound. We need to celebrate. Welcome our comrade home."

"And the planes here undamaged," Russ added. "Big plus in my book."

Newkirk ran his hand over his coal-black hair, shook his head. "Pop the cork on that thing." He turned to Ed. "This story better be good."

****

Instead of the usual dining arrangement, they had cleared the Governor's banquet hall of tables. Beneath the chandeliers, people gathered in groups around the floor, discussing the current events in Burma. Unlike the usual festive atmosphere these gatherings provided, no one laughed or chuckled. Instead, urgent and concerned tones filled the air.

To one side, near a table containing several liquor bottles and a crystal punchbowl, Ralston cornered one of the aid directors. After Ralston described the situation at the asylum, he frowned. "We can assist with delivering food, but I'm afraid taking your people is out of the question."

Ralston hung his head. "We need at least three meals a day. Can you supply that?"

The gray-haired man stroked his mustache. "We can provide one. That should prevent total starvation for at least the next week. But once the evacuation commences..." The man shrugged.

Ralston placed his hand on the man's sleeve. "But who will take care of them if we leave?"

The man thrust back his shoulder. "The Burmese, of course. They wanted their country back. Soon they'll get their wish."

A uniformed Brigadier standing at their side nodded. "Naturally, the army will be here, but we shan't be responsible for the civilians. Unless they are in the army, it'll be their own lookout."

Ralston turned back to the gray-haired man. "Can they start food delivery in the morning?"

The officer caught Ralston's sleeve as he turned to go. "You might consider the solution we implemented with a situation like yours."

Ralston frowned. "I beg your pardon."

The officer nodded. "Similar situation to yours. Colonel Thackeray. Chap over there in the corner." The Brigadier pointed towards a group in the banquet hall's corner where a group, including his wife, gathered around an officer. "Ask him. He might have a suggestion."

As he approached, Thackeray's words drifted over the gasps from some women in the crowd. "The army will be here to the end, but the police have their hands full. They'll be little help, I'm afraid. Especially if the phones stop working."

"The phones?" A man wearing a black swallow-tail jacket at the group's edge inquired.

The officer shrugged. "Electricity as well. With the Indians leaving, soon, all utilities will shut down. What remains needs to be seconded to the military."

"This is outrageous." A red-faced, gray-haired man glared through his pince-nez, released his tweed jacket's lapels, thrust a finger in the air. "What's happened to the empire?"

Thackeray shrugged. "Like French Indochina, it may wind up under Japanese stewardship for the duration. Once we lick the Hun, it will be a different story."

A woman placed her hand to her chest. "So, what should we do?"

Thackeray sipped his drink, appeared to ponder the question. "I suggest you move your dependents out as soon as you're able."

As Ralston joined the group, Sylvia leaned close to him. "Everyone's leaving. What shall we do?"

He took her hand, nodded to the man. "He may be right, but there are still the patients to consider. I was told this man might have a solution." Ralston waved his hand in the air. "Colonel Thackeray?"

Thackeray arched his eyebrows as several others turned in Ralston's direction.

"Herbert Ralston, sir, Director of the Lunatic Asylum."

Thackeray nodded. "You have a question, sir?"

"I'm in a bind with the patients in my care." Ralston gestured back to the uniformed officer in the opposite corner. "The Brigadier claims that you recently solved a similar situation."

Thackeray rolled his eyes, moved to Ralston, and leaned close. "He must mean the zoo. Damnedest thing I've been a part of. All the zookeepers had skedaddled, leaving the animals untended."

"What did you do?"

"What could we do? We slaughtered all the dangerous beasts. Lions, tigers, and such. Even the poisonous snakes. Then let the rest of 'em loose. Quite a sight, it was."

****

Inside the Ralston's home on the asylum campus, Thant and Thiri sat side by side on a couch.

"But what about her?" Thiri nodded to Sanda perched in an easy chair, her cast propped on a footstool drawing with a pencil. The Ralston's two girls lay on the floor beside Sanda, similarly occupied with crayons. "I promised to take care of her. Would Professor Cho have room for her too?"

Thant chewed his lip. "I will ask. If not, I will find you both something nearby. With so many fleeing, there are many vacant dwellings. There may even be empty apartments in Cho's building."

"Have you seen Ed recently?"

Thant shook his head. "He may be one they moved to an airfield outside town. The Japanese bomb the Rangoon field almost every evening."

"I still can't believe you are doing this."

Thant shrugged. "The boss always treated me with respect."

Thiri hung her head. "I fear I have not always been a good friend to you. And here you are taking such a risk.

Thant chuckled. "That's not true. You played with me when we were little. Nobody else did. Not even the other girls. And the boys..."

He said no more, merely shook his head.

She took his hand. "I'm sorry for all that now. We just didn't know how to treat someone different."

Thant smiled. "Remember that doll you gave me?"

"The ugly one? The one with blond hair and blue eyes?"

"I still have it."

She gave him a weak smile and shook her head.

Ralston and Sylvia's entrance interrupted their conversation. With giggles, the girls put down their colors and rushed to their parents. Victoria hugged Ralston's leg, while Julie held up her sheet. "See?"

Ralston placed his pince-nez on his nose and studied the drawing. "Beautiful."

"It's supposed to be a scary python."

Ralston's brow furrowed. "They are quite beautiful, but you're right, they are deadly. What made you think about them?"

"Remember, I saw them at the zoo. Doreen took us last month. Can we go again soon?"

Victoria released Ralston's leg to clap her hands and dance beside her sister.

Ralston and Sylvia exchanged glances before he turned back to his daughters. "I'm afraid they took all the animals away."

"No-oo," both girls howled.

Ralston reached down, scooped them both up in an embrace. "They had to. To keep them safe from the bombs."

"Will they bring them back?"

"As soon as it's safe." He extended his hand to Thant. "Good to see you, young man. But, as I said before, I would appreciate it if you confine your visits here to times when we can provide appropriate supervision."

Thant shot Thiri a glance as he shook Ralston's hand. She bit her lip to suppress a chuckle. Thant shrugged. "I am sorry. But rest assured, I would never abuse your trust or dishonor my fiance'."

Ralston tapped Thant's chest. "I realize the heat of passion pre-nuptial is always the highest, but the opportunity to quench it will come often enough after the proper service."

Sylvia's face flushed. "Really, Herbert." She turned to Thiri. "How were the girls?

She grinned. "The girls were wonderful. Did you two have a pleasant evening?"

"The situation in town is disastrous." Sylvia turned to her husband. "We've much to discuss." She held out her hand to the girls. "Now come along you two. It's time for bed."

Julie grinned up at Thiri. "Can we hear a story?"

Thiri arched an eyebrow. "Perhaps your mother might want some time with you two tonight. But perhaps tomorrow?"

As the two girls skipped along with their mother out the door, Ralston turned to Thant. "It appears most of the government is leaving. What are your plans?"

"This is our country, Thiri, and mine."

"So, you'll remain?"

Thant shrugged. "Where would we go? If the British keep the Japanese out, then things will be as before. If the Japanese come? Well, they promise an Asia for Asians, so things might improve."

"Sylvia and I have grown quite fond of this country. Hate to leave, but there is the children's safety to consider."

Thiri placed her hand on Ralston's sleeve. "So, you may leave?"

He nodded. "A passenger liner will arrive in the next few days. I'm certain we should go. Would you and your young man consider coming along?"

"But what of her?" Thiri nodded to Sanda. "I promised to stay with her until she healed."

Ralston frowned. "You mean the leg?"

Thiri nodded, "You may not understand, but I am fond of her. She is like the sister I never had."

Ralston ran his hand over his bald spot. "Would you consider staying then until we get everything packed? It will require a good deal from Sylvia. I'm sure she would appreciate the assistance with the children."

Thiri's brow furrowed. "Of course. But what of the other inmates here? What will happen to them?"

Ralston shook his head. "I'm not sure. In the next few days, a sensible solution might present itself."

At that moment, Thackeray's description of the zoo crept into his mind. The man's words describing the action crept into his mind. "We killed the dangerous ones and let the rest go."

But who had the right to make that decision with human beings? All his life, he believed that only God had that right. But again, humans had the responsibility to do the right thing. What could be the right thing in this case? Never had Ralston more respect for God than at this moment.

****

The next morning, Ralston paced in the women's ward foyer, while Eka, seated at the desk, trailed him with her eyes. He paused to peer through the ward door porthole.

"You know the women better than anyone, Eka. What do you think would happen if we let them go?"

The stocky, Burmese woman scowled. "Most would run away."

Ralston turned away from the porthole in the door where he observed the ward. "What about the rest?"

"Walk away?"

"You mean they would all leave?"

She nodded. "A few might linger. Fear leaving, but with everyone else gone, they might eventually wander off."

He turned back to the window.

She turned to him. "What are you planning?"

"They ordered my family and me to leave. We sail in four days."

"What does that mean for this place?"

"I only have commitments to feed them for the next few days. After that, there is nothing. I can't let them starve."

Her brow furrowed. "And this place?"

"Do you mean, will you still have a job?"

She nodded.

"With the civilian government folded, there will be no one to pay you. I'm sorry."

She hung her head.

He moved to her side. "I realize I'm asking a lot, but will you help me release the women?"

"Is that the only answer?"

"Believe me, I have worked to find another way, but nothing has borne fruit."

Her brow furrowed. "How do you plan to do it?"

"For safety reasons, I want to release the women first, probably today. Hopefully, most will be safely away when we release the men on the final day."

Eka stood. Walked to the door. Peered through the porthole. She turned to Ralston. A tear streamed down her cheek, and she nodded.

CHAPTER NINETEEN

Newkirk peered at the map as he spoke to the pilots seated behind him in the alert shack. "We got half the planes out at Highland Queens, and the rest we got disbursed around the field. At least the Japs can't take us out like they did at Pearl."

As Newkirk finished his briefing, the Alert Shack phone rang. All the pilots' heads turned in its direction.

Closest to the phone, Tex Hill picked it up, listened for a moment, then slammed it down. "We got bombers comin' in from the North."

Ed, along with the pilots assigned to Mingaladon, raced to their planes. While those assigned to the disbursal field, Highland Queens, leaped in the three cars assigned to deliver them there.

After take-off, Ed formed up on his element leader. At twenty-thousand feet, they scanned below for the Japanese. Once the second element from Highland Queens joined them, they banked to intercept the bombers. Flying above the clouds, no other planes appeared in the vast blue sky.

"Lost contact with base." Newkirk's voice came over Ed's headset. "If anybody else has contact, sing out."

No one responded in the affirmative, but several cursed the radios. Designed for low flying general aviation planes, the group's transmitters regularly failed. In fact, the poor reception had contributed to Ed's forced landing and subsequent kidnapping.

"S`pose the Japs are under this cloud cover?" Tex's drawl prominent over Ed's headset. "They couldn't hit shit through these clouds."

"Frank, take your element East and Bert take yours West. Drop through the clouds." Newkirk replied. "If you spot something or pick up a signal, sing out. The rest of you remain on me."

Ed steered his plane off the right wing of the element, heading Westward. As they dropped into the clouds below, they spread their formation. At eleven thousand feet, they passed through the cloud cover. With his head swiveling to check his position with the others and scan for threats, he relaxed until a tracer stream zipped past him from the right.

"Bandits. Oh, shit, must be a hundred of the fuckers." A voice he didn't recognize crackled over his headset.

At the same time, Ed found himself in a swarm of Japanese fighters. They seemed to be everywhere at once. Eager to pounce on the Americans, the Japanese failed to coordinate their attacks. While his plane shuddered when struck by an occasional bullet, the Japanese could not keep him in their sights long enough for a killing burst as they dodged each other. He rolled and swerved, nearly colliding with two attackers as he swiveled his head to look for the next threat or an opportunity to escape. The entire thing reminded him of dodge ball they played in school, except here they tossed more balls aimed at him than he could count. Plus, the consequences of an errant move more severe than a body blow delivered by a rubber ball.

On his right, a P-40 spiraled down in flames, while his element leader barrel-rolled into a burst from a swooping Japanese fighter with fixed landing gear. As a child, he saw sparrows chase a hawk. The big bird soared while the tiny birds dove and swooped around him. At that moment, Ed became that hawk with the Japanese, like those angry swirling sparrows, swarming him.

Unable to gain the advantage with any of his opponents, he needed to break off. Ed glanced up towards the overcast. With the altitude advantage, several Japanese fighters blocked this avenue. Even if he could out climb his nearby attackers, the Japanese above would swoop down on him. Obviously, the American formation above the clouds had not heard their radio messages. They would hardly ignore the perfect chance to ambush so many enemy planes, leaving Ed and the others to fend for themselves.

In his training sessions, Chennault preached a mantra; never get into a turning battle with the more maneuverable Japanese fighter. Shoot and dive away, until you can find a safe way to gain altitude to get back into the fight. At this moment, he understood what the old man meant. The light and maneuverable Japanese planes performed aerobatic miracles. The only thing saving him now, their inability to get a shot at him that did not endanger their comrades.

He barrel-rolled, came out head-on with a Japanese fighter. He jerked back on the stick. As his opponent swerved beneath him, Ed's plane stalled. Upside down, a bullet passed through his canopy and passed out the other side. Like a rock, his plane dropped, spiraling, his right wing nicked another Japanese aircraft as it swooped around him. On his left, an opposing pilot anticipating Ed's dive banked to lead his dive. Ed braced himself as this plane's shells slammed into the armor plating behind his seat. Gravity and the P-40's inherent characteristics took over as he swooped out of the melee headed for the ground.

As his speed increased with the dive, he kept his eyes glued to the altimeter. How low to go to escape? At one thousand feet, he eased back the stick, slowly bleeding off the dive's speed. His head swiveled, spied no nearby threats, so he leveled off at five hundred feet and banked towards the base.

He wondered about the others. One P-40 had gone down in flames. What about the others? He had not fired a shot. What a fuckup.

****

After the day's disaster in the air, the pilots gathered in the bar. Several gathered around a pilot with bandages on his face holding a beer bottle. "Got no engine, just glidin, so I belly into this rice paddy. Plane's on fire. I figured the tank's gonna blow any second, so I take off runnin'. Suddenly I'm dodgin' bullets everywhere." After taking a long pull from his beer bottle, he shook his head.

The pilot beside him at the bar frowned. "Jap strafe ya?"

"Nah, it was the shells in my plane cookin' off in the fire." He shook his head. "Imagine. After all that shit, get shot up by my plane? Ain't no justice in this damn world, that's for sure."

He turned to the man beside him. "Where the hell were you guys while the Japs jumped our asses."

"We had no idea. Fuckin' radios."

Ed tried to tune out the discussion. His hands still trembled, recalling the encounter that afternoon. When he stepped from the cockpit, the gaping holes behind his seat made his knees weak. The rear of the fuselage had so many bullet holes, it resembled Swiss cheese. Recalled the noise and shuddering as bullets slammed into the plane. Thank God for the armor plate behind his seat.

Still, his attention had been outside the cockpit, unaware his aircraft had this much damage. With the control lines exposed through the gaping holes, miraculously none had been severed.

As he turned to walk away from the plane, his crew chief grasped his sleeve. "Ya better have that arm looked at."

Ed glanced down at his torn flight jacket. Blood oozed from the rip. His jaw dropped. "Didn't feel a thing."

Light-headed, his stomach churned as he walked to the medical tent.

After a medic stopped the bleeding, he bandaged the wound. "Just a graze."

Now, as he tossed down his second drink, his arm stung, the shock wearing off. They lost two planes, but no one had died. A sullen mood filled the barroom. The usual glib atmosphere following a scramble absent today.

Newkirk's entrance prompted them all to turn in his direction. He tossed his hat on the bar, slouched as the bartender filled a shot glass for him without being told. He shook his head as he raised the glass. "Besides the two we lost, we got two more shot up bad. Might have to write one off."

"And we didn't get one a the fuckers."

Newkirk tossed back his drink, held the glass out for a refill. "When no one called back, I shoulda brought the rest a the squadron down."

One pilot at the bar shook his head. "Shit, skipper. Wouldn't made a damn bit a difference for us. Japs had us outnumbered and altitude advantage."

A second nodded. "Yeah, mighta ended up worse."

Newkirk shrugged. "It's gonna happen again unless we figure out a way to prevent it."

****

KUNMING, CHINA

Since Joe had never done escort duty, Greenlaw placed Boyington in charge of the detail. Boyington split the four-plane element into pairs, with each pair flying a zig-zag pattern above the transport in a scissoring pattern. The tactic ensured one twosome had the airliner in sight, and below at all times.

"Blue Fin 3 commence turn." Boyington's voice came over Joe's headset.

"Roger." He banked, glanced down at the CNAC DC-2 they escorted, as Boyington's pair passed over it.

Who rode in the plane they shepherded? Unlike other airliners passing through the area, this one rated extra security. At the pre-mission briefing, Greenlaw only told them the course to fly to intercept the plane. When asked who might come, Greenlaw replied, "A real honcho."

After the Chinese invited several high-ranking Generals to the celebration following their first combat, none of these officials required any special consideration or security measures. Not even Tiger Wang, the Chinese air commander. Also, starting two days ago, the office staff, including the Old man, had cleaned and organized their offices. They had added extra staff from the locals to make sure the hostels and the surrounding grounds appeared spic and span. Not a single cigarette butt lay on the tarmac. No longer the flower attracting the bees, Olga dressed more like a missionary and shooed away her usual office visitors.

Except for the instructions they called between them to coordinate turns over their escort, their orders had imposed almost complete radio silence. Whoever rode in the plane below must be important.

While maintaining his pair's position rested on Joe's shoulders, he still scanned the surrounding sky for threats. No clouds above or below to provide cover for a lurking attacker. Nothing but a vast blue ocean above with the green patchwork below.

"Blue Fin one, commence turn" Joe spoke into the microphone in his oxygen mask as his pair passed over the airliner. On his left, Boyington's unit banked as Kunming appeared on the horizon.

"Maintain top cover," Boyington replied as the airliner turned on its landing approach. Now they must maintain their zig-zag cover over the airfield until ordered to land.

As his pair passed over the city, he glanced toward Ann's hospital. While at Rose's last night, he learned that the Morgan's would leave today. He wondered how the inspection had gone. More importantly, he wondered about Ann and Johnathan.

Once the airliner landed, the order to land came over Joe's headphones. After they parked, Joe climbed down from his plane. Struck by a chill breeze, he zipped his flight jacket to the top, shivered, and trotted over to where Boyington stepped down from his craft. After the big man tossed his parachute into the cockpit, he beckoned Joe to follow. "Let's get the hell outta this cold."

Next to the parked DC-2, Chennault, in full uniform, shook hands with a short bald Chinese man in a brown wool suit. The man's wire-rimmed spectacles caught the sun as he stole a glance at Greenlaw. Greenlaw stood at almost what might pass as attention beside Chennault, his ever-present pipe now peeking out of his khaki shirt's pocket. The Chinese man sneered as he gave Greenlaw an appraising glance, before striding off with Chennault. Greenlaw trailed along like Chennault's pet dog.

Boyington reinforced the image. "If old Harvey had a tail, it'd be hangin' between his legs."

"I wonder who the Chinese guy is?"

"Don't know, but the Old Man looks ready to kiss him. Ain't seen him wearin' that outfit since General Wang came."

Inside the hangar, they joined a group of pilots gathered around a coffee urn. Boyington tapped one, dispensing a mug of steaming coffee on the shoulder. "Who's the big-wig?"

The man wrapped his fingers around the steaming mug to warm his fingers. "Hell, if I know."

Another at Boyington's side poked him in the ribs, nodded to the side. "Check that out."

As one, the group turned. A gorgeous Chinese woman, her thin silk dress, topped with a fur stole and high heels, scampered inside. Wide-eyed, shivering, she halted, then smiled. "Y'all got a warm spot outta this cold?" Her Southern drawl obvious.

One pilot beckoned her to join them. "The coffee oughta cut the chill."

As she joined them, one passed her a mug. Her teeth chattered as she accepted it. "Thank you. Is it always this cold here?"

One shoved his hat back on his head, grinned. "Except for this here breeze, today's about the warmest day we've had in a week."

Another nodded. "You shouldn't be out, dressed like that. How about we take you to a spot where it ain't so darn cold?"

She arched an eyebrow. "Oh?"

He turned to the others. "This young lady appears in distress, we would be remiss if we didn't offer her some hospitality, right, guys?"

When several voiced their agreement, she beamed. "It is freezing out here."

"We got an officer's club, but we can invite guests." He pointed to a car parked outside the hangar. "Come on with us. We'll get ya outta this cold."

She glanced back at the parked airliner, shrugged. "Why not?"

As the woman climbed into the passenger seat, five of the pilots packed into the back seat. After the car sped away, Joe turned to Boyington. "Wonder who she was?"

"I have no idea. Gorgeous. Almost as sexy as Olga. She looks Chinese, but sounds like a Georgia peach."

"You oughta head on over. Who knows? Even an old guy like you might get lucky."

Boyington grinned. "Gotta check in first. Then maybe so."

Together they marched to the administration building. Inside, Olga stared out her window. She turned away at their entrance. "Flight go, okay?"

Boyington nodded. When she turned back to the window, Boyington and Joe peered over her shoulder. Outside, the Chinese man they saw earlier sat in a P-40's cockpit. He nodded as Chennault standing on the wing pointed out features inside.

Boyington nodded to the window. "Who is that?"

Olga turned, arched her eyebrow. "You don't know?"

"Nah, must be a big shot judgin' from all the hoopla. Who is he?"

"It's the Generalissimo himself."

"No, shit?"

"Yep. Chiang Kai-shek. His wife's supposed to be with him, but I haven't seen her yet."

****

In the dining room at Rose's hotel, Joe raised his glass as a waiter passed by.

"She said what?" Ann covered her mouth, chuckling.

"She said, this is my Air Force, how can I run it properly if I do not know the pilots?"

"Not exactly the demure little Chinese wife."

Joe shook his head as he leaned back at the table. "I've never met this Generalissimo fellah. Don't think I've seen a picture of him before, but the look on his face when he and the Old Man walked into the officer's club?" Joe shook his head, grinned. "Not inscrutable. More like: We will discuss this later, dear."

She placed her hand on his sleeve. "Oh, Joe, I wished I had been there. Did you talk to him? Chiang?"

He pointed to himself. "Me? I'm a simple peasant. I'm sure he wouldn't even know I exist."

"But we support him. Man must have charisma or charm. Like Roosevelt, but not as tall."

"The way I understand it, the only reason he gets all this aid from the U.S. is he's put together a coalition of warlords, and he's not a communist. Frillman claims the man's got this huge portrait of Mussolini over his desk."

"You're kidding."

"Nope. He sent his son to Germany for military training. Kid marched into Austria with the Wehrmacht."

Ann placed her hand on his sleeve. "But what about Madame Chiang? Rose is a big fan of hers."

Joe nodded. "Who wouldn't? She's fun to listen to. Went to college in Georgia. You should hear how she gets rollin' when she puts on her Southern accent. The guys love her."

"And she claims it's her Air Force, not her husband's."

"Yep, said her father talked Roosevelt into forming the AVG. Rich guy apparently has a lotta clout in Washington."

"And her husband didn't disagree?"

Joe shrugged. "Not at the time. He stomped out. The Old Man said there were other things he wanted to see, so he sent him along with Harvey Greenlaw."

"The Chinese put great value in what they call face. He probably didn't want to make a scene."

"Anyway, I wouldn't doubt what she said, cause, after that, the boss stayed with her. They were still talkin' when I left a couple hours later. Boss looked like that dog in the RCA poster."

"You mean the one who sits staring at the gramophone?"

Joe nodded. "Got that caption on it, says: His master's voice. So, what happened with the Morgans?"

Ann described the inspection and Johnathan's sit down with her father.

"And your Dad suggested that Johnathan stay with you at the hospital after they complete the inspection tour?"

"Then, we could have a normal courtship and engagement."

She nodded. "His mother agreed. She offered to appoint him as a province director, so he could support himself." Ann chuckled. "I thought Johnathan would pass out when she did."

Joe cocked his head. "Really?"

"Believe me. I'm a nurse. I almost doubled him over, put his head between his knees, so he wouldn't faint."

CHAPTER TWENTY

RANGOON, BURMA

Outside the window, women filed out the asylum's gate towards Rangoon. "Where are they all going?" Sanda asked as she turned to Thiri, peering out over her shoulder.

"Away from here."

One outside paused at the gate to glance back. Sanda waved, but the woman turned back as if not seeing her. Sanda frowned. "That was Gwen. She and I came from the same city."

"Where was that?"

"Quandong. It is near Mandalay."

Sylvia folding clothes before placing them in boxes behind them turned. "Please, girls, come away from the windows. For our safety, Herbert wants no attention drawn to the house."

Sanda hobbled on her crutches to an easy chair. Seated, she sighed. "I lived with them for years. There are no dangerous ones left on the ward."

"They killed the attendant, so at least one must be."

Thiri and Sanda said nothing to Sylvia's statement, merely exchanged glances.

Julie scampered into the room, trailed by her sister. As they danced at Thiri's feet, Julie held up a sheet of paper. "See I wrote the whole alphabet, from memory, now will you tell us the story?"

Thiri frowned as she studied the sheet. "What comes between the L and the N?"

Victoria nudged Julie, climbed up on her tiptoes and whispered into her sister's ear. Julie's eyes opened wide, and she nodded. With a grin, she turned back to Thiri. "Is it M?"

Sylvia's head snapped around. Her jaw dropped as Thiri nodded.

"So, what story would you like to hear?"

Julie arched her eyebrows, glanced at her sister before replying. "The story of the tiger and the monkey." Victoria danced and clapped her hands. Seated at her feet, next to Sanda's chair, Thiri told the story. When she finished, Julie laughed, but Victoria tugged on Thiri's sleeve, frowning. "So how did the monkey get the tiger to come to the python?" the little one asked. "And how come the python didn't just eat the monkey?"

"You remember," Thiri's brow furrowed. "You tell me, so I know you remember the lesson."

Victoria frowned before her face lighted up with a smile. "Because monkeys lie!" Julie nodded with a grin.

Thiri sat up straight and shook her head. "No, he was a trickster. He told each what they wanted to hear, but he did not tell them everything. He told the tiger he would take him to a much bigger friend. One so big, he could feed his entire family. Remember what he told the python?"

Julie's eyes lit up. "Yes, he promised to bring him something bigger to eat, too!"

"That's right. He didn't tell him the food had sharp teeth and claws, and while they tried to eat each other, the little monkey scampered away."

"Honestly, dear, do you think that is a story that should be told to proper young ladies?" Ralston said to his wife while hurrying past, a suitcase in each hand. The two girls laughter pealed.

Ignoring her husband, Sylvia came to Thiri's side. "My dear, you have been a godsend. I don't know what I would have done without you."

"Please, you have been most kind to me and my fiance. Helping with these little delights has been a reward in itself."

"Well, when my husband told me about the predicament between your family and your intentions, I couldn't in good conscience let them persecute you like that. Christianity has more than enough martyrs."

Thiri nodded. We must learn to accept that there are many paths to God and not hate people because they chose another way."

"Oh dear, those are such beautiful words. There are many similarities between the Catholic Church and our own Church of England."

"Oh yes, I listened well when you let me bring the girls to church. There are many ways they are much alike."

"Well, I am glad you found it comforting."

"I did. I have also found comfort in the practice of other religions we have here in Burma."

Sylvia sighed. "They brought you up Buddhist, and our previous governess often told me of things from that faith that seemed comforting. She attempted to teach me meditation."

Thiri's eyebrows rose. "Did it work for you?"

Sylvia shrugged. "I could never quiet my mind enough."

"You are aware we have Muslims, Sikhs, and Hindus here as well."

"But besides those ferocious Muslims, I know little about the rest."

A mischievous grin crept over Thiri's face. "I often find great joy and comfort in the evenings from a Hindu holy book. The *Kama Sutra*. It emphasizes spirituality through postures and movement. It is something you can do with your husband that might lead to his spiritual growth as well. Perhaps if you could tell me where you are going, I could send you a copy later."

"Oh, Thiri, that is too much. Really. I feel so guilty abandoning you here like this. With the Japanese coming and all the chaos, I worry so about your safety."

"I am confident that things will eventually calm down here once the panic is over. A few Burmese are leaving, but mostly it is the foreigners. The Japanese promise to return Asia to the Asians, and many of my fellow Burmese look forward to that. Not that all British are bad, but many have not been as kind as you and your husband."

Sylvia brushed her hair back. "I am not sure where we will end up, but I am sure you can reach us through the British Consulate in New Delhi."

"Please, then, I will send you a copy. I will also mark the lesson I enjoy the most, but you must promise to share it with your husband as soon as possible. You might give him a little brandy first to help him relax. Experience full joy in the practice."

****

Outside the main house, Thiri and Sanda watched as Ralston piled luggage into the car.

"I wish you could come with us," Julie whined as she hugged Thiri's knees.

Kneeling, Thiri tousled the girl's curls, before giving her a peck on the cheek. "I will miss you too. But I will write once things settle."

Sylvia took the little girl by the hand. As she led the tot to the car, she glanced back. "As I mentioned earlier, send it on to the British consulate in New Delhi. They will make sure we receive it."

Thiri nodded. "Yes, and I will send you the book as soon as I secure a copy."

Victoria, clutching a stuffed bear, gave her a wave as she climbed into the back seat of the waiting car, while Ralston loaded suitcases in the trunk.

Ralston glanced up and scowled. "Book?"

Sylvia nodded. "A Hindu holy book." She turned back to Thiri. "The *Kama Sutra*, correct?"

"Yes, that's it."

Ralston arched an eyebrow. "Hindu, you say?"

"Yes, dear. Thiri says it aids spirituality through postures and movement. You must do it with another person."

Ralston frowned. "There's plenty of Hindus in India. I am certain we could obtain a copy when we get there."

Sylvia turned to Thiri. "That would spare you a great expense, and with the war, private mail might not be reliable. What did you say was your favorite exercise?"

Thiri grinned. "Number twelve."

"Number twelve? I can remember that."

While leaning on her crutches beside Thiri, Sanda's eyes rolled up in her head. "Carl hopes you all have a safe journey. He will miss having you around too."

Ralston stole a glance at Sylvia, rolled his eyes. "Tell Carl we were happy to have met him too."

The ambulance with Thant at the wheel pulled through the asylum gate. After parking next to the car, he and Cho strode to Ralston. "I understand you intend to release the rest of the patients."

"That's right."

Thant cocked his head, "Some of them might be violent, yes?"

"It's hard to predict, but there is a danger."

Thant nodded to the car. "If your wife could accompany Thiri and Sanda into town, I will assist you in the release. Once we finish, I will drive you to the dock in the ambulance."

Ralston turned towards his wife, chewed his lip as he pondered the situation before turning back to Thant. "That would put them out of harm's way here, but I've been told they had emptied the jails yesterday. I'm not sure I want my wife and the girls in town, unescorted."

Thant nodded to his companion. "This is Professor Cho, he is proficient with firearms."

Cho nodded, opened his topcoat to reveal his shoulder holster.

"He can drive your family to the dock then take Thiri and Sanda to where they will stay."

Ralston turned to Sylvia. She frowned. "I'm uncomfortable leaving you here, but it sounds sensible."

With Thiri and Sanda in the back with the children, Sylvia left with Cho at the wheel. Ralston turned to Thant. "I suppose we should get started."

As Thant drove the ambulance, Ralston directed him to the wards still occupied.

"How many patients remain?"

"I'm uncertain at the moment. Our official census in these wards is two hundred eighty-two, but there have been fatalities in the last few days. How many? I'm not sure."

"How do you plan to do it?"

"Until you came, I would have Sylvia wait in the car with the engine running outside the building. I would unlock the doors at each building, and then we would have raced away."

Thant's eyebrows rose. "Without telling them, they were free to go?"

Ralston shrugged. "I imagined the more adventurous would discover the unlocked door. Once they found it, the rest would merely follow."

****

Not a cloud appeared above as they drove through Rangoon.

"So, Newkirk covered for Burton with Kunming." Frillman shook his head as he rode next to Russ in the Jeep towards the docks.

Russ shrugged. "But he still expects his pound of flesh. Ed's confined to the airfield."

"Can't go searchin' for his girl?"

"Nope. Newkirk says, if she's there, she's probably safe. He just needs to stick to his duties for now and can head on over there when things quiet down here."

Frillman gazed off, pondering Ed's situation. "While he hasn't talked to me about her, I understand he's really taken with this woman."

"Yeah. Imagine, workin' with that bandit to save her?"

"Think Ed'll sit still for it?"

Ang Su leaned forward from the back. "If she is the right one for him, he will do something. I would have done anything to save my wife, even if it might have cost my life."

Russ slammed on the brakes as an elephant emerged from a side street, nearly toppling Ang Su into the front seat. Wide-eyed, Russ shoved his hat back on his head. "What the heck?"

As the elephant trudged through the intersection, a pair of zebras trotted behind. Frillman shook his head. "Place is becoming a real circus."

With the intersection clear, Russ resumed their travel to the harbor.

Frillman turned to Ang Su. "You lost your wife?"

"Yes. She and my daughter were visiting relatives in Nanking when the Japanese seized the city. I never learned the specifics of their demise, but I pray they were spared the rapes."

As a tear glistened in his eye, Ang Su turned away. At a loss for words, Frillman turned to the front.

At the dock, as Russ and his crew loaded up supplies, Frillman roamed the dock. Finished with loading, Ang Su nodded to Frillman, who conversed with a British officer at the pier's end. "Do you suppose that man objects to our requisition?"

As the two strode back to their Jeep, Frillman ended his conversation and joined them.

Russ nodded to the departing officer. "Guy givin' you grief?"

"No, I asked him for directions."

"Directions?"

Frillman gave them a sly smile. "To the asylum."

"What?"

Frillman turned to Russ at the wheel. "I keep thinking about Burton's situation."

Russ nodded. "Newkirk told him to not be concerned, but havin' her locked up in someplace with a bunch of loonies is not somethin' I'd want for anybody I cared for."

Frillman's eyes narrowed. "My thoughts exactly. Since we finished our scrounging for the day, Good Samaritans, such as we, might mosey on over to that asylum place."

Russ grinned. "At least we can make sure she's okay."

"You got the Tommy gun?"

Russ's brow furrowed. "Why?"

"In case they don't respond to a polite inquiry."

Russ shook his head. "Should we be singin' Onward Christian Soldiers as we go?"

"Early clergy often had to be warriors too." Frillman replied.

As they sped down the road toward the asylum, they passed a packed car speeding in the opposite direction. Close to their destination, they met an ambulance heading towards town. Ahead, the walled institution loomed on the horizon. A naked man stood at the gate. As the Jeep slowed, the man sprinted away.

Frillman pointed towards one building where several men wandered. Some clothed in canvas smocks, others wore nothing. "What the hell?"

Russ slammed on the brakes, pushed his cap back on his head as he scanned the grounds. "There're guys wanderin' all over the place."

Frillman nodded. "Don't think they're staff. I understand some a these places out here in the sticks, experiment with different treatments."

"The naked guys gettin' some kinda sun remedy?" Russ asked. "Well, the gates wide open. We might as well see about Burton's lady friend."

As they pulled up to the administration building's entrance stairway. Several patients gathered there scampered away.

Frillman turned to Russ. "You two stay here and keep an eye on the Jeep. I'll go inside and talk to the man in charge. See what I can find out. What's the girl's name?"

Russ turned to Ang Su. "Thiri, right?"

Ang Su shrugged.

"That's it?"

Russ nodded. "I think so. Not sure how it's spelled or anything. He never mentioned a last name."

"Not much, but we can try it." Frillman trotted up the stairway.

Down a hallway inside the entrance, a European man wearing a canvass smock like the other patients sat at the desk outside the Director's office, tapping keys on the typewriter. He brushed his disheveled brown hair back from his face and smiled as Frillman neared.

"Doesn't this make a wonderful sound?" He pointed to the machine, which had no paper in its roller before he resumed his tapping. "Hear that, laddie? Tap-tap, tap-tap."

Frillman nodded to the sign on the door. "Excuse me, I'm looking for the Director."

The man at the typewriter frowned. "Director?"

"Yeah, the boss."

The typist's eyelids fluttered as his frown deepened. "The boss?"

"Yeah, the man in charge."

"That would be King Randal."

Frillman stroked his chin. "Where might I find him?"

The man at the desk nodded towards the door. "Right through there."

Frillman turned and knocked. When he got no answer, he turned the knob and stepped inside.

There a man paced. Shoulder length black hair, with a matching beard, the tall Asian wore a low-cut gown, unzipped at the back, and barely reaching his knees. While he paced, his lips moved as if reading from the leather-bound book open in his hands. As if sensing Frillman's entry, he glanced up from his book. "Wie Gehts?"

"I'm sorry. Do you speak English?"

The man's eyebrows rose. "Ich bin ein Englander?"

"Uh, am I English?"

"Ja."

"No. I'm an American."

The man frowned. "I speak English, but I don't speak American."

Frillman chuckled and shook his head. "Then, English it is."

"You are new to me. Which ward are you from?"

"Excuse me?"

The man cocked his head, sighed. Repeated the question only this time more slowly.

"Uh. I'm not a patient."

The man arched an eyebrow. "A visitor?"

Frillman shrugged. "I guess you might say that."

"Who did you come to see?"

"It's Thiri I believe?"

The man rolled his eyes. As the dress slipped from one shoulder, he set the book aside to pull it back up. He turned his back to Frillman then held his hair up, exposing his bare back. "Could you do me a favor and zip this up?"

Frillman stepped forward and did as the man asked. "You are King Randal?"

The man turned to face Frillman, tossed his hair back over his shoulder. "Thank you, that's much better. I'm Randal Von Jergen, yes. Actually, I'm the Queen."

"The man outside told me you are the boss."

"Pfft! He has a very active imagination. Wouldn't believe a thing he says."

"But, you're the Queen?"

Randal spread his arms wide. "Yes, now. As you can see, they set me free. Burma's not the most benevolent place for people like me. They put me here several years ago to see if they might persuade me to give up my tendencies. But at last, I'm free."

"Are there women here?"

"Besides myself? No, liebchen I've not seen one since they unlocked the door. At last, I don't have to put up with competition from a lot of hussies." Randal pointed to the cart with crystal decanters in the corner. "Would you care for a drink, handsome?"

Frillman passed his hand over his head. "Thanks, but like I said, I'm here to find a woman."

Randal's lip thrust out in a pouty frown. "Well, if you're going to be that way. Go ahead. Don't let me keep you."

As Frillman left the room, he passed the man tapping on the typewriter. The man glanced up. "Would you like to hear me play chopsticks?"

As he neared the door, a burst of automatic fire came from outside. Frillman ducked behind the doorway. When no further gunfire occurred, he peeked around the door frame. Outside Russ and Ang Su stood next to the Jeep, Russ held the smoking Tommy gun pointed in the air. "Is there trouble?"

Both turned towards the door, Russ lowered the gun. "Buncha, these guys tried to climb on the Jeep. Had to fire off a few rounds to get 'em to back off. What did ya find out?"

Frillman shook his head as he descended the stairs. "The staff have abandoned the place."

As the three scanned the grounds, men wandered out the gate. Russ shrugged. "Guess they let 'em all go."

"I'm not sure how reliable the guy I spoke with was, but he claimed there weren't any women."

"We could always look around and make sure. Hate comin' all this way without findin' something."

CHAPTER TWENTY-ONE

As the car sped down the road, Julie giggled, pointing out the window.

"What's that funny-looking bird?" Julie asked as they passed an ostrich standing next to the road.

Sylvia's hand rose to her mouth as the giant bird scampered away. "Oh, my. It's an ostrich."

Julie turned to her sister; her face pressed against the glass. "It was in the zoo last time. Why is it out here?"

Her mother reached over the car seat and patted her shoulder. "It's probably migrating. Birds do that in winter."

Sanda giggled. "It looks funny. I've never seen one before."

"They come from Australia," Thiri added. "They can't fly, but they run fast."

Victoria pointed to the sky. "Are those birds migrating too?"

As Thiri looked in the same direction, one from the flock overhead split off from the rest. As it swooped down, the red balls on the wings became obvious. Thiri's jaw dropped. "It's an airplane."

Behind the wheel, Cho slowed to glance in the same direction. "It's Japanese. He might shoot at us."

As flashes appeared from the plane's wings, a tree on their right shattered. With a clang, one bullet ripped through the car's roof, before smashing the passenger side rear window as the plane roared overhead.

Cho skidded to a stop. "Quick, everyone out of the car." After opening the rear door on his side, he grabbed Victoria. "Run into the trees."

As Thiri exited, she scooped Julie up in her arms before racing after Cho.

Sylvia thrust out through her door, yanked open the rear passenger door. Sanda's eyes rolled up. "Carl, what should we do?"

Sylvia held out her hand. "Tell him to come with me."

"You stay here. I need to go help your mother with Sanda." Thiri told Julie after setting her behind a tree on the road's other side. "Stay down and no peeking no matter what you hear until I come back."

On the car's other side, Sylvia tugged on Sanda's arms. Tears filled Sanda's eyes as she reached for her crutches. "Carl wants to stay in the car. He says it's not safe out there."

The Japanese fighter banked for another strafing pass.

Wide-eyed, Sylvia glanced over her shoulder. "Let him stay then, but he would want you out of the car and safe."

The machine guns' chatter filled the air, as a trail of lead kicked up dust toward the stopped car. With a metallic clang, the shells ripped a large hole over the driver's seat. A glass splinter grazed Sylvia's cheek as she took Sanda's hand. Sylvia flinched but held onto Sanda.

Sanda pivoted on the seat. As her feet touched the ground, Sylvia's head exploded, blood fountained, as she toppled onto Sanda.

At the same moment, Thiri sprinted across the road. As she raced around to the car's passenger side, Thiri's knees weakened. Mustering all her strength, she staggered forward and pulled Sylvia's limp body off the screaming girl.

As the Japanese fighter passed overhead, it soared up in a banking turn, preparing to make another pass.

Thiri reached out to Sanda. "Take my hand."

Tears streamed from Sanda's eyes. Wide-eyed, she stared at Sylvia's bloody body. "They killed her, Carl. Do something."

Thiri grasped Sanda's collar and tugged. "Carl wants you to save yourself. Now come."

Sanda wiggled, tugged to free herself. "No, it would be wrong to leave her and Carl."

Thiri drew back her fist. With all the strength she could muster, she hit Sanda in the face. Stunned, Sanda's eyes glazed. Thiri yanked her out of the car. With her arms locked under Sanda's shoulders, she dragged her to the trees on the passenger side of the road as bullets ripped into the car. With a whoosh, the fuel ignited, flames engulfed the auto. As smoke billowed up from the flaming vehicle, the Japanese fighter swooped up and banked away. Its mission accomplished.

****

Thant swerved the car, stopping it below a tree that branched over the road as the fighter soared above them. Both he and Ralston stared skyward, tracking the plane's path towards town.

"It appears to be clear."

Thant nodded as he pulled the car back onto the road, while Ralston craned his neck, searching for more threats. A column of smoke rose down the road. Ralston clutched Thant's arm. "Oh, no."

Thant sped up. "It could be another vehicle. This is the main road to Rangoon."

"Did you notice any other traffic while I released the patients?"

"No, but it might be a vehicle coming from town."

Ralston eased back in his seat. Appeared reassured. "Yes, yes, of course."

"No, No." Ralston wailed as they rounded a bend. The flaming car sat in the road's center. The two girls on the left side of the road tugged Cho's hands as if dragging him to the fire.

As Thant slammed on the brakes, Ralston leaped from the ambulance.

"Mommy, mommy," Julie screamed at the top of her lungs. On the opposite side, Thiri tugged Sylvia's nearly headless body away from the fire.

As Ralston rushed towards the flaming car, he stumbled and slid in the dirt. Once back on his feet, he rushed to Thiri's side.

She pointed to the children. "Go to them, there is nothing you can do for her."

His lip quivering, Ralston's hand covered his mouth. As a tear formed in his eye, he turned and trudged toward his screaming children. As he neared, Julie slipped from Cho's grasp, but Ralston snagged her before she passed him. Still struggling to free herself from her father's grasp, she screamed. He clutched her to his chest, turned her away from the gruesome sight across the road. "No, you mustn't go over there."

Tears ran down the tot's cheeks. "Is Mommy hurt? Will she be okay?"

With her face buried against his chest, hoping to spare her the vision across the road, Ralston glanced over his shoulder at the flaming wreck. What to say to his child? Tell her nothing will ever be okay again? He turned back to her. "Mommy is not in any pain, darling."

She wiped a tear from her cheek. "Are you sure?"

Ralston nodded. "She's not there. She's with God now. It's time for you to be brave."

After setting her back on the ground, he clutched her hand. With Julie at his side, he shuffled to where Cho continued holding Victoria's hand. Tears streamed down her face as she gazed up at her father. He kneeled, held out his arms, and the girl rushed to his embrace.

****

Once Frillman and the others boarded the Jeep, they roared away from the asylum's administration building.

"What are we gonna tell Burton?" Russ asked as they drove out the gate, swerving around the men walking on the road.

"I don't know. All we learned is there aren't any women there."

"Do you suppose there's another asylum for women?"

Frillman shrugged. "Might be. I should have asked."

"Back home if you needed directions or wanted to find somethin' you asked at the police or fire station. We might check there."

When honking failed to clear a path through the men wandering down the road, they settled on moving along, trailing the walkers. A column of smoke rose ahead on the horizon.

Ang Su leaned forward. "That place disturbed me. I would want no one I cared about there. If there is no other place, at least we found out she is no longer there."

Russ shook his head. "I've seen farm animals housed better. They musta had fifty, sixty people in each of those enormous rooms."

Frillman scowled. "And the beds? Nothing but planks, no bedding, and the stink?"

Ang Su wrinkled his nose. "Pig sties smell better."

Frillman sighed. "Still, I wish we had something else to tell him. But all we had is a first name, and I not sure how it's spelled so I couldn't even go through the records to see if she had been there."

Russ nodded towards the men trudging before the Jeep. "And these guys. What the heck is gonna happen to 'em."

Frillman shook his head. "What we have here is more than any kind soul could deal with. It may sound weak, but it's up to God now."

Finally, an open field near the road allowed them to pass the wandering men. As Russ swerved back on the road, he accelerated, leaving the procession behind. Around a bend in a long straight stretch, Ralston's car burned. Stopped about a hundred feet from the flaming wreck, the three approached on foot. The car's paint now blistered or peeled in areas exposing bare metal. The only flames now rose from the burning tires with the wheels resting on the road's dirt.

Russ pointed with the Tommy gun towards the car. "Looks like it got strafed."

He turned to scan the surrounding trees.

"Anybody here?" Frillman called out. "Hello. We're Americans."

Ang Su pointed at the blood pooled at the roadside. "Someone hurt bad."

Russ nodded. "Don't think they're still around. They might walk on up ahead."

Frillman reached down to pick up a rag doll that lay on the roadside. "Car with kids." As he walked back to the Jeep, he shook his head. "Fuckin' Japs."

****

With its bell pealing, the ambulance entered Rangoon's outskirts.

Thant drove with Cho at his side, while the others crowded around Sylvia's covered body in the ambulance's rear.

"Carl is angry," Sanda growled as she massaged her swollen jaw. "He wanted to stay in the car."

Thiri rolled her eyes. "Tell him if he did, he would have burned up."

Ralston clutched both girls, who stared at their mother's covered body as the ambulance rocked down the road. A tear in her eye, Victoria glanced up. "Do you suppose she is watching us now?"

Ralston nodded as he placed his arm around her shoulder. "So, let's make her proud."

On his other side, Julie sniffled. "If I cry, will she be ashamed?"

"No, honey, but she will not be proud if we don't go on with our lives. Be the good people she wanted us to be."

Sanda cocked her head. "Do all mothers watch their children from heaven?"

Ralston pursed his lips. "I would think so."

Sanda's eyes rolled up. "Don't worry Carl, I will always listen to you too."

Thant called over his shoulder from the driver's seat. "We are at the harbor. What wharf do we go to?"

"I'm not sure. We must ask. The ship is the Mary Celeste."

As Ralston finished talking to Thant, Julie peered up at him. "Are we taking mommy's body on the ship?"

"I would suppose." He glanced at Thiri. "You must think I'm foolish for not wanting to leave her back there on the road."

Thiri shook her head. "It would be hard to leave a loved one like that."

"She deserves a proper service. I couldn't just leave her."

Thant slowed near a British officer standing at the harbor entrance. When Thant stopped, the officer stooped at Thant's window. "You have a pass?"

As Thant glanced to the back, Ralston slid forward. "We're seeking the Mary Celeste."

The officer nodded. "She's docked at pier three, but, as I said, you need a pass to go down there."

"Our car was strafed by the Japanese and set ablaze. We lost all our papers."

"Jappos, ya say?" He nodded towards the back. "Them your little uns?"

"Yes, and the body in the back's my wife. They killed her in the attack."

He gave Thant and Cho an appraising glance. "And these other folks, they travelin' with ya as well?"

Thant shook his head. "We merely gave them a lift after the attack. We are staying here in Rangoon."

The officer beckoned to a soldier passing by. The man trotted over, snapped to attention, and saluted. "Accompany these folks to the Mary Celeste. The gentleman and the children are sailing on her." He turned back to the ambulance. "And the body?"

"I'd hoped we could take it aboard as well. Arrange a proper service."

The officer turned back to the soldier. "Hear that, Private."

"Yes, sir."

"Once they're aboard, escort the others back here."

As the private stepped onto the ambulance running board, the officer turned and saluted. "Carry on."

As the ambulance pulled up at the Mary Celeste's gangplank, a man wearing a peaked hat slipped his clipboard under his arm while marching to the vehicle. The soldier stepped off the running board and nodded to the van. "Got some folks here claiming they have passage on your ship."

The man with the peaked hat turned to Ralston, carrying Victoria in his arms. Wide-eyed, the child sucked her thumb as she studied the ship's officer. "Herbert Ralston, Director of the Rangoon Asylum."

The ship's officer scowled. "You have your passports?"

"The Japanese attacked our car. They killed my wife, and all our papers and luggage were destroyed in the car."

The man grimaced. "Bloody savages." He pulled out the clipboard. "Ralston, you say?"

"Yes. My wife Sylvia and two daughters."

Sanda poked her head out from the ambulance's back. The man peered at her and frowned. "Other daughter?"

"Uh, no. She's with the people who brought us to town."

"I have a Ralston listed on the passenger manifest. Do you have any identification? Or someone who can vouch for you?"

Victoria removed the thumb from her mouth. "He's my daddy."

The officer gave her a weak smile. "And I fine man, eh?" He turned to Ralston. "Is there anyone else who can vouch for you?"

The governor appeared at the railing. "Herbert, old man. We'd almost given up on you."

The officer called up. "You know this man, sir?"

The governor rushed across the deck and down the gangplank. When he arrived at their side, he glanced at the soldier first and then back at the officer. "Is there a problem?"

"Yes, the Japanese attacked our car on the way here." Ralston then described the attack. When he finished, the governor frowned. "And Sylvia? My God."

"Her body is in the back of the ambulance. I hoped we could bring her aboard."

The governor turned to the officer. "Have some of your people fetch Mrs. Ralston."

The officer scowled. 'The body? But…"

The governor leaned close to the officer, their faces almost touching. "Good heavens man can't you see what these people have been through?"

The officer glanced at Ralston clutching his child. "But…"

The governor's eyes narrowed. "We're not bloody savages. Now get these people squared away chop-chop. Once we're underway and things settle, we can handle this in a civilized manner."

The officer nodded, and the governor turned back to Ralston. "After we're underway, we'll arrange a proper service."

Ralston's brow furrowed. "You mean?"

The governor patted Ralston's shoulder. "Only thing we can do under the circumstances, I'm afraid. No proper facilities for storing bodies. And in this climate?"

"A burial at sea?"

The governor nodded.

Victoria glanced up at her father. "What does that mean, daddy?"

Ralston bit his lip, hung his head. "I'll explain later, dear, but for now, let's be brave like your mommy needs us to be."

CHAPTER TWENTY-TWO

KUNMING, CHINA

"Put us under the British?" Joe scowled as he stared into his glass on the bar. "Their brass don't know their asses from a hole in the ground."

Boyington shrugged. "That's the latest word."

"Where did you hear that?"

"Didn't. Snuck a peak at a cable on Olga's desk. Some Limey Rajah named Stevenson wants the AVG inducted into the Army. Once that's done, they'll be ordered to stay in Rangoon."

Joe shook his head. "Put us under the British?"

"Yep. S'pose that would make me eligible for a knighthood?" Boyington raised a pinky as he hoisted his glass. "That's me, Lord Kick-Ass. Sound right?"

"Jesus, Greg. Remember the RAF guy in Rangoon."

"The one I punched?"

"No, the other one. Guy that flew in the Battle of Britain."

"Nah." He nudged Joe and winked. "If you recall, I was gettin' acquainted with one a the hostesses."

"Well, he claimed they'd ordered 'em to not dive away from combat. Instead, they were to stay with the enemy and dogfight. Anyone who failed would be court-martialed."

Boyington shook his head. "Poor bastards. Remember that show Schilling and the Brit put on for us back in November?"

"Schilling's a hell of a pilot."

"Well, the Limey was an ace. Schilling whooped his ass three times. Hell, those damn Buffaloes they're flyin' can't even out dogfight a P-40. Japs are eatin' 'em alive down there. Court-martial the poor bastards for divin' away. Shit, what would they do, shoot 'em for desertion?"

Joe shook his head. "No doubt."

"So, they could either stay and let the Japs kill 'em or have their own guys put 'em up in front of a firin' squad." Boyington scoffed. "Typical military logic." He tossed back his drink, wiped his mouth with his sleeve. "Well, we ain't in the military, we're the AVG, right?"

"You mean the American Volunteer Group?"

"Right. Volunteers, right? Barkeep how about another here?"

"Volunteer group." Joe scoffed. "First thing I learned when I joined the Army was don't volunteer for nothin'."

****

Chennault gazed into the reporter's eyes' waiting for the man to begin. After shoving his hat back on his head, his pen poised over his notebook, the man glanced up. "Colonel Chennault, is it true your men are now the sole air defenders in Rangoon?"

"Indeed, the British have sustained heavy losses, but I understand reinforcements are scheduled to arrive."

The reporter's eyebrows arched. "But I was told they were getting bombers."

"If the British take the fight to the Japanese, that might ease the pressure on Rangoon. Word is they might get a squadron of Hurricanes too. Should give `em a better footing."

The reporter nodded. "Ah, Hurricanes. They did a fine job during the Battle of Britain. You're right, that might stem the tide. Anyway, back to your command here. You realize what you and your men have accomplished has been well received in the States. Also, Churchill compared your pilots with the men who flew in the Battle of Britain."

Chennault shrugged. "It's sure brought in a bunch of reporters. Since you got the ears of folks back home, how about deliverin' a message for me?"

The man smiled, sat up straighter, his pen once again hovering over his notebook. "Fire away."

"Tell `em that once we get the supplies we requested, our combat effectiveness could increase tenfold."

"You're having problems with supply?"

"Problem is there is no supply."

"But I understood you have support from the President and the general staff in Washington."

Chennault waved his hand dismissively. "I get promises, but little more. I've got planes bein' grounded because we're short on parts. We're runnin' low on ammo, the pilots are worn out. Right now, I gotta crew down in Rangoon scrounging stuff from the docks. At this rate, we might not continue past this month."

The reporter leaned back, frowned. "You guys are the only good news coming out of this damn war right now. This won't make folks back home happy."

Chennault narrowed his eyes. "Then tell `em to do somethin' about it."

****

As Dr. Ross slipped on his smock, gagging sounds came from behind the bathroom door.

"Are you all right, dear?" Dr. Ross leaned towards the closed door. Ann failed to reply, but the retching sounds continued. When it subsided, she opened the door. "I'm sorry. Rose and I ate at this new cafe in town last night. Might be something I ate."

"You sure? You look peaked."

She removed a water pitcher from the counter, poured a glass, and sipped. "I'll skip breakfast this morning. Drink lots of fluids." She gave him a weak smile. "I'll be fine."

As he buttoned the smock, he nodded. "We have little going on today, besides the walk-in clinic. Perhaps you should take the morning off."

"Really, Dad, I'm fine."

As they walked together to the hospital, a brisk breeze prompted him to hunch his shoulders and shiver. "Even though winters here are not as fierce as the ones back home, I don't much care for this chilly weather."

"Does it snow here?"

"Not usually just these cold spells."

Concerned about her vomiting this morning, Dr. Ross kept a close watch on her throughout the day. Perhaps she had been right, just a mild case of indigestion, but often foreigners found themselves vulnerable to local diseases. The rest of the day, Ann seemed fine, just resting more frequently than her usual self.

As they returned to the cottage that evening, she clutched his hand. "I'm not sure why, but I suddenly feel scared. Like something bad is lurking."

Dr. Ross chuckled. "Might be what your mother called women's intuition. Claimed she sensed things. Especially problems."

She squeezed his arm, smiled. "I've never placed much stock in stuff like that."

"Perhaps, you should. Could be the Morgans sneaking back to see if we are rolling in sin once they left?"

She laughed. "Seriously, though, it's weird."

"Sometimes normal worries that you've shoved to the back of your mind creep out like that. Perhaps worries about your young man. Flying is a hazardous occupation, even when they are not engaged in combat. Have you heard anything from him?"

"He called yesterday. Said he might come tonight."

"Will they send them to Rangoon, like the others?"

She shook her head as they climbed the cottage steps. "He said most of the guys are eager to go, but they aren't sure when."

Suddenly she quickened her pace as she scurried across the porch. "Sorry, I feel an urgent need to powder my nose."

As she disappeared inside, Dr. Ross chuckled. Powder her nose. Why couldn't women admit they had to pee like men do? He shook his head. Men had their own euphemisms for the act. Like, tapping a kidney or draining the bilge. Just not as delicate as the feminine jargon, he supposed. A car pulling up to the cottage in the dark prompted him to turn. When he recognized Rose's car, he smiled. At least this visitor carried less of a threat than the Morgans. Possibly, they might be in for a pleasant evening.

Rose's voice came out of the darkness. "I thought you might run low on scotch."

"That and pleasant company."

As Rose climbed the stairs, she called over her shoulder. "I believe we are welcome. Bring along the food basket from the backseat."

As she gave Dr. Ross a hug, Joe followed carrying a wicker basket and a bottle. As Dr. Ross extended his hand, Joe tucked the bottle under his arm.

"Ann told me the Generalissimo and his wife visited." Dr. Ross said

"You ever met him?"

Dr. Ross's eyebrows rose. "Once, when I first came. Blustery little fellow, but his wife? There's a charmer."

Rose scowled. "She is a married woman. You would be wise to keep comments like that to yourself."

Dr. Ross gave her a grin. "But she couldn't hold a candle to you."

"Oh?" With her eyelashes fluttering, Rose took his arm. Gave Joe a smile. "Maybe you and Ann should go see that new movie in town tonight."

****

Ann squeezed Joe's hand as they strolled down the hotel hallway, chuckled. "New movie? Pooh. *Blood and Sand* has been here for a month."

"You suppose that was Rosie's code for us to get lost? Give her a chance to be alone with your Dad?"

She snickered. "I hope so. Can't imagine her being that excited about a bullfighting movie?"

"I thought all the girls had the hots for Tyrone Power. And those matador trousers with the tight crotch."

She slapped his shoulder. "It's his eyes that drive women wild."

"Yeah right. Bullfighters."

"She didn't ask you to bring the car back for her later tonight?"

"Actually, she gave me a wink when she gave me the keys."

Outside the door, they kissed. Ann smiled up at him. "Like the great lady, herself said. Is that a pistol in your pocket or are you glad to see me?"

He pressed against her. "Believe me, it's a real friendly weapon."

She caressed the bulge in his trousers. "Is it ever."

"You keep this up, and we won't make it inside. Might make the other guests complain."

Inside the room, Ann set her purse on the bed while Joe drew the curtains. She sighed as she glanced around the room. "I wonder if Rose holds this particular room for us?"

Joe stepped up behind her, slipped his hands around her waist. "If you like, I can ask her for a different room for our honeymoon."

As he nuzzled her neck, she stroked his cheek. "I haven't said yes yet. Might be premature making those kinds of arrangements."

"What? You're gonna toss me over for Johnathan?"

"Perhaps I'd still see you on the side. Add to the excitement."

"I'd be your gigolo?"

"Sounds deliciously exotic."

His hands cupped her breasts. "Hmm. I suspect my lady arrives unfettered?"

"Be gentle, they seem tender."

He stepped back to unzip her dress. As it slid down the track, a lascivious smile spread on his face. "As I suspected. Did you also neglect the rest of your undergarments?"

As he slipped the dress off her shoulders, he resumed nuzzling her neck.

"Oh, Joe, I care deeply for you, but you make me feel so wicked."

"I feel the same. Probably that thing poets call love."

"So, you don't think I'm merely some hussie?"

"While at this moment, I have the basest intentions, I truly respect you."

Once her dress dropped to the floor, she undid his belt. As he tugged at her girdle, she pushed him away. "You'll never get this damn thing off. Let me do it while you get out of those clothes before I rip them off you."

Undressed, Joe swept her up and set her on the bed. His eyes roamed over her as he lowered himself beside her. "Now, Miss Ross, let's get down to serious business."

As light streamed through the window the next morning, Joe sat up, rubbed his eyes. He brushed his hair back out of his eyes as he scanned the room, searching for Ann. Her clothes, piled on the floor beside his, suggested she hadn't gone far. The warmth in the sheets showed a recent departure. He leaned back with a contented smile as he heard her moving in the bathroom.

The sounds of gagging bolted him upright. He leaped from the bed and tapped on the closed door. "You okay?"

Again, the sounds of retching resonated from the door's other side. "Ann?"

She gasped. "Just a second."

As he stepped back, she peeked out. "I'm sorry. Not sure what's going on."

"You're sick?"

"I might have a bug. Happened yesterday too, but other than that, I'm fine."

He took her hand, led her back to the bed. "Maybe you should lie down a bit till it passes. Let me nurse you back to health."

She shook her head and grinned. "Said the spider to the fly."

****

MENGTZU, CHINA

Two days later the squadron moved from Kunming to extend their range into Indochina. Before the mission, Boyington leaned against a tree smoking, with Joe at this side, while the Chinese ground crew refueled their planes.

"Is there some kinda rule about pilots being married?"

Boyington shrugged. "I think the boss frowns on it."

"Are any of the other guys married?"

"Your girl givin' you grief? Wants ya to make her an honest woman?"

"Nah, it's not that. Ann keeps puttin' me off. Yesterday she said she heard that the old man might discharge me if we get married."

"Where'd she hear that?"

"Rose, I guess."

Boyington's brow furrowed. "Then it's probably the truth. So, if you go through with it, keep it quiet."

"Whattya mean?"

Boyington glanced around to make sure no one nearby could overhear. "There're guys in the unit that's married. They just don't broadcast it."

"Really?"

Boyington glanced around once more. "I'm married."

"What? But..."

Boyington moved close to Joe. "No one knows but you, so if the word gets around, I'll kick your ass like you wouldn't believe. Only reason I'm tellin' you is, cause if I don't keep your mind off this woman business, some Japs gonna flame your butt. So, if that's the only thing holdin' her back, go ahead, but don't broadcast it around."

"I know the Army wouldn't take married guys into flight training. The Marine Corps different?"

"Hell no."

"Well then, how...?"

"It's a long story. I'll tell you later, after the mission, but keep it to yourself like I said. Shit, here comes Sandy, I guess we're gonna get the word about this operation."

As Sandel joined them, he kneeled. "We're escorting Chinese bombers outta Chungi."

Boyington nodded. "Where they headed?"

Sandel kept his eyes on the refueling as he talked. "Supply dumps in Hanoi. Boss figures that might remind the Japs we're here too."

Boyington flipped his cigarette away. "Also, it might keep us from gettin' high-jacked by the British. 'Cept I'd like to get down to Rangoon and collect some a that bonus money."

Sandel rose, glanced over at the crews around the P-40s. "Well, you might get your chance today, if the Japs spot these bombers."

After take-off, they met the Chinese formation within already headed towards their target. Since the Chinese had broken into two groups, Sandel covered the lead squadron with ten planes. At the same time, Boyington, along with Joe and two others, protected the trailing planes.

An hour into the flight, Boyington's voice came over Joe's headset. "Bluefin leader, this is Redfin one. Where the fuck these Chinese goin'?"

"Roger. Guess they forgot to correct for the crosswind, plus you can't see anything through these clouds. Lemme go down, and let 'em know."

With no common radio frequencies between themselves and the bombers, Joe wondered how Sandel would accomplish this. Breaking off his scan for threats, Joe leaned over as Sandel wove before the lead bomber. Sandel then drew abreast of the leader. Finally, the lead bomber banked to follow his lead, the remaining craft followed.

Once the formation altered course, Sandel's plane rejoined the escorts above the bombers.

Joe checked his own compass. By his reckoning, the bombers had to follow a course of 150 degrees, they had been flying at 130. With the unbroken clouds below, they had no landmarks to guide them. Ahead, on his right, Boyington led their element out of the escorting zig-zag pattern to parallel the bomber formation.

Again, Boyington's voice crackled over this headset. "Bluefin leader, this is Redfin one. They're off course again."

Sandel's voice replied, "With the clouds below hard tellin' where they are. Let 'em go their way. Do their thing while we maintain cover."

"Fuck" While no call sign came, the speaker had Boyington written all over it.

After about a half an hour, black smudges from anti-aircraft fire appeared around the bombers. As if using this firing from below as a signal, the bombers dropped their loads through the clouds. After turning for home, the lead plane increased its speed, spreading out the bomber formation for miles, making it impossible for the squadron to cover them all.

As they neared Mengtzu, the P-40s broke off from the bombers to land and refuel.

As Joe taxied to the refueling area, Sandel marched across the field from his plane to Boyington's. After parking his ship, Joe hopped down and strolled over to where the two men talked. Both turned as he approached. Sandel placed his hands on his hips and scowled. "As I told your section leader, I expect our pilots to maintain radio discipline at all times. Profanity may be appropriate, but I expect you to follow proper protocol. Joe nodded. "Sure, Sandy. Whatever you say."

Sandel sighed and stomped off.

Joe turned to Boyington. "He pissed cause I didn't salute."

"Nah, he expected ya to kiss his ass. Whattya think. We blast `em?"
"Whoever might have been under those bombs had guns. So, what the hell."

CHAPTER TWENTY-THREE

RANGOON, BURMA

"She wasn't there?" Ed sank down on his cot buried his face in his hands after Frillman told him about their visit to the asylum.

Frillman placed his hand on Ed's shoulder. "They let them all go."

"And no one has any idea where they might have gone?"

"I inquired with the police. They weren't helpful. The city's in chaos. Criminals running unchecked, wild animals roaming the street, and now they have all these people wandering around from the asylum."

Ed shook his head. "And no one knows where she went?"

"I checked the administration building. Found no one, except some patients. Wasn't sure about your girl's name, so I couldn't check the records to see if she'd even been there."

"Damn. Listen, I'm on alert tonight. So, tomorrow I might be able to cut loose."

Frillman frowned. "Alert? At night?"

"Yeah, the Japs are tryin' a new tactic. Guess they've been losin' too many ships to our fighters and anti-aircraft. So, they come in the dark. After midnight, sometimes just before dawn. That way, they can get back to their airfield in daylight."

"But there's no lights on the runways here."

"Ground crew worked out a system. Anyway. Do you think you could talk to Newkirk? Ask him if I could go with you to town."

Frillman stroked his chin. "Help with the scrounging?"

"Sure, do some pokin' around on my own. I've gotta try something."

"I guess. Since you know her name, we might head out to the asylum again. See if there's any records."

After Frillman left, Ed strode across the darkened airfield to the alert shed. Inside, he found a cot and settled in for the night. As he rested his head on the pillow, Thiri's face rose before him. Her smile, her laughter. What he would give to see that once more. To run his hands over her smooth skin. To rock again with their bodies entwined, seeking release.

Petite, he often wondered if a stiff breeze might blow her away, but she had an inner strength. Her cunning often surprised him, especially in her dealings with Thiha. Thiha, the bandit and killer. The fear etched on Thiri's face as the man groped her in the car, as he negotiated for Ed's services, made him bolt upright on the cot.

Yes, she had an inner strength, but with all the chaos surrounding them, had she fallen victim to another predator?

What had Frillman said? Not only had they released the people from the asylum, but now criminals and wild animals roamed the streets. A beautiful woman alone? With sleep out of reach, he rose from the cot. After putting on his flight boots, he slipped out, not wanting to disturb the other two pilots.

Outside, he strolled up the runway past the parked aircraft. He had not prayed in years. But now, as he stared up at the stars, he asked God to watch out for her. Though brought up a Christian, he believed that the real God, wherever he might be, looked out for all. Not only Christians but Muslims, Hindus, Sikhs, and even Buddhists like her.

As he fought back tears, he hoped that at this same moment, she gazed up at these same stars. And no matter where she might be at this moment, she felt safe and happy.

After taking a deep breath, he continued his stroll. In the dark, shadows moved around the planes assigned for the alert. A starter whined as one plane's engine roared to life. The ground crew would repeat this every hour, making sure they stayed warmed up, ready to take off at a moment's notice.

Ahead, a man squatted next to a lantern. As Ed approached, he rose. "Are those the landing lights?"

"Yep. Red on the starboard side of the field and green on port."

Ed chuckled. "Shouldn't it be the other way around?"

"You must be one a them Navy guys."

"Yep."

"Well, this ain't the Navy."

Without another word, the man marched off.

Back inside the alert shed, Ed once more sat on his cot. After kicking off his flying boots, he lay back down. As he drifted off to sleep, he hoped the little talk he had with God on his walk had been heard. That somewhere at this moment, she sat safe and happy.

The hand on his shoulder shook him awake. "We got bandits. Man, your plane."

As he slipped on his flight boots, he glanced around. They roused no one else. As he marched to the planes, Jenson appeared out of the dark. "You goin' up too?"

Jenson shook his head. "Just you. When you reach twenty-thousand feet orbit and call in. A British air traffic controller will guide you to the targets."

Once airborne and on-station, Ed notified British Air Control. Now nothing broke the silence except his engine's roar and his breathing. Not equipped for night flying, the instruments had no lights, forcing him to operate the plane by feel and sound while navigating by the stars.

"Bombers coming in from the North," Air Control announced over his headphone. With a quick glance at the star's positions, he adjusted his course to follow the air traffic controller's instructions. While scanning the sky for signs of the enemy formation, he avoided glancing forward where the flames from the exhaust ports might ruin his night vision.

He glanced left, right and above, searching for the enemy formation, but saw nothing. As the call came directing him to the South, flashes appeared on the ground in his rearview mirror.

"Situation normal, all fucked up," Ed grumbled to himself as he banked. In all likelyhood, the bombers headed to Thailand or Indo-china, West of Rangoon. As he set his course to intercept the enemy, his plane rocked, shrapnel zipped through the canopy inches from his face.

Some trigger-happy gunner searching himself for the Japanese must be firing at him. While shouting his position to Air Control, he jinked his P-40 into a zig-zag path as more bursts thundered around him.

As quickly as it started, the firing stopped. "Sorry old man." A voice said over his headset. "Bombers have moved off our radar."

He thumbed the send button. "Make sure your gunners know I'm up here."

No further calls came in before the low fuel indicator light flashed. "Nightwatch to Control, heading back to base."

As he scanned the darkened city below for landmarks leading back to Mingaladon, the airfield's beacon flashed twice. Once he turned towards the signal, he descended to five hundred feet as instructed to let the ground crew below know his location. On his left, the red and green lanterns lit one by one, revealing the airstrip's location. As he glided down to set his craft on the field, headlights lit up, illuminating the runway. At least this part seemed to go as planned, he told himself as he touched down.

Parked and shutdown, Ed cursed as the canopy, holed by the shrapnel, jammed after only sliding back three inches.

Outside, Jenson climbed on the wing. "Let me give ya a hand with that."

When neither succeeded, two mechanics with pry bars worked it loose. Free from the cockpit, Ed examined the plane's skin with the aid of a flashlight. "From now on, I'm carryin' a hammer. Bust out the fuckin' thing. Be damned if I go down with the ship."

One ground crew shook his head. "Friendly fire?"

Ed shrugged. "British anyway."

The crewman handed Ed a flask. "You look like you could use a hit."

Ed nodded his thanks as he accepted the flask, flicked off the cap, and took a long drink. Finished, he returned the container, then turned to Jenson. "Anybody else up?"

"Carlson took off about half an hour after you. Listen, we got a bottle over in the car. Since you're done for the day, you can keep me company while we make sure he gets down safe."

After sliding into the passenger seat, Jenson, behind the wheel, passed him a bottle. "Any luck?"

"You mean besides surviving the Brit's gunnery?" After taking a drink, Ed shook his head. "Controller sent me on a wild goose chase. First North, then South. Finally, spotted bomb blasts behind me."

As he finished his story, a plane roared overhead. Once the ground crew lit the lanterns, a car at the runway's end turned on its headlights. Jenson shook his head. "Real sophisticated setup we got here."

As the P-40 swooped down, it bounced on the airstrip, too close to the car lighting the runway to stop. To avoid hitting it, the pilot swerved in their direction. With the fighter roaring toward them, both leaped from the car. As the P-40's prop chewed into the parked vehicle, both hugged the ground as the plane's propeller hurled metal splinters and car parts like shrapnel. Once stopped, the plane's pilot leaped from the craft as flames crackled from the spilled fuel. A firetruck raced to the scene. Its foam smothered the fire before they completely engulfed both the car and aircraft.

Jenson and Ed joined the plane's pilot watching the ground crew climb over the twisted wreckage, rubbing his eyes.

He turned to them. "Fucking hydraulic line busted on approach. Sprayed all over the cockpit. Couldn't see a damn thing."

Jenson nodded. "At least you didn't hit the car at the end of the strip."

He nodded. "Didn't see you guys."

"We got out in time. Lucky nobody got hurt."

One ground crewman peering inside the car stepped back and turned to them. "Shit, there's somebody in the back seat."

****

As Thiri stretched and yawned, Thant passed her a steaming teacup. "Were the sleeping mats satisfactory?"

She nodded as she brushed back her hair before taking a sip. On the other side of the room, Sanda poked her head up from beneath the blanket on her mat. She took one look around the room before lying back down. Thant chuckled. "It appears she slept well, too."

Thiri smiled. "You must thank the professor. The dinner he cooked last night was marvelous."

"With all the students gone, the harvest at the University garden is abundant."

Cho came through the apartment's front door carrying a cloth bag. After setting the sack on the floor, he pulled out a flowered smock and passed it to Thiri. "I guessed on the size. I also secured fresh undergarments for yourself and your friend."

Seated cross-legged on her sleeping mat, she held the dress up. "It's beautiful." She nuzzled the fabric against her cheek, smiled. "I had almost forgotten what real fabric felt like. Thank you."

She turned to Thant. "What shall we do next?"

"Now that you are here, we can find the boss."

She stifled a chuckle with her hand. "It is amusing to hear you call Ed that."

Thant frowned. "He always treated me with respect. Made me his bodyguard and driver."

She nudged his shoulder. "I'm teasing. But honestly, what should we do next?"

"We should go to the airfield. The guards have grown accustomed to me, so we could get in without question."

"They would let me in?"

Thant nodded. "I would tell them you are a nurse if they question it."

She glanced down at the smock. "But this dress is not one would see on a nurse, is it?"

Cho stroked his chin. "I have some trousers. They might be a bit baggy, but after we roll up the legs, it will work. That and an old shirt would do nicely."

Sanda bolted upright on her mat. "What about me?"

Cho turned to her. "You could stay here." He pointed to a record player. I have a gramophone and wonderful records from the States."

"Records?"

Cho scratched his head, gave Thiri a beseeching glance. Thiri turned to Sanda. "They are plastic disks that play music. The music from the States is wonderful."

"The States?"

"Yes, the United States of America. It is a country like Burma, but it is a long way off across the ocean."

"And if you like, I have some splendid books," Cho interjected.

Sanda made a pouty frown. "I can't read."

Cho cocked his head, Thiri turned to him. "Sanda came to the asylum quite young."

Cho's face dropped. He turned to Sanda. "How about games?"

Sanda gasped. "No! I don't do that. That causes bad hands."

Sanda frowned, she glanced back and forth between Thiri and Thant. Her eyes rolled up. "He is a nice man. You saw how he took care of the children." She sat silently, as if listening, then turned to Thiri. "Carl says I must go with you."

Thiri turned to Thant. "We'll put her in the back. Tell them she is a patient."

Thiri shrugged. "Then, it is settled. But I am filthy. Let me take a quick shower." She turned to Sanda. "How about I help you with a bath like we did before, so you don't damage your cast."

Sanda grinned as she nodded.

Thiri grinned. "Then, we'll slip on our disguises and rescue the prince."

Sanda's brow furrowed. "Prince?"

She patted Sanda's hand. "Yes, a fearless man, who gave up much to save myself and Thant."

Once both women bathed and dressed, Thiri trailed Thant and Cho, as they helped Sanda down the stairs.

After placing Sanda in the ambulance's back, she grasped Cho's hand. "You are a nice man, but I have to listen to Carl. He keeps me safe."

He patted her hand with his free hand. "Of course. I wish I had someone to watch over me like that."

"Really?"

He nodded.

"Maybe you should come with us today. Carl will protect you."

Cho stole a glance at Thant, arched an eyebrow. "Would that help?"

Thant nodded. "Having a patient in the back alone would be suspicious. With you in back, Thiri would provide an extra pair of eyes in our search."

At the airfield, they passed through the gate without problem. As Thant cruised around the base, Thiri scanned for Ed among the men moving around the base. Near the airstrip, workers used a tractor to pull the plane from the car. An officer standing next to the crew waved them over.

Thiri frowned. "That must have been a bad accident."

Thant nodded as he pulled up next to the wreck. "I wonder what they might want. They only use our hospital if it is a local. They deal with the British casualties at the base hospital."

Once the officer arrived, Thant rolled down his window. The officer leaned down. "One of the Americans died last night in that. Would you be able to deliver his body to the mortuary?"

Thiri gasped. "An American?"

"One a them fellahs came down from China. I hate to impose, but all our vehicles are tied up with other things. This climate bodies don't keep well."

As Thiri clutched Thant's arm, he patted her hand before turning back to the officer. "What's the American's name?"

"Merrick, Merrit. He's gotta tag on his toe."

Thiri pressed her fingers to her forehead as Thant continued talking to the officer. "Any locals injured?"

"We got nothin' right now. Japs been leavin' us alone." As he said this, the air-raid siren wailed. As pilots sprinted from the alert shack, Thiri and Thant craned their necks, hoping to catch sight of Ed in the crowd.

The officer glanced up at the sky. "Damn, sounds like the honeymoon's over. You folks better find shelter. Park that thing under one a the trees over there. Might keep it outta sight from the air. You'll find trenches all over. Use those."

As the officer jogged away, fighters roared down the runway. Thant swerved the ambulance around the men rushing around the field, seeking shelter or manning anti-aircraft guns. Once he pulled the vehicle beneath a spreading banyan, he and Cho carried Sanda between them as they dashed to a sandbag pile, they hoped surrounded a slit trench.

Once they lifted her over the sandbags, all crouched down in the slit trench. With the fighters scrambled, the siren's wail continued, drowning out all but the loudest shouts from men, preparing for the attack.

As they huddled in the trench, planes roared overhead. The ground shook as bombs exploded around them, tossing dirt into their hiding place, like a gravedigger finishing his duty.

Machine guns rattled, while the ground trembled with each blast. Smoke, punctuated by screams, filled the air, as Thiri wrapped Sanda in her arms.

Sanda's fingers dug into Thiri's arms. "Carl, make them go away."

Thiri ran her fingers through Sanda's hair. "They will stop soon. We are safe here."

"No. No. I must get out before it buries me." She wrestled free from Thiri. As she rose, Cho leaped up, wrapped his arms around her waist, and wrestled her to the ground. Trapped beneath him, she kicked. Yanked his hair. Bared her teeth, snapping at him like an angry beast. "No, bad hands."

In pain, Cho raised up. She pummeled his face. When that failed, she clawed at his eyes. "Get off me, no!"

Scurrying crab-like to the battle between Cho and Sanda, Thiri trapped Sanda's hands. "Please, Sanda, he only wants to protect you."

Trapped beneath Cho, Sanda turned to Thiri. Tears streamed down her cheeks. "You said you would protect me." Her head turned to Cho. Once again, she bared her teeth. Snarled. "Carl will fix you like the other one. You'll see."

A bomb exploding next to the sandbags lifted Cho in the air, allowing Sanda to slip free. Dazed by the blast's concussion, neither Cho nor Thiri could keep her from crawling over the bags. As Thant pursued her over the sandbags, a second bomb struck the ambulance parked nearby. Like leaves blown by the wind, the blast's shock wave hurled them back over the sandbags. As their bodies came to rest on the grass, the bombing and shooting stopped. Except for moans and the flame's crackle a veil of silence settled over the field.

To So Few

CHAPTER TWENTY-FOUR

As the sun's disk appeared on the Eastern horizon, the Jeep roared through Rangoon, trailed by four trucks.

As they neared the harbor gate, Russ, at the wheel, called over his shoulder. "You didn't know he was in the back?"

As if reinforcing Russ's question, Frillman glanced back at Ed in the back next to Ang Su.

Ed hung his head, unable to meet Frillman's glance. "Nope, neither did Jenson. Guess he couldn't sleep in the alert shack, so he climbed in the car. Musta did it while Jenson was tryin' to get me outta my ship."

Russ shook his head. "Merrit was a decent guy. What a mess. So, we lost one ship with the crash, and yours needs repair."

"Must be why Newkirk let me come. He's still pissed about my trip to the village."

Ang Su clapped Ed on the shoulder. "Must be an exceptional woman. I hope to meet her."

Ed nodded. Said nothing more. Even if he could find the right words, they would not bring her back to him. To share all his feelings and thoughts about Thiri would take hours, if not days. Instead, they needed to finish the scrounging, then rush to the asylum. Perhaps they'd find her trail there.

Frillman turned back to him. "This is the last of our drivers. So, once we get these loaded and headed off to Lashio, we'll run out to that place you think held her. With luck, we might catch some clues."

After the convoy stopped at the wharf, Frillman posted a guard at the Jeep. Finished, he and Russ strode past the crates piled everywhere on the massive pier. With his finger on the submachine gun's trigger, Ed surveyed the surrounding area for threats.

As he read the stenciled labels on the wooden boxes, Russ glanced at his clipboard. He paused near one stack and marked boxes with chalk.

"Lots of stuff for the Brit's planes, but nothin' here labeled for CAMCO," Russ said as he rechecked his clipboard. "Lots of food and ammo. Should be enough to fill these four trucks."

Finished with this wharf, they resumed their examination at the next pier, where a ship cast off its mooring line preparing for departure. Finished with their survey, they walked back to the Jeep. Russ paused and scanned the surrounding area. "Streets in town are jammed, but this looks like a ghost town."

As they turned the corner, Frillman put out his arm to pause them. Wide-eyed, he pointed ahead to the lane loaded with trucks setting on wood pallets without wheels. "Is that for real?"

The men strode ahead. Near the vehicles, Russ kneeled to peer beneath one. "Wheels are under here. Other than that, they look good to go" He turned to Ang Su. "S'pose the guys can put 'em together?"

Frillman grinned. "With all these, we can haul even more stuff back to Kunming. Just need more drivers."

As Russ stood, he nodded. "Buncha guys hangin' around Kunming with nothin' to do. Bet the boss could fly 'em down."

Frillman clapped Russ on the back. "This'll make his day for sure. Let's head on outta here."

As they approached the Jeep, the guard pointed to a pair of trucks being loaded from a warehouse. A man wearing a khaki suit directed the men carrying boxes to the vehicles. "Isn't that Rice? I thought he headed home, back in September."

Frillman nodded, "I heard a lot of guys that left earlier stuck around here to do business instead of going home."

With his hand, Ed visored his eyes, following the action at the warehouse. "Guys in the unit are helping themselves. Cigarettes, booze,...."

The khaki suited man turned in their direction, smiled as he stepped into the truck and waved as it roared away, swaying slightly with its load.

As they climbed in the Jeep, Frillman turned back to Ed. "The drivers can load up the trucks Russ marked. Let's go find your girl."

As the asylum appeared on the horizon, they met two men on the road. One, wearing a canvas smock, shuffled beside a man in a dress, strutting down the road on high heels with a multi-colored parasol over his shoulder.

Wide-eyed, Ed stared at the pair. "What the..."

Frillman turned to Ed. "That's King Randal. I guess he prefers Queen Randal."

"You know them?"

Frillman grinned. "When we were here last time, they were the only ones in the administration building. Claimed to be running the place, but most likely, they were patients. Since he and his assistant are here, I assume no one must be in charge. But we can manage without them, I'm sure."

Once the Jeep stopped outside the administration building, the four men climbed the stairs. Frillman paused at the door, scanned the grounds. "The other day, there must have been hundreds of 'em wandering around out here. Now it's like a ghost town." He pulled open the door called over his shoulder as he led them down the hallway. "Hope the records are still intact."

Inside the quiet, vacant building, their footsteps echoed as they marched to the Director's office. Ang Su scowled as he fanned his face. Russ shook his head as Frillman opened the Director's office door. "Place smells like an unflushed toilet."

Frillman nodded. "From what I saw on the wards, not sure they used the commodes."

Inside, Frillman pointed to the file cabinets lining the wall. "I suggest we look first for admission records. That might give us a path through her stay here. What was her name again?"

"Thiri."

Russ frowned. "That's it. No last name?"

Frillman nodded. "That's common in Burma. How's it spelled?"

After Ed told them, Frillman pointed to the cabinets. "Well, let's get started."

While the three Americans searched the files, Ang Su strolled around the office, examining portraits and objects on the shelves as if in a museum. At the desk, he pulled open drawers until he found the cattle prod. As Russ turned with a folder in his hand, his jaw dropped. "Jesus, what's that doing here?"

Ang Su scowled as he examined it. "What is it?"

"A cattle prod. Farmers use `em to drive cows through loading chutes and stuff. Don't touch the prongs, it'll shock the shit outta ya."

Ed's stomach churned. "Who would use something like that on a human being?"

Frillman shook his head as he read from a file. "Welcome to modern mental health practice. Thiri, you said? How's it spelled again?"

After Ed spelled her name, Frillman grinned, held the folder out to Ed. "Says here they discharged her into her fiancé's custody a week ago."

Ed's knees trembled. He put his hand on the edge of the desk to maintain his balance. "Her fiancé'?"

Frillman nodded. "Says here admitted after attacking her brother. According to her fiance', the dispute arose because Thiri desired to convert to Christianity, and the family objected. The patient exhibited no further signs of violence. Since she is no longer a danger to herself or others, we discharge her."

Ed shook his head. "The part about her attacking her brother fits, but the rest?"

Frillman remained holding the open file. "When did you get arrested?"

"December twenty-third."

Frillman held out the file to Ed. "That's the day they admitted her."

After taking the folder, Ed studied it himself. A frown creased his forehead. "It says her fiancé's name is Thant."

"You know him?"

Ed nodded. "He was my driver and bodyguard." Ed didn't mention Thant's sexual preference. Except the only evidence he had of that had been Thiri's word. She also claimed to have arranged Ed's kidnapping. What about her had been real? he wondered. "What the hell?"

A sound like thunder came from outside. Ang Su went to the window. "The bombing has started again."

As they marched back down the hallway to the Jeep, Russ turned to Ed. "This Thant guy. He one a the folks kidnapped ya in the first place?"

"Yep, from the same village."

"S'pose he took her back there?"

"Right now, Russ, I don't have a clue."

Frillman pointed to a twin-engine plane formation passing on the horizon. Bombs dropped from the swarm. "Looks like the airfield is catching it."

As they raced back to town, thoughts raced through Ed's mind. "Wheels within wheels had been an analogy she often used. If his kidnapping had all been part of her plan, what about the rest? Shrewd at business, her ability at running the company even impressed a bandit like Thiha. Could this all have been some elaborate plan to get the money? The cash hoard she accumulated in U.S. currency, which she used to purchase the gold. Thant, his trusted driver, and bodyguard. Had this all been some conspiracy they hatched to fund their escape from her village or this country where they lived as second-class citizens? Her brother had been a spy. Did treachery run in the family?

He massaged his forehead as if to wipe these thoughts from his mind. They needed to check the apartment. Earlier, he replaced the boards covering the stash after removing it. She would be the only one who knew its location. If someone had removed the planks would he need to know more?

****

As the bombing ended, people emerged from their shelters. With the ambulance engulfed in flames, Cho dropped to his knees beside Thant's body. His hands clasped before him like a supplicant kneeling at the altar, tears streamed down his face.

Thiri staggered to where Sanda's body lay tossed against the sandbags. Her chin rested on her chest as if sleeping. Thiri dropped to her knees, cupped Sanda's chin. As she raised Sanda's head, Sanda rewarded her with a cough. When her eyelids fluttered open, Thiri's head snapped around to Cho. "She's alive. What about Thant?"

After drying his tears on his sleeve, Cho grasped Thant's wrist. A smile crept over his face. He tapped Thant's cheek. "Please wake up."

A British soldier with a red-cross armband dashed over and kneeled next to the men. After checking Thant's eyes, he turned to Cho. "Concussion." Examined the rest of Thant's body before rising. The medic removed a capsule from his bag. "Crush this, then wave it under his nose. It'll bring him around. But he should take it easy for a while."

As he approached the women, Sanda curled up in a ball. The soldier stopped. "She got any wounds?"

Thiri shook her head. "She is frightened, though."

He nodded as he pulled a flask from his bag. "Ain't we all. Here missy, take a nip a this. Settles the nerves."

Thiri took the flask and turned to Sanda. Thiri held out the container. "Here, drink some of this."

Sanda frowned cocked her head. "Why are you moving your lips like that?"

The soldier shook his head. "Blast probably cocked up her hearing. Have a doctor check her. If the eardrums not punctured, she'll be okay. Just have to give it time."

With gestures, Thiri finally got Sanda to take a sip. After doing so, she smiled. "That warms my tummy." She frowned. "Why can't I hear my talking?"

Thiri shook her head. Picked up a stick from the shattered tree beside the burning ambulance, pointed to Sanda's ears, and snapped the twig.

"My ear's broke?"

Thiri nodded.

"Then what's ringing?"

The medic grinned. "She'll be okay. Just needs time for the pressure to equalize. Might be a few minutes or a few hours. Either way, she'll be fine." He waved to a passing military ambulance. When it stopped, he rushed to it, climbed in back, and reappeared with a folded stretcher. Once he unfolded it next to Sanda, he turned to Thiri. "Japs will probably hit us again. You folks need to get off the field. Transport her with this." On his feet, he rushed off to the military ambulance before it drove off.

Revived, Thant coughed as Cho helped him sit up. He rubbed his eyes, glanced at the blazing ambulance. He extended his hand. "Can you help me up?"

With Cho's help, Thant made it to his feet. After taking a few tentative steps, he stumbled to the stretcher. "As the soldier said, we must move away from here."

Thiri stood, brushed dirt from her clothes. With gestures, she directed Sanda to slide on the stretcher. "Cho and I will carry her. You lead the way."

As Thiri and Cho hoisted the stretcher, Thant brushed the dirt from his hair as he followed them. "Where are we going?"

Thiri glanced over her shoulder. "To the road. If we carry her down it, perhaps some kind soul might give us a ride. Are there more ambulances?"

"I am uncertain. But with the bombing, they are probably out."

Cho glanced up at the sky. "For now, I suggest we return to the apartment. It is four kilometers, but I believe we can carry her that far."

After traveling but a few blocks down the street, a flatbed truck driven by a Burmese man slowed beside them. A boy in the passenger seat called from the passenger seat. "Can we help?"

At the stretcher's head, Cho nodded. After giving the boy directions, they loaded Sanda on the flatbed and climbed aboard. With all aboard, the truck chugged off.

At the intersection leading to Cho's apartment building, the truck stopped. Bombs had hit the neighborhood. The structures on either side now crumbled wrecks or engulfed in flames. Cho's apartment building, minus most of its front wall, still stood, leaving his apartment and most of its furnishings exposed.

Wide-eyed, Cho stared up at the ruin. "My books, papers. My God. There might as well be nothing left."

Thant wrapped his arm around him, drew him close. "At least we have each other."

The boy hung out the truck's window. "Is there another place you could go?"

****

As the four men left the Jeep in front of Ed's old apartment building, Frillman scanned the neighborhood. "Nice area."

Ed nodded. "Gangster I worked for arranged it. Wanted us to entertain clients here. We never got around to it."

Frillman turned back to Ed. "You think she's here?"

"Either that or I might find out if she is worth looking for."

"You mean because of the fiance' thing?"

Ed shrugged. "Partly."

Russ retrieved the Tommy gun from beneath the seat.

Frillman frowned. "That necessary?"

"With all the crazies loose, not sure what we might run into."

Frillman turned to Ed. "We'll follow you up."

As they moved up the stairs, doubts ran through Ed's mind. Did he want to go up there? If he discovered someone disturbed her cache, what then? Accept he had been the ultimate patsy?

At the top of the stairs, he stopped. The closed apartment door undamaged. She and Thiha possessed the only other keys, and Thiha knew nothing about her stash. Could she and Thant be inside now? As he fumbled in his pocket for the key, he held his breath, straining to hear any sound from the other side. He took a deep breath as he shoved the key in the lock. Quick movements to his side made him turn. Russ and Frillman, like cops preparing for a forced entry, stood now on the doorway's edges as if fearing gunfire through the door. Russ, the submachine gun, his finger on the trigger. God, what melodrama, Ed said to himself as he turned the knob, but Thant carried a pistol. Would he use it?

Like always, the upper hinge creaked as the door swung open. Uncertain what lay inside, he stepped through the open doorway. His eyes scanned the room. Inside, everything appeared as he last saw it. Her clothes scattered everywhere, drawers overturned and dumped on the floor. Broken glass in the corner where the police had hurled her perfume bottle. The musty smell of disuse had replaced her fragrance, the only difference now. Everything now coated with a layer of dust.

The others slipped inside behind him. As their eyes roamed over the destruction, Frillman turned. "Is this how you left it?"

Ed nodded. "Pretty much."

"Looks like someone searched. And not delicately."

"Cops, after my arrest. Really tore the place up."

Ed moved to the closet. Inside, the floorboards he'd torn up and replaced remained in place. If they had come back, they would not have bothered.

Puzzled, he roamed the apartment, going from room to room. No sign that anyone had been here since he left. What had happened? This thing with Thant, what did it mean?

Back in the living room, the others stood by as he scanned the room. Frillman broke the silence. "Well, what do you think?"

Ed shook his head. "Doesn't look like she's been here."

"Any other thoughts where we might check?"

Ed ran his fingers through his hair, shook his head. In this city, where could she be? Perhaps Thant had taken her back to the village. He wished he knew more about his driver. Where Thant went on his time off? Who he saw? But Ed never bothered with those things.

Like an addict seeking his drug of choice, he felt compelled to press on. "We might try the warehouse."

As they moved down the stairway, Russ slung the submachine gun over his shoulder. Outside, as they climbed into the Jeep, a flatbed truck driven by an old man with a boy in the passenger seat pulled up. In the back, a girl with a cast on her leg lay on a stretcher. At her side, holding her hand, sat another girl. Her shoulder-length black hair tangled and caked with dirt. Her face, a mud mask. Like the two men leaning against the truck's cab, all appeared rescued from the grave.

Ed glanced at the truck. His jaw dropped as he stepped back. A grin spread on the girl's face as she dropped the injured girl's hand. One man bolted upright on the flatbed. "Boss?"

"Thiri?"

Thiri leaped down from the truck, rushed into his arms.

As they embraced, Ang Su turned to Russ, shrugged. "Perhaps she cleans up well."

CHAPTER TWENTY-FIVE

KUNMING, CHINA

Chennault wadded the radiogram before tossing it in the wastebasket.

"Now wait. I need it for the War Diary." Olga grabbed the trash can. After securing the crushed note, she unfolded it.

He stood, strode to the window. "After you transcribe what you need, hang it in the can. We're short on butt-wipe."

Finished reading, she looked up with a puzzled frown. "Who is this Stillwell fellow?"

"Never met him personally, but I know the type."

"Type?"

As a P-40 soared off the runway outside, he turned. "Word is they're concentrating on the European Theater. For now, the Pacific is a sideshow. Burma will be a sideshow of a sideshow."

"And your point?"

"They wouldn't put one of their shining stars in charge of it. Probably somebody they shuttled out of the way, so the stars can get down to business."

"So, if they place the AVG under American command, he'd be our boss?"

"Yep. I ask for supplies, more men, and this is what they hand me?"

Olga moved to his side, placed her hand on his shoulder. "But they promised. The Kittyhawks and the pilots."

"Believe me, if, and I mean if with a capital I, they arrive they're comin' with strings."

"The induction?"

He nodded. "And when it does, this thing we've built might all fall apart."

Both turned as a clerk clutching a radiogram rapped on the door frame. "Sir, this just came in."

As he read it, a frown crept over his face. "Damn, what next?"

"Will there be a reply?" the clerk asked.

Chennault sighed. "Not yet." As the clerk exited, he turned to Olga. "Bad things come in threes might as well wait for what comes next."

"What now?"

"A radiogram from Madame. The air commander in Burma is requesting our guys be placed under his command."

"Will Chiang do it?"

Chennault rubbed his chin, his eyes narrowed. "Not if the good Madame has her way. I'll remind her that if she does that, she's givin' up her air force."

"You could go to this Stillwell fellow. Maybe get him on your side."

Chennault shook his head. "I'm not supposed to know he's here. Things seemed easier when all we had to fight was the Japs."

****

As Joe, Ann, and Boyington sat in dining room at Rose's hotel, busboys scurried by carrying trays laden with either food or drinks. Ann pointed with her fork at Boyington's untouched steak. "You gonna eat the rest of that?"

Boyington shrugged. "Go ahead. I don't wanna eat too much on an empty stomach." As a waiter passed, he held up his glass. "How about a refill?"

As Ann slid the plate before her and dug in, Joe gave Boyington a scowl. "You should ease up on that."

Boyington scoffed. "Why? All we do is patrol, or follow those Chinese squirrels around while they bomb the shit outta the jungle." He turned to Ann. "Pardon my language."

As she cut into the steak, she shook her head. "I've heard worse."

Joe frowned as she took a bite. "Where are you puttin' all that?"

After she swallowed, she sipped from a glass. Placed her hand on Joe's sleeve. "I can't figure it out. It's like I've developed a hollow leg or something. Can't seem to get enough." She pointed with her fork at Joe's plate. "Can I have the rest of your potatoes?"

As Joe shoved his plate towards Ann, he turned to Boyington. "Scuttlebutt claims we're gonna head down and reinforce the Pandas in a week." He turned to Ann. "You haven't touched your wine."

She gave a dismissive wave. "Doesn't taste right. I'll stick to the water." She rose. "Excuse me, I'll be right back, don't let them take my plate, okay?"

As she left, Joe trailed her with his eyes, then turned to Boyington. "When we were up at Mengtzu, you promised to tell me about that marriage thing."

Boyington looked around as if searching for eavesdroppers. "I was working at Boeing as a draftsman when I flew the first time. After that one ride, I got hooked."

Joe nodded. "Same thing happened to me. Barnstormer came to Sabetha offered rides for two bits in an old Jenny."

"Well, I was married with kids, couldn't afford lessons on my pay, so I checked on joinin' the service."

"None of 'em take married men in flight training."

Boyington shrugged. "So, gave it up. Then one day, my boss comes to me. Says they gotta have a copy of my birth certificate. Some kinda background check for security." He winked. "Compliant fellah I am, I go down to the courthouse. Well, all my life, I figured my last name was Hallenbeck. Instead, I find out my real last name's Boyington. My stepdad, Hallenbeck, never officially adopted me. He and my mom just let me believe my last name was Hallenbeck."

"What?"

"Yeah, I never knew my real dad. My stepdad and mom got married when I was a baby. I never knew any different."

"But you were a Marine."

Boyington nodded. "Yep. I go find a recruiter as soon as I found out and signed up."

"How'd that work? You're married."

"That's the beauty of it. Greg Hallenbeck was, but there was no record of a marriage for Greg Boyington."

Joe shook his head. "What the hell?"

Ann re-entered the dining room as she approached the table, Boyington nodded in her direction. "We'll finish this later."

Before Ann reached the table, Rose intercepted her, took Ann by the hand, and led her to the kitchen. Joe turned back to Boyington. "Looks like she's busy. So, spill."

"Well, I quit Boeing, put my family up in a little apartment near the base where I took flight trainin'. Helluva strain, but I made it through."

"So, here you were, a Marine pilot with his family stashed off base."

Boyington nodded. "That wasn't the only thing. You know how they ship ya around. Plus, bein' an officer you hardly break even with the officer's club dues, even had to rent a room in Bachelor Officer's Quarters. Officers have to buy their uniforms. Bad enough with the Army or the Navy. The Corps also requires them Dress Blues. Expensive as hell." He held up his glass. "Plus, I developed a taste for this."

"Musta been rough."

"Marriage went to hell, and my wife goes to the Corps and turns me in. So, now on top of all the bills I got, they dock my pay for dependent support."

He tossed back his drink, held up his glass for a refill. "That's the reason I volunteered for this. Need the money to get me outta debt."

As Ann and Rose approached laughing, Boyington tapped Joe's arm. "Like I said, not a word about this to anybody. If you wanna marry this dame, keep it quiet."

As Ann settled back in her chair, she clutched her side as she erupted into giggles. With a scowl, Rose shook her finger in Joe's face as if scolding a child. "No more drinking for her. I said nothing funny, just asked about her father, and she laughs like a hyena. You bad influence. She not behaving like responsible missionary lady."

Joe's brow furrowed. "But..."

With a deep breath, Ann choked back her giggles, gave a dismissive wave. "Rose, it's not Joe's fault, and I haven't had a thing to drink. I don't know why it's like suddenly I feel silly. Guess I have a bad case of the giggles." Her eyes grew wide. She jumped up, squeezed Joe's shoulder. "Excuse me. I need to powder my nose again."

****

As they replaced a child's bandage in an examination room, the Chinese nurse assisting him turned to Dr. Ross. "Is your daughter unwell?"

"Excuse me?"

"Today, she seemed so tired. Not like her at all."

He nodded as he wound the gauze around the child's thigh. "Had a stomach bug. Probably recovering."

"I hope it is not something local. There are many diseases around that we who live here are immune to."

"Might be, but it seems to have passed. Lost her appetite for a while, but now it's back with a vengeance."

Which reminded him, he needed to call Rose to arrange a second grocery delivery. He didn't mention another concern that leaped into his mind during her recent ordeal. In fact, it still nagged at the back of his mind. Like waiting, as they say, for the other shoe to drop. Could she be with child?

While he had not discussed her relationship with the young pilot, he felt confident they had an intimate relationship. Nor had he ever discussed contraception with his daughter. As her father, not his role. Such discussions, the responsibility of a mother.

Uncertain how to proceed with such a delicate topic, he never broached the subject. Told himself that as a trained nurse, she possessed the needed education in this area. Perhaps, as a physician, he read too much into what might be going on. It had been a small bout with a stomach bug or a touch of food poisoning.

But, the idea of grandchildren appealed to him. Especially as he recalled Ann as a child, the thrill of watching her grow and learn. What a joy that would bring to this stark posting.

It would also bring problems. Ann bearing a child out of wedlock? Not with the Morgans lurking about the countryside with their morality inquisition.

Marriage between Ann and Joe would not solve the problem either. Not that he disapproved of the young man, but Mrs. Morgan expected the eventual union between Ann and her son. Anything else might toss her into a vengeful fury, destroying everything he built here.

But perhaps he worried about nothing. A parent's worries never ceased. In fact, as the child grew, so did the consequences of a misstep. As he finished applying the fresh bandage, he sighed. Being a parent, never a simple thing.

****

Greenlaw scowled as he glanced up at the briefing room clock. "Goddamnit, where's Boyington?"

Joe shrugged. "It's a routine patrol. I can fill him in if there's anything special."

"If it had been up to me, I would have sent you guys to Rangoon instead of the Pandas. Got him outta my hair."

Joe chuckled to himself. Figured the man probably meant Olga's hair. After the Generalissimo's visit, Boyington had been drawn once more back to her office. As he often claimed, if it could be had, he'd have it. Men have needs, and unlike himself, most of the guys in the group believed she might be the most available supply nearby.

"We need to watch for anything special, like transport not on the regular schedule? Or have the spotters reported Japs headin' this way?"

"No, just the weather report." Greenlaw shoved a sheet at Joe. "Here's the forecast. Now go find your flight leader."

Dismissed, Joe sauntered towards the most likely place to find Boyington. As he moved down the hallway, he recalled his evening with Ann. While she still fussed about her breast tenderness, her passion seemed boundless. Everything normal, until this morning. As they dressed, she turned to him with tears in her eyes. He'd not seen her like this since he told her about Russ's wife's death.

He drew her to him, and the tears rolled down her cheeks. After sobbing for what seemed an eternity, she pulled away. Gave a weak giggle. "You must think I'm silly."

He shook his head. "What's wrong?"

"I don't know. It's like a blue wave swept over me. Out of the blue, and I just cut loose."

She sniffed. Joe offered her his handkerchief. Once she finished, she gave him a weak smile. "Let me take this and wash it. Okay?"

"But what's wrong? Was it me?"

"No, like I said, it came out of nowhere."

Later, as he drove her back to the hospital, things seemed normal. Last night he and Greg talked about their upcoming move to Rangoon. Even though she said nothing at the time. Perhaps it had been that, and she didn't want to say anything about it. Didn't want to sound like the worrying wife. Whatever caused it passed.

As he neared Olga's office, the sound of Boyington's voice drifted down the hall. "Pull out of Rangoon?"

As he stood in the doorway, both Boyington, perched on her desk, and Olga, toying with her collar, turned to him. "Junior, you ain't gonna believe this."

"What's that?"

Olga leaned back as Greg held out a radiogram. "The Generalissimo is orderin' our guys outta Rangoon by the end of the month."

Perhaps this might end Ann's worries. After his last combat experience, he did not feel that eager himself to go back to it.

Joe turned to Olga. "So, we're not goin'?"

Olga shrugged. "Don't ask me. This involves stuff going on way above my head."

Chennault appeared at Joe's side. "What's all the commotion?"

Olga's face flushed, Boyington slid off the desk. "Nothin'. Joe and me were headin' out and stopped to say hi."

Chennault nodded. "Well, since you're here, maybe you can help spread the word."

Boyington cocked his head. "Word?"

"Yep, Lamison and Frillman are down in Rangoon scroungin'. They found a buncha trucks. I'm sendin' every available body I can down there to drive those trucks back up the road once they're loaded."

Boyington stepped forward. "You know those guys down there might need a break." With a twinkle in his eye, Boyington continued. "How about sendin' down some fresh pilots, and then those Pandas down there can drive the trucks back?"

Chennault looked like a parent whose child just offered to guard the cookie jar. A smile tugged at the corners of his mouth but failed to crease his leathery face. "I'll give that careful consideration. Now, don't you two have morning patrol?"

CHAPTER TWENTY-SIX

RANGOON, BURMA

Once leaving Ed's apartment, the Jeep carrying Frillman, Russ, and Ang Su roared through the airbase's front gate. A few fires still smoldered from the earlier bombing, while men still clustered in the bunkers around antiaircraft guns or lounged on sandbags near the trench shelters. After the Jeep pulled up outside the alert shack, Frillman turned to Russ. "You guys better head out for chow."

Russ frowned. "What about you?"

Frillman glanced at the shack. "I'm goin' in and inform Newkirk about Burton."

"Alone?"

"He's got to see Ed had no choice. He needed to get the girl settled. It's the right thing to do."

"At least let me come along. Moral support."

Frillman rolled his eyes. "I heard how you and Jenson went with Ed when he pulled that stunt with the flight to her village. Newkirk still feels you hood-winked him."

"But he never told Greenlaw, just got all over Burton's case. This is gonna really get him... uh."

Frillman shook his head. "Pissed off, the words you're lookin' for?"

Russ hung his head. "Yeah, I'm sorry if it offended ya."

"Offended me? I said it, not you."

"But bein' the chaplain and all..."

Frillman scoffed. "Russ, I use dirty words, probably worse than you. Have evil thoughts like anybody else. Ministers aren't saints. I'm just a man doin' a job I love."

"Still, it's gonna upset Newkirk."

Frillman glanced back at the alert shack once more. "Hard telling what he might do. Anyway, if it's just me, Newkirk might view this as an ecclesiastical intervention. I am the Chaplain. Means more than preparing folks for heaven. Need to be God's hands here on Earth too."

Russ shook his head. "I promised to go back in the morning. Find out what he needs to do next."

"I'll let you know if he gets to come back with all sins forgiven or whether he should go back to being an outlaw like the other deserters down here."

****

As Thiri shampooed Sanda's hair in the apartment she and Ed had once shared, Sanda leaned back in the tub with her cast dangling over the side. She turned to Thiri. "I hear better, but there is still ringing."

"Can you hear Carl?"

"Not since the bombs. I hope he is all right. I thought the prince would be handsome."

Thiri chuckled, recalling how often she teased Ed with almost the same comment. "He's not Burmese, but he will do. He is courageous. He flies airplanes."

"Like the one that killed Sylvia?"

Thiri shook her head. "Those are his enemies. He goes up and shoots them down, so they don't hurt people like her."

Sanda frowned. "He didn't do a very good job."

"He is but one. The bad ones are many. Close your eyes, I will rinse out the soap."

Finished with the bath, the two women dressed and returned to the apartment's living room. As they entered, Thant rose from the couch. "The boss and Cho are out looking for food."

As Thant limped toward the bathroom, Thiri frowned. "Are you all right?"

Thant nodded. "Stiff."

"There is plenty of warm water, perhaps a bath might help."

As Thant ambled off, Cho entered carrying a cloth bag. Ed trailed lugging a crate. He smiled as he raised the box. "Liberated this case a Champaign from a shop down the street. Figured we might be due a celebration."

After settling Sanda onto an easy chair, Thiri moved to Ed's side. He took her into his arms. She nuzzled his neck. "I was so frightened for you. Did the British treat you poorly?"

He stepped back from her, stroked her cheek. "I saw that place where they had you. Compared to that, I've had a picnic."

While Cho chopped vegetables at the kitchen counter, Ed opened a bottle. After pouring a glass for Thiri, he brought one to Sanda. As he passed her the glass, she cocked her head. "Is it hot?"

"No, it's not chilled either."

She studied the glass. A curious frown on her face. "Why does it bubble?"

Ed shot a puzzled glance at Thiri. She raised her glass. "They make it to have bubbles in it. It's sparkly, like its taste."

Sanda took a sip, winced, giggled. "It tickles your tongue." Then sipped again.

Thiri leaned close to Ed. "Sanda lived at the asylum most of her life. She has much to see and learn."

Ed raised his glass as if offering a toast. "Well, in that case, you must learn to drink this properly."

Sanda frowned. "Properly?"

"Champaign has a ceremony with it called a toast."

"Toast?" Sanda asked.

Thiri patted Sanda's shoulder. "Not holding bread over a fire, it's another word for ritual."

Ed nodded. "Yes, you touch glasses like this." And he tapped Thiri's glass with his, then raised his glass. "To the return of the other half of my heart."

Thiri squeezed his arm as she sipped. Ed stepped to Sanda. Hoisted his glass again. "Is there something you feel good about at this moment? We can salute that now?"

"Oh, yes." Sanda raised her glass. "To Carl, may he soon return."

After clicking her glass, she drank. Ed gave Thiri a puzzled frown. "Carl?"

"We'll talk about it later."

After pouring a glass for Cho, Ed and Thiri seated themselves on the couch near Sanda. While they discussed what each had experienced since their separation, Cho stir-fried at the stove.

As they finished, Thant returned from his bath. Ed turned to him. "So, you are Thiri's fiance'?"

Thant's face colored as he shot a glance at Cho, while Thiri erupted in giggles. She nudged Ed. "It was brilliant. You mustn't tease him."

After sipping again, Ed shook his head. "And we don't know what happened to Zeya."

Thant shrugged. "I am thankful he stopped lurking around. But he seems to have disappeared."

Cho shrugged. "There were rumors among the comrades that several went to Thailand to join Aung San."

Thant nodded. "Also, instead of arresting the others, he arranged for them to return to the village."

Ed squeezed Thiri's shoulder. "If you hadn't argued with him, he might have sent you there too."

She shrugged. "Brothers and sisters argue it's what we do. Besides, I never did what he told me. Why should I have started then?"

Ed drew her close. "But when he sent the others away, that would not be what his British bosses would have expected."

Thiri frowned. "But Thiha claimed Zeya worked for the British."

Ed nodded. "When they arrested me, the officer called him a constable, so that part is true. But he sent Thant and the others home."

Cho nodded. "When he pressured me to betray Thant, I never doubted for a moment about him being a policeman. And now these rumors that he might have gone to Thailand to join Aung San? I am uncertain what he may be up to."

Outside a siren wailed, airplanes rumbled overhead. All but Sanda glanced upward as if they could see through the ceiling. Cannons roared, and ack-ack coughed as bombs whistled down. Sanda screamed as the building trembled each time an explosion occurred nearby. The lights flickered as if the connection might fail. Like a giant striding away, the explosions faded before stopping.

As the attack ended, Ed drew Thiri aside. "We need to talk about what comes next."

"Next?"

He nodded upwards. "Rangoon's dangerous. Criminals and wild animals roam the streets. There's looting and killing everywhere. And now the Japanese started bombing again."

"What are you saying?"

"You can't stay in Rangoon."

She gasped. "But..."

Ed Put his arm around her. "Remember, I wanted us to be together after we got free from Thiha?"

She nodded.

"I still want that. Do you?"

"Yes, but does that mean we leave together?"

Ed ran his fingers through his hair, sighed. "I don't know. We'll work something out. I know we can."

He turned to Thant. ". What about you? You can't stay here either"

Thant stole a glance at Cho, cleared his throat. "I want to go somewhere I can be myself. Openly love whom I choose."

Ed glanced at Cho who continued cooking without glancing up, Ed massaged his forehead. "Oh, man. This is such a screwed-up world." He turned back to Thant. "Where would that be? After all you've done, I'd do anything to get you there."

Cho paused in his cooking, sipped from his glass. "Because of the bombing, staying here is not a good idea."

Thant frowned. "But the Japanese. They will come soon. Drive the British away. With the comrades in power, things might change."

Cho scoffed.

"The comrades promised to make things better for people like us." Thant protested.

Cho shook his head. "The Japanese claim they want to give Asia back to the Asians, but this bombing?"

Thant marched to the kitchen counter, peered into Cho's eyes. "They warned us before it started. Told us to leave so we would be safe while they drive the British out."

Cho rolled his eyes as he stirred the sizzling vegetables. "What then? Crawl back in to live in this rubble heap they created?"

"What if we go to my village?" Thant turned to Thiri. "Your father is a kind and just man. He would surely give us sanctuary while we waited for the liberation."

"Also, I promised your father to find you. Make sure you were safe." Ed turned to Thant. "How would you get to the village?"

Thant shrugged. "The bombing has damaged the rail lines. We would need a car."

"No, I am not going back to the village." Thiri planted herself before Ed. Narrowed her eyes. "I am staying with you."

Ed tossed his hands in the air. "Where? Here? The bombs fall constantly. They just unload on the city. Don't think they bother aiming."

She shook her finger under his nose. "And you? Up there in the air, you are safe?"

"That's different?"

She placed her hands on her hips, scowled. "How? Bomb falls on you? Japanese shoot you down? Either way, you're dead."

"This is my job." He placed his hands on her shoulders, "What if I could get you to Kunming?"

Thiri's brow furrowed. "Kunming?"

Ed nodded. "It's our home base in China. The guys from our outfit are hauling supplies there up the Burma Road."

"Where will you be?"

"Here until they send relief, then I go back to Kunming. We would be together then. From there we can start our life together. Look, it's not ideal, but this gives us a chance of being together."

She tossed back her head. "So, I go to this place in China, where I know no one."

"There's the guys I was with today."

"The mechanic and his Chinese friend?"

Ed nodded. "Plus Frillman. Remember, I told you about him before."

"The holy man?"

Ed shrugged. "He is the chaplain. I'm sure he would help settle you there. Plus, this swell lady works for the Colonel. Her name's Olga. She'd help ya out too. You'd like her."

Thiri turned to Sanda. "What about her?"

****

While the others ate breakfast the next morning Ed talked over his shoulder as he led Thant down the apartment building's stairway. "There's a Buick dealership just down this street, maybe they have a car you guys can use." Before stepping out on the sidewalk, Ed checked his shoulder holster. "You still have yours?"

Thant spread his jacket, exposing the revolver's handle.

As they stepped into the sunlight, smoke drifted up from a smoldering building across the street. A man and two boys picked through the building's rubble while a woman sobbed on the sidewalk.

"Damn, that was close."

Thant nodded and pointed down the street where another building had collapsed. "It appears as if the bombs almost walked down that side of the street."

"From the damage, it looks like the plane flew in that direction along that side of the street. If he'd drifted this way a few feet, it would have landed right on us."

After turning the opposite direction, the two strolled towards the intersection. Around the corner, a crowd milled before a shop. Near the door, a line had formed. At the entrance stood a man with a shotgun while another barred the door with his arm. Once a person emerged from inside with a package, the man blocking the door allowed the first person in line to enter.

Ed pointed down the street where a large sign atop a building showed half of a Buick emblem. A chain-link fence surrounding the building's empty lot now folded back in several places large enough for a vehicle to pass through. While the building's vast display windows had been shattered, several cars remained inside. After passing through a fence opening, they approached.

At the window, both stepped over the knee-high window ledge. Inside, the glass crunched beneath their feet as they moved across the showroom floor.

"That's a Buick Roadmaster. My old man would kill for one of those babies. Wonder why the looters never took 'em."

Thant ran his fingers over the smooth leather seat and nodded. "Perhaps they wanted one with a roof. It often rains here."

"They're convertibles." Ed pointed to a leather cover at the back of the passenger compartment. "There's a cloth top under there. Has a motor that makes it go up and down. It covers the entire passenger compartment."

As Thant slid behind the steering wheel, Ed strode to what appeared to have been an office. "I'll see if there're keys back here."

"It is a beautiful machine. And you say there is a cloth top that folds up to cover it?"

Ed nodded as he returned, clutching a handful of keys on chains. "Found these on the floor back there." He passed them to Thant. "See if one of 'em fits."

While Thant sorted through the keys. Ed strolled around another, parked beside it. "If we get it runnin', you suppose you could use it to drive back to the village?"

With his hands on the wheel, Thant leaned back with a contented smile. "This is truly a chariot of the gods."

The sound of a vehicle pulling up outside prompted both to glance out the window. Outside, Frillman, with Russ at the wheel, sat in the Jeep outside, surveying the building's damage.

Ed strolled to the window. "How d'you guys find us?"

"We stopped at the apartment. They said you were down here scroungin' for a car." Rus replied.

Ed pointed with his thumb over his shoulder. "You guys gotta see this."

After they joined Ed at the window ledge. Russ shoved his cap back on his head, while Frillman stared wide-eyed at the shiny vehicles setting on the showroom floor. Frillman turned to Ed. "They're abandoned?"

Ed shrugged. "Nobody's around. Not sure if they run, Thant's checkin' through a batch of keys. If we find the right one, we'll know more. Is Newkirk ready to have my hide?"

Frillman shook his head. "I convinced him you needed the time here to further God's work. So, he cut you some slack for now, but you've used up his patience. What's the car for?"

"Thant's gonna drive back to the village."

Frillman smiled. "So, your girl will be safe?"

"She's not going with `em."

"Now wait." Frillman massaged his temple as if fighting a headache. "She's staying here?"

"No, but she needs to go somewhere safe."

Frillman sighed. "What's she going to do?"

Ed gave Frillman a sheepish grin. "I'd like you to take her with you guys to Kunming."

The Chaplain's eyes opened wide. He stepped back, held his hands up as if he could shove aside Ed's request to take Thiri with them. "What? Now wait."

"And the other girl, Sanda?"

Wide-eyed, Frillman stared at Ed. "The one with the broken leg?"

"She would go too."

Frillman placed his hands on his hips, scowled. "I can probably buy the idea of your girl, but... What's going on, Burton, you building a harem?"

"No, it's like this. The girl saved Thiri from some terrible stuff in the asylum."

Frillman shoved his cap back on his head. "She was a patient?"

Ed nodded. "Been in that place most of her life. She seems harmless, but she's real naïve. Thiri feels responsible for her."

Frillman rolled his eyes. "You don't ask too much." He cast his eyes skyward. "Oh, Lord give me strength."

Russ stood on his toes to glance over Ed's shoulders. "God those cars are gorgeous."

Ed nodded. "Nobody around. Think they're abandoned."

Frillman sighed. "Come on then. Let's have a look."

After stepping over the window ledge, they trailed Ed to the car, where Thant continued checking keys. He glanced up as they came to his side. "I have yet to find one that fits in the ignition switch."

Russ shook his head. "Don't worry, I can find out if these babies run pronto." He opened the driver's door. "Scoot over."

Once behind the wheel, Russ reached beneath the dash, then exited the car. With his hands on his hips, he scanned the surroundings before striding off through a door at the store's rear. He returned shortly with a length of wire and pliers. After removing the ignition switch from the dash, he crossed two of its poles with the cable. As static growled from the car's radio, Russ switched it off. "It's got juice."

He depressed the clutch, then the accelerator, and the engine roared to life. As he peered at the instrument panel, his brow furrowed. "Ain't got much gas, but she sounds good."

A grin spread over Thant's face and then evaporated. "The boss says this car has a top."

Russ grinned. "Hey, fellahs, can ya undo the boot cover? I need to show our customer this vehicle's fine features."

Once Frillman and Ed removed the boot cover, Russ operated the top. Thant's jaw dropped as the top's motor hummed, and the top unfolded over them. "Once it's up, you clip these here, so the wind won't rip it off and your set."

Ed leaned in and grinned. "Till we can get it gassed up, let's put the top back down. No sense advertising this beauty to the looters."

Frillman strolled to the other Roadmaster. "How about we get them both fueled? After that, we can take them back to the base. They'll be safe there."

Russ turned to Frillman. "What would we do with the other one?"

"Since we have to travel all the way back to Kunming on the road, we might as well ride in style."

Ed turned to Frillman. "What about Thiri and Sanda?"

"A bunch of the locals are billeting fliers near the dispersal fields. For now, I can get them set up there so they should be safe from the bombing."

"And what about taking them to Kunming?"

Frillman stroked his chin. "Let me talk to the Lord about this. I'll get back to you."

CHAPTER TWENTY-SEVEN

After the scramble the next day, Ed and the others swooped down on a bomber formation, without warning the bomber's escorts dropped from out of the sun.

As tracers zipped past Ed's canopy, he barrel-rolled the P-40. The Japanese fighter on his tail swerved past, banked. Once again, in the agile plane's sights, Ed yanked back on the stick, throwing his aircraft into an inverted dive. With the ground rushing to greet him, he flipped the P-40 right side up.

"He's back on your tail. Break right, if he follows, I'll nail him." Tex snarled over Ed's headset.

Still diving, he jinked to the right. At the same moment, tracers again streamed past his canopy from behind. He drew his elbows into his side, trying to make himself as small a target as possible as shells slammed into the armor plate behind him. "Come on, Tex, nail the fucker."

With his engine screaming, the ground rushed up to greet him. So low now, details of the landscape below loomed ahead. If he continued this path, in seconds he would slam into the ground. Desperate, he pulled back on the stick. As its shadow passed over his canopy, the Japanese plane behind him appeared ahead. As the Japanese swooped upwards, Ed raised his plane's nose and squeezed his triggers. As if directing a firehose, he swept the tracers across the enemy's path. When they intersected, the other plane turned into a fireball.

Ed yanked harder on the control stick to avoid the debris from the exploding Japanese. At treetop level, he scanned the sky, searching for a safe spot to gain altitude. Like buzzards, the Japanese circled above, waiting for anyone who dared rise to meet them.

To the West, a bomber formation unloaded on the dock area. As their bombs rained down, black smudges from anti-aircraft below appeared in the sky surrounding them. He'd had enough from the trigger-happy gunners on the ground before. To avoid this firestorm, he turned on a course that might allow him to intercept the bombers, before their escorts could swoop down in defense.

As he neared the bombers, two, trailing smoke, fell behind the others. Like sharks drawn to blood, the gunners below now concentrated their firing at the stragglers. Occupied with these cripples, Ed hoped he might now close with the others without risking ground fire.

A glint from above made him glance up. "Looks like I'm not the only hunter up here today, he said to himself, as a P-40 swooped toward the formation from above his one o'clock position. Already in range, this fighter sent a stream of lead into the formation's leader. Gunners from the others bracketed the diving P-40, and it burst into flame, trailing smoke as it passed through the bombers.

Now in range, Ed walked a long burst through two bombers. As he swooped beneath the Japanese formation, his windscreen cracked as bullets whizzed through the cockpit.

Weaving back and forth, he swooped away from the bombers as the other P-40 slammed into the ground below in a blinding flash. No parachute drifted down. He wondered who the poor bastard had been. With his low fuel indicator flashing, he changed course to return to the base.

****

Outside on the bungalow's porch, the tall, balding man in the flowered shirt sipped his scotch as the P-40 roared overhead. Seated with Sanda at his side, he turned to her. "Do you suppose that might be her young man checking up on us?"

"The prince?"

The man's eyes opened wide. "Didn't think Yanks went in for that stuff."

Sanda cocked her head. "Yanks?"

"Pardon. He's American, right?"

"That's right," Thiri called from inside as she came to the door leading to the porch. "What is this stuff, you mentioned?"

The man hoisted his glass as if saluting. "Royal titles. Fought their bloody revolution and all, to get rid of our King and what goes with it."

Thiri thrust back her shoulders. "He is my prince."

The man sipped his drink again. "Sounds serious."

"He is earnest. And a brave warrior."

The man chuckled. "No, I meant your feelings about him."

"I find him more than suitable. Do you need anything? Perhaps a sandwich or some tea?"

The man shrugged. "No, I'm quite content."

"I am most grateful for you opening your house to us. Mr. Bishop."

"Oh please, call me Stanley or Stan. And for havin' ya here, it's my pleasure. Need the company. Takin' you two in is a far better deal than the others got."

"The others?"

"Yeah, the neighbors are all billetin' the Yanks. Need someplace to be when they aren't up their givin' The Jappos what for, eh?"

A black Great Dane lumbered onto the porch. After setting down next to Bishop, it whined, snuggled its head into his lap. Bishop scratched behind the dog's ear while refilling his glass. "We enjoy havin' these lovelies around right, Rolf?"

The huge dog's tail thumped on the porch as it nuzzled against Bishop. "Now ease up, boy. You ain't no pup anymore. Can't hold ya in my lap."

Stanley turned to Thiri. "Japs ain't gonna bomb here except by accident. Old worn out journalists have no military value, I guess."

"Is the newspaper still printing?" Thiri asked.

"One of the first things got hit during the Christmas attack. Got nothin' to do now, but head into town occasionally and file a dispatch if the military will allow it. Newsflashes have little priority, even from a man here on the ground."

Thiri frowned. "But you spent most of the morning typing."

"Keepin' a journal. Writtin' up what I see here every day. Who knows might even get it published sometime. That is if I get outta here."

Thiri's eyebrows rose. "You plan on leaving?"

"If the military skedaddles. I'll go with them. Cover the story on my way out the door."

"What do you write about?"

He waved his glass toward Sanda seated at his side. "Today, I wrote about you and your friend here."

"Like what?"

"How you came to stay with me." He bent down to retrieve a notepad at his feet. After retrieving a fountain pen from his shirt pocket, he removed its cap. With the pen poised over the paper, he turned to Thiri. "How did you meet the Yank?"

As Thiri talked, Bishop scribbled on the pad. She described Ed's forced landing near the village, his kidnapping, and later their working for Thiha. He laughed and shook his head when she confessed about her part in arranging Ed's kidnapping. Set the pen aside for a moment, tossed back the remains in his glass. "Damsels are a devious bunch, but this takes a prize."

"In Burma, it is customary for the woman to have choices."

He chuckled. "But kidnappin' a fellah?"

Thiri arched an eyebrow. "I might be a bit more assertive than most. But it suits me."

"And the Yank knows all this?"

She grinned. "Men have big egos. I believe it flattered him."

He leaned back, gave her an appraising smile. "This story alone would make a best seller. Damn exciting adventure and all."

She sighed. "It has been an adventure."

With her hand Thiri visored her eyes as a wave of twin-engine planes passed overhead. "Another attack?"

"Yep, looks like they're really gettin' serious about takin' Burma."

After the planes passed, two British Hurricane fighters passed overhead. Bishop grinned. "Looks like it's our boys turn to head into the fray. You missed the Yanks go at the last bunch."

"What happened?"

"Think the Jap's escorts got to 'em before they could attack the bombers. Your boys gave it to 'em, I think, but there were too damn many Japs. In the end, one buzzed right over the house. Told Sanda here, it mighta been your beau."

Sanda nodded. "He flew by too fast. Plus, he had a thing covering his face, so I could not tell if it was him."

From the city's direction came a rumbling like thunder. Bishop shook his head. "Be nothin' left in the city, this keeps up."

****

After rolling back his canopy, Ed stepped out onto the wing. He shuddered as he examined the holes in the fuselage left from the Japanese attacker. The crew chief shook his head. "The self-sealing gas tank saved ya."

"What about the windscreen?"

"Hard tellin' might have to check with Lamison and his crew on that. One thing we don't have spares for."

"One of our guys got nailed by the bombers. Didn't see a chute, and it went in hard."

The Crew chief nodded. "Don't know who it might be at this point. Might have been a guy from the Highland Queens. The one we lost from here got outta his ship, okay."

As he hopped down from the wing, Jenson arrived in a jeep. "Can't you bring one back without tearin' it all up?"

"What a furball. You do any good?"

Jenson grimaced. "Nah, guns jammed. Damn near blew the wings off. Somebody fucked up. Mixed a few Brit rounds in the thirties' belts, and they got stuck."

"We gonna have to put the belts together ourselves?"

"Not sure that would be better. Ain't much difference between the thirty-cal and the Brits three-o-ones. Have to mike 'em all to be sure."

"But they had to come from different boxes, right?"

Jenson scratched his head. "Maybe the armorers had a rough night. Anyway, the boss wants a word with all the guys. Hop in."

The crowded alert shack buzzed with conversation as the pilots talked about the day's action. Tex Hill greeted Jenson with a smile, but it faded when he noticed Ed. "Listen, I'm sorry about that, Jap. I had him in my sights, but ran outta ammo."

Ed shrugged. "We tried."

Hill clapped him on the back. "But you got him. Also, the boss said you nailed two bombers. He's tickled."

Jenson nudged him in the ribs. "Keep this up, and he might even get to likin' you."

Newkirk's entry brought a hush over the room. He stepped over to a large map showing the Rangoon surrounds. "Since the Japs are bombin' the shit outta

Mingaladon, we got a new dispersal arrangement. At the end of the day, you bring the plane back here. Ground crews will patch up what they can. If the ship can still fly, they'll gas it up and re-arm it. Once that's done, you'll take your plane to one of these outlying fields for the night. The airstrips will be close to your outlying billets, and the Jeeps stationed there will deliver you to them.

The following morning you bring your ship back here, where we will make each day's combat assignments. The crew chiefs have each plane's field assignment, so when you finish here, check with them. Questions?"

One pilot raised his hand. "What if the plane's not fixable in time?"

"We'll put it in one a the camouflaged revetments. Hopefully, if it doesn't get hit, we can fix it and get it back in the air."

"And the guy flyin' the damaged ship?" A pilot in the front row asked.

"We'll transport 'em to their billets. Got enough Jeeps for that. While your ships bein' repaired, you can provide relief for the guys who still got planes. I'll keep a rotation schedule, and hopefully, the phones continue working. Anything else."

"Hallet bailed out North of here. Any word?" A pilot called out from the back of the room.

"Yeah, he walked to the train station and called in. We got no way to pick him up, so he has to wait for the next incoming train to bring him. Anything else?"

When no one said anything more. Newkirk dismissed them, but as the pilots rose, he called out. "Burton. We need a word."

As the others filed out, Ed's stomach churned. Tex mentioned he'd shot down three today. Perhaps he might be in line for congratulations, but the look on Newkirk's face reminded Ed of a teacher he had in grade school. Had the same expression when he kept rowdy students after school for what he called additional instruction. These tasks usually included clapping erasers or sweeping the room with a whisk broom in winter, but in the warmer weather might comprise washing the man's car. As he pondered what might be in store, Frillman entered grinning. "Ah, good, now we can get this matter of your dependents squared away."

Puzzled, Ed frowned. "Dependents?"

Newkirk nodded. "Your wife."

****

As Ed clung to the Jeep's seat to keep from being tossed out the back on the bumpy road, he leaned close to Frillman perched in the front passenger seat. "You told Newkirk she was my wife?"

As Russ, behind the wheel, slowed for a cyclist wobbling down the road's center, Frillman nodded. "Only way the Boss would okay her traveling up the road."

"But that's not true."

"Technically, yes."

"You lied?"

Frillman shrugged. "From what I understand of your relationship, in the Biblical sense, you two have been married for a while. It's just not legally sanctioned."

"So, we need to keep that fact quiet."

"Nope. You gotta legally marry her, or you will be responsible for me committing a grave sin. Not to mention, in Greenlaw's eyes, a court-martial offense. Might get me discharged from this fine unit."

"But..."

Frillman thrust a finger skyward. "Don't worry." He patted his jacket pocket. "Got the papers right here that will make it official."

"What?"

"Yep, all we need to do is have you and her sign off on it. When I sign off on it, I'll date it for some time before today, and we're good to go."

"You mean we'll be married?"

"Yep. I am ordained. My duty, even here." Frillman turned back to Ed. "See? Problem solved."

Jenson, seated beside Ed, clapped him on the back. "How 'bout me and Russ standin' up for ya. He can be a groomsman, and I'll be the best man."

Russ shook his head. "How come you get to be the best man? And what about Ang Su?"

Ang Su, also in the back, on the other side of Jenson, shook his head. "I am unsure I should partake in this heathen ceremony."

Ed rolled his eyes. "But I haven't proposed. What if she says no?"

Frillman shook his head. "Then, we're in trouble."

As the Jeep pulled up outside the bungalow, Thiri strode onto the porch. For a moment, her smile warmed his heart until he remembered his mission. As she rushed down the stairs, his hands trembled. His throat dry. Icy fingers gripped his throat. Precisely like this morning's combat, fear coursed through his body. Except now, he had no parachute.

CHAPTER TWENTY-EIGHT

KUNMING, CHINA

Joe scanned right, left, and up, searching for threats as he trailed Schilling's plane. Boyington had finally got his wish. Detailed to relieve the Panda's, he and several others from the Adam and Eves departed two days ago for Rangoon. Now, this morning, Chennault sent Joe and Schilling along with four from the Hell's Angels on escort duty.

Since the bombers would target Hanoi again, they gassed up at Mengtzu before meeting the bomber formation headed for Indochina. Relieved to be flying and away from the boredom in Kunming, he wondered if this would be as easy a run as last time. Or, as Boyington described it, a quick trip to Indochina to watch the Chinese bomb the hell outta the clouds. At least with him gone, Joe didn't have to hear the big man complain. Hoped the man finally got a chance to rack up the bonus money he craved.

Unlike the other missions, today's sparse cloud cover allowed them to follow the Michelin road. Perhaps today, they might see what the Chinese bombed.

"Bandits at two o'clock." George McMillan, the Hell's Angel assigned to lead the mission, announced over Joe's headset. Below, and on his right, three large tailed twin-engine bombers in a V formation appeared heading towards them.

"Form up on me," McMillan ordered over the radio. As Joe trailed Schilling in a dive on the bombers, the enemy formation banked. Now headed in the opposite direction, the Japanese increased their lead.

"Shit, they spotted us," Schilling growled over the airwaves.

Joe shoved the throttle in as far as it would go. Glanced down at the gauge, measuring manifold pressure. Increased it to the forty-pound maximum, but still, the bombers sped away. As Joe scanned his gauges to make sure this boost to maximum power didn't strain the engine, Schilling's plane pulled away, closing on their quarry. In fact, Schilling's plane raced ahead of the entire formation.

Once more, Joe checked his engine's gauges, wondering where Schilling got this extra speed boost. None of the others drew away from him, so Schilling must be doing something special to get this advantage. What? Joe had no idea.

Tracers zipped back from one bomber's tail gun. In response, Schilling swooped down away from the guns' arc, before lining up with the plane's unprotected belly. As a burst from Schilling's guns raked the bomber, smoke trailed from its left engine. Slowed, it dropped back from the rest. Schilling wove to pass it before firing at the lead plane in the formation, leaving the straggler to the P-40 swarms trailing him.

Without a clear shot at the straggler, Joe held his fire, while one Hell's Angel turned the damaged plane into a fireball. At the same moment, Schilling's gunfire tore the wing from the enemy's lead aircraft. The third banked to avoid Schilling, allowing another Hell's Angel to close within range. The P-40's tracers slammed into the Japanese bomber, shredding its tail. With its vertical stabilizer gone, it flipped over and plunged into the jungle below.

"Fun's over. Form up on me." McMillan called over the air.

After joining the Chinese bombers, they proceeded to Hanoi, where the Chinese bombers dropped their loads on several massed supply depots. Once they refueled at Mengtzu, they returned to Kunming. While the pilots claiming victories on the mission celebrated with barrel rolls over the field, Joe buzzed the hospital. Not for celebration, but to let Ann know he returned unharmed.

****

As the plane roared overhead, Ann rushed onto the cottage's porch. Unsure whether she might be visible to the pilot, she waved on the plane's second pass, sure Joe piloted the low-flying craft. With his smock draped over his arm, Dr. Ross joined her. "Think your young man might visit tonight?"

"Oh, I hope not. I don't have a thing to wear."

"What?"

"Not sure, but all my clothes aren't fitting right. Everything seems too tight and uncomfortable. Either they're shrinking in the laundry, or I'm gaining weight."

After years of living around females, Dr. Ross learned to avoid comments on women's weight gain. The wise man either needed to say nothing or dismiss the notion entirely. Possibly change the subject or go for the safe diversion.

While her increased appetite failed to worry him, this would not be the moment to mention it, so he sagely chose the latter alternative. "Probably the laundry. Noticed the same with my own clothes."

"The way I've been stuffing myself lately, I worried."

Dr. Ross cleared his throat. "Everything else all right? Any other changes?"

Ann yawned. "Not really. We've had a tough day, I'm bushed. If you don't mind, I'll head on up to bed now."

"But..."

"If you're hungry, I made sandwiches. They're in the icebox along with a nice salad, okay?"

After she ascended the stairs to her room, Dr. Ross called Rose at the hotel.

"I was just there yesterday, you needing groceries already or are you lonesome?"

He chuckled. "Neither, but it is always nice to hear your voice."

"Perhaps when I make the next delivery, we can send the kids to the movies again, eh?"

"Ann already commented that she'd seen that movie enough. We might need to come up with another excuse."

"I own this fine hotel. Perhaps instead you should come to town and let me take you to the pictures. What you say to that?"

"And leave my daughter here alone and unchaperoned? If the Morgans pulled one of their surprise inspections, what then?"

Rose cackled. "I merely make suggestions. You must work out details."

"You're correct. I haven't seen that movie yet. Perhaps we can see it one night when she has the late shift. That would appear appropriate even to the Morgans. But that's not the reason I called."

"Oh?"

He paused before continuing, hoping to avoid a lot of questions from this woman. "Yes, I need a rabbit."

"Rabbit? Not much meat. A goose would be better."

"It's not to eat."

"No? Then what you do with it?"

Unprepared for an inquisition, Dr. Ross's mind whirled as he pondered excuses for needing a live rabbit that might satisfy this woman's curiosity. Besides, a live rabbit hanging around would arouse Ann's too. "It's for the children. It would provide a superb source of entertainment. Get their minds off their discomfort. Any other animal might be too boisterous or aggressive. A rabbit would be ideal."

"If you are keeping it, you will need a hutch and food too. I have a farmer in mind who would help you."

"Excellent, once again, I am in your debt."

"I will bring the rabbit and its equipment with the regular grocery order on Friday. Perhaps after, you can take me to a picture show, eh?"

****

Finished with the debriefing, once he showered and changed, Joe headed to the officer's club. Alone at the bar, Schilling sat nursing a drink. He seldom talked to Schilling. The man's nearly legendary prowess as a former test pilot intimidated him. But after the day's mission, Joe's curiosity about Schilling's plane's performance got the better of him, so he settled onto the stool next to the man. Schilling acknowledged his presence with a nod, Joe broke the ice. "Did you have the X-plane today?"

"Nah, it's down for an overhaul."

"I had everything runnin' at max, and you pulled away."

Schilling set his glass on the bar. "Ran the boost to fifty."

"Fifty? Mines got a wire on it keepin' it from goin' past forty. They install it at the factory, so we don't blow the engine."

Schilling shrugged. "I cut the wire, first thing when I use one of the other ships."

"But..."

Schilling nudged him. "You know what you're doin' and what to watch for you can get away with it."

Schilling had grown used to testing the limits of the planes he flew as a former test pilot. Probably even more in tune with the plane's performance than most. He wouldn't need a lot of the devices that the manufacturer put in place to make the planes what they called "idiot-proof."

Joe shook his head. "Not all the guys know what you do. What about the next guy to use the plane?"

"I always tell the Crew chief to fix it when I get back."

"And they don't figure out you cut it?"

"When you're busy flyin' a lot of stuff breaks. They're probably pleased I tell 'em what might be wrong."

McMillan sauntered up to Schilling and clapped him on the back. "How in the hell did you manage to catch up with 'em?"

Schilling gave Joe a sideways glance before replying. "Mighta had a lighter fuel load or a tailwind. Happens sometimes."

Wow, Joe said to himself. He wondered why Schilling shared this with him and not the others. Did he now belong to some club of elites unknown to him? But then again, they flew in the same squadron, and Schilling probably knew of his friendship with Lamison. That might be the connection. Whatever the reason, he might need to hang around more with this squadron mate instead of Boyington. He'd surely be a better influence.

McMillan hoisted his glass in a salute. "I had Greenlaw credit you with not only the one you got but a piece of the others."

Schilling shrugged. "Thanks."

When Schilling said nothing more, McMillan strolled off to rejoin his fellow Hell's Angels in a corner.

Schilling turned to Joe. "As if that makes killin' any easier."

"God damn if it weren't for bad luck I'd have no luck at all." A familiar gruff voice called out behind them.

Both turned as Boyington waved for the bartender's attention.

Joe frowned. "Thought you were down in Rangoon, becomin' our first ace."

"Ace? More like ass."

Schilling chuckled. "What, the Japs surrender when they heard you might be in the neighborhood?"

Boyington scowled, then poked Joe. "See, I let you get mouthy with me, and the rest take liberties. I shoulda kicked your ass in Frisco when you deserved it."

Joe grinned. "Honest, Greg, whattaya doin' here?"

"We got to Rangoon, and there weren't enough ships for all the guys. So, we drew straws to see who stayed and who came back."

Joe chuckled. "Let me guess. You pulled the lucky straw."

He gave Joe's chest a gentle backhand tap. "Lucky. Damn, I need the dough. Then I get back here and find out you guys struck pay dirt on one a these Chinese missions." He turned, waved to the bartender. "Dammit, I need a drink. Wouldn't give ya nothin' on the flight up either. What a goddamn war."

Joe clapped Boyington on the back. "If it's any consolation. Word's out we move down there in a week."

****

As Dr. Ross placed groceries in the kitchen cupboards, Ann held the black and white rabbit up to her face. "It's darling, Dad."

At her side, Rose nodded. "She has a husband as well." Rose reached into the box and pulled a second. The older Chinese man at her side grinned. "I built a large hut, so when babies come, there will be lots of room."

Dr. Ross paused in his work. Turned to the man. "The rabbits pregnant?"

When the man nodded, he held his long stringy, gray beard to keep it from flapping like a flag in the breeze. "If that is more than you want, I will come back and take the babies away. They very popular. Taste good as chicken, but cleaner."

Ann nuzzled the rabbit, turned to her father. "The children will adore them." She turned to the old man. "Can I take this one out to the hospital now? The kids are waiting for supper, so they'll be rowdy right now. This little lady might distract them while we get it done."

The old man gave her a half-bow. "While you do that, I will finish setting up the hutch. Then I can show you how to take care of them. Where would you like me to place it?"

Rose turned to Ann. "You have vegetable garden, yes?"

Ann frowned as she stroked the animals head. "Yes, but wouldn't that be cruel to put them so close to something they can't have?"

"No, the hutch has an open mesh bottom, so their droppings fall to the ground. The hutch then stays clean."

Ann frowned. "Okay, but why the garden."

Dr. Ross shook his head. "I believe Rose is trying to tell you that allows the droppings to fertilize the vegetable garden."

Rose grinned. "That's right. You move it every few weeks to fresh spot, turn over droppings in old site, and have a fertile patch ready to plant."

Ann held the rabbit up to her face. "You hear that? For that much work, you should get a share of the harvest." She turned to Rose. "This one will be in bunny heaven. Lots of loving pets and fresh vegetables. I'll get you fat as me in no time."

Rose frowned gave Ann an appraising glance. "You? Fat?"

"Either I'm getting thicker, or the laundry is shrinking my stuff. I'm off Saturday, how about you and I go shopping?"

Rose turned to Dr. Ross. "Can your bank account cover such an excursion?"

Dr. Ross scoffed. "If you discount the scotch once in a while, I'm sure we can get by."

Rose turned back to Ann. "Then for sure. We have date."

As Ann carried the rabbit to the door, Rose called to her. "So, you know, your father is taking me to movie tonight."

Ann turned, cocked an eyebrow. "You haven't seen it yet?"

Dr. Ross shot a glance at Rose before replying. "Uh, no." He shrugged. "You know me. Just an old homebody."

She grinned. "Well, good for you. I'm dying to know what you think of it. I've seen it so many times, I feel like I can recite the heroine's dialect from memory." She turned to Rose. "Get him back at a respectable time, though. He has a clinic tomorrow."

After Ann left, Dr. Ross turned to Rose. "I'll show Mr. Chan here where to put the hutch, and then I'll join you in the car."

As he and Mr. Chan walked behind the hospital to the vegetable garden, thoughts swirled through his mind. These rabbits would not be suitable. How to explain to this man he needed one not pregnant for the test. Could the man arrange it without alerting Rose? His stomach churned. He needed to do this without drawing attention, but how?

CHAPTER TWENTY-NINE

RANGOON, BURMA

As he swooped down on the bomber formation, Newkirk's voice came over his headset. "Escorts comin' down, outta the sun. One pass and dive."

Instead of diving on through, Ed leveled off briefly to continue hammering the bomber in his sights. Stupid, he knew. Not only ignoring Newkirk's orders but also the training Chennault drummed into their heads in Toungoo. Dive in, shoot, and dive away. Never tangle with the agile Japanese fighters. But one more kill would make him an ace. Not only that but on his wedding day? Too much temptation.

With his target streaming smoke, he now pushed the p-40s nose down, sending it roaring earthward. Guess he expected too much. At least he damaged the bomber. But he pushed his luck. Time to get the hell outta here.

From the moment she agreed to his proposal, Ed felt invincible. He could do anything. He chuckled, recalling his fear when he asked her. How his knees trembled when she initially said nothing at his entreaty. Worst of all, he'd blurted it out in front of the others. Not only Sanda and that Englishman who owned the bungalow, but Frillman, Lamison, and that Chinaman that shadows Russ everywhere. What would they do if she refused? Life without her in it, he could not imagine. But add the humiliation of a public refusal?

Instead, a mischievous smile spread over her face. She tipped her head back, placed one hand on her hip, and shook her finger in her face. "I will, but I must have a ceremony."

His jaw dropped. He clutched her in a smothering embrace. A ceremony? Hell, he'd give her the damn world.

But now he had to get the groom back in one piece. Get his mind back in the game. As tracers zipped past his canopy, he glanced in his rear-view mirror. Shit, two fixed gear Japanese fighters set on his six. As one poured lead in Ed's direction, the second trailed in a weaving pattern ready to pounce if Ed changed course.

Out of altitude, he could not continue escaping in a dive. To give him a little time, he raised the ship's nose, bleeding off airspeed. The lead plane on his tail roared past, as Ed banked to face his trailing comrade. Unable to avoid Ed, the second attacker's propeller tore through his right wing, sending Ed's plane into a gyrating spiral towards the ground.

Without hesitation, he shoved back the canopy, undid his seat harness, and kicked out of the plane.

With a jerk that shook every bone in his body, the parachute opened. As he dangled beneath the vast white umbrella floating down, a Japanese fighter banked in his direction.

How did Jenson collapse his before to avoid getting strafed? As the Japanese opened fire, Ed tugged on one side's shrouds. "If that don't spill it, I'm fucked."

As the Japanese gun's chattered, he strained on the lines. Nothing, the damn thing stayed full. His leg jerked as a shell tore off his boot heel, and the Japanese passed overhead. Helpless, he followed the plane's path with his eyes. It spun around in a banking turn for a second pass. Again, he tugged at the shrouds, but no luck. Just a meager swing. Not enough to avoid the Japanese guns.

As the Japanese passed again from behind, he braced himself, preparing for the bullets to tear into his flesh. Instead, a few rounds from the enemy fighter struck the canopy. Not enough to speed his descent. Perhaps the damage might now let him collapse the parachute. Avoid the bullets. He tugged one set of shrouds again. Nothing.

Could he release the harness? Freefall the rest of the way? A glance down assured him he would wind up splattered like a bug on a windshield.

Like a giant bird of prey, the Japanese again turned in his direction. He mouthed a prayer as the Japanese's tracers reached out to him.

****

In the bungalow's bedroom, Thiri hummed and swayed in her wedding gown. Seated on a nearby bed, with her glasses perched on the end of her nose, a gray-haired lady from the house next door pawed through the jewelry box on her lap. As she held a strand of black pearls to the light, she squinted as she peered at them before handing them to Thiri. "These might prove suitable." The woman's Highland brogue rolled off her tongue.

Thiri beamed as she clasped them around her neck, then turned to the full-length mirror. "They are exquisite, Mrs. Thornton."

"But are ya sure, lass? When we put together that gown, ya wanted no black in it."

Thiri nodded. "True. Black is a somber color, and this is a festive occasion. But look at how they sparkle and shine, like stars in a dark night. They shouldn't dampen the mood."

Mrs. Thornton fumbled again inside the box before holding up a sparkling brooch. Thiri gasped. "That's gorgeous."

"We can use it as a clasp to keep that thing from falling offa ya. That gown hugs your curves nicely, but I worry that off the shoulder thing might part. Then where would we be, eh? Enough of ya is showin' to make the other women envious, and the men wish they'd seen ya first. More than that might appear unseemly."

Sanda perched on a chair nearby, her cast propped up on a footstool, nodded. "You look like a sparkly flower."

Mrs. Thornton placed her finger to her chin as she studied Thiri, then again rummaged in the jewelry box. "Earrings next. Since ya don't have piercings that presents a bit of a conundrum." With a grin, she held up a pair of diamond pendants. "Present from my first husband on our twentieth anniversary will go nicely with the brooch and the tiara."

Thiri frowned. "Tiara?"

"You said the Buddhist bride wears lots of colors and jewels. We need ta hang `em all over ya."

Mrs. Thornton set the jewelry box aside and rose. "Let me see. Now, where did I put that box."

Inside her closet, she shuffled through boxes on a shelf above the hangars. She pulled one down, peered inside, grinned, before replacing the lid and returned it. "Humph, not that. Hardly suitable for a nuptial."

Bishop entered, trailed by the Great Dane. He paused, removed his pipe while giving Thiri an appraising glance. "That young man don't get here soon I might make a pitch for you myself."

As Thiri spread her arms, she smiled. "This is all so wonderful. Thank you both so much."

Mrs. Thornton came out of the closet, peered down her nose at Bishop. "When Stanley told me this morning, I knew we had to do this up right. Not been anything worth celebrating here for months."

As if conducting an orchestra, Bishop gestured with his pipe. "I figured Lottie here would do you up proper."

Mrs. Thornton turned to Thiri. "What's this young man of yours like?"

As the dog nuzzled Sanda, she scratched behind his ear, grinned. "He's a prince."

Mrs. Thornton's eyebrows rose. "He's not a Yank?"

Thiri giggled. "He's my prince."

"Not handsome, but Thiri says he's adequate."

Sanda's statement elicited a puzzled frown from Mrs. Thornton. "Well, I hope he has better manners than the ones stayin' with me."

Thiri chuckled. "He is learning. Almost civilized."

Mrs. Thornton gave a dismissive wave. "No matter how princely they seem before the wedding, they all turn back into frogs once the honeymoon's over."

Stanley cocked his head. "That chap that arrived with him and his friends last night, chaplain, is he?"

Thiri nodded.

"He officiatin' this thing?"

"I believe so. He said he might try to bring a monk from a temple in town." Thiri paused, stared off. "I only wish my father could be here."

Stanley frowned. "He lives in the outback, right?"

"Yes, it is a small village. And the nearest phone is in a village a half-day walk away."

"What about that young Burmese chap who brought you to my place? Could he tell your pop?"

Thiri shook her head. "They left right after they delivered us here. At least he will tell my father I am safe and going to Kunming. That will have to be enough for now."

As Bishop pulled his pocket watch from his pocket, a plane roared overhead. "I figured it to be about time for `em to show up."

Two more planes in succession now roared overhead. "We better shake a leg if everything is going to be ready."

As Mrs. Thornton returned to the closet, she called over her shoulder. "Give me a minute. I know that tiara is here. Won't take a moment."

Bishop frowned. "Tiara?" Wide-eyed, he turned to Thiri. "I must say, she's sparkling enough there, old girl. Sure we need it?"

Mrs. Thornton returned, cradling an enameled wooden box, grinning. After setting it on the table, she raised the lid. With a flourish, she hoisted the jeweled crown, before placing it on Thiri's head. It immediately slipped down over her eyes. Mrs. Thornton stepped back, her hand to her mouth. "Oh, dear. You are a tiny little thing. But don't worry." She slipped it off Thiri, peered at it down her nose, then twisted it slightly. Now it set perfectly on Thiri. "There that should do nicely."

****

After the mission, Jenson leaned against Newkirk's desk in the alert shack. "No one saw Burton after the attack?"

Newkirk shook his head, walked to the chalkboard, where they listed planes and duty assignments. Stared at it, as if this might somehow conjure up their missing plane and pilot. "He was on Tex's wing on the pass. Tex said even though I told everyone to do one pass and dive through, Burton leveled off after a bomber."

Jenson scowled. "He what?"

"Went after one."

"Shit, I dove straight through, mighta got a piece a one, and even then, their fighters were all over my ass."

Newkirk turned from the chalkboard. "Anti-aircraft battery said one of our guys mighta gone in around that time, North of town. Said he collided with a Jap, but nothin' more."

"The Brits came in right behind us. Figured with the escorts bustin' our asses they could take on the bombers without problems. One a their guys chased a Jap off my tail, or he mighta flamed my butt."

Newkirk nodded. "The AA guys get us and the Hurricanes mixed up. Coulda been one of their guys." He walked to the desk, picked up the phone. "I'll give 'em a holler, find out if they know anything."

"What a fuckin' mess. Who's gonna tell her?"

With the phone to his ear, Newkirk gave Jenson a puzzled frown. "Oh yeah, his wife." Newkirk held the phone up to his mouth. "Newkirk here, listen one of our guys is missin' from that afternoon scramble. Any of your guys see anything?"

He glanced at Jenson as he listened. "Well, thanks, let us know if he turns up, and I'll check with our guys."

Newkirk shook his head as he replaced the phone in its cradle. "None of their guys mentioned seein' a downed P-40, but he'll double-check. I guess they've got one missing too."

"But what about his wife?"

Newkirk shook his head. His face a grim mask. "Tell Frillman. That's his job."

"But I've gotta head out to the same dispersal strip. He's billeted right next door."

Newkirk shrugged. "You guys are at Seagram, right?"

"Yep."

"Like I said, unless you wanna do the honors, tell Frillman. He's got that new slick car. He can drive out there and get the job done. But make sure he tells her he's missing. We have nothing more, but we'll keep her informed."

Jenson hung his head. "What a shitty deal."

"It's what war is. One shitty deal. If he's bought the farm, at least they had a week of married bliss. More'n most get nowadays." Newkirk glanced at his watch. "We better get goin'. No lights out on those fields, so unless you wanna find your field in the dark, we gotta get rollin'."

As Jenson slogged to his plane, his heart sank. To cover for Ed, they kept this ceremony away from Newkirk. What could he say? Frillman would already be out at the bungalow near Seagram along with the others preparing to celebrate their friend's wedding. Now instead of attending a party, he might be headed to a wake. Shitty deal? Understatement of the Century.

****

As the sun sank low on the horizon, they parked Frillman's Buick before the bungalow's stairway. After opening the car's trunk, Russ lifted out the Champaign crate. "Do they do a lotta drinkin' at Buddhist weddings?"

The bald young man draped in a yellow robe standing beside Frillman smiled. "Only if it brings you closer to harmony and the Buddha."

Russ smiled as he set the crate on the trunk's edge. "That's why you're here, right? To sanctify the wedding?"

The monk shrugged. "Marriage, to us, is not a sacrament. Merely a secular arrangement. I might bless the couple if they wish." The monk turned to Frillman. "As I understood, you have the authority in that regard."

Frillman nodded. "Gee, I guess that means I've got the buck."

The monk frowned. "The buck?"

"It's a term that comes from card games."

The monk's brow furrowed. "I have seen the Europeans play with cardboard; they call cards. Is that what you mean?"

"Yeah, that's it. One game's poker. When guys played in the old West."

"You mean cowboys?"

"You know about cowboys?"

The monk nodded. "Before I took my vows, I saw movies with cowboys. Bad guys wore black hats, and good guys white. Easy to find out who to avoid. But what about this buck?"

"When cowboys played cards to keep track of the deal, they passed around a knife. Whoever had the deal would stick it in the table nearby, then when their turn ended, they'd pass it to the next guy. Prevented fighting."

"That is always a good thing." A grin played on the monk's lips. "So, it means you are dealing here tonight."

"Exactly."

Russ hoisted the crate. "If the lesson's done for the night, how about grabbin' the suit we got for Ed, padre? Ang Su's got the food scrounged up." He nodded to the monk. "Anything special we need from your end?"

The monk frowned. "End?"

Russ rolled his eyes. "Sorry, I meant from you and your beliefs."

"Nothing really. As I said, I must bless the couple if they desire."

As they trudged up the stairs, Bishop met them on the bungalow's porch. When he spotted the Champaign case, his eyebrows rose. "I should have mentioned I have a well-stocked wine cellar. Not sure we need much more."

With the suit draped over his shoulder, Frillman nodded to the man. "Nice of ya, but since we're celebrating for our friend, we felt we needed to contribute." He nodded to Ang Su, clutching a basket. "Also brought some local delicacies. Help soak up the celebratory libations."

After lugging their items inside, Russ scanned the room. "Where's the bride?"

Bishop grinned. "Next door, finishing her preparations. Believe she plans a dramatic entrance."

Frillman held the suit up. "Groom not here yet?"

Bishop shook his head, "Four planes flew in a short while ago. Two more due. They usually wait until all return before ferrying them over to the billets. In the meantime, can I interest you, gentlemen, in something from the bar?"

As Russ lugged the crate to the bar, Ang Su set the food basket beside it.

Frillman scanned the room. "Got someplace I can hang this suit up? Had it pressed. Shame for it to get wrinkled before he puts it on."

"There's a closet through there, plenty of space." As a plane roared overhead, Bishop glanced up. "There's another. With the sun going down, the other should be along shortly. Field here isn't lighted." He stepped behind the bar. "So, what'll it be gents?"

Russ glanced at Ang Su. When he nodded, Russ turned back to Bishop. "Ang Su, and I'll pass, think I need to stretch my legs, though."

As he exited, Ang Su trailed him out the door. After Frillman returned, he moved to the bar, while Bishop filled a tumbler with an amber liquid. "I'm havin' a scotch. Do either of you imbibe? If not, I can make tea."

Frillman smiled. "Scotch is fine with me."

The monk gave a slight bow. "If it is not too much trouble, tea will be welcome."

Outside in the dark, Russ and Ang Su stepped behind shrubs bordering the bungalow. From inside his shirt, Ang Su retrieved his opium pipe. After charging it, Russ handed him his lighter. Once Ang Su lit it and took a puff, he passed it to Russ.

"Except for a beer with us on occasion, I have never seen you drink liquor."

Russ nodded as he exhaled. "Dad was a drunk. He got liquored up one night and killed himself and my mother in a car wreck."

"Cars are dangerous. Operating one under the influence would be deadly." After taking a puff, Ang Su returned the pipe to Russ.

Russ hoisted the pipe as if saluting. "Heard somewhere that alcoholism runs in families, like hair and eye color, so I make a point of avoidin' it."

"That sounds wise." Ang Su toked once more before passing the pipe back to Russ.

The sound of a vehicle pulling up to the bungalow prompted them to extinguish the pipe. As they emerged from behind the bush, Jenson stepped out of the Jeep. Paused at the stairs base, Jenson gazed up at the bungalow's lights. as the Jeep pulled away. He turned as Ang Su and Russ joined him at the stairs base. Puzzled Russ gazed after the Jeep before turning to Jenson. "Where's Ed?"

Jenson hung his head. "Ed's missing. Is the padre here?"

Russ nodded.

Jenson doffed his Stetson, ran his fingers through his hair. Turned back to the house. "Good."

CHAPTER THIRTY

KUNMING, CHINA

As Ann trailed her father's pacing with her eyes, she chewed her lip to stifle a smile. "If you're looking for the cornflakes, I moved the box to the pantry where the mice can't get to it."

"Not really hungry this morning. Thought I'd have a coffee, then head on over for the clinic."

He glanced in her direction as she struggled to keep from grinning. "What?"

"Enjoy the movie?"

"Spellbinding. Must see it again."

Struggling to keep a straight face she turned away. "I thought you would like it. You enjoyed *Beau Geste*. Figured you might enjoy another movie about the Foreign Legion."

Dr. Ross paused, turned towards her. "True, but I liked that movie because of Gary Cooper. Splendid actor. Would have liked to see that other one he was in when it came through before you arrived but couldn't get away, with the daily bombings too much work."

"*Sergeant York?*"

"Uh, yes, exactly. But this *Blood and Sand* thing. With what's his name?"

"Tyrone Power?"

"Yes, him. I understand the girls all love him, but he doesn't hold a candle to Cooper. But some might consider a movie about the French Foreign Legion a treat, fascinating bunch."

"So, you didn't care for it?"

Dr. Ross frowned. "No, I intend to go again. But I still prefer Gary Cooper." He filled a mug with coffee. "Walk-in clinic is about to start. Love to chat more about the movie, but I need to get going."

As Dr. Ross descended the porch steps, he made a note to himself. True, before he and Rose left, Ann said she wanted to talk to him about the movie. Perhaps they should have at least gone by the theater before heading to Rose's hotel. Checked on the pictures they post outside showing scenes from the movie. Given him a rough idea about the plot, at least. But for now, he navigated safely through her initial inquisition. Needed to call Rose later, check with her about the movie. Since she lived in the city, she must have gone herself.

But for now, he had other plots to hatch. Mr. Chan promised to bring the un-bred doe later today, along with a second hutch to prevent her untimely compromise.

He needed to find a plausible reason for the additional livestock. Something to keep Ann's inquisitive mind at bay. Then came the second part. How to get a urine sample from her for the test?

Doubts now crept into his mind. Like an angel sat on one shoulder whispering in his ear, while a devil perched on the opposite side making its case. Was he being too sensitive to this? Why not just level with her? Share his concerns. Talk with her as an adult about the situation. She might take precautions, or perhaps her relationship with Joe had not yet progressed to intimacy.

The demon on the opposite side kicked him. "That's stupid, it hissed. Only a fool would believe such a thing. They sneak off like newlyweds, and you know it."

On the other hand, if he set her down, shared his thoughts and concerns that might drive a wedge between them. Granted, she always favored him. His shadow since her first step, hanging around his clinic in the evenings. Claimed she merely wanted to play with the children while he worked with their mothers.

They separated so many years ago when he fled here. Had only begun to re-establish their relationship. Should he risk that because of his worries?

Not for one minute. For now, he must stick to the plan. Run the test discreetly. Once he had the results, perhaps his mind would be at rest. Move past this. Let them get on with their work.

He almost pictured the demon on his shoulder, leaning close. Whispering "or not."

****

Olga snatched the radiogram from Chennault's grasp. As she studied it, a smile crept over her face. "General?"

Chennault nodded. "Brigadier."

"How many stars is that?"

"One."

She tossed her head back. "Does that make Harvey a full Colonel?"

Chennault cleared his throat. "They've not mentioned specifics in that yet."

He had not discussed the full induction process with anyone, including his adjutant. Not mentioned MacGruder's recommendation to replace the current administrative staff with regular Army officers. Since it had been a recommendation instead of a fact, he kept it to himself. Knew the induction would prompt a mutiny among the rest of the men. He didn't need that turmoil coupled with the desperate battle they faced in Rangoon. Not only with the Japanese, but the British command, too.

She held out the radiogram. "Who is this Bissell character? You know him?"

"He was junior to me before my retirement."

She waved the message in the air. "But it says here he will take overall command of the air arm here in China. He'd be your boss?"

Chennault nodded. "We both worked in the war college. He had this idea that fighters should drop balls and chains on bombers instead of shooting."

"What?"

"The head of the Air Corps, Hap Arnold, favored him. Part of the reason I left."

"But why?"

Chennault winced as the questions persisted. "Stillwell believes we might get more cooperation from the Army if a regular is in charge."

"They don't trust us?"

"No, me. I quit and came to China. We built the ground observer network and this unit without their help. Figure I'm some kinda maverick. The military frowns on loose cannons."

She placed her hand on his shoulder. "You've done all those things, and the men all swear by you."

He shook his head. "This keeps up they'll swear at me instead."

****

With a frown, Ann slid the dresses across the rack as she checked labels. "I have put on weight. It's not the laundry."

Rose shrugged, shook her head. "You were already too skinny. Not healthy. Plus, men like more cushion when they ride."

Ann's scowl prompted Rose to giggle. "It's no laughing matter. I've always maintained a healthy weight."

"Perhaps you might cut back on the noodles."

Ann stepped back, placed her hands on her hips. "Go on a diet?"

"As we get older, things change."

"Doesn't slow you down much."

"I am a woman supporting myself. That takes much work."

Ann threw back her head and laughed. "That's not what I meant."

"Oh?"

"I heard all about the movie you and Dad saw the other night."

"Yes, even though I saw it before, sharing it with your father brought new joy."

Ann rolled her eyes. "Yes, dad told me all about it."

Rose's eyes opened wide. "He enjoyed it as well?"

"Since he saw *Beau Geste*, he's been quite fond of Foreign Legion tales. Even has some books on it. But he said it wasn't as good as *Beau Geste*."

"Foreign Legion? What has that got to do with *Blood and Sand*? That is about bullfighting."

Ann smirked. "Perhaps he didn't watch it as close as most people. Might suggest he get glasses."

Rose blushed, sorted through a nearby dress rack, feigning disinterest. "Perhaps he dozed in parts. He seemed tired. I thought he liked it."

212

"Anyway, have you noticed Dad acting differently?"

"Different? In what way?"

Ann selected a dress from the rack, stepped up to the mirror, and held it up before her. "What do you think?"

Rose glanced over. "Nice color. But have I noticed anything different about your father?"

"Maybe it's me, but I catch him watching me a lot."

"Watching?"

"Yes, I'll be busy with something, and turn around. There he is staring like he's studying me. When I notice he turns away like he's doing something he's ashamed of."

"He's your father. Has not seen you for many years. It would be unnatural if he ignored you."

Ann selected a second dress from the rack, held it up. "How about this?"

Rose wrinkled her nose. "Not good color for you. Try the peach one beside it. Make your eyes bluer."

"What about the thing with the rabbits?"

"Having them for the children to pet is a wonderful idea. Plus, they will give you a healthy garden."

"But, they brought two more."

Rose shrugged. "Perhaps he goes into business with Chan."

"Chan?"

"Yes. The rabbit broker. He always looking for places to put more hutches. His yard is nearly full. You get more fertilizer. Chan gets an additional hutch making rabbits for him to sell. Perhaps I should discuss this with Chan myself. Increasing cash flow always a good thing."

"Humph. You're probably right. After I try these on, let's go grab a snack. I'm starving."

"Humph. You do eat more. Maybe you got bun in oven."

"What?"

Rose nodded. "Baby on way."

"But..." Ann's mind raced back to New Years'. Both she and Joe had drunk too much. Had literally ripped each other's clothes off. That night they failed to use a condom. But that couldn't be it. She shouldn't have been fertile then. Didn't fit her menstrual cycle. Should have been safe regardless. She turned to Rose. "Don't be silly. It's probably all this stress with the Morgans." That had to be it. Worry and stress also interfere with the menstrual cycle. That would also explain the late period, she said to herself. A week late often nothing unusual.

"She took Rose's arm. "Like you said. I'll skip the noodles. Stick to protein and vegetables."

****

The next morning, Dr. Ross moved his stethoscope across the young girl's bare stomach. With his breath held, he stared off while listening. As he slid the scope lower, the young girl flinched, uncomfortable with his hand's presence so near to her private areas. He remained in place, again holding his breath, intent on discovering the faint rhythm showing life inside her womb.

The older Chinese woman at his side smoothed the girl's hair back from her forehead. "Lie still. He is seeking the child." She turned to Dr. Ross, who silently maintained his scope's position on the young woman's belly.

As he leaned back, he turned to the older woman. "I believe I hear it, but I need one more test to confirm." He gave the girl a smile. "You may close your gown now. If you both excuse me, I need help with the rest of the procedure."

After stepping outside the curtained examination area, he strode to where Ann put medical instruments in a cupboard. "I need your help with one of my female patients. A test."

She frowned. "And you can't explain it to her?"

"Uh. It's complicated. My Cantonese is not the best."

She chuckled. "How did you manage before I arrived?"

"Not as well."

"Let me finish putting these away while they're still sterile. She's where you just came from?"

After nodding, he squeezed her shoulder before returning to his patient. Inside the examination room, he pulled down two sample cups from the supply cabinet. The patient and her mother, silent, trailing him with their eyes. "My daughter is coming in shortly. She'll accompany your daughter to a more private area where she can finish the examination."

As Ann entered, both women greeted her with a half bow. After returning their greeting she turned to her father. "What do you need, dad?"

"I need a urine sample from her for a pregnancy test. I thought if you could take her to the lavatory. Perhaps show her what we need."

"How?"

"By providing one yourself."

She chuckled. "Now it makes sense. Not something you could do yourself. Pfft. Language barrier."

After taking the sample jars from the counter, she beckoned the girl to follow her.

Dr. Ross trailed them with his eyes. With luck, he would soon have the answer to the conflict he wrestled with. Did he really want to know? And what would he do when he got the result?"

CHAPTER THIRTY-ONE

RANGOON, BURMA

Silent, Thiri sat on the bungalow's porch as the sun rose, staring off at the horizon. Still dressed in her wedding gown, the only jewel remaining the brooch at her shoulder. Seated at her side, Frillman said nothing. Merely studied her profile.

When they told her about Ed, she collapsed into this chair. Said nothing, just gazed off, like now, as if searching for Ed in the distance. After the others left or retired, Frillman remained. Uncertain what to do or say, hoping his presence alone provided the comfort she needed right now.

The only time he had notified anyone about a loved one's demise had been Russ. At the time, he had Olga at his side, and she supported both himself and Russ. What more to do, he didn't know. The strange girl with the broken leg had at least cried. Mrs. Thornton now sat with her in her bedroom. But what about Thiri? What could he do?

The other planes stationed at this airfield took off right before dawn. Before take-off, Jenson stopped, asked about news, then assured her he would call if he heard anything more once he got to Mingaladon.

Thiri said nothing. Just stared off as Jenson spoke, lost in her own private world. That had been over an hour ago. No word came from the airbase, so they knew nothing more at this point.

The aroma of coffee brewing drifted out the bungalow's door. Soon Bishop appeared with two steaming mugs. After handing one to Frillman, he placed his hand on Thiri's shoulder. "Here, dearie, I'm makin' some eggs. Ya need ta eat. Keep up your strength. He wouldn't wanna see ya wastin' away. Any news?"

Silent, Thiri shook her head. Her first movement since planting herself in that chair. Bishop squeezed her shoulder. "He'll turn up. You'll see. Any man lucky enough to snare a lovely like you's got all the luck in the world. He'll be along soon, and we can get on with the weddin'."

With the steaming mug clutched in one hand, she patted his hand, never taking her eyes off the horizon.

Frillman placed his hand on hers. "Mr. Bishop is right. We had a guy shot down the other day. Only way we knew he was all right was when he called from a train station. Plus, we had no way to get him. Took two days for him to get back by train. Probably the same for Ed."

Her lip quivered. A tear rolled down her cheek, which she wiped away with her sleeve. "I will see him again."

On crutches, Sanda appeared in the doorway. After hobbling to an empty chair next to Frillman, she settled in it. Her eyes rolled up, a smile crept over her face. "Carl says the prince will be back soon."

Frillman bolted upright in his chair, gave her a curious frown. Thiri turned to her. "Carl's back?"

Sanda nodded. "He says with all the friends around me, he can go elsewhere once in a while."

Frillman glanced around. "Did someone else come?"

Sanda shook her head. "You can't see him. He only talks to me. He said you are a good man."

The telephone ringing inside prompted them all to turn. As he answered the phone, Bishop murmured to the caller. After ending the call, he appeared at the door. His jaw set, his eyes on Thiri. She turned to him.

"That was that young Lamison chap. They found Ed's plane, about ten miles from here."

"Anything else?" Frillman asked, his eyes locked on Thiri.

"That's it. No sign of him, but they're still searching."

Thiri said nothing. Returned to her vigil, studying the horizon as if her eyes could pierce the jungle surrounding the clearing across the road.

A cart drawn by a water buffalo and led by a thin man emerged from the trees on the clearing's opposite side. As the black pajama-clad man drove the buffalo along the road, a slight breeze puffed up white fabric piled in the cart. Thiri leaned forward, her eyes narrowed as she tracked the cart's progress. As she visored her eyes with her hand, a head rose from the cart's back. She stood, shuffled down the porch stairs. Followed the path to the road where she continued watching the approaching wagon.

Frillman stood. "What is it?"

Bishop shrugged. "One a the honey bucket collectors. Come around once in a while and scoop out the loo."

"The loo?"

"Guess you Yanks call 'em toilets. The locals prize our cesspool contents."

"What's he got in the back?"

"Hard tellin' the guys collect a lotta stuff in their travels. Whatever it is, looks like he's got one a his kids ridin' in back to weigh it down."

As the cart neared, the cart's passenger rolled out of the back and limped towards the bungalow. Thiri rushed to him, and they embraced.

Bishop's jaw dropped. "I'll be damned." He scurried after Frillman, who rushed to the pair locked together near the grinning man at the cart. With tears streaming down her cheeks, she smiled. "You're limping, are you hurt?"

"Nah, Jap shot off my boot heel."

Still clutching Thiri to his chest, Ed nodded to the cart. "I need help with him."

Frillman and Bishop stared inside the cart. "He's dead. Who is he?"

"His papers say he's Flight Officer Riley Evans."

"But..."

Ed shook his head. "Man saved my life. I couldn't just leave him."

****

Barefoot, with a burgundy, terry-cloth robe draped around him, Ed stepped into the bungalow's living room, still toweling his wet hair. The British officer, leaning against the bar, set down his drink. "Flying officer Burton, is it?"

Ed stopped toweling, cocked his head. "We don't have ranks beside squadron leader in our outfit. Was a Lieutenant Junior Grade in the Navy before I joined the outfit."

The officer adjusted his Sam Brown belt, cleared his throat. "On behalf of His Majesty's government, I want to thank you for retrieving Flight Officer Evans' body."

"Man was a hero. Couldn't just leave him for the scavengers."

"Well, we should consider all who serve heroes. The ones who give their lives, more so."

"Not this guy. Because a him I'm standin' here. He didn't have to do what he did, and it cost him his life."

The officer cocked an eyebrow. "Yes?"

"We got jumped by a swarm of Nates. I collided with one. Had to bail out. While I floated down, one decided to plug me. But Evans dove in and took him out. Stayed with me till I landed."

"I see."

"There's more."

"Go on."

"By the time I landed, the Japs regrouped and swarmed him. Musta been at least a half dozen. He got two, but didn't stand a chance." Ed strolled to the bar, poured a drink, stared off. "When his plane caught fire, he hit the silk. Of course, the Japs machined gunned him on the way down."

The officer threw back his shoulders. "I see. So, he gave his life to save yours."

"About the size of it."

"I will share that with command. I'm sure this story will comfort his next of kin."

At that moment, Bishop entered carrying a pair of riding boots.

Ed tossed back his drink. "No, he deserves more. Recognition. A medal." He turned to Bishop. "What's the big jackpot decoration in the British Military?"

"Victoria Cross."

Ed nodded to the officer. "Yeah, that one."

"Certainly, I will share your feelings with my superiors. While the actions you describe sounds heroic, we call our people upon daily to go above and beyond. Its award will rest with them."

As Ed poured a second drink, he nodded to Bishop. "Stanley here's a journalist. I told him the story."

The officer turned to Bishop, scowled. "All his dispatches must go through our network."

"Not necessarily. See, our main headquarters up in Kunming is crawlin' with reporters huntin' grand stories. Stan already sent it up through our channels. Boys up there jumped all over it. I suggest your people oughta get out in front of it before it rolls over 'em."

The officer's brow furrowed. "Humph. I will share that as well. If there's nothing else?"

"Yeah, there's more. I wanna notify his next of kin personally. Tell them how their loved one died."

"I will send those details on to your command as soon as I have them."

Ed thrust back his shoulders. "Also, if you plan to hold a service for him, let me know. That's it."

The officer set his empty glass on the table, donned his peaked cap, and marched out.

After the officer left, Bishop held out the boots. "Removed the spurs, they should fit."

As Ed took the boots, he shook his head. "You think that guy'll get Evans a medal?"

"That story about informing Kunming might leverage it. Pity we can't get it done."

Ed shrugged as he slipped the boots on. "I'm countin' on the unit's loose cannon image to get the job done." He stood. "Little loose, but an extra pair of socks, and they'll be perfect."

"Not sure they can mend your flight boot."

****

Jenson shook his head as Ed described his bailout. "Do you think that guy'll get him a medal?"

"Newkirk claims Churchill is really pleased with the AVG. Compared us with the guys that flew in the Battle of Britain."

"How would that help?"

"The Brits are gettin' their asses handed to 'em all over Southeast Asia. What Evans did might get 'em some decent press from here for a change."

"But you bluffed that officer when you said you sent the story to Kunming."

Ed shrugged. "It was a bluff then, but Newkirk liked it so much he passed it on to the old man. Guess he's gettin' interviewed by some guy from the London paper tomorrow."

"What about the old guy with the cart?"

"Met him on the road. He comes on me cartin' Evans over my shoulder draggin' that damn chute. He asked me for it, so I offered it to him if he brought us here."

Bishop joined them, hoisted his glass. "Plus, I allowed him to have the contents from my cesspool. He seemed pleased with the entire arrangement."

He turned to Ed. "Is the groom all set?"

Ed hoisted his glass. "I guess so. After the last two days, this should be a piece of cake."

Bishop shook his head. "As a man who has been to the altar on three occasions, I need to warn you. The challenge of marriage begins after the ceremony, not before."

****

With Jenson playing the *Wedding March* on a kazoo, Thiri entered the bungalow's front door on Bishop's arm. Frillman, with the monk at his side, stood at the back of the room before the fireplace. A log smoldered in the hearth, and while smoke rose from incense sticks in a jar on the mantle.

With Russ and Ed standing to one side of the two clerics, both trailed Thiri with their eyes as she entered. As Mrs. Thornton stood beside Sanda seated on the couch, she dabbed tears from her eyes. She leaned down to Sanda. "She's gorgeous."

Sanda nodded. "Sparkly. The prince looks handsome too."

When the procession made its way to the hearth, Jenson set the kazoo aside to stand beside Russ.

Frillman held out his hand. "Who gives this woman to this man?"

Bishop patted Thiri's hand. "She informed me nobody gives her away, but herself."

Frillman's eyebrows rose. "Is this all okay then with you?"

Thiri gave Ed a sideways glance. A mischievous grin played at her lips. "I believe him to be adequate, but only time will tell. So yes."

Frillman turned to Ed. "Since we're improvising here. How about you?"

Ed retrieved a sheet of paper from his suit coat pocket. Thiri smiled as he passed them to Frillman. "While they raised me in the Friends Church, I don't follow all their strictures. But in honor of my parents and with Thiri's approval, we would like to use these vows."

After unfolding the sheet, Frillman peered at the sheet. Shrugged. "Okay, here goes."

He turned to Thiri. "Repeat after me. In the presence of God and these our friends, I take thee, Ed, to be my husband."

Once Thiri repeated the words, Frillman continued. "Promising with Divine assistance to be unto thee a loving and faithful wife so long as we both shall live."

Once Thiri finished her vow, Frillman turned to Ed. "In the presence of God and these our friends, I take thee, Thiri, to be my wife."

After Ed recited his part, Frillman continued. "Promising with Divine assistance to be unto thee a loving and faithful husband so long as we both shall live."

When Ed finished, Frillman turned to the couple. "At weddings in our country, it is customary for the couple to kiss. Is that what you two want?"

In answer to Frillman, Ed swept her up in an embrace. As their lips met, the others gathered around, applauded.

FROM THE AUTHOR

I hope you enjoyed this story as much as I did bringing it to you. Authors live and die by reviews. If you liked it please leave a review online. It might guide someone else to this same pleasurable experience. To discover when the next book in the series is due out follow me on Facebook or Twitter. You can also get updates and find other books I've written on my website at: https://richardpowellauthor.com/

On the website you will also find links taking you to the historical roots of the series.

Also, you may email me through the contact tab on the website. I love hearing from readers and personally answer my email. As an added bonus I am including here the opening chapters of another work of mine from a different series. It's historical fiction set in Post War Europe. If you enjoy espionage conspiracies this might be for you. Turn the page to begin enjoying it.

PACT WITH THE DEVIL

CHAPTER ONE

MAUTHAUSEN, AUSTRIA MAY 1945

An ideal spot for an ambush, Captain James Ross thought as he shifted in his seat. The main highway packed with surrendering German soldiers fleeing the oncoming Russians clogged up the road. Prevented his column from speeding to their destination. But since turning onto this side road, they encountered no one. No one rushing to abandon their target. Perhaps, like other fanatics, the waiting garrison intended to fight to the death as ordered by their Fuhrer. Or did they lie in wait along this road waiting to deal out death to any who ventured near?

With the mass surrenders, they encountered little resistance in the last few days. Had he been foolish for leaving the offered armor behind? Too caught up in the need to press on with this mission of mercy? Instead of eating dust behind a half truck with a mounted fifty cal., he led this column in an open Jeep. Despite his stupidity he survived until now. His hand tightened around his carbine His eyes strained to pierce the surrounding foliage. Could his luck hold?

The towering pines lining the road obscured the surrounding country. As his Jeep sped down the dirt road, the only view of the horizon came from ahead. Going up hills, they saw only sky. If trees blocked the way, a curve would be ahead.

Overhead branches provided alternating sunlight and shadow, like a tunnel with a damaged roof. The alternating brightness and darkness prevented the soldier's eyes from adjusting to the light.

A rut in the road bounced the Jeep. Ross turned to make sure his passengers had not been tossed out. Not that he cared for either man. The older man, wearing a brown three-piece suit, sat hunched, holding his hat, preventing the wind from blowing it away. The other, chained and handcuffed, sneered at him with contempt. He sat ramrod straight, appearing almost proud despite his flowery gown.

As the Jeep slowed, approaching a curve, a rifle volley roared ahead. The Jeep slid on the dust-covered road as the driver slammed on the brakes, forcing the ambulance behind to swerve, stopping only inches from a collision. Ross leaped from the vehicle. Once on the ground, he rolled into the roadside ditch.

"Cover the flanks!" he shouted as he crawled forward, hugging the ground. "Harrison, take the left! Johnson, Forney, follow me!"

After retrieving the small metal mirror from his shirt pocket, Ross eased it above the ditch's rim. On his side, he slowly turned the mirror, viewing the tree-lined road. If a sniper spotted the mirror, he sacrificed his hand instead of his head. The only sound the detachment's vehicles idling on the road.

No obvious danger in the mirror. No telltale flashes of metal from the trees or gun barrels protruding from the brush. Ross expected Sergeant Harrison on the opposite side of the road, also scanned the surrounding plant growth. Except he would use his gunsight in case a sniper exposed himself or fired at Ross's mirror.

"All clear this side!" Harrison called from the road's opposite side.

After rolling out of the ditch, Ross slithered into the roadside cover. Inside, a path paralleled the road. His move triggered no gunfire. As he crept forward, he scanned the nearby woods. The bush behind him thrashed, alerted he turned, preparing to fire. He lowered his carbine as Forney and Johnson emerged from the shadows. Both also peered into the forest to the right as they approached Ross. As they joined him, they dropped to their knees. One removed his helmet to wipe his brow while the other continued scanning the nearby trees. Ross tapped his chest with his index finger, then pointed down the path ahead. While inching forward in a crouch, he led them forward.

Brightness ahead suggested they approached an open area. Stopped at the clearing's edge, the two riflemen peered into the surrounding brush as Ross studied the clear ground ahead through his binoculars. Tallgrass covered an area about 100 yards across. The clearing formed an open semi-circle next to the road. Near the center stood a lone tree with a small body wearing a Wehrmacht uniform tied to its trunk.

"You stay here," he whispered, pointing to one man. "Forney and I will check the perimeter. Wait until I come back, or you see me on the other side before you go into the clearing."

The man nodded while scanning the surrounding brush. Ross and Forney crept around the clearing's border, staying in the surrounding bush.

After finding no one lurking on the other side, Ross gestured to Forney to remain undercover, then slid from the forest on his belly. Halfway to the tree, his hand brushed clothing. The coppery aroma of blood and feces drifted to his nose as he touched the wet earth near the clothes. A groan made him drawback. After pushing the grass aside, he peered ahead.

"Mir helfen." A voice ahead mumbled, then groaned again. Ross inched forward, then raised his head. The man's tunic bore the twin SS lightning on its collar. His trousers pulled down to his knees, blood dripped from his exposed groin. Crab-like Ross moved to his left. His hand touched a second pair of boots, except the toes faced downward, and gray-green trousers draped around them. This man had experienced the same fate as the first but seemed still in death. As the blood had yet to congeal, the wounding must have been recent.

After skirting the blood pool, he resumed his crawl to the tree to examine the small, bound body. The body's chest peppered with bloodstains. The rifle volley must have been a firing squad. Apparently, they spared him the agony meted out to the Master Race's Elite.

Sergeant Harrison, his adjutant, called from the road, "All clear."

Ross rose, then walked to the tree. An emptied knapsack near the tree's base and the bound figure lacked boots. His killers must have searched him for items of use. As he raised the body's chin, Ross shook his head. A boy, not over twelve years, still in death.

"Probably the partisans they warned us about getting even," Harrison said as he surveyed the carnage on the ground. "Guess they aren't all bad, though," He added, nodding to the boy tied to the tree, "Killed him quick."

Behind Ross and Harrison, a medic with red crosses on his helmet kneeled by the man groaning on the ground. Harrison retrieved a blanket lying on the ground next to the boy's spilled knapsack. He tossed it to the corpsman.

"Thanks!" The medic said, pressing the cloth against the injured man's groin, "Only way to stop the bleeding here is with pressure."

The man groaned again, and the medic turned to Harrison, "Can you hold this for me while I get bandages to bind it. He needs morphine too."

"Have him hold it himself or tie it with his belt. We gotta get goin'. There are people up ahead who need all the supplies we got, so forget the shot and the bandages. Johnson use your Kraut Lingo. Tell him he needs to hold it tight to prevent bleeding. We'll pick him up on our way back," Harrison replied over his shoulder as he walked towards the vehicles.

As ordered, one rifleman kneeled by the German and whispered Harrison's instruction. The soldier looked up and called to Harrison, "Sarge, he wants us to shoot him!"

"Tell him that would violate the Geneva Convention. All we can do is offer aid." Harrison continued his stroll to the vehicles on the road. "Mount up, we gotta get rollin'."

Silent, Ross shouldered his carbine as he returned to his Jeep. The man in the dress remained in the back of the Jeep. Despite his shaved head and apparel, the man dripped arrogance. He held his head back, watching Ross return. His posture and expression, as if he viewed something distasteful. He peered behind the Jeep and barked in German. The older man stood clutching his hat to his head. Wide-eyed, he stared at his surroundings as he climbed back into the Jeep.

"I guess some of your guys stayed in uniform when they took off, Commandant," Ross said as he climbed back into his seat. The driver restarted the vehicle, and Ross nodded to him. As the Jeep rolled forward, Ross waved the rest to follow, then studied the map he pulled from his pocket. After taking a compass reading, Ross scanned the road ahead. "After we round this curve, we should find the camp about a mile ahead." The driver slowed for the curve, and as they headed West, the smell of death drifted to them on the breeze.

*****

With the convoy's engines roaring just out of sight around the road's bend, Justine scanned the surroundings for suitable cover. "Hans set up over there. Joseph, use those trees on the right for cover." Finished positioning her men, Justine tied the white cloth to the five-foot stick. "If I drop the stick on the road, do nothing. Just go back to the camp after they pass. If I wave it in the air, Hans, take out the vehicle in front and Joseph the next. Then cover me so I can make it back to the trees."

The men she addressed wore civilian clothes, held Schmeizer machine pistols, and Panzerfaust rockets slung over their shoulders. Both nodded before trotting to their concealed positions.

Finished tying the cloth to the stick, she walked to the roadside. With her hand, she shielded her eyes from the sunlight, enjoying the early spring warmth while she waited. A deep rumbling, much like thunder, came from the East. Not heralding an approaching storm. Instead, it announced the Russian's advance, meting out revenge for the German's rape and pillage of their homeland. They vowed to make the Germans pay for their atrocities. As the Jeep appeared over the hill, she stood holding the flag above her head.

The vehicle stopped only a few feet from her. Wide-eyed, the young soldier behind the wheel's jaw dropped as if seeing an apparition. His passenger stepped out. Cocked his head as if puzzled. Soldiers in the vehicle behind scanned the woods around them while the click of gun safeties being released mixed with the idling engine's rumbling.

As the soldier approached, he touched his helmet visor as if saluting. "Captain Ross, United States Army, Ma'am." While dust covered his face and clothing, he still seemed handsome.

"Justine Rothstein." She extended her hand, which he took in his own.

"May I be of assistance, Ma'am?" His blue eyes, intent, locked on hers. Like he had had not seen an attractive woman up close for a while.

"My people are guarding the camp ahead. We want to make sure that the living inside are not harmed further."

"My orders are to proceed to the camp ahead as quickly as possible. Inside that ambulance are people here to provide medical care. We also have food and medicine in the rest of the vehicles, and likewise, we're here to protect and help the people ahead."

"Good, with your permission, I will accompany you to make sure you arrive safely. Once your people are in place, then we can go."

"Marston, take the Commandant and His Honor in the truck. Miss Rothstein will ride with me," Ross shouted to a large soldier carrying a carbine. After uncuffing the man in the dress, he herded him to a truck down the line while the man wearing the suit scurried behind.

She chuckled as her eyes trailed the man being led down the convoy's length "The man in the dress, who is he?"

"Claims he's the Commandant of the camp ahead."

"Why is he dressed like that?"

"That's what he wore when we captured him. I didn't want to waste time looking for something else for him to wear before we set out to the camp. I figured the people up ahead might need us more than he needed his dignity. If it's like the others I've seen, they can't wait." Ross gestured to the back seat of his Jeep.

"You know he probably killed to get those clothes," Justine replied as she dropped the stick with the white flag and climbed in.

"I'm sure he's done worse."

As the Jeep moved forward, Ross turned to Justine. "That your folk's handiwork up the road?"

She nodded. "I regret the boy. We planned on shoving him in with the crowds marching back to Germany, but he was vicious. Like a mad dog."

"The young ones still have zeal."

"He stabbed my adjutant with a dagger after we took away his gun. Bit and kicked, so we tied him to the tree. Even then, he persisted." She sighed. "I am afraid my people lost their patience and shot him."

"How did you come to be a partisan?"

She tightened her headscarf to prevent it from blowing away. "Part of a young girl's rebellion, I guess."

She said no more. did not expect this American to understand what happened. Besides, why tell all this to some stranger. Many Germans hated them for their religion. Her neighbor's violence had forced her family into exile in the Warsaw ghetto. Her mother, father, she and her brother elected deportation to escape the torment and bullying. While being transported, she jumped from the train. She hid in the forest, traveling at night. Finally, during her sojourn, she found the band of partisans in the woods. They treated her as an equal and let her fight along with the others as they harassed the Germans. As the years passed, she became a leader.

CHAPTER TWO

As the convoy crested a hill, the camp appeared below and ahead. The smell of decaying flesh now washed over them like a wave as the vehicles descended into the valley approaching the barbed wire enclosure. Two armed men in civilian clothes stood at the barbed wire barricade blocking the road. The men moved this gate aside as they approached before waving the vehicles through. Inside the fence, bodies covered the ground except on a path wide enough for the trucks. Most still in death, but a few with a faint light in their eyes peered at them as they passed. Soon a few emerged from the buildings. They shuffled towards the vehicles looking like clothed skeletons. The living held out their hands in silent supplication.

"Make sure the men do not feed the prisoners, Sergeant," Ross ordered as he climbed out of the Jeep. Earlier, the medical staff briefed the men on the danger of giving these poor wretches GI food. Their long-starved systems need gentle turning to regain normal function. Until then, the GI's rations would poison them.

His men came forward from their vehicles. Ross ordered Harrison to set up a defensive perimeter with one squad. The remaining riflemen assisted the medics. With tenderness, they led the walking prisoners to clear areas away from the bodies, lining them up near tables being set up by the corpsman. Weakened, many of those standing collapsed to the ground. The riflemen rushed to the trucks. They retrieved blankets, which they spread on the ground, so those who could not stand had some relief from the cold mud.

The doctor, a short, bald man, directed the activity of the medics and riflemen. Gradually organization emerged. One corpsman staffed each table. The riflemen transported those who could walk to the tables. They stayed nearby to make sure the prisoner did not collapse again during the assessment. Several others carried stretchers to the medics working with the men on the ground. Grim, but gentle, they eased the living onto the pallets, giving them some relief as they awaited examination.

The doctor now moved among the medics, treating the prisoners on the ground. With some, he squatted to place his stethoscope on a patient's chest. He then examined the patient's eyes. Finished with his initial examination, the doctor moved on to the next or motioned a medic to his side. He would whisper both to each patient and the corpsman. Ross could not hear what the doctor said but guessed he gave instructions on starting care. Ross wished he had more physicians and corpsman, but his gruff rifleman, not assigned to guard the area, helped without orders. It still seemed like too little.

Ross had accompanied two previous camp liberations. Still, the sight and the smells he experienced as he looked around this camp sickened and shocked him. Harrison came forward, accompanied by the Mayor and the Commandant. The Mayor, still clutching his hat, scanned the area. He held a handkerchief to his nose, and his eyes appeared wide behind his wire-rimmed spectacles. The Commandant also studied the suffering mass, but with a proud smirk.

Justine moved to his side. "Your men need not stand guard. My comrades have cleared the area of Nazis." The woman now carried a stubby submachine gun with a large drum magazine. She slung its strap over her shoulder, allowing this weapon the GI's called a "Burp Gun" to hang at her side.

He studied her profile, attracted by this woman who commanded soldiers. "Where are the guards?"

"Most ran away into the forest to escape the approaching Russians. The ones who stayed, we let the stronger prisoners take care of them." She pointed to a small brick building with an over-sized chimney. "Their bodies are over behind the crematorium. Those we found in the woods we dealt with as you saw by the road."

"Not all Germans are Nazis," Ross said he recalled the boy tied to the tree, "Many just couldn't resist the bullying and intimidation."

She pointed to the Mayor and the Commandant. "Like those two over there? The weasel and the hyena?"

He faced her now. Her eyes seemed filled with fire. Ashamed, he looked away. It had been hard growing up an American Jew, but it did not compare to what the Nazis had done across Europe. "I am sorry if you think I criticized or judged what you may be doing. We've been here less than a year, so I can't imagine what it may have been like in the last fifteen years under these butchers." He removed his helmet, ran his fingers through his sweaty hair. "We want the same things, you know. My men and I are working to bring justice back."

"Justice! I hope we both agree on what that word means. If not, you will just be another enemy to my people and me. The camp is now in your hands. My people must leave to continue our work." She pointed to the prisoners. "Bring these poor souls, justice, and we will be friends.".

After stomping off, she beckoned her people to follow.

"Where are you going?"

His call prompted her to turn. She threw back her shoulders, scowled. "Back to the wood to keep hunting Nazis. Good luck, General, in your quest for justice." Silent, she and her people disappeared into the surrounding forest.

Ross turned to the Mayor, who still clutched the handkerchief to his face as he surveyed the area. "Once my people have the area secured, and the care here started, we will return to the village. Mr. Mayor, I want you to assemble all the people in town that can walk. I mean men, women, and children if they are not near death. I want them gathered in the city square. Our vehicles will bring them here, and they can bury the dead. I want them all interred properly."

"But sir, we knew nothing of these things." The Mayor's voice a shrill whine. My people did not do this terrible thing." He shook his finger at the Commandant. "It was him and the rest of those Germans who came to my country."

With a sweeping gesture that covered the area, Ross snarled. "These people came here through your town. You knew they were here. I am sure someone reported the odor from this place to you. You all turned away. Pretended you didn't know."

The Mayor clutched his hat's brim. "But... but..."

"I don't wanna hear excuses. The Supreme Commander ordered every person living near one of these Hellholes to come and see it for themselves, so later they can never say: I knew nothing. I intend to make sure we follow the order. By giving these souls a decent burial, God may look a little kinder on you when you meet him."

He shoved the Mayor aside. "Sergeant, take these two back to the Jeep. Make sure the Commandant's cuffs are locked tight. I need to secure the camp's records. Maybe we can make sure these bastards hang themselves!"

Harrison nodded and shoved the Commandant towards the Jeep. The Mayor scurried after him, continuing his whiny protestations.

He walked to the best-maintained building in the camp, assuming it contained the office. Inside, several desks and file cabinets lined the walls. Satisfied they remained locked and intact.

They would load them for transport to headquarters. There the Judge Advocate's people could extract the evidence they needed to prosecute the people responsible for this camp's horrors. He hoped this satisfied Justine and others like them. End this wickedness forever.

*****

After setting the town's people to work burying the camp's dead, Ross drove the Commandant to Mauthausen for processing. Stopped before the city hall's front entrance, Ross unchained the man in the dress. An MP, who hurried down the steps, came to an abrupt halt, his jaw dropped as he saluted, staring wide-eyed at the Commandant.

As he returned the salute, Ross nodded to the Commandant. "Corporal, before you lock this man up, make sure he's searched."

"Sir, we don't have any individual cells. We're only taking SS here. The Colonel wants the rest just turned over to the civilian authorities."

Ross smiled and winked. "He's SS. This is their new camouflage uniform. He commanded the death camp outside of town. So, treat him with all due respect."

"Yes, sir. Be my pleasure." The MP grinned, grabbed the Commandant's arm before dragging him up the building's grand staircase. Inside, Ross crossed a large open area with several desks occupied by Military Police personnel. A short man with graying hair, wearing a Colonel's eagles, sat next to one talking to a Sergeant. The Colonel leaped to his feet as the Commandant's escort passed. "Corporal, what is that man doing here?"

The MP turned. "Sir, he's SS." He nodded to Ross. "The Captain here ordered me to take him to a cell."

Ross stepped between the Corporal and Colonel. Turned to the Colonel, whose face now flushed crimson. "Sir, that man's my prisoner. I captured him this morning, and we just returned from the camp he commanded."

With a scowl, the Colonel eyed the Commandant, who thrust his shoulders back as if at attention and sneered.

Ross continued his narration. "Locals cornered him at the train station. Looked like they wanted to lynch him. He rewarded us for saving him by showing us the camp's location."

The Colonel placed his hands on his hips. "Captain, we're no longer processing prisoners here. All captured Germans are to march back to Germany for processing. You will find a column of them now on the main road outside of town. Take him there and turn him over to the men escorting them. Once he reaches the detention centers, they'll process him."

"We have enough troops to guard these guys, Sir?"

"Captain, the surrounding forest is full of partisans hunting these people. If any escape them, the Russians are not far behind. I don't believe any of them want to take their chances with that outcome. Our need for an escort right now is minimal." The Colonel turned to the MP. "Corporal, go with the Captain and make sure he finds the appropriate people."

They marched together through the deserted streets occasionally stepping to the side as a vehicle sped past. The Corporal and Ross moved swiftly, but the Commandant wobbled on his high heels. He sometimes stumbled in the dark, but neither Ross nor the Corporal reached out to steady him. Instead, they continued their pace, knowing the German did not desire to be left behind.

At the edge of town, men wearing what appeared to be every sort of German uniform marched West on the highway past the city. Vehicles coming from either direction relied on their horns to scatter the marchers as they raced towards their destinations. Two men wearing Military Police helmet emblems stood at the intersection watching the passing traffic.

As the three approached the intersection, the MPs turning to face them stared wide-eyed at the sight.

The Corporal chuckled. "Been a while since you guys seen a good lookin' babe. Thought you might want to meet one of the local lovelies to break up the boredom in your cold and lonely vigil."

One shook his head as he gave the Commandant an appraising glance. "You ain't even beginning to be funny, Johnson."

The other nodded. "Nah, I'll bet this is Johnson's way of announcin' he's movin' up from sheep."

The Corporal clapped the Commandant's back. "This here's a big shot SS guy they captured near here." He nudged the Commandant's ribs. "What's your name, honey?"

"Standartenfuhrer Gerhart Mundt!" As he thrust back his shoulders, he gave the Nazi salute.

"No, heel clickin'? You worried you might break a heel, darlin'?"

Commandant Mundt turned to Ross and bowed his head. "Despite the circumstances, I appreciate your saving me from that mob. I know you might not agree with how we treated the people in the camp, but it was better than they deserved."

Ross frowned, "What do you mean?".

"In other camps, we killed them. Here we gave them a purpose in life. To provide a service to the Fatherland. These Jewish vermin should consider it an honor."

"You mean you just worked `em to death instead of gassing them. Maybe the Jews should give you a medal instead of stretching your neck?"

Mundt smiled, extended his hand. "I knew an Aryan such as you would understand."

"Actually, I'm Jewish. Hope I didn't make a mistake pulling you away from that mob earlier cause I want a front-row seat when they hang you after your trial."

Mundt scowled, spit in Ross's face. Muttered a curse in German.

Ross wiped the spittle from his cheek, smeared it back on Mundt's face, then shoved him to the ground. "Make sure he gets to the next stop in one piece. I want to see him dancing at the end of a rope." Then marched off.

CHAPTER THREE

At city hall, a scowling Sergeant stood guard on a truck blocking Ross's Jeep. When the man turned to face him, Ross nodded toward the vehicle. "Can you move this thing?"

As he saluted, the Sergeant's scowl deepened. "Not without orders."

Ross pointed to his Captain's bars. "Okay? Then move it."

"I meant from someone with clout."

"You, Captain Ross?"

Ross turned to the building. A man with a Major's gold leaf on his helmet trotted down the stairs. As the officer approached, Ross stood straighter while the Sergeant snapped to attention and saluted. "I'm Ross."

After returning the Sergeant's salute, the Major glared at Ross. "You got a problem with rank, Captain?"

"Sorry?"

"You didn't salute."

"No, saluting helps snipers pick their target. Highest rank goes first."

The Major scanned the surroundings. "They assured me they had cleared the area."

Ross snapped to attention, saluted. Your funeral asshole, he thought to himself. "You're lookin' for me?"

"You've got a company near the camps, right?"

"They're helping with the prisoners."

"Your unit's assigned to me."

"To you?"

The Major nodded. "We'll follow you to the camp. After that, you are to provide security for our mission."

"Mission? And what will that be?"

"What I tell you to do. Now let's get goin' we need to get this show on the road."

*****

After rounding up his unit from the camp, they roared down the road trailing a convoy of flatbed trucks.

Sergeant Harrison, perched in the Jeep's back, leaned forward. "We're escorts?"

Ross shrugged.

Harrison's eyes roamed the roadside. "If we're escorts, what are we doin' in the back?"

"Don't seem worried about ambush."

"You see that Kraut they had with 'em?"

"Guess he's leadin' 'em somewhere. Might be another camp."

Harrison shook his head. "But there ain't any ambulances."

As the sun rose, the convoy halted. Ross reached for his carbine as he scanned the roadside. The only sounds the rumble of Russian artillery in the East and the vehicles idling.

After several minutes Ross turned to his driver. "Let's go find out what's goin' on."

After pulling out around the truck ahead, the Jeep traveled to the convoy's front. Beside an abandoned guard post outside a cave, the Major talked with a man wearing a German uniform. The German pointed to the cave several times as he spoke.

As Ross stepped from the Jeep, he turned to Harrison. "Let's go find out what this party's about."

As Ross and Harrison approached, a squad from the trucks pushed the guard post's gate out of the way. The Sergeant accompanying the Major waved the vehicles forward. Dust clouds rose as the trucks roared ahead. The Major and the German turned to Ross and Harrison as they approached.

The German, his dirty tunic torn in places, turned toward the sound of Russian guns. As in town, Ross snapped a salute, which the Major acknowledged before he turned toward the rumbling in the East.

"Sounds close."

The Major turned back to Ross. "Not over twenty miles. Should be here tomorrow."

As the last flatbed passed, a Jeep pulled up beside them. Before boarding it, the Major turned to Ross. "No need for your men to go inside."

"What are we here for?"

"Set up a defensive perimeter."

"That's it?"

"Make sure no one follows us in."

"No one?"

"That's right. Especially the Russians."

"But..."

"They're our allies?"

Ross nodded.

"For now."

Once the Major's Jeep disappeared inside the cave, Ross's men piled out of their trucks. Ross stretched. No sleep since the day before yesterday. He longed to curl up inside a truck bed. But not yet.

After Harrison dispersed the unit, he joined Ross. "What the fuck's goin' on?"

"According to the Major, we're to make sure no one else enters."

Harrison tipped his helmet back on his head. Nodded towards the cave. "He say what they're after?"

"Nope. You got any thoughts?"

"All the way through France we heard about the Nazi's lootin' shit. Artworks, paintings, gold. S'pose that's what this is? Some kinda treasure horde?"

"Whatever it is, this bunch ain't sayin'."

"You look dead on your feet."

Ross yawned. "How 'bout the men?"

"Despite all the bouncin' around in the trucks, guess they got some shut-eye."

"Set 'em on two-hour watches then. I'll take the first shift. You can spell me when you get a little rest yourself."

"That an order?"

"Damn straight. But you could rustle up some coffee first. That shit you make would wake the dead. Might help me make it through the first shift."

*****

Tank treads rumbling jarred Ross awake. Disoriented, he sat up. The men in the next foxhole switched the machine gun's position towards the tank's sounds. After donning his helmet, Ross glanced skyward. The sun's position suggested afternoon, Harrison must have let him sleep through a double shift.

Harrison dropped in beside him. "Tanks."

"Whose?"

"LP says they're not ours, but don't look like any Kraut tank they've seen."

As an engine roared on their right, trees on that side crashed to the ground. A lumbering khaki-colored behemoth rolled into the road beside one of their trucks. Men wearing uniforms much like theirs, except with high-topped black boots, rolled off the back of the tank. Some carried stubby burp guns like Justine's.

"Fuck. It's the Russians." Harrison turned to Ross. "What do we do?"

"We got a bazooka?"

"Fuck, no."

Ross removed his white handkerchief from his pocket. "I guess I better talk to 'em."

"Keep 'em covered!" At Harrison's command, safeties down the line clicked, and rifle bolts snapped.

As Ross rose, he held both hands above his head, hoping the breeze would furl the handkerchief he stepped into the road. "We're Americans."

Two Russians slipped behind the tank, while another drew a bead on Ross. The tank's turret swiveled, leaving Ross to stare down its massive barrel.

One Russian stepped forward. "You got cigarettes?"

"You got vodka?"

"Shit yes, cowboy."

Ross turned back. "Any a you guys got smokes?"

"I got a carton a Luckies in our truck. I'll get 'em."

The Russian grinned. After he spoke with his comrades, they lowered their weapons. One mounted the tank, tapped his gun butt on the hatch. A man emerged wearing a padded helmet. After the two spoke, the tanker disappeared, returning shortly with a bottle filled with a clear liquid. The man on the tank passed the container to the English speaker, who approached Ross grinning. "Are you General Patton?"

Ross shook his head. "Not hardly."

"An aide, perhaps?"

"Never laid eyes on the man, why?"

Uncapping the bottle, he handed it to Ross. "We heard he might be sympathetic."

"Sympathetic?"

"Might help free our country from these Russian assholes."

"You're not Russian?"

"Russian?" The man scowled. "No. Lithuanians. But we got this fine tank. Much better than yours. Patton needs us."

After the soldier with the cigarettes gave them to Ross, he handed them to the would-be defector. Sergeant Harrison joined them. After he and Ross took a drink from the bottle, Harrison shook his head. "So, you ain't Russians?"

"No, we volunteered for the spearhead. That way, we could find Patton. With luck, he might defeat them and get rid of Stalin. That crazy Georgian ruins everything."

Harrison scratched his head as he peered at the tank. "How much gas you got in that thing?"

"We got filled up about an hour ago. Should be okay until sundown."

Harrison nodded toward the road. "Well, Patton is not too far down that road. You might catch up with him by then."

A broad grin spread on the man's face as he spoke with his comrades. After remounting the tank, they handed down another bottle, waved as the tank sped away in the direction Harrison indicated.

*****

As the sun set, the Major's Jeep emerged from the cave. After pulling to the roadside, the first flatbed trucks rolled out with tarps concealing their cargo. The Major dismounted and joined Ross and Harrison standing near the road's edge.

As the first truck rolled by, the Major turned to Ross. "Any activity?"

Ross gave Harrison a quick, sidewise glance. "An element of the Russian vanguard came through."

The Major scowled. "The Russians?" His head swiveled to the artillery rumbling in the East, then scanned the area. "Any problems?"

"No, sir. Helped them a little with directions, and they moved on. Others might move in soon, though."

"Our work here is complete. With the Russians lurking about, I would feel more comfortable with your people stationed at both the front and rear of the column. Once we reach Mauthausen, your people can report to the area commander. We can take it from there."

"Give us some time to form up."

After the Major returned to his Jeep, Ross turned to Harrison. "I'll take the first platoon as the lead escort. You bring the rest in trail."

"Heavy weapons in back?"

Ross shrugged. "If we hit trouble, you'll be able to come to the rescue."

"Makes sense, but have Murph take the point Jeep." Harrison nodded toward the flatbed. "Any ideas what's under the tarp?"

"I'd guess a Ford sedan, rounded like that, but with the side overhang hard tellin'."

That night as they rolled into Mauthausen, Ross's contingent pulled over to let the flatbeds through. The Major's Jeep pulled alongside Ross's. "Any word from your Sergeant, Captain?"

Ross nodded. "They got the tire changed and are about fifteen minutes outside town."

"Very good. As I said earlier, we can take it from here. When the last one arrives, your men are relieved."

"What did we pick up from the cave?"

"All I can tell you is it might be the key to our country's future."

Soon the last flatbed arrived with the rest of Ross's company escorting. As the flatbed convoy rolled out of town, Harrison joined Ross near his Jeep. "What's next?"

"I checked with the boss at city hall. We head out in the morning. Make way for the Russians. This is theirs now."

"Tarp came off that truck while they worked on it."

Ross's eyebrow rose. "Yeah?"

Harrison nodded. "Was real tense for a moment. Smitty tried to take a picture, and one a their guys threatened to take his camera."

"So, what was it?"

Harrison leaned close. "If I tell ya, I might have to shoot ya."

"What?"

"You got top-secret clearance?"

"Shit, Sergeant. You and I've seen it all. So, what was it?"
"Remember those funny lookin' rocket planes we saw on that Kraut airfield?"
Ross nodded.
"Looked kinda like one a these."

To continue the tale, click or follow the link below you will not be disappointed:

https://www.amazon.com/gp/product/B087W7FJN6/ref=dbs_a_def_rwt_h
sch_vapi_tkin_p1_i5

ACKNOWLEDGEMENTS

As always I need to thank my critique group from Malice in Memphis for the input they had on this manuscript. On this one they stepped up with even more help than usual. In addition to the excellent feedback from the Legendary Larry Hoy and Mother of the year Kristina Holmes. Lynn Maples designed the cover. Also, Jackie Ross Flaum did a Beta read on the completed manuscript. They deserve all the acclaim for the good parts. Any screw ups are my responsibility

Made in the USA
Las Vegas, NV
06 December 2021

36290289R00142